CRETACEOUS

WRITTEN & ILLUSTRATED BY
Tadd Galusha

EDITED BY
Charlie Chu and Desiree Wilson

DESIGNED BY
Sonja Synak and Hilary Thompson

AN ONI PRESS PUBLICATION

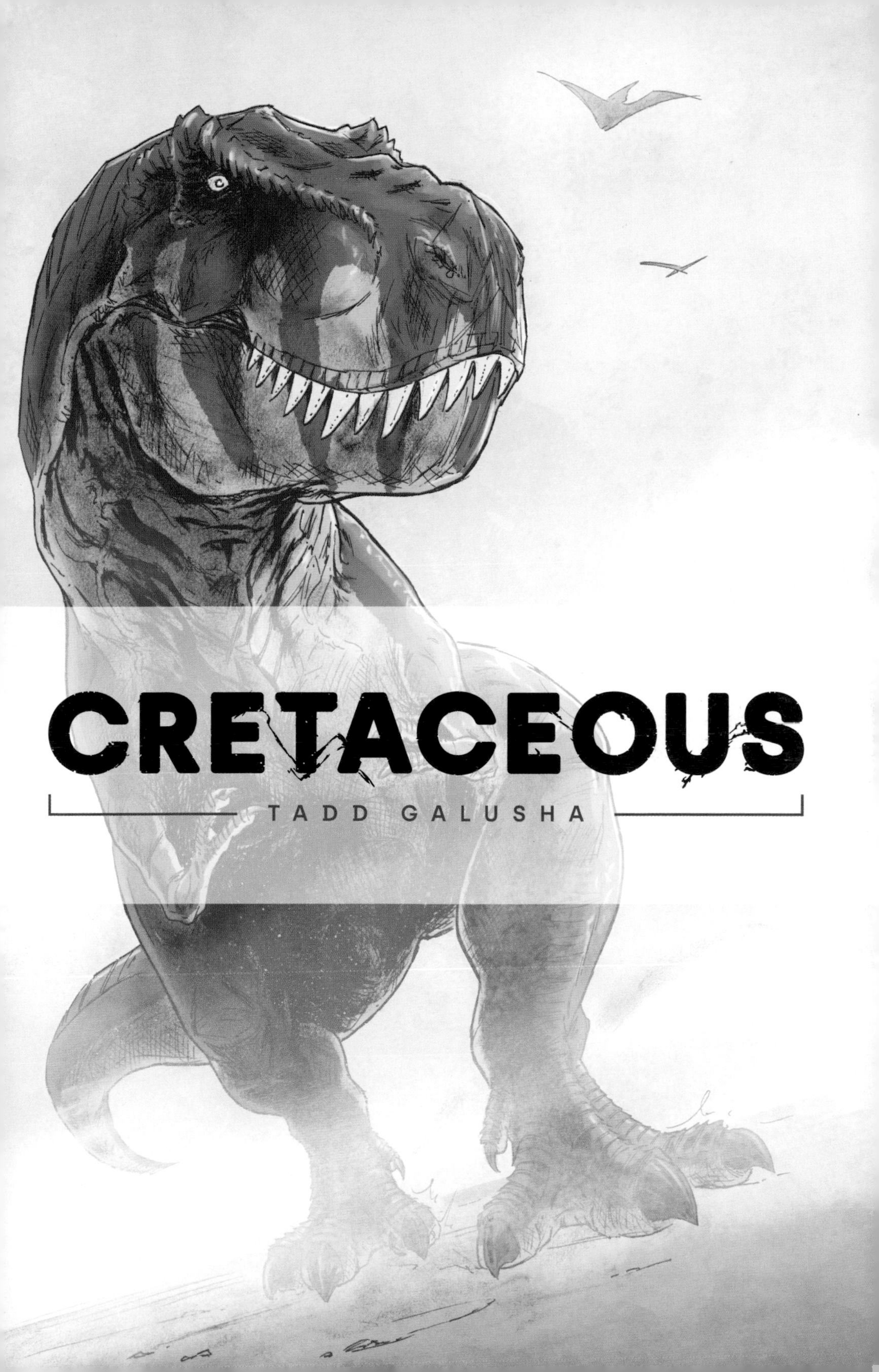
CRETACEOUS
TADD GALUSHA

Published by Oni Press, Inc.

Joe Nozemack, founder & chief financial officer
James Lucas Jones, publisher
Charlie Chu, v.p. of creative & business development
Brad Rooks, director of operations
Melissa Meszaros, director of publicity
Margot Wood, director of sales
Sandy Tanaka, marketing design manager
Amber O'Neill, special projects manager
Troy Look, director of design & production
Kate Z. Stone, senior graphic designer
Sonja Synak, graphic designer
Angie Knowles, digital prepress lead
Ari Yarwood, executive editor
Sarah Gaydos, editorial director of licensed publishing
Robin Herrera, senior editor
Desiree Wilson, associate editor
Michelle Nguyen, executive assistant
Jung Lee, logistics coordinator
Scott Sharkey, warehouse assistant

onipress.com
facebook.com/onipress
twitter.com/onipress
onipress.tumblr.com
instagram.com/onipress

@taddgalusha

First edition: March 2019

ISBN 978-1-62010-565-8
eISBN 978-1-62010-566-5

PRINTED IN CHINA.

Library of Congress Control Number: 2018940558

To my loving wife,
Erin.

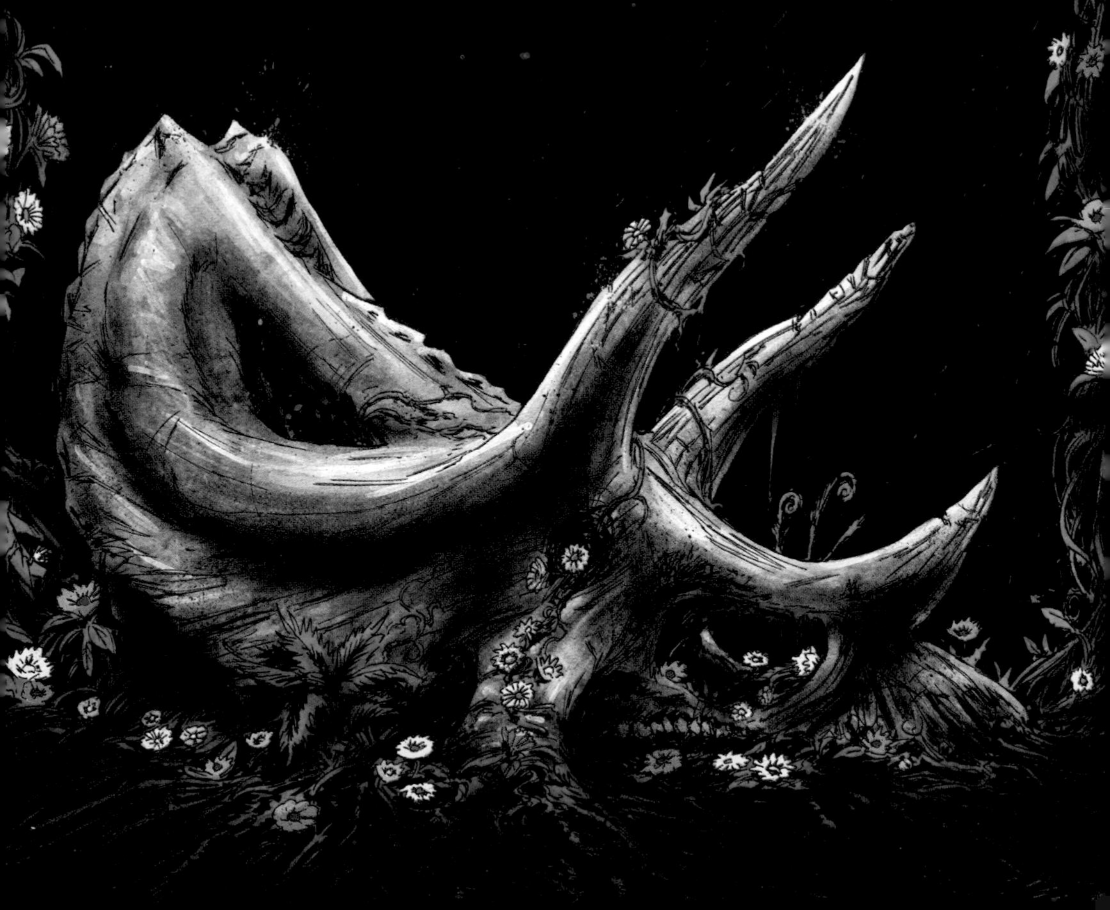

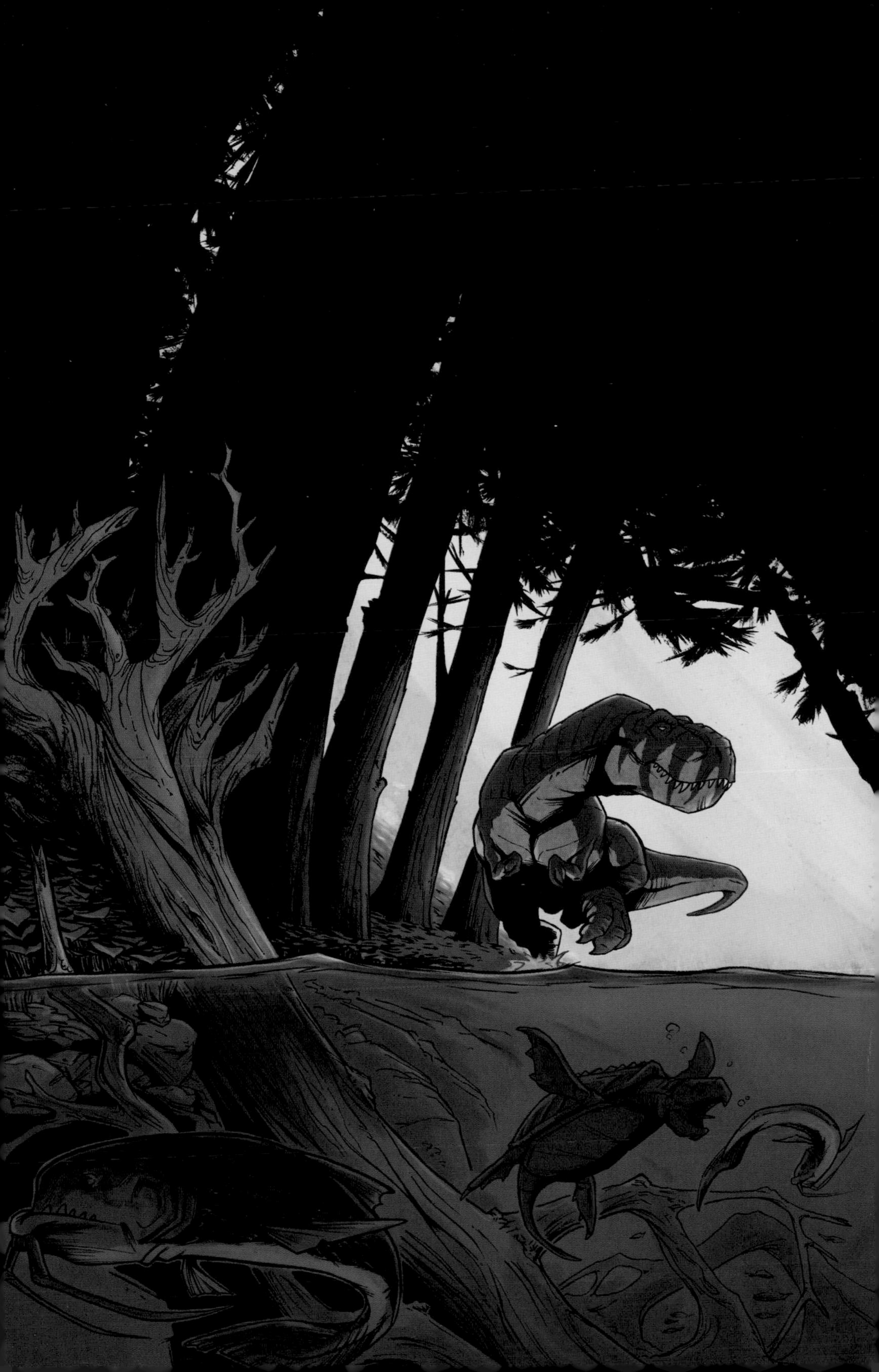

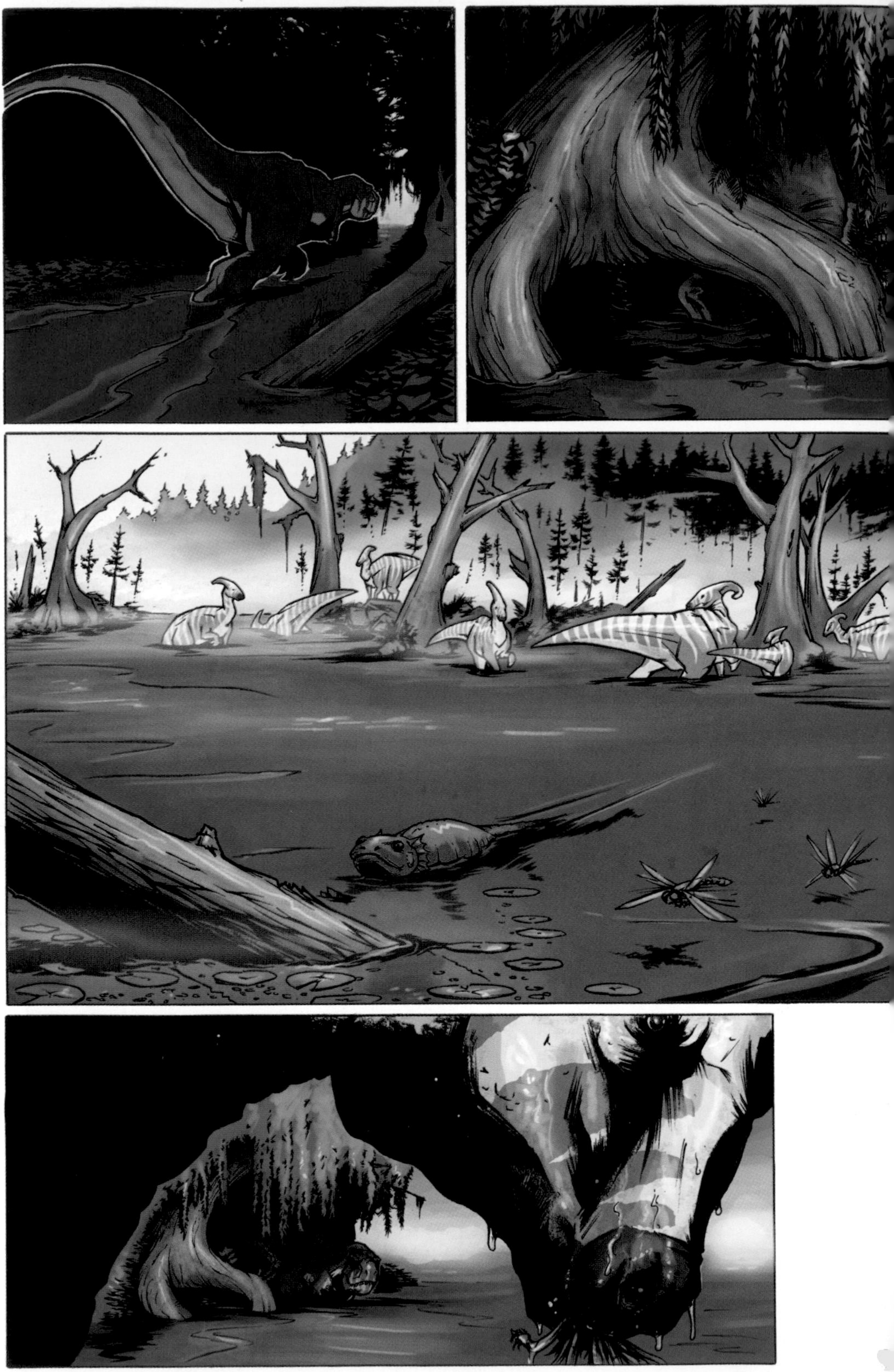

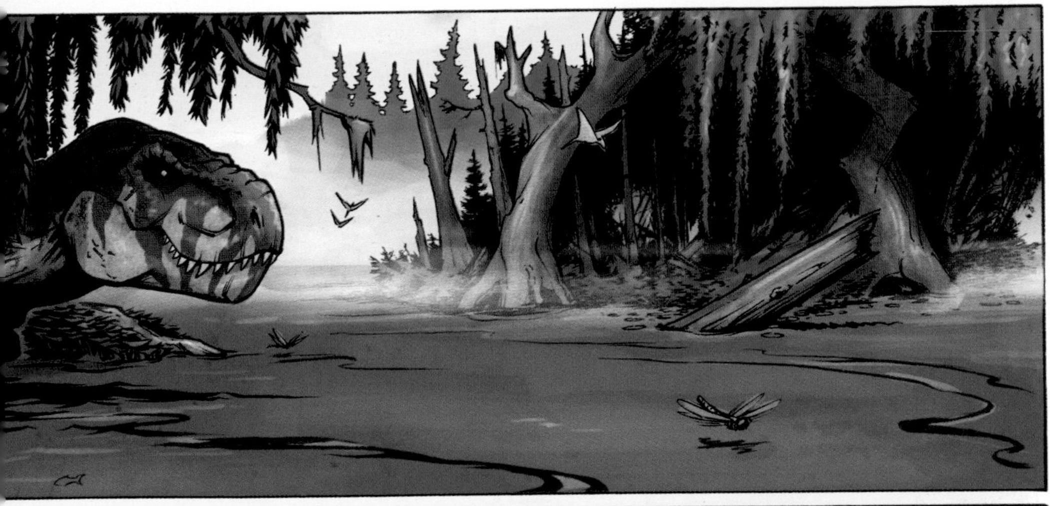

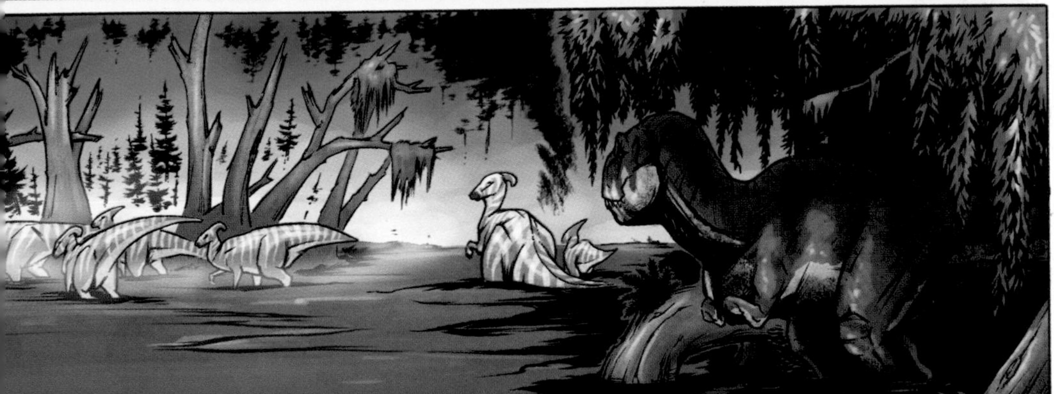

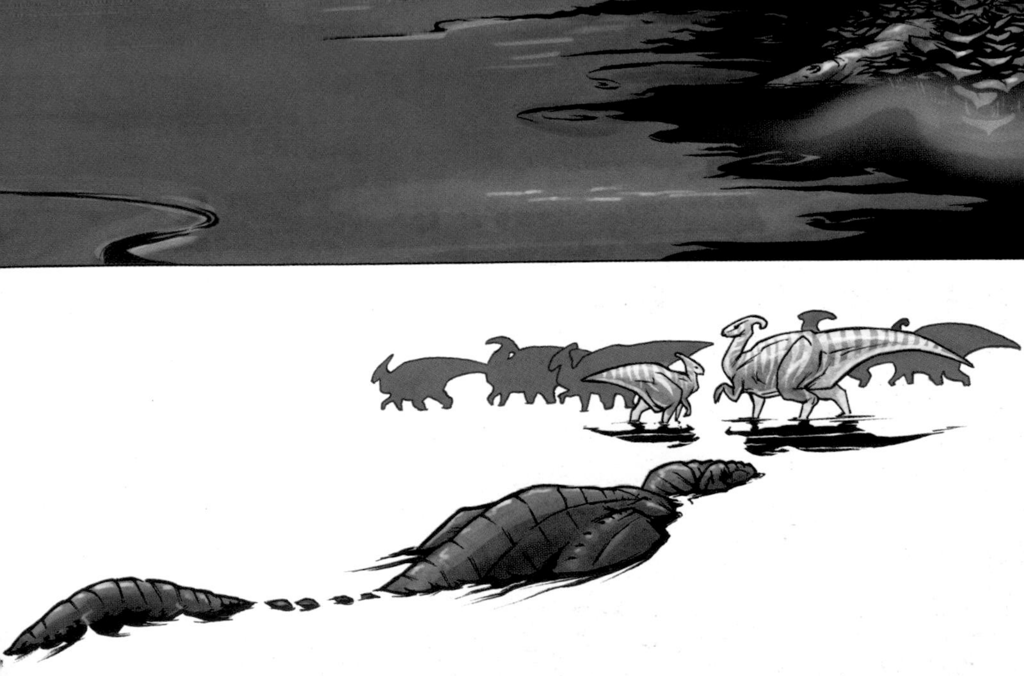

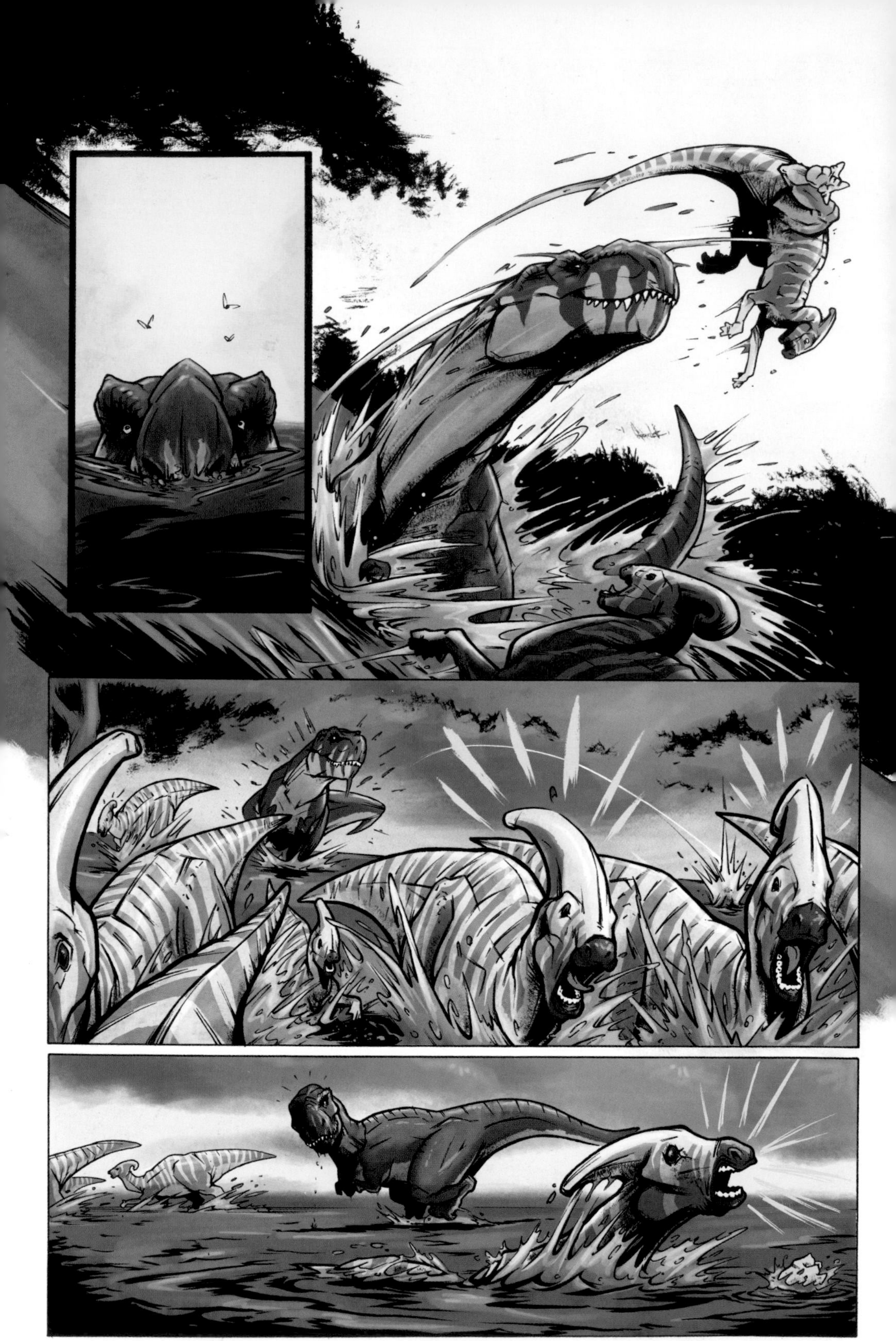

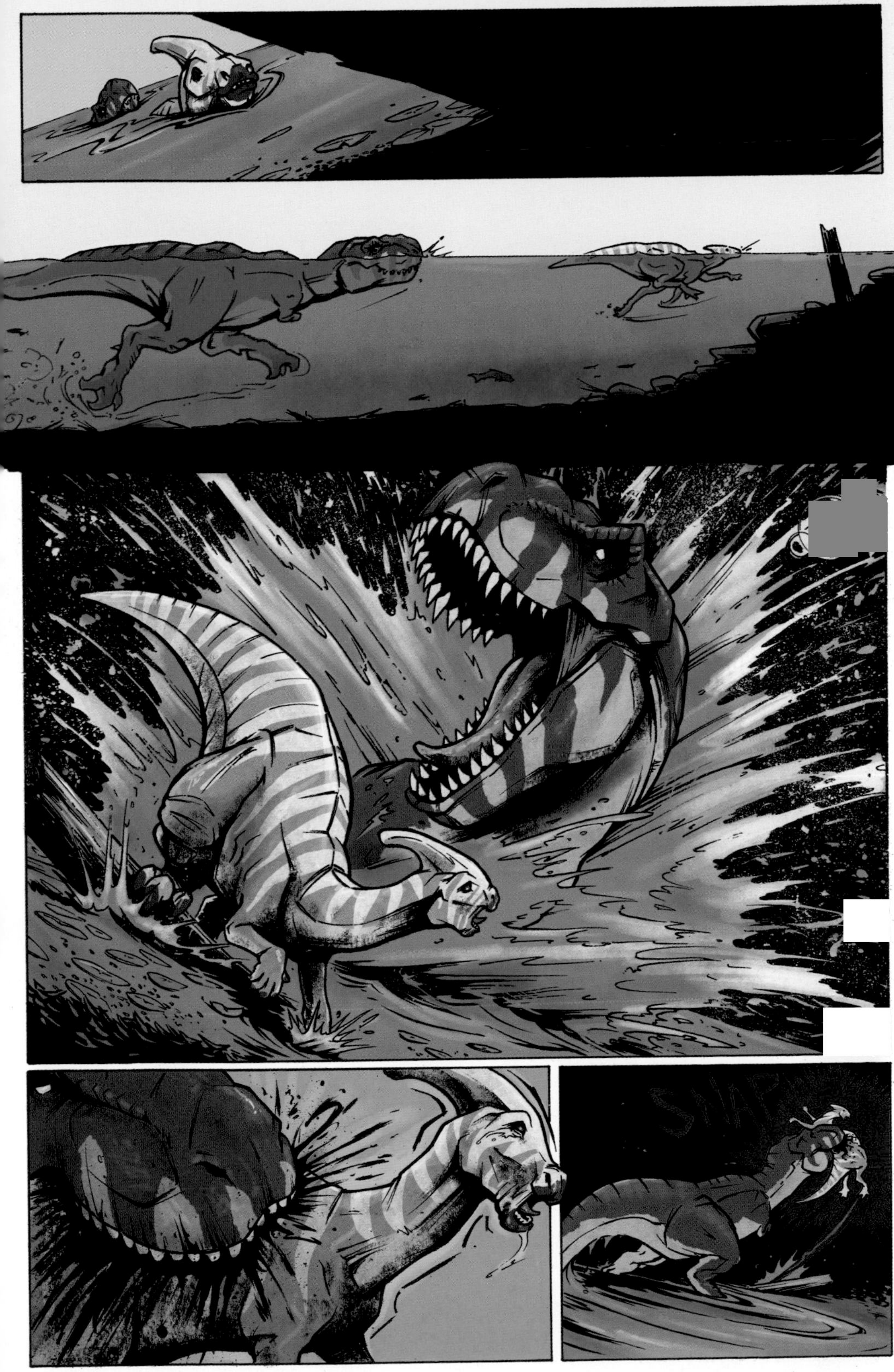
SNAP

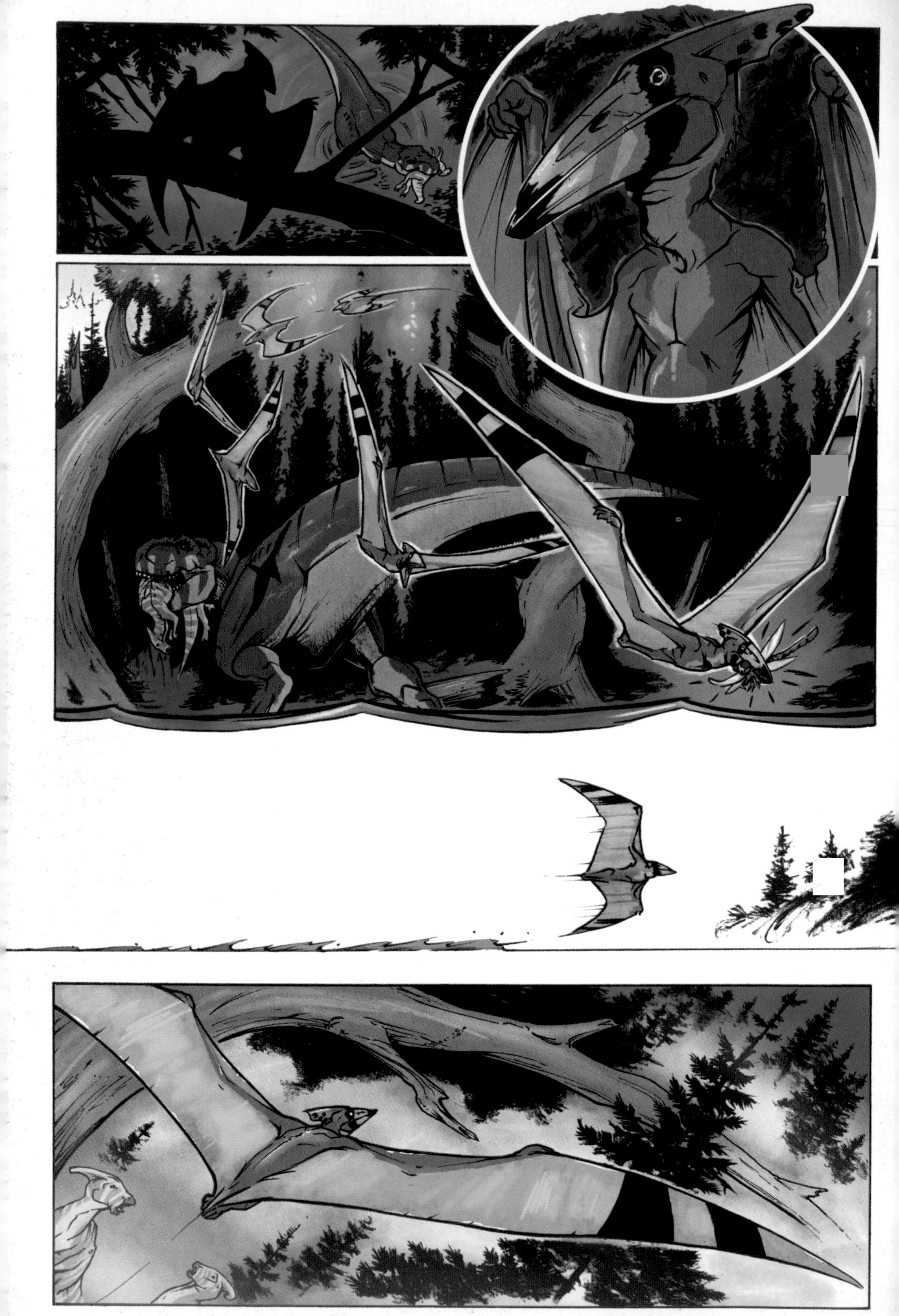

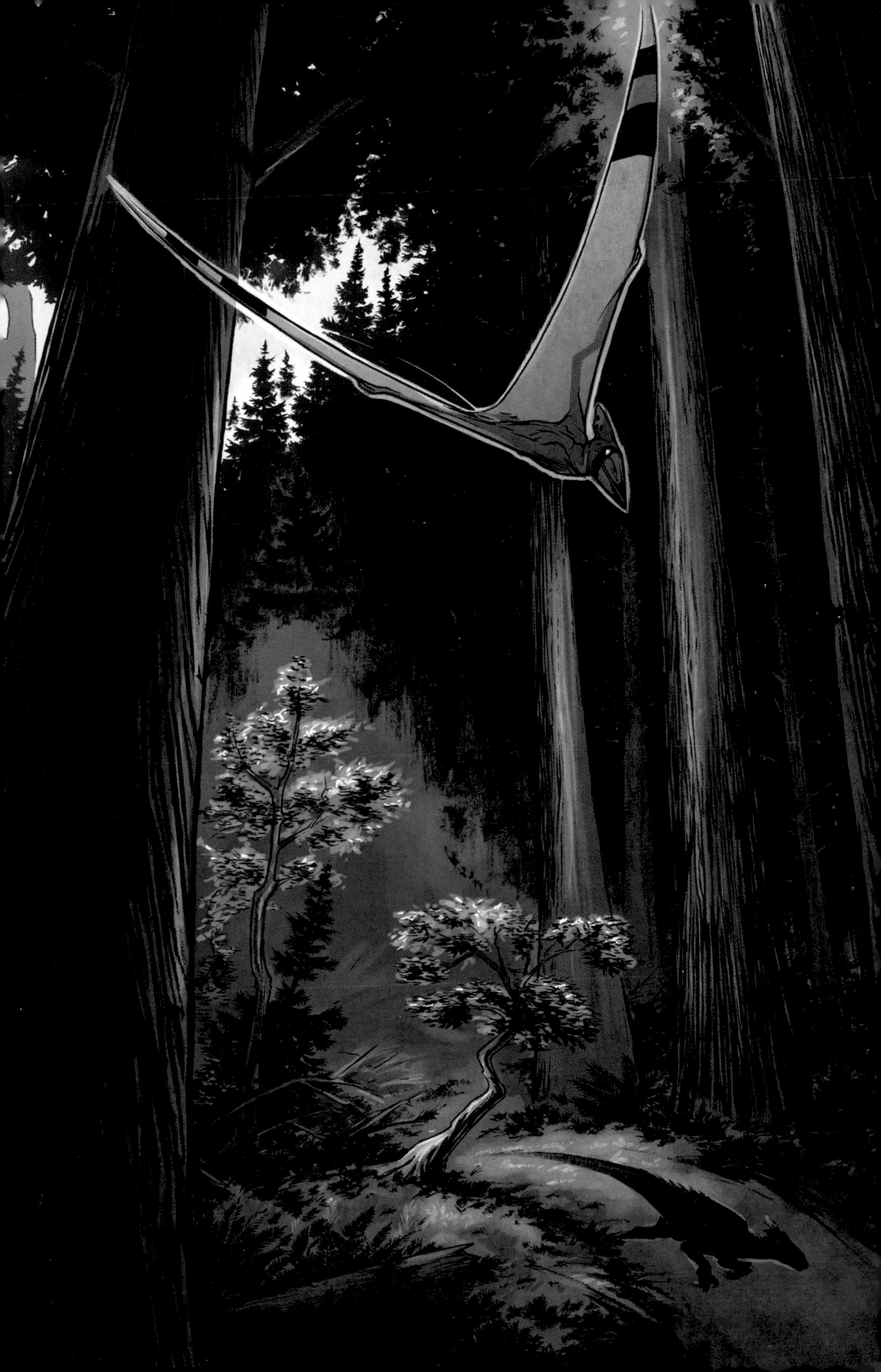

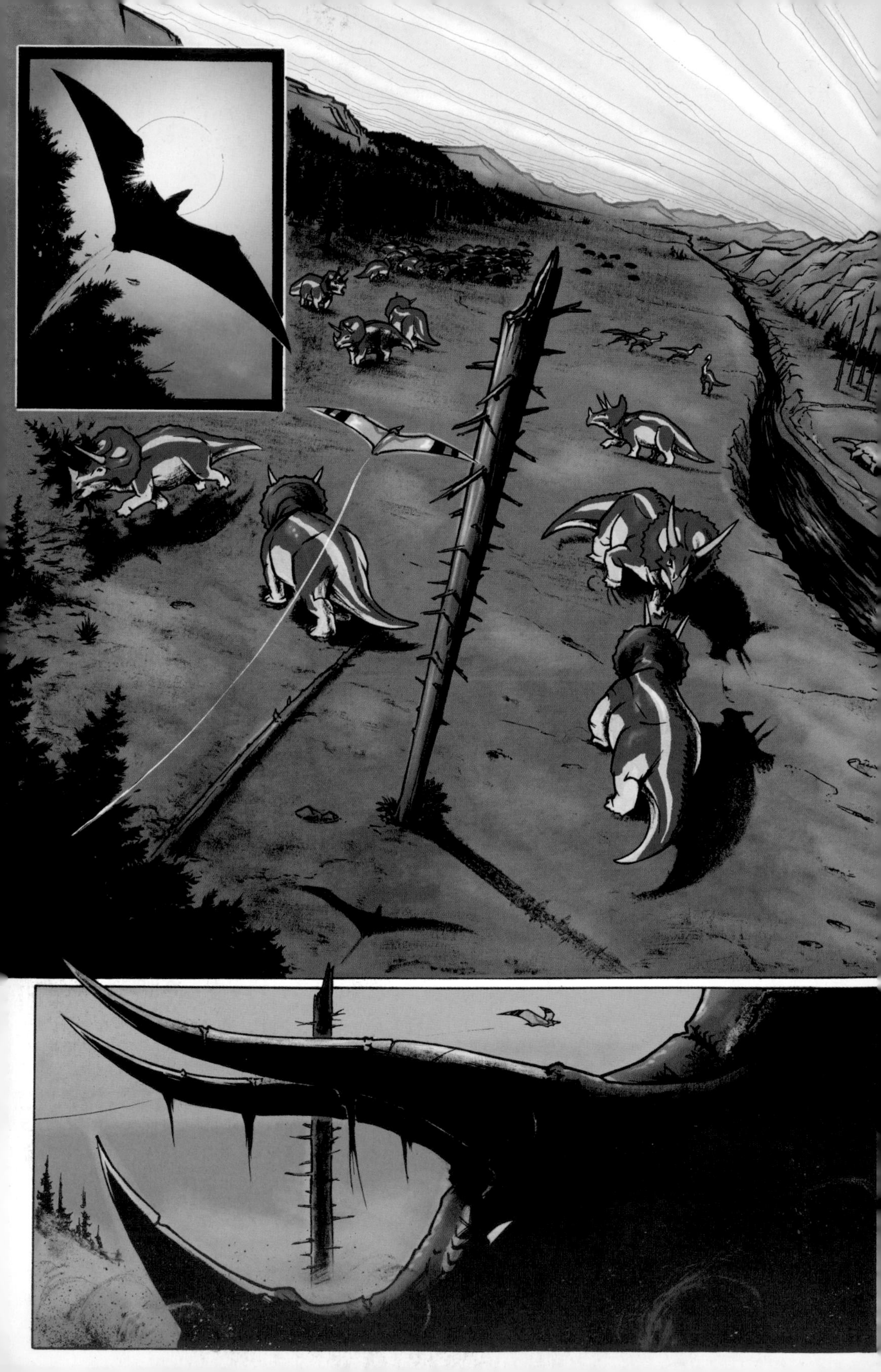

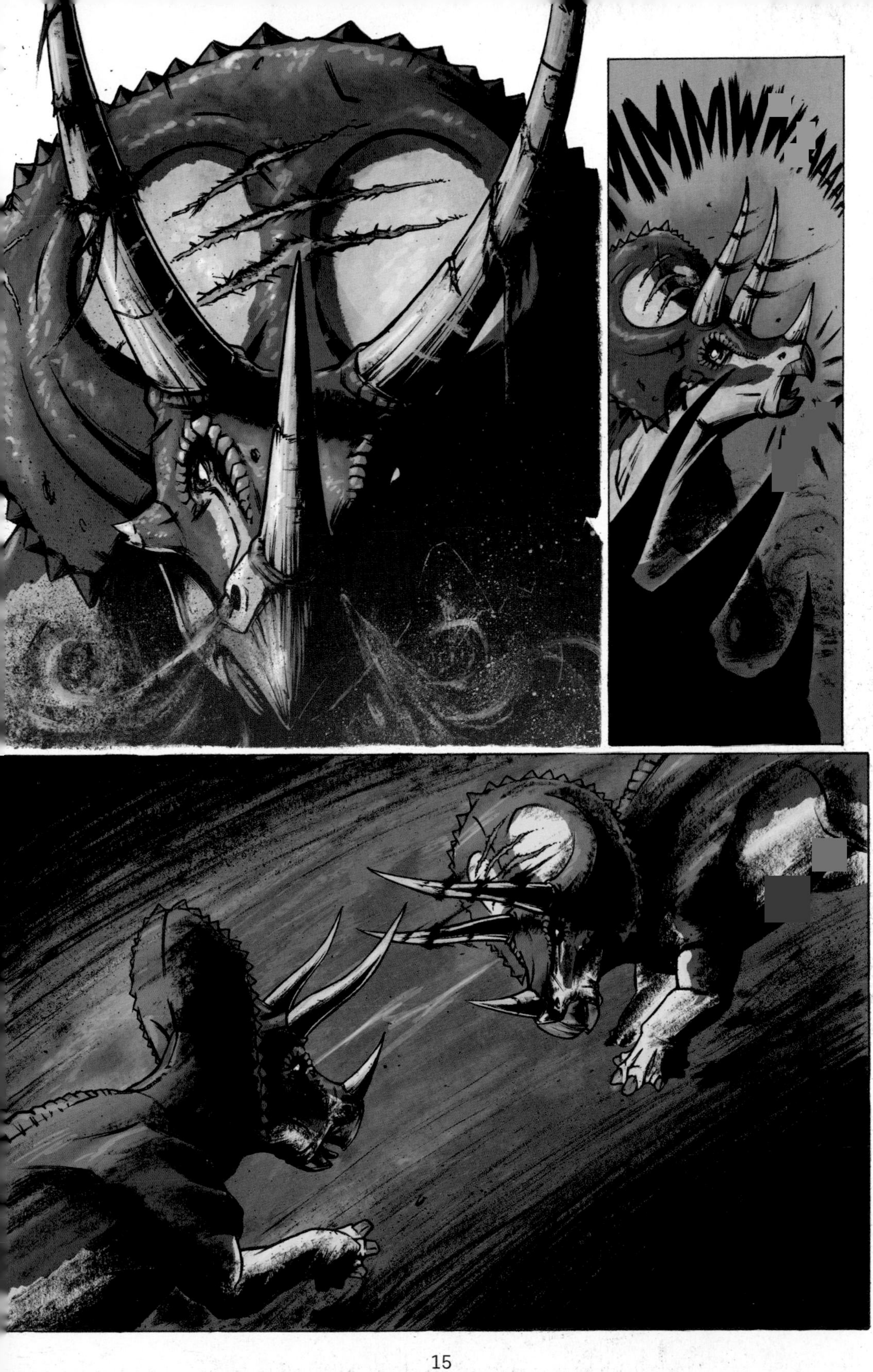
MMMW
AAAA

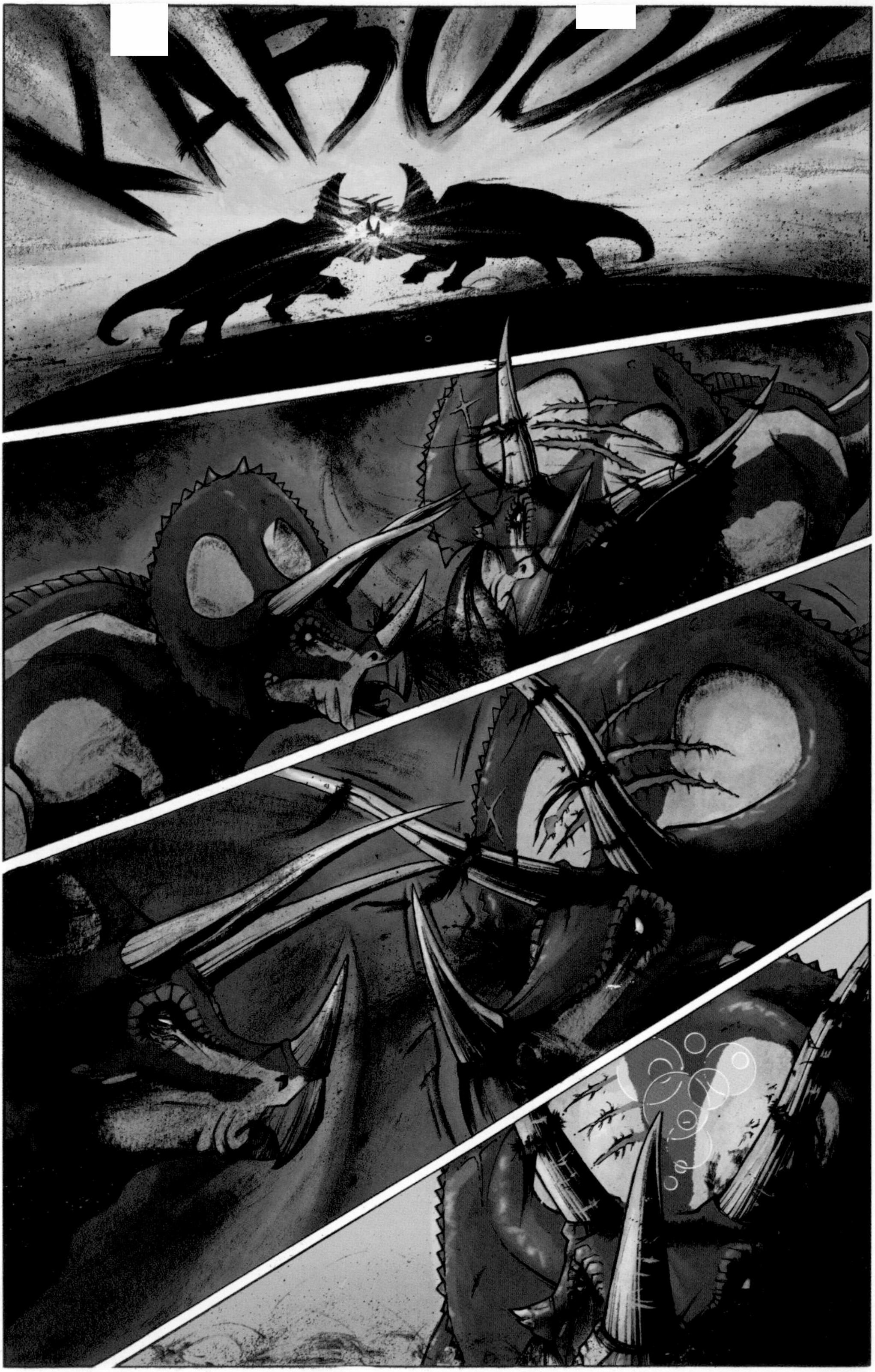
KABOOM

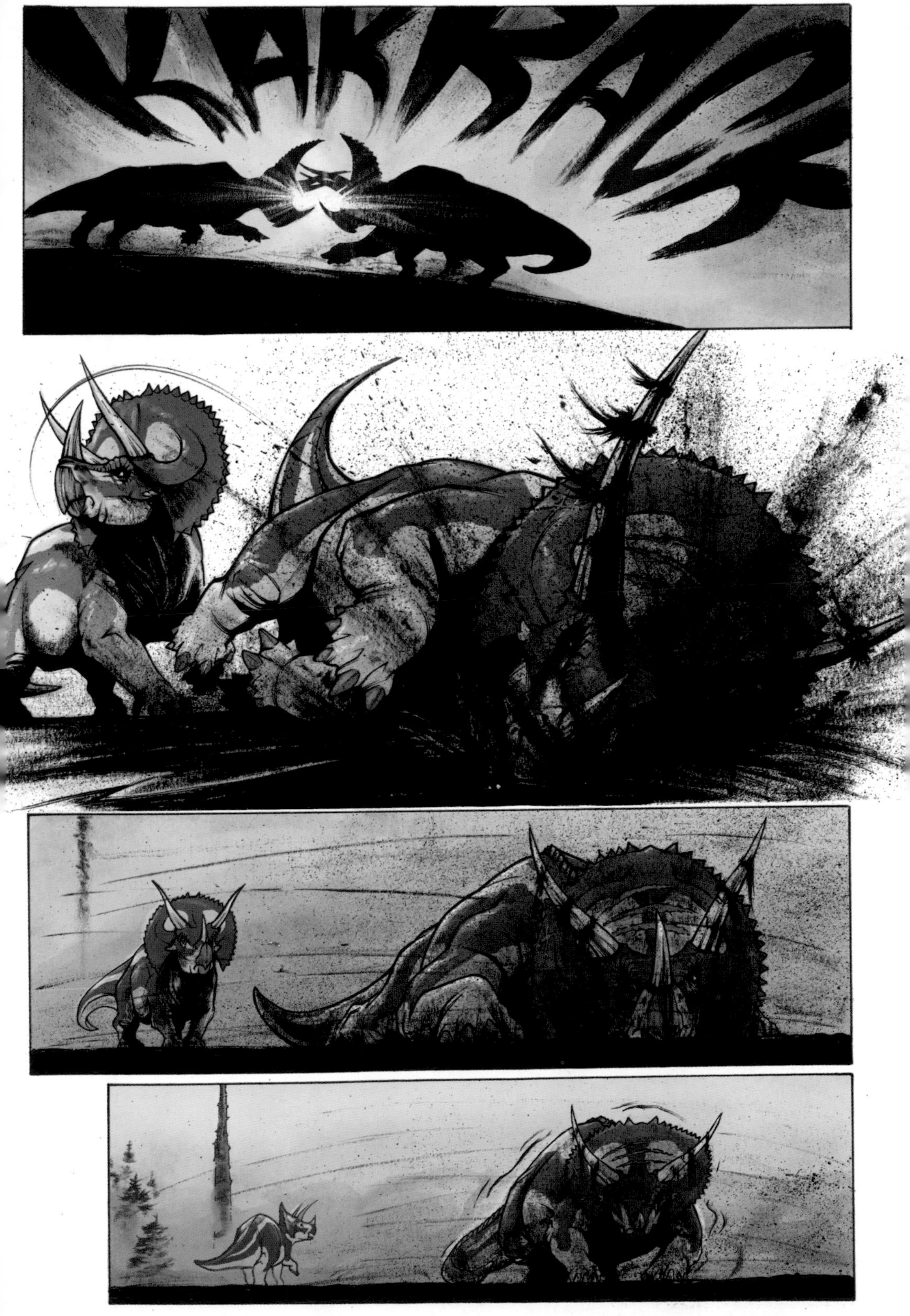

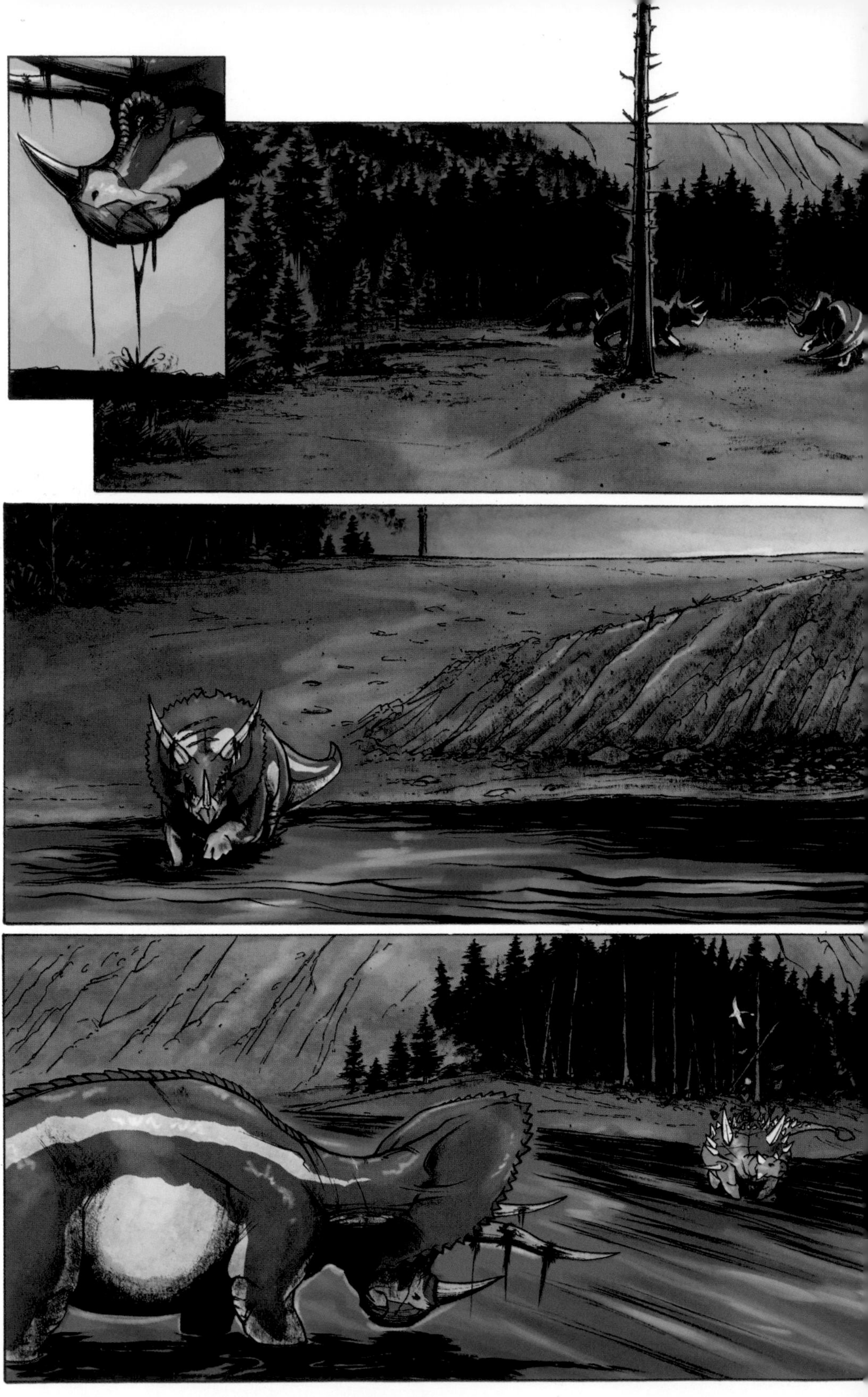

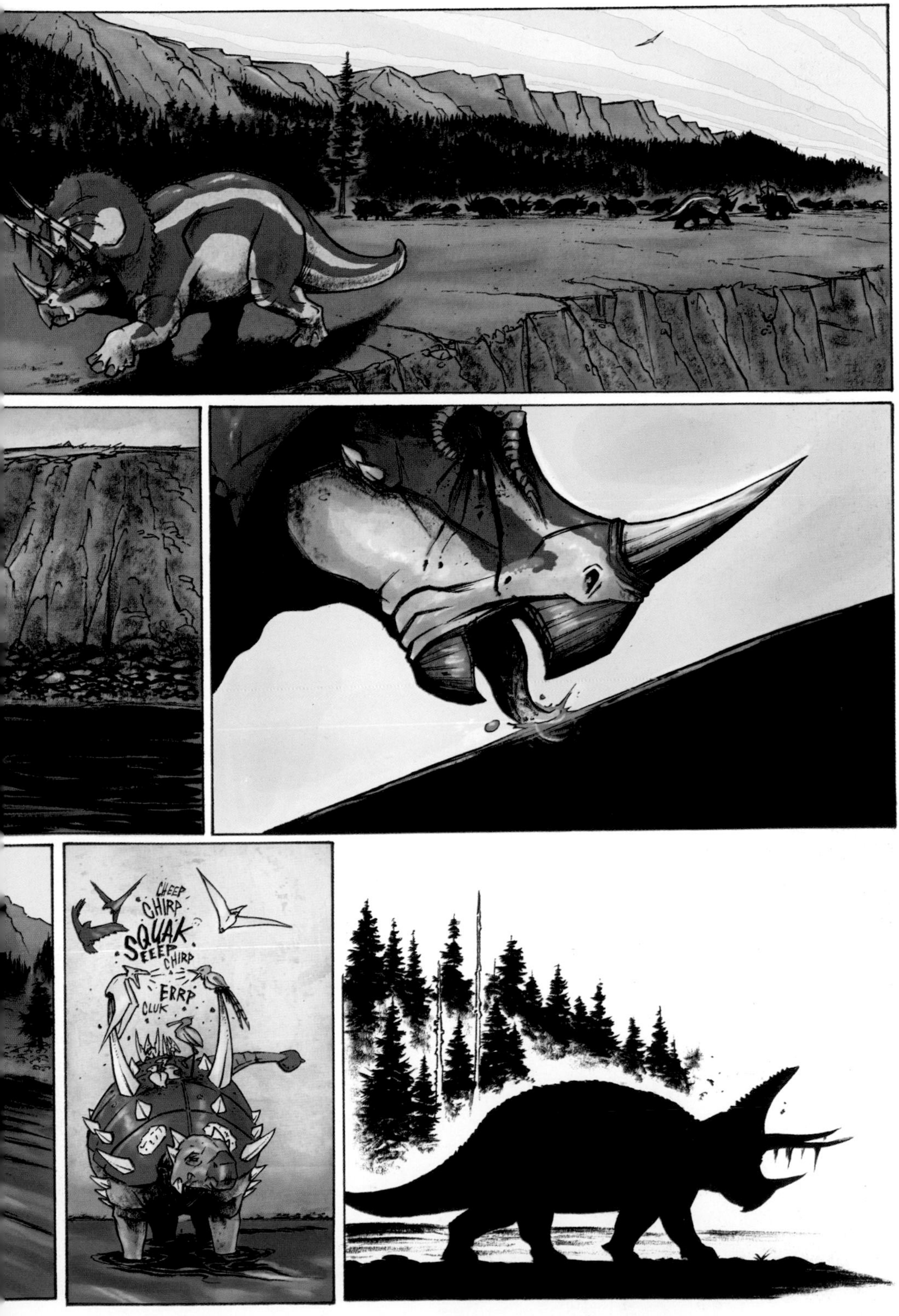
CHEEP
CHIRP
SQUAK
SEEEP
CHIRP
ERRP
CLUK

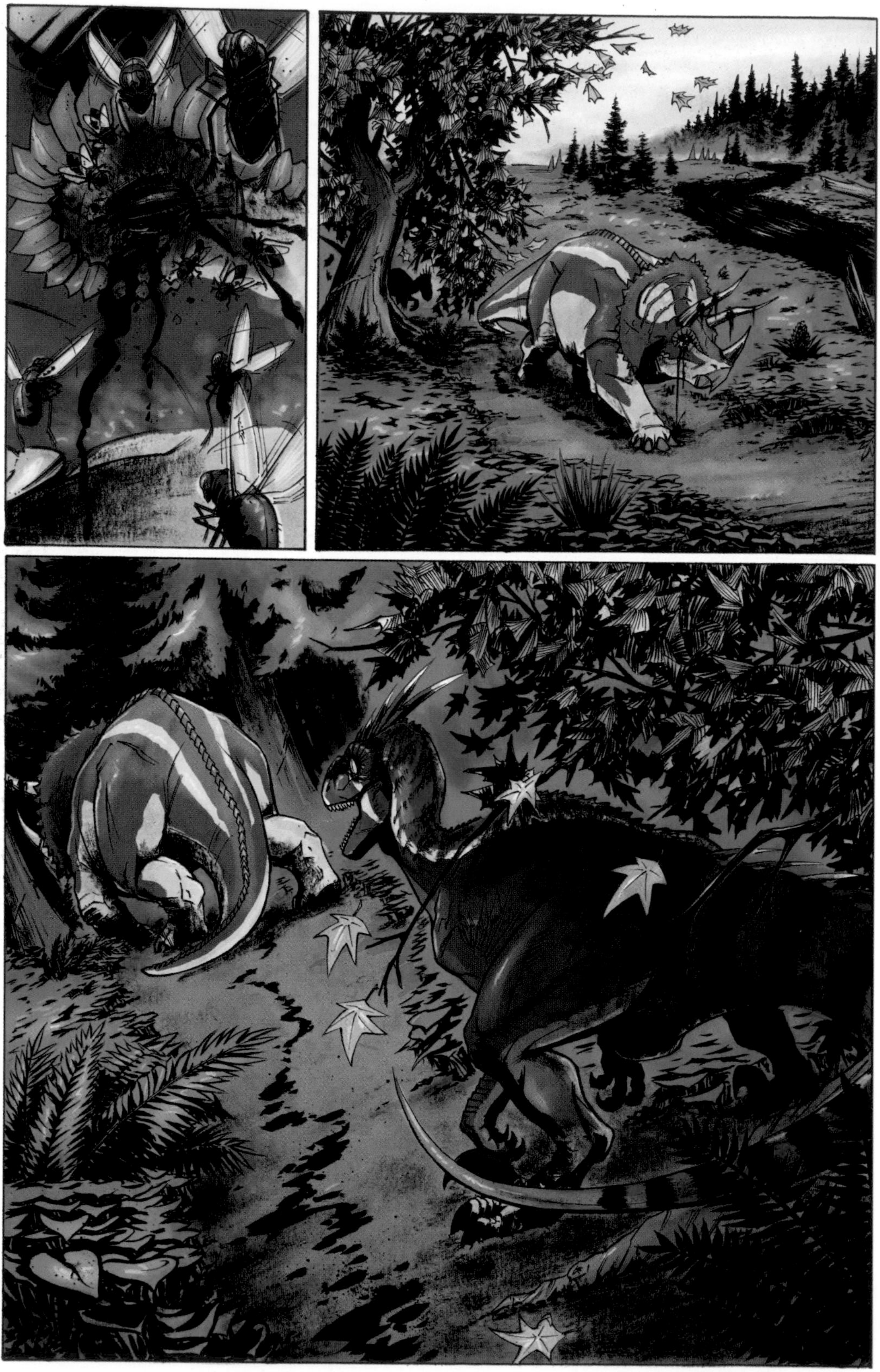

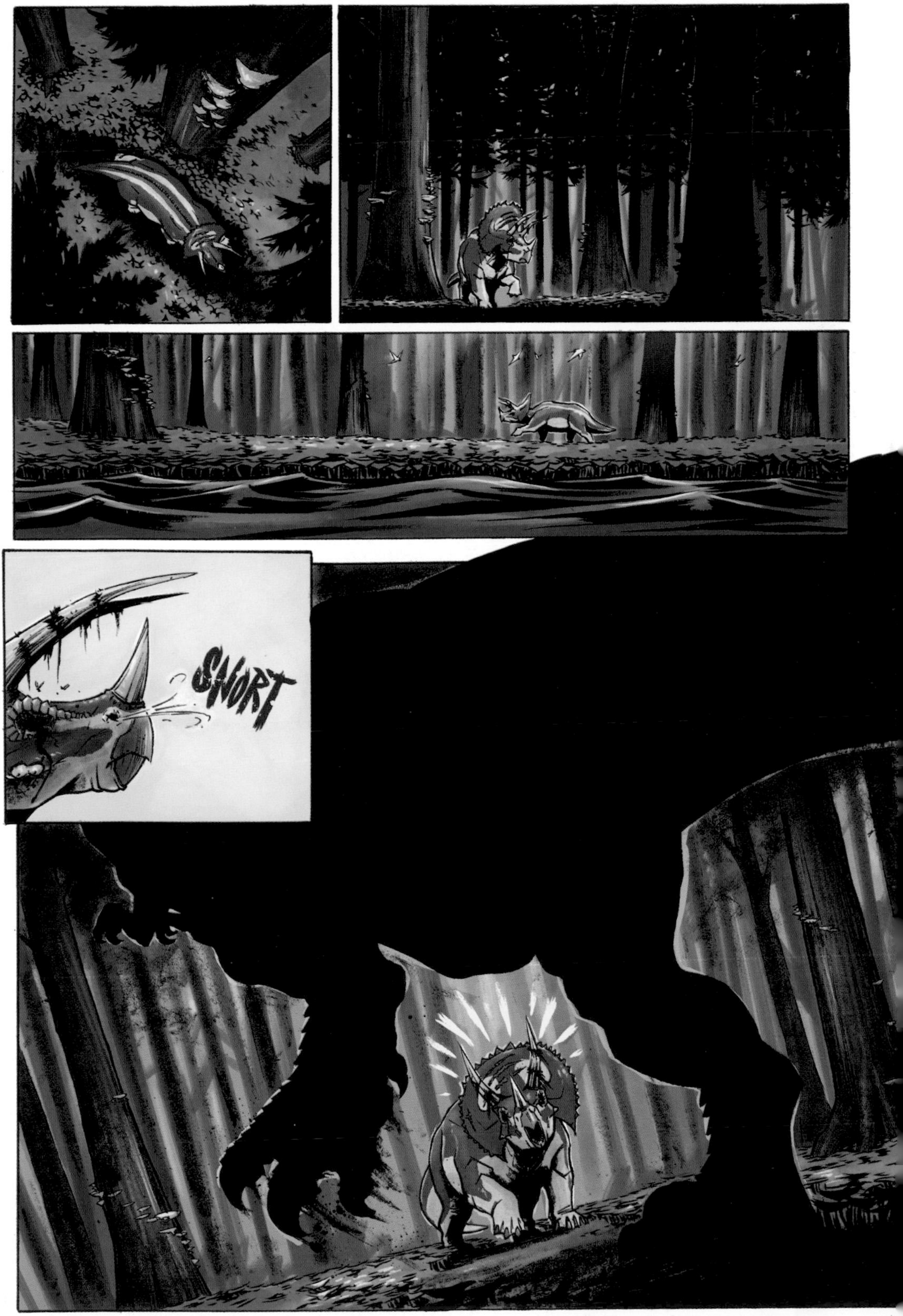
SNORT

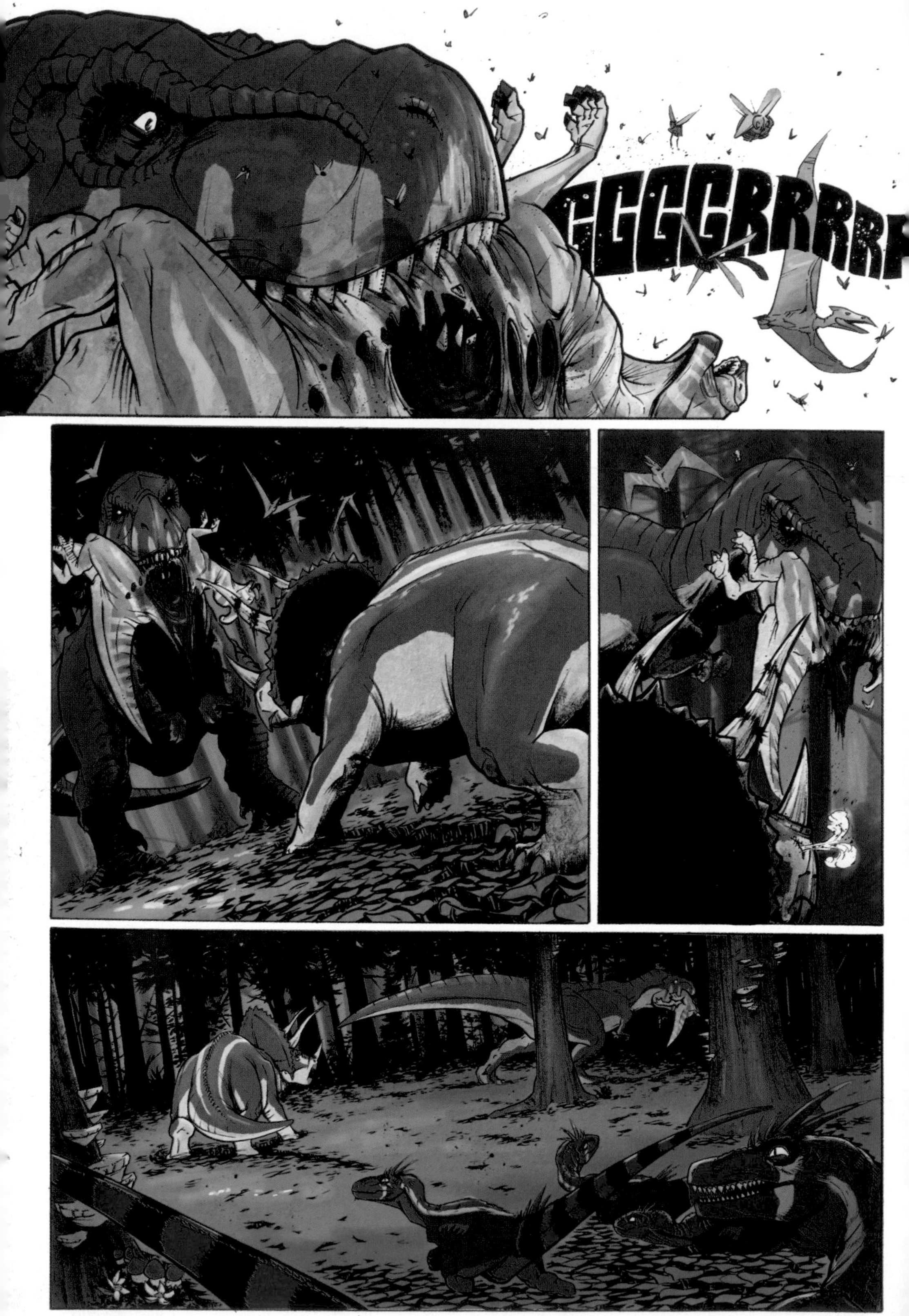
GGGRRRRR

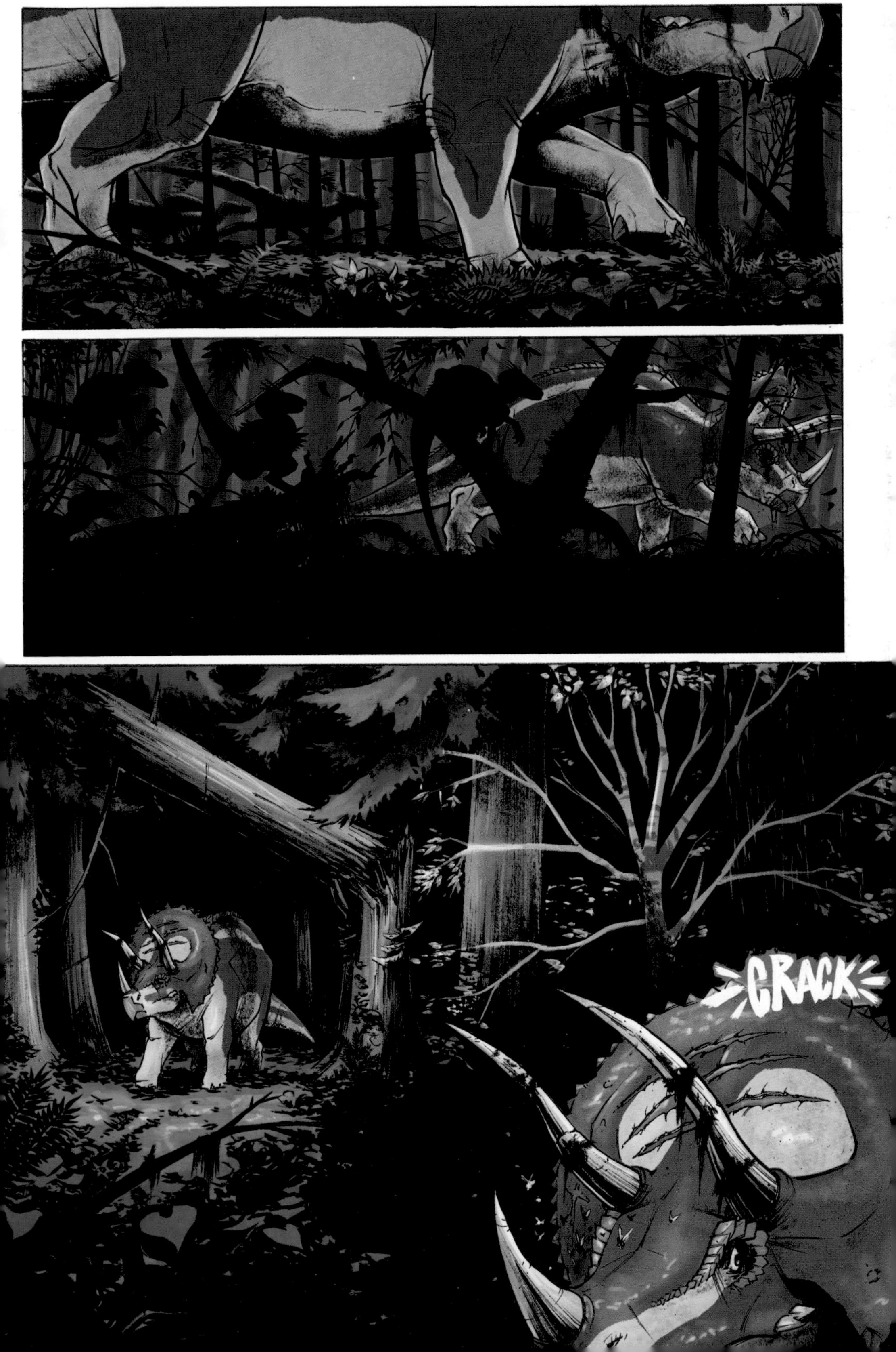
CRACK

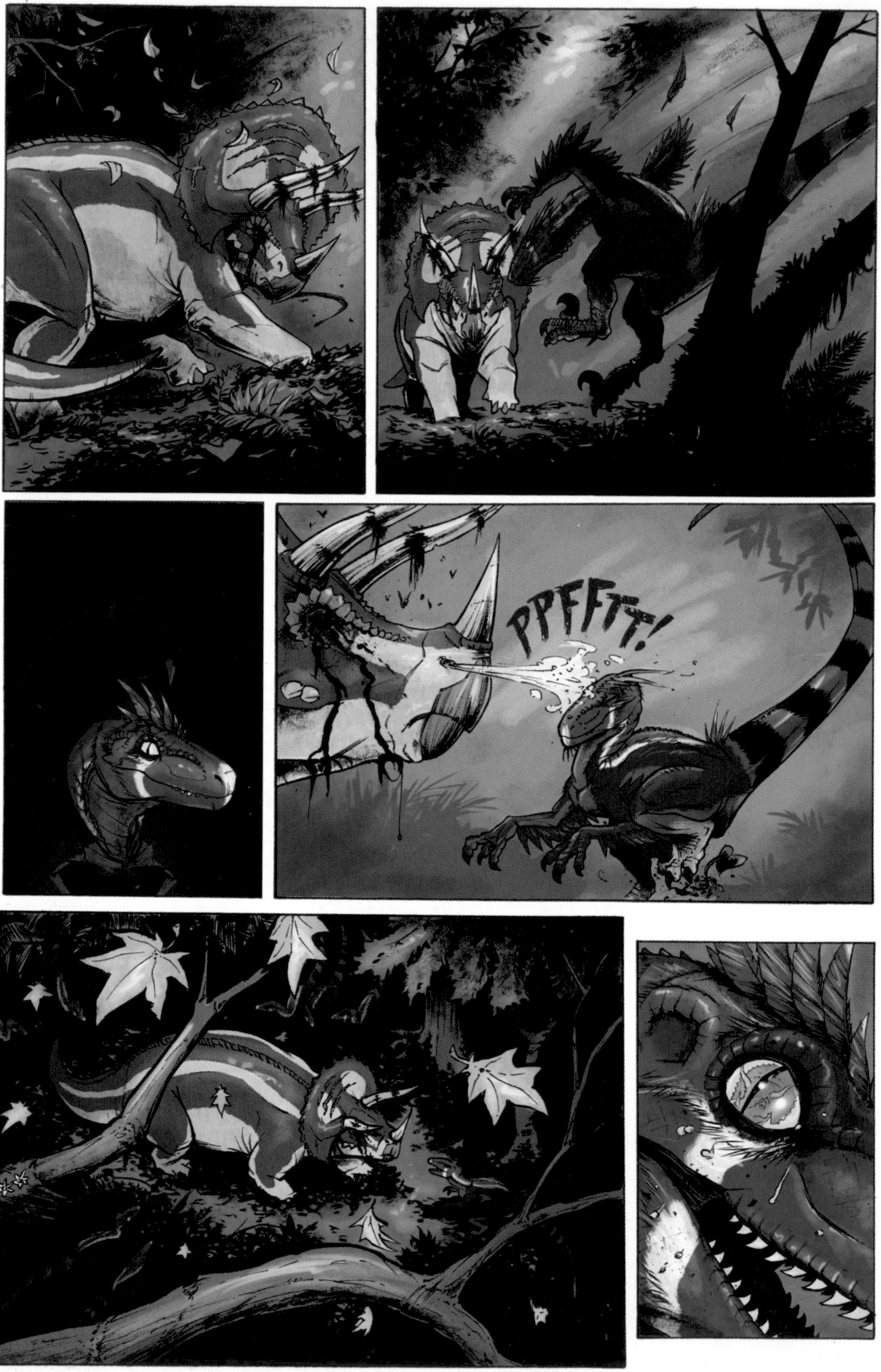
PPFFTT!

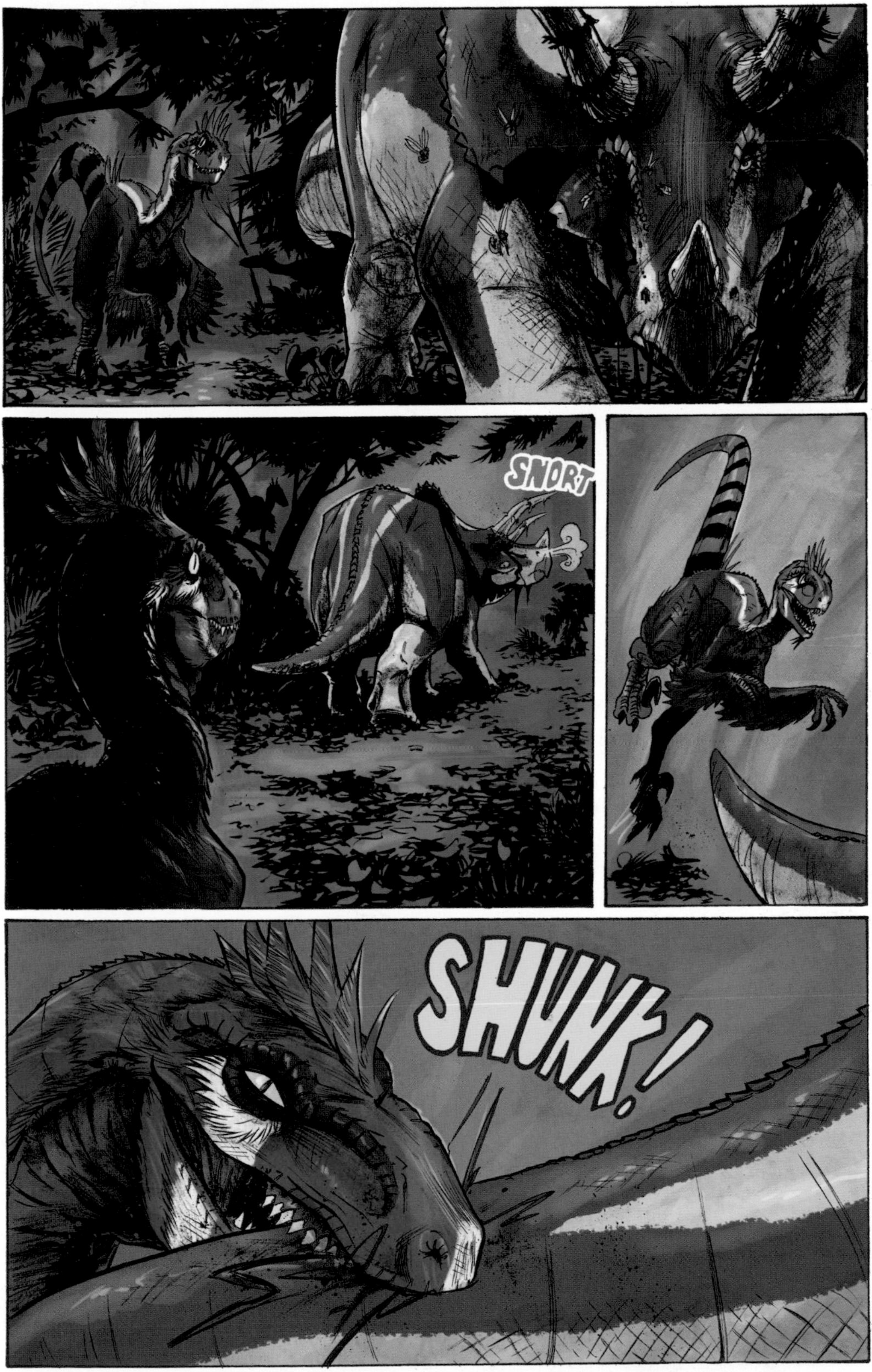
SNORT
SHUNK!

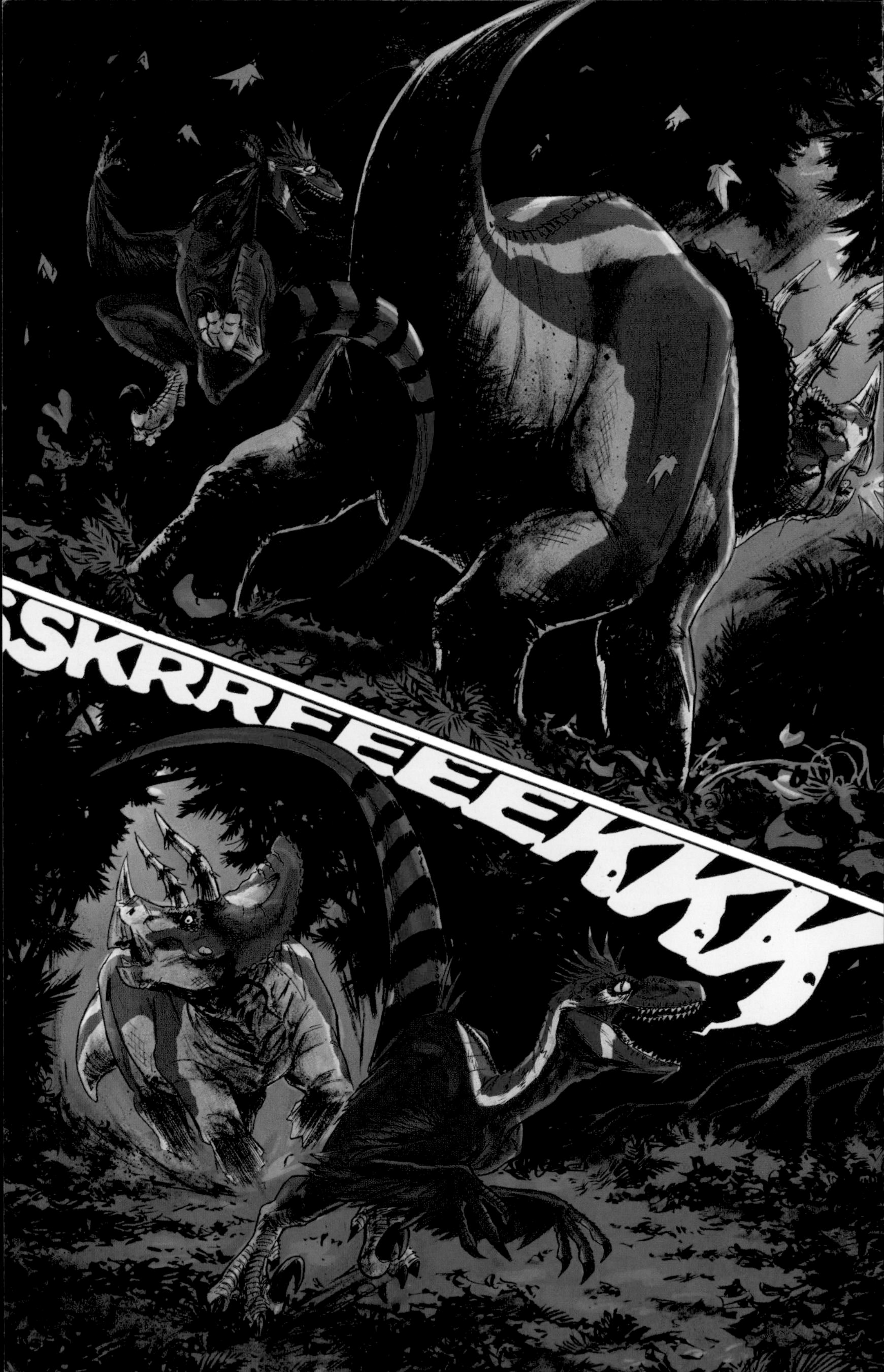
SKRREEEEKKK

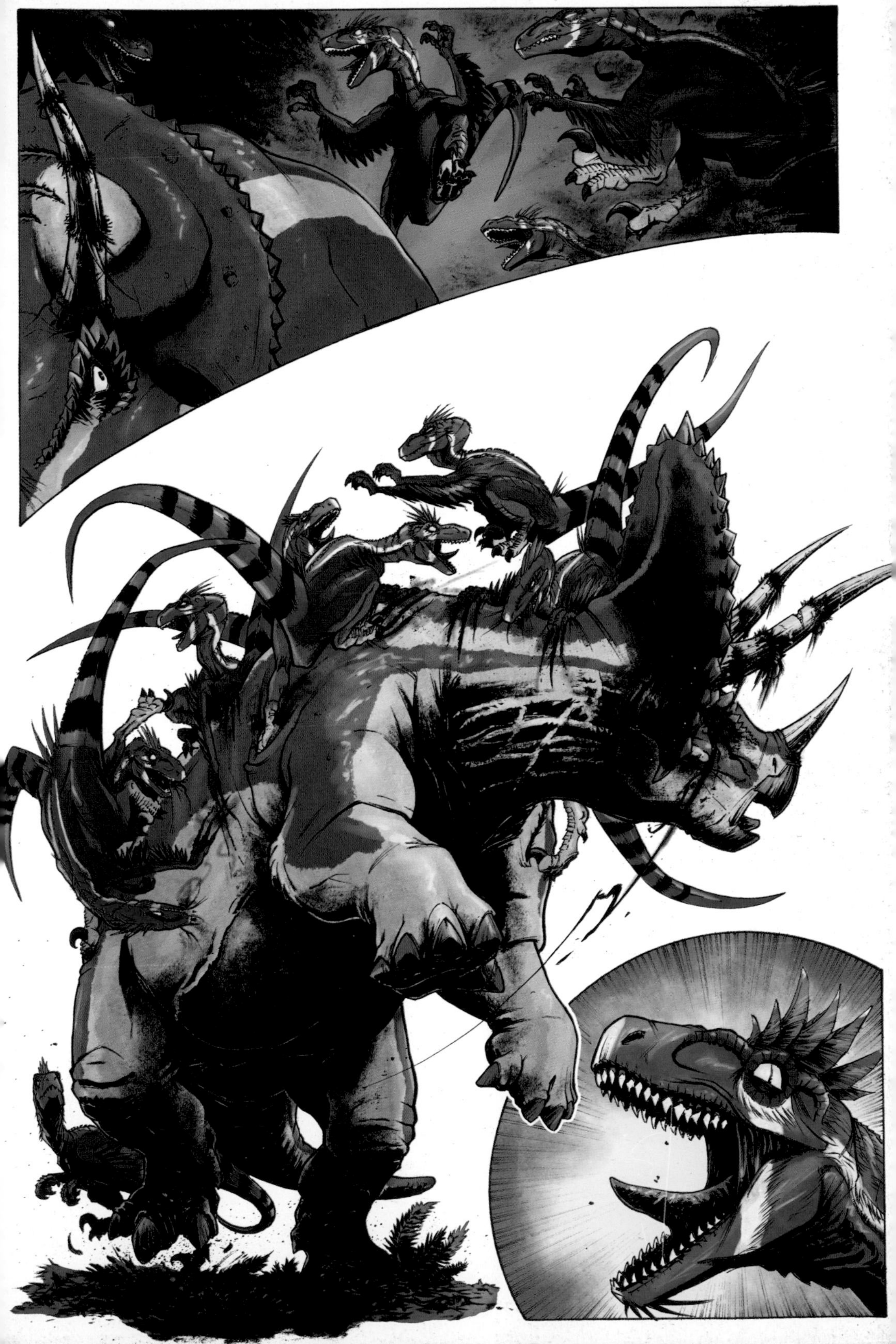

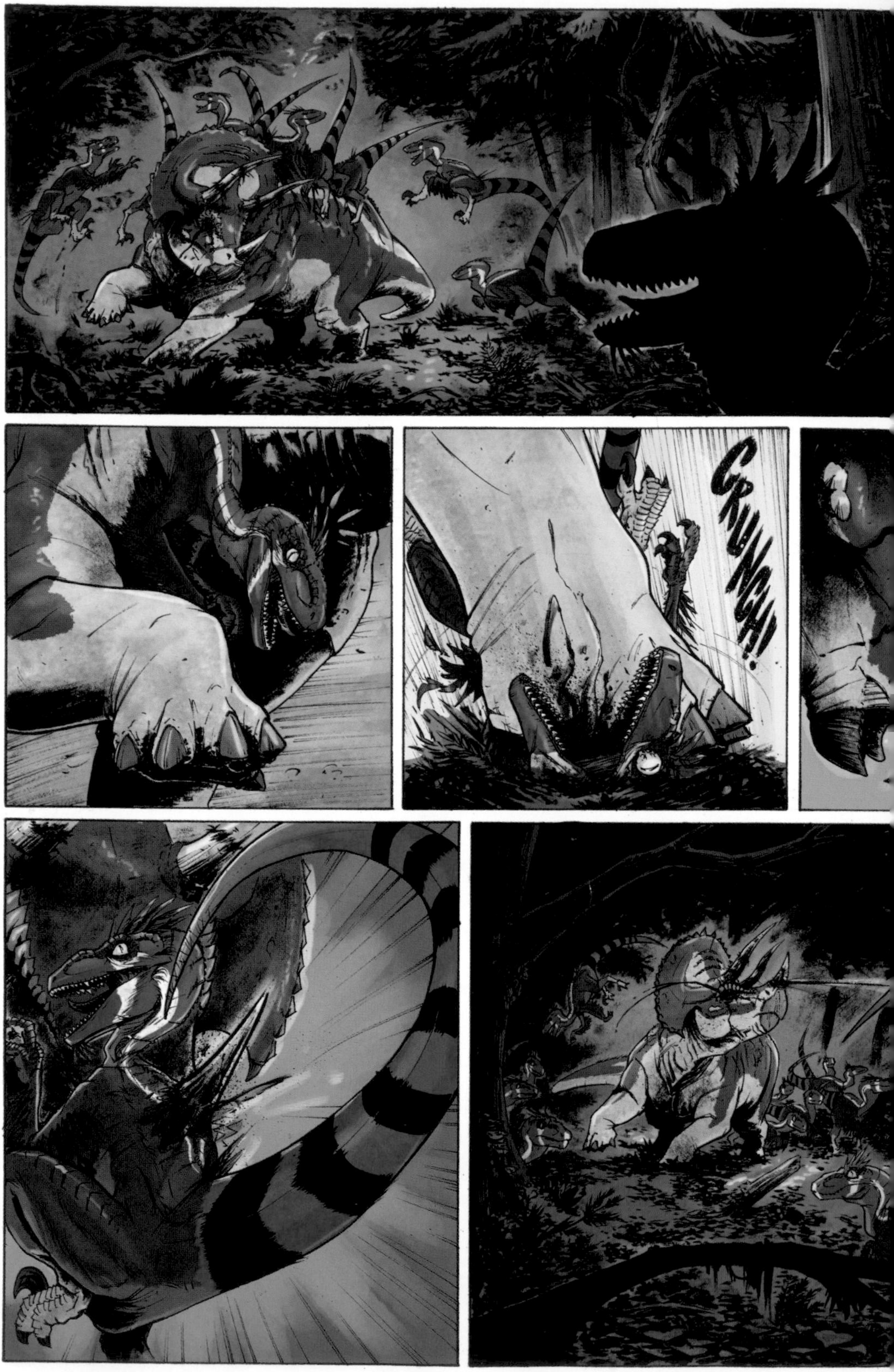
CRUNCH!

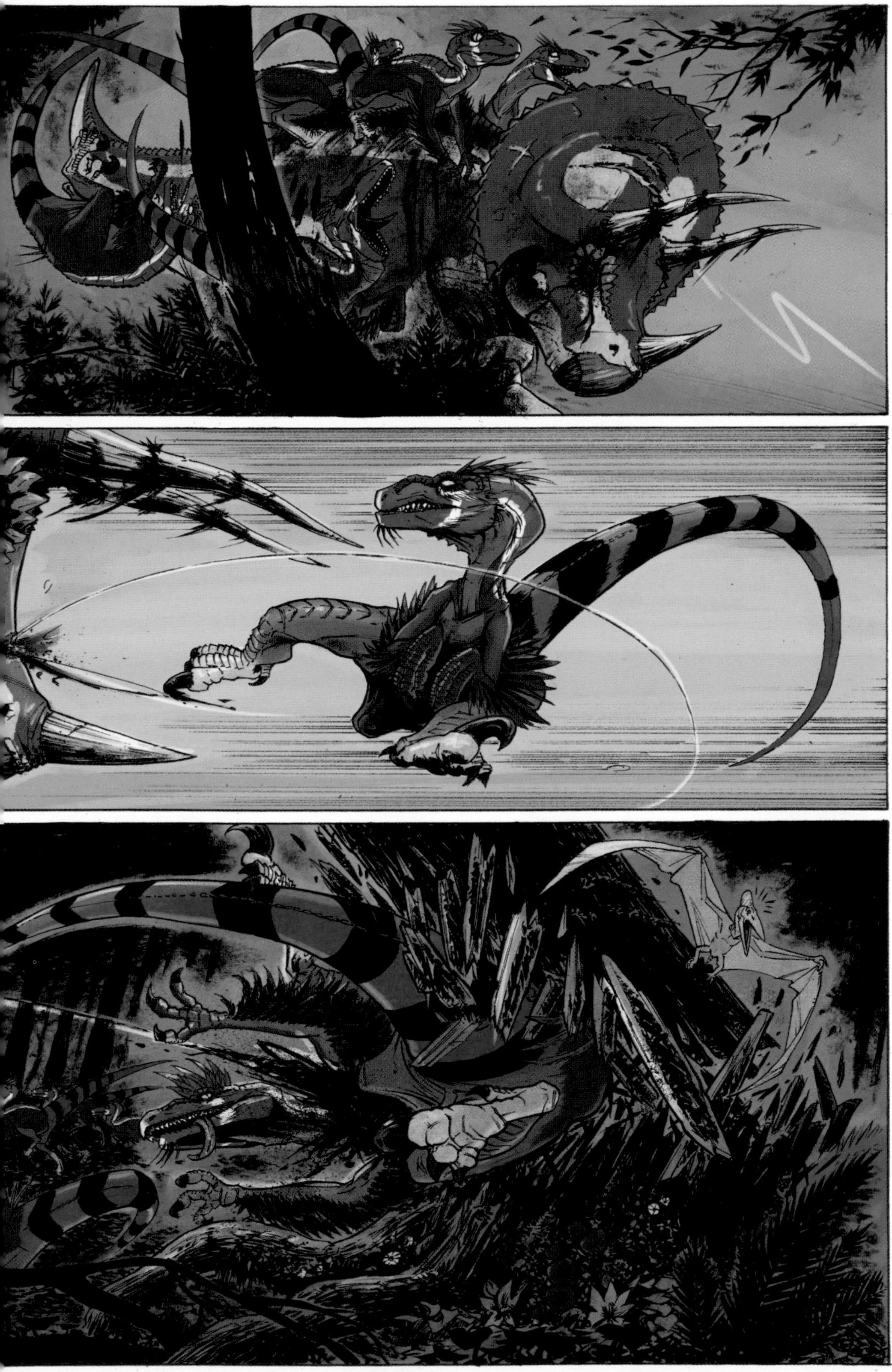

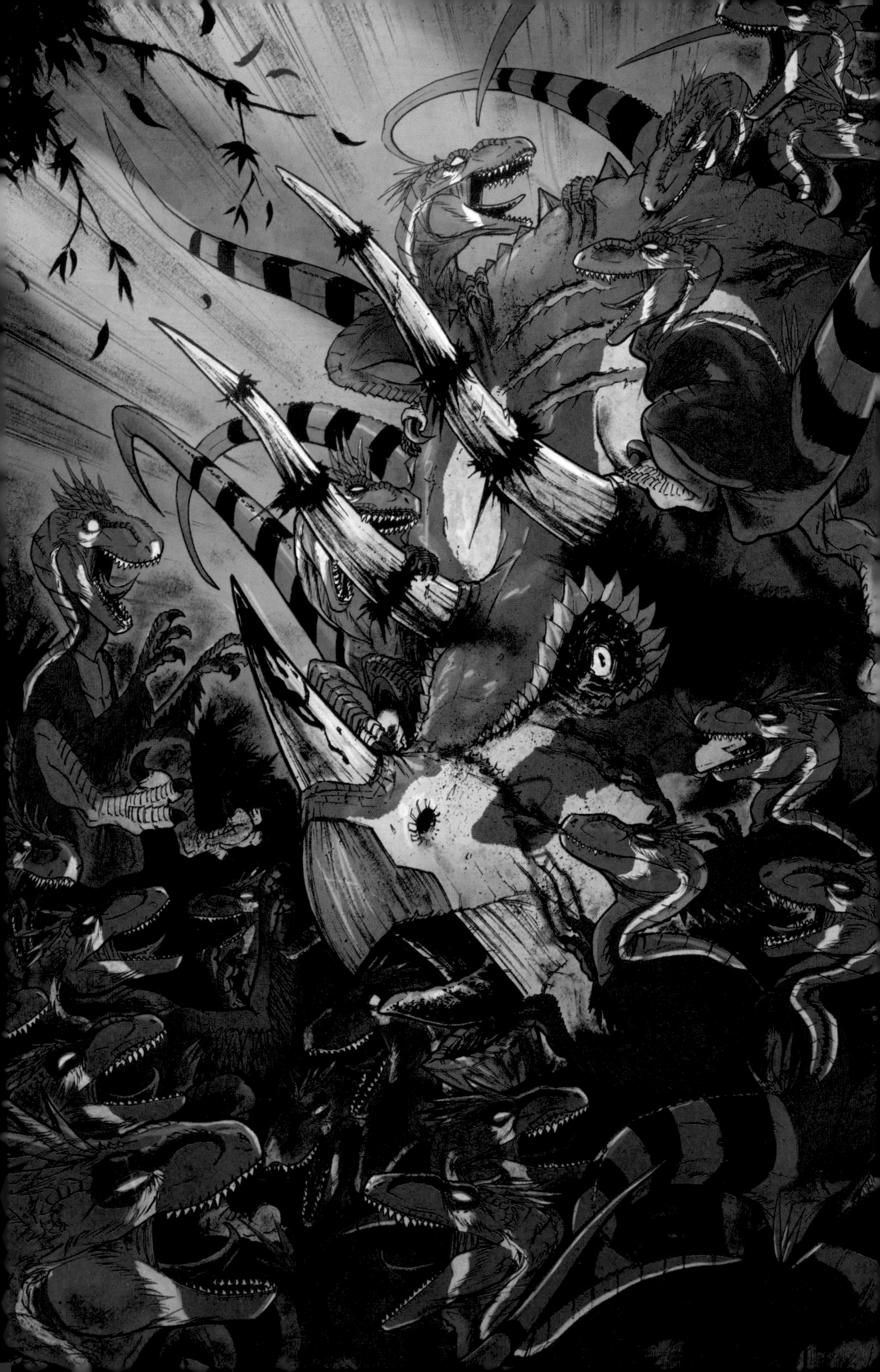

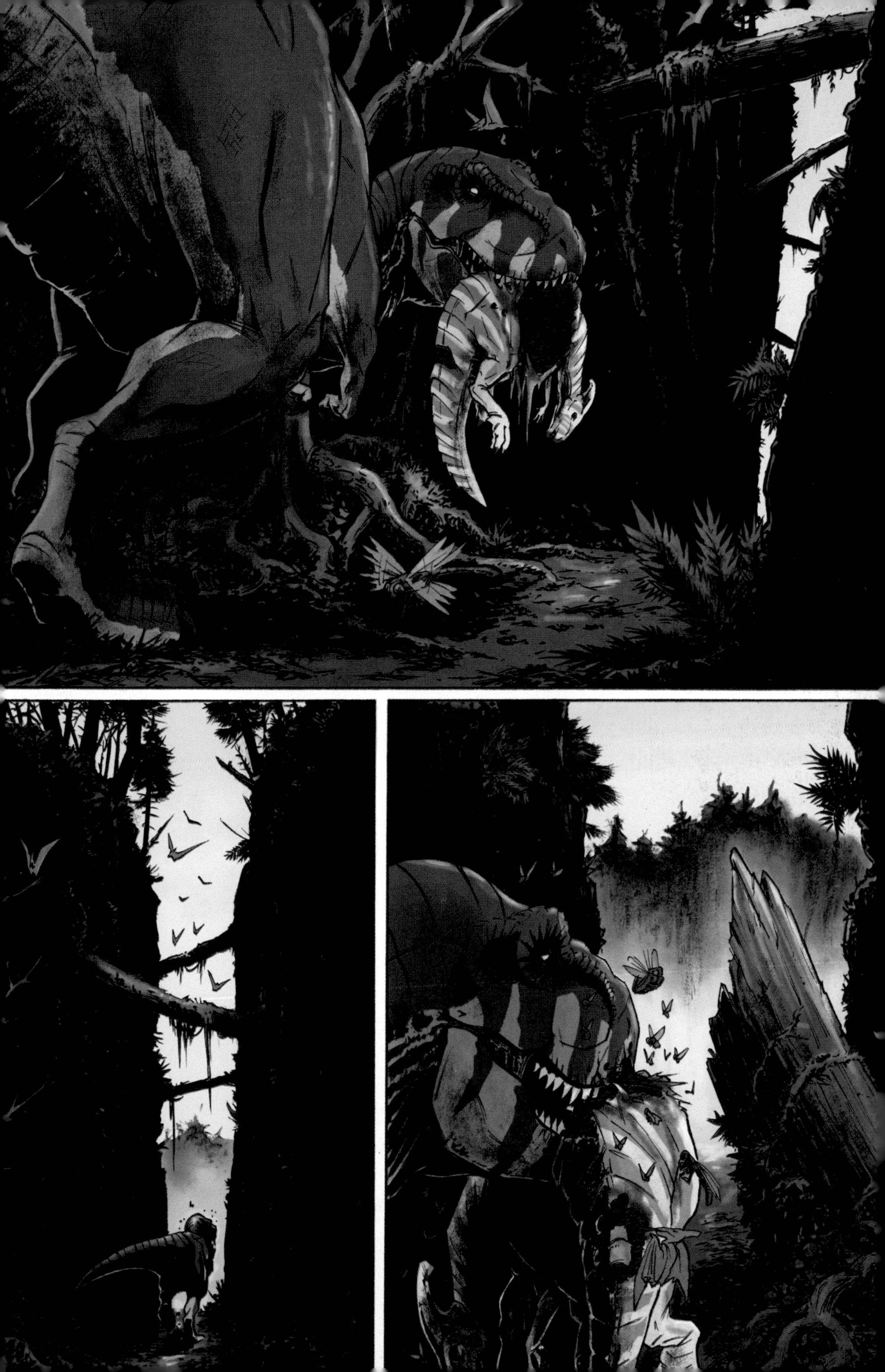

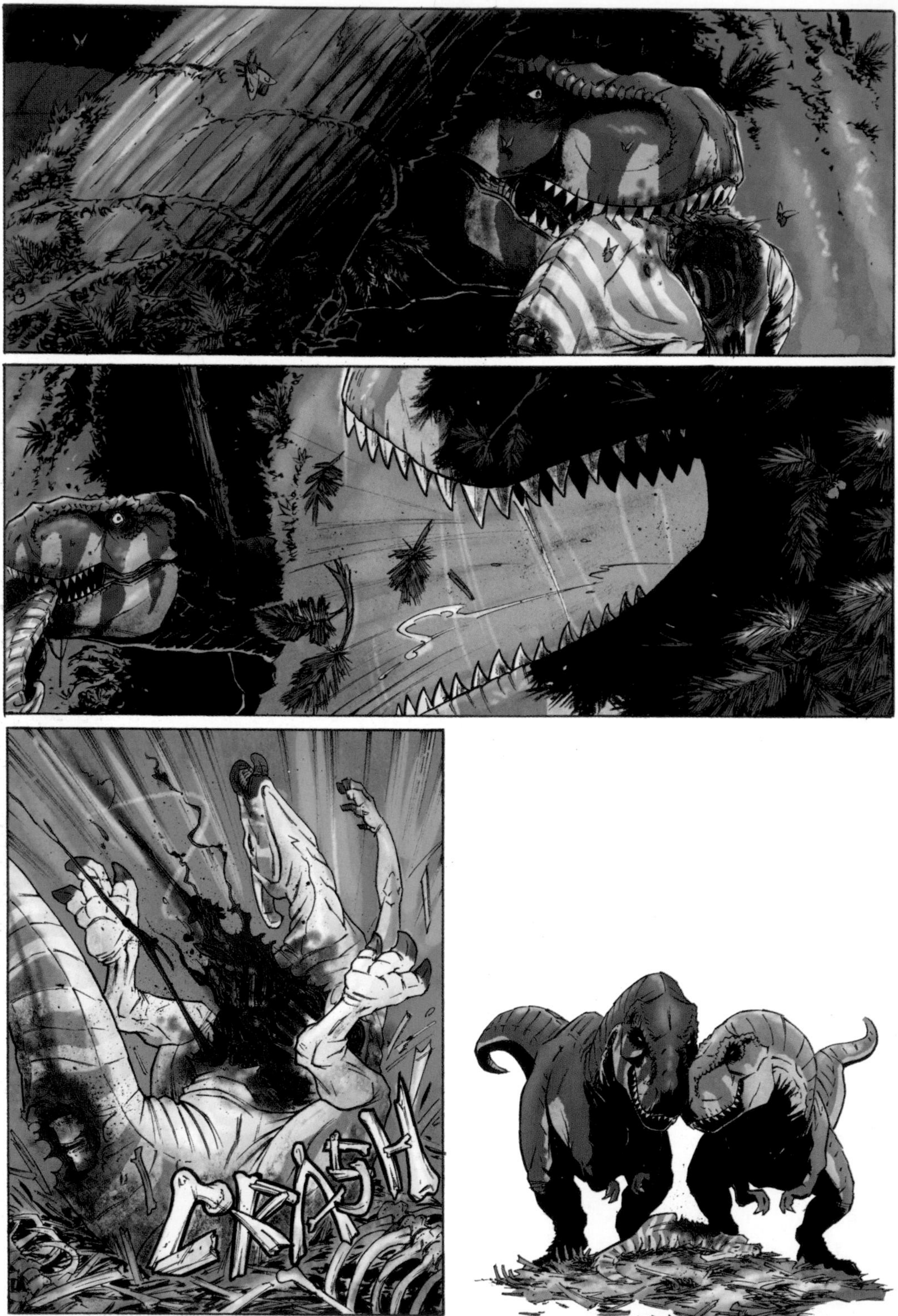
CRASH

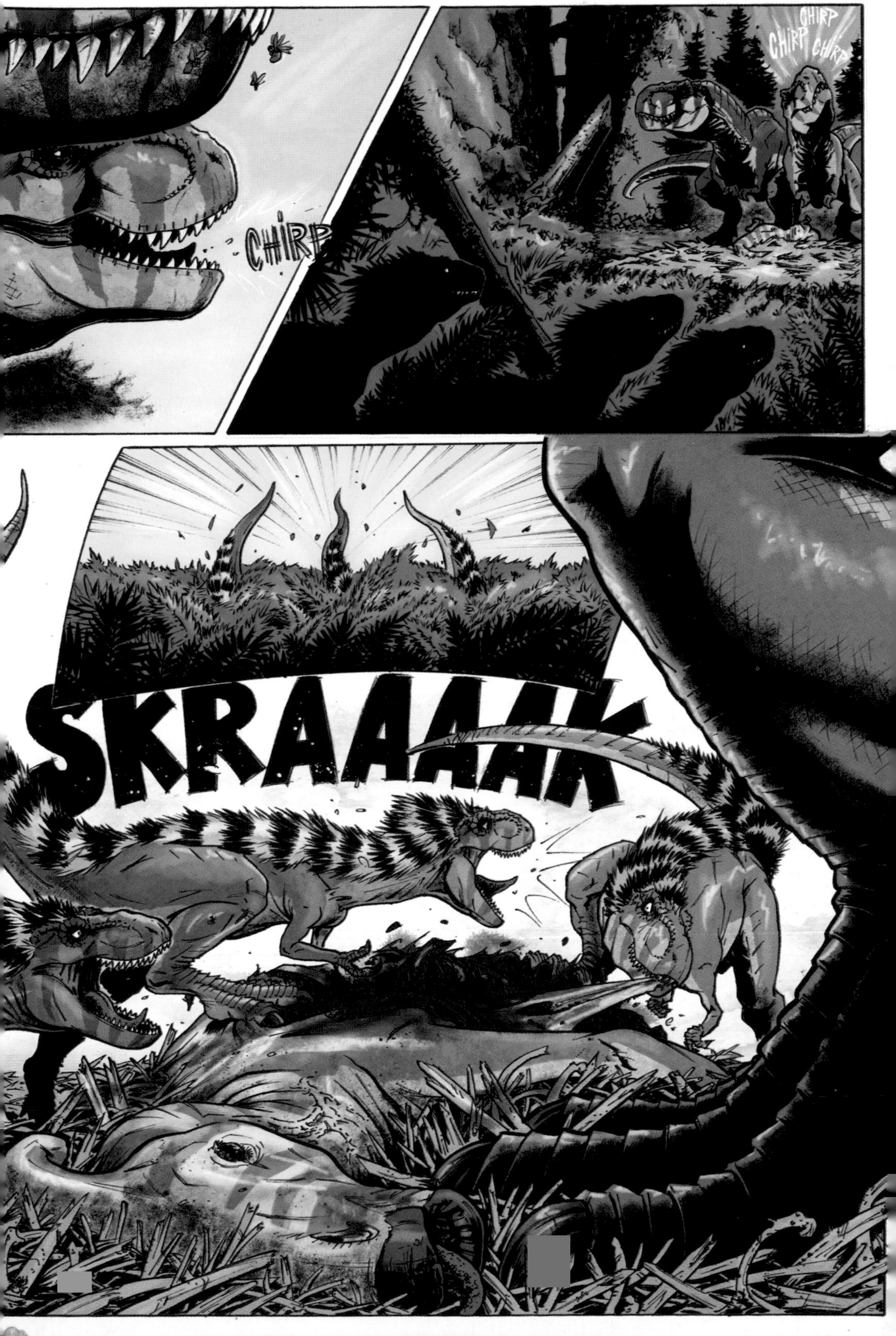
CHIRP
CHIRP
CHIRP
CHIRP
SKRAAAK

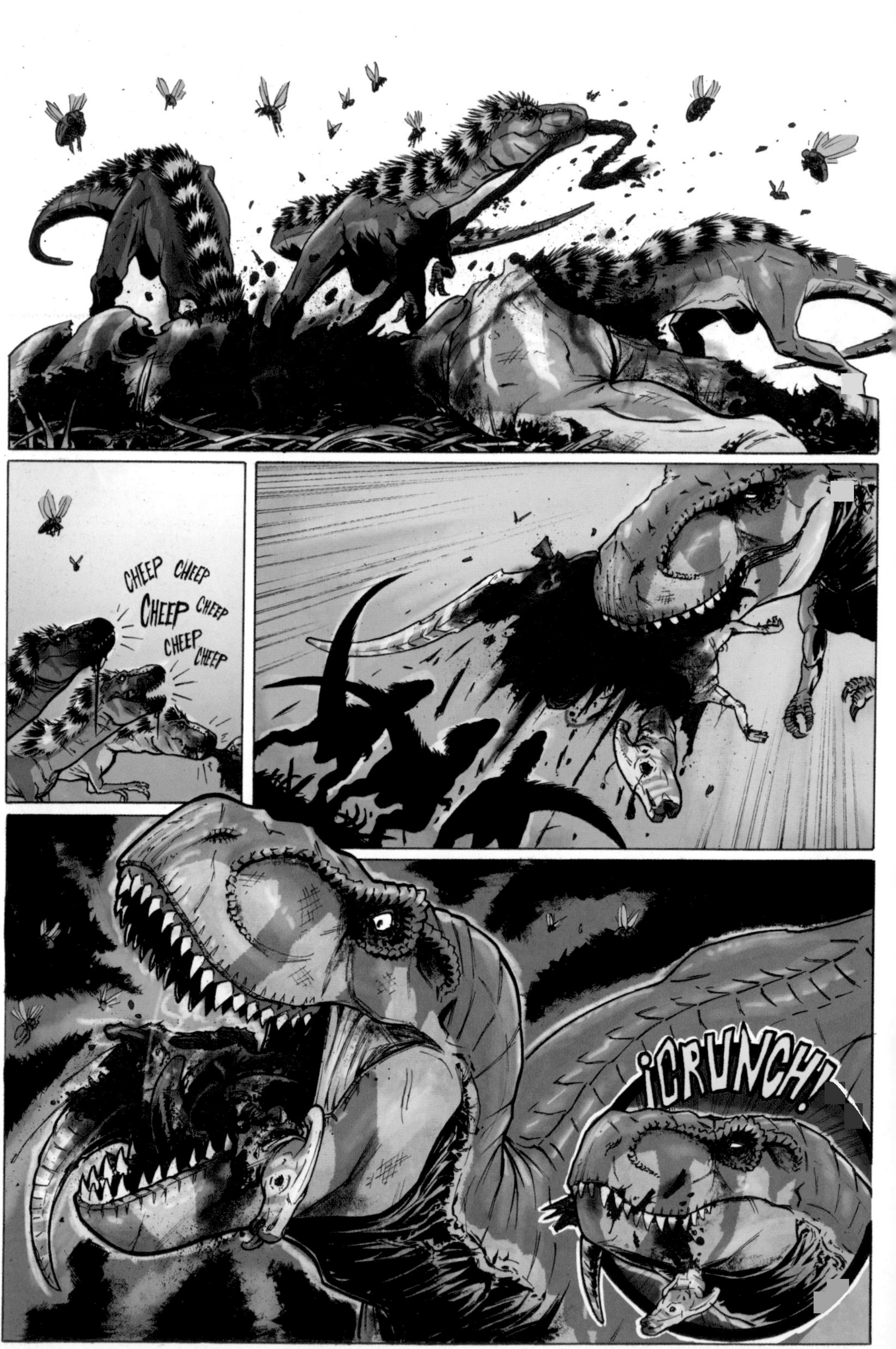
CHEEP CHEEP
CHEEP CHEEP
CHEEP
CHEEP
¡CRUNCH!

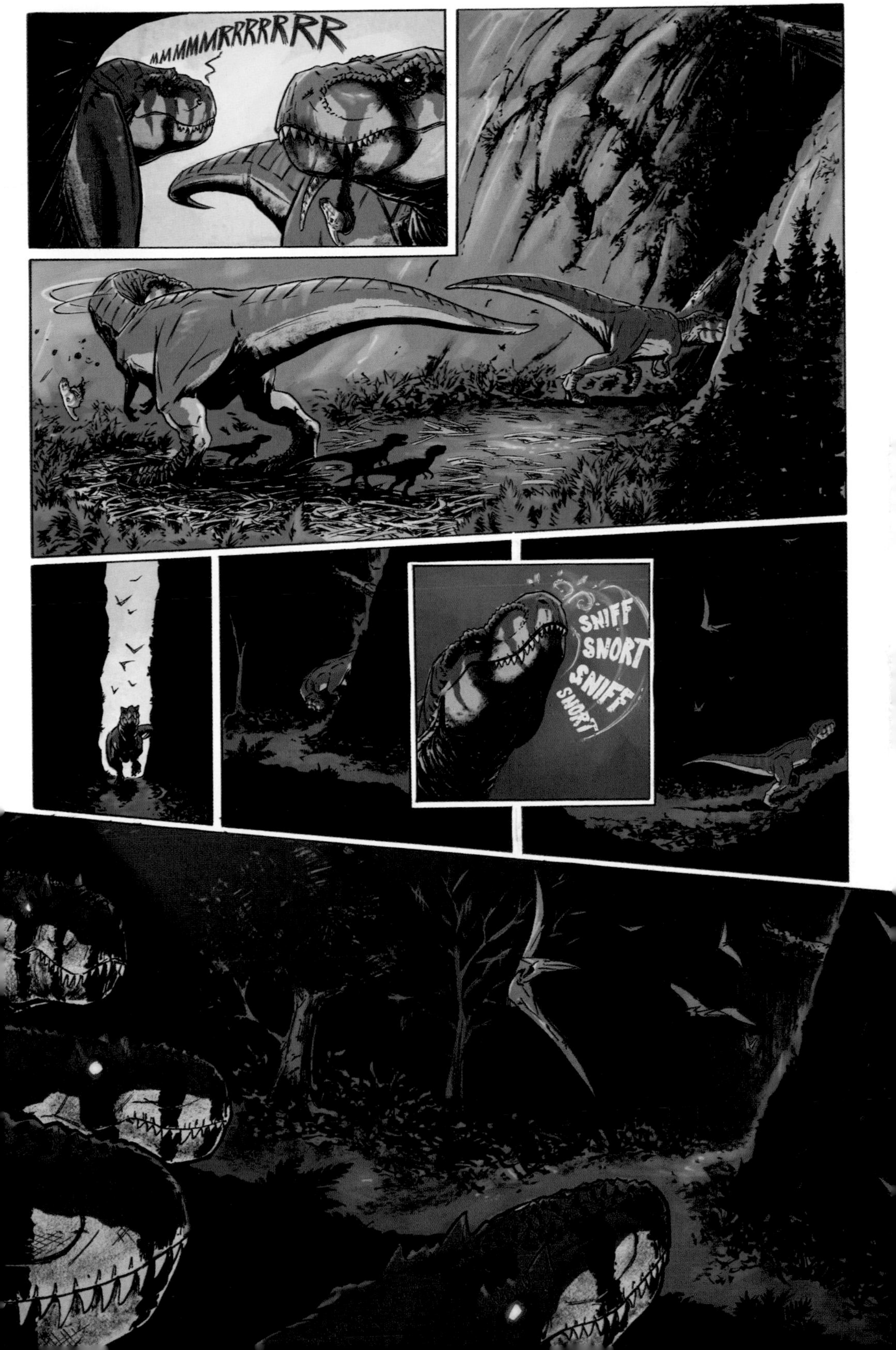
MMMMMRRRRRRR
SNIFF
SNORT
SNIFF
SNORT

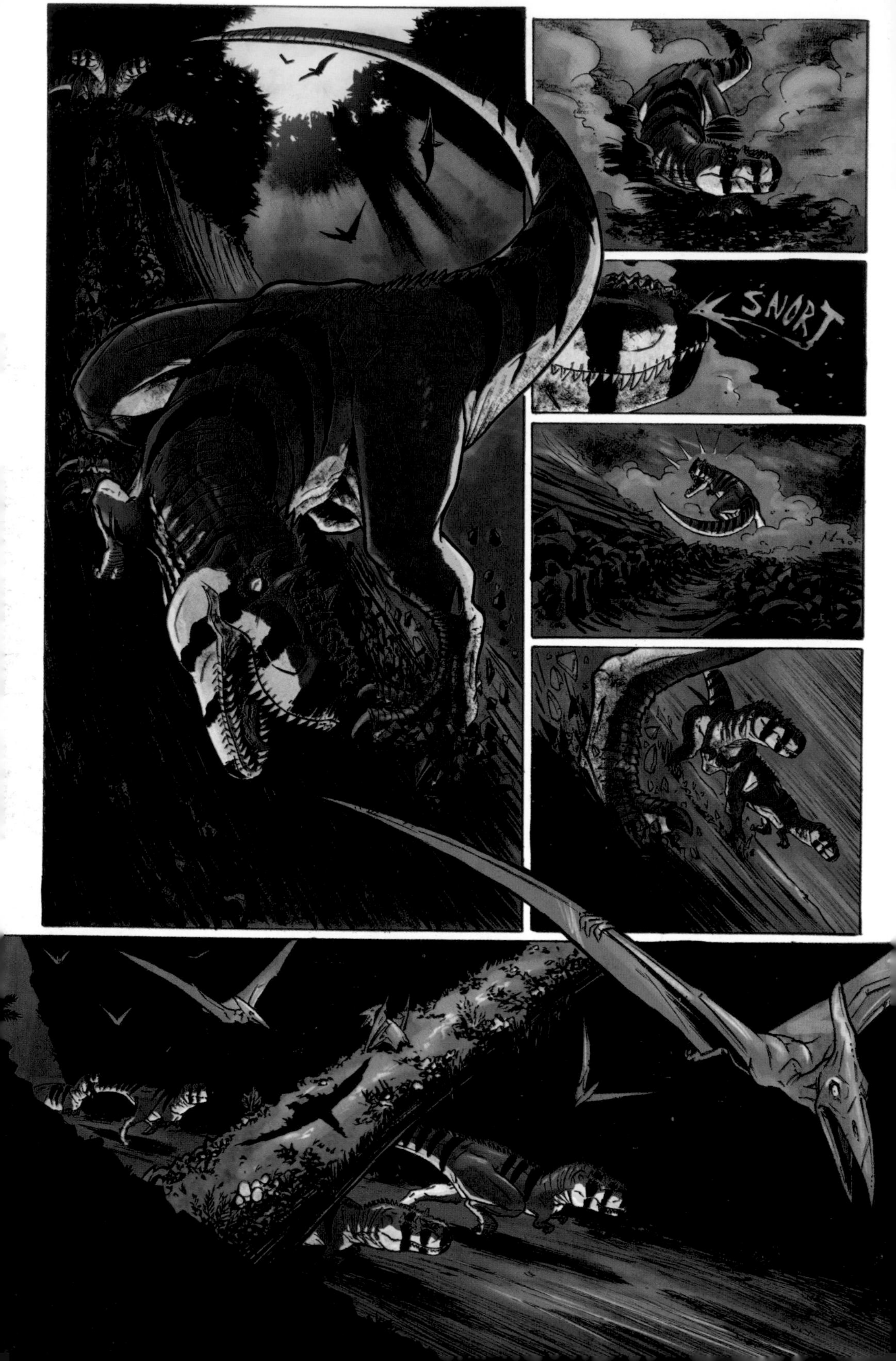
SNORT

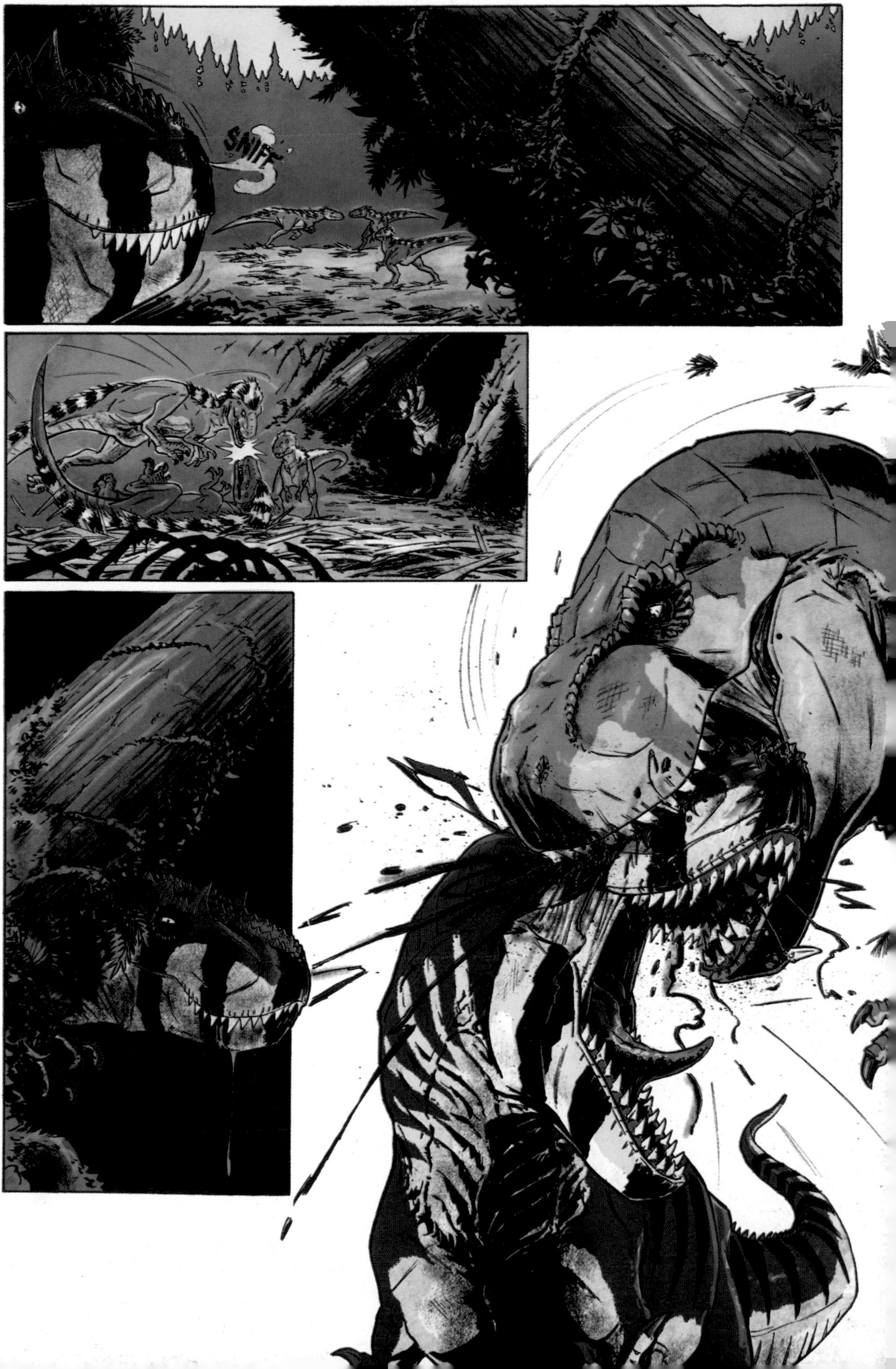
SNIFF

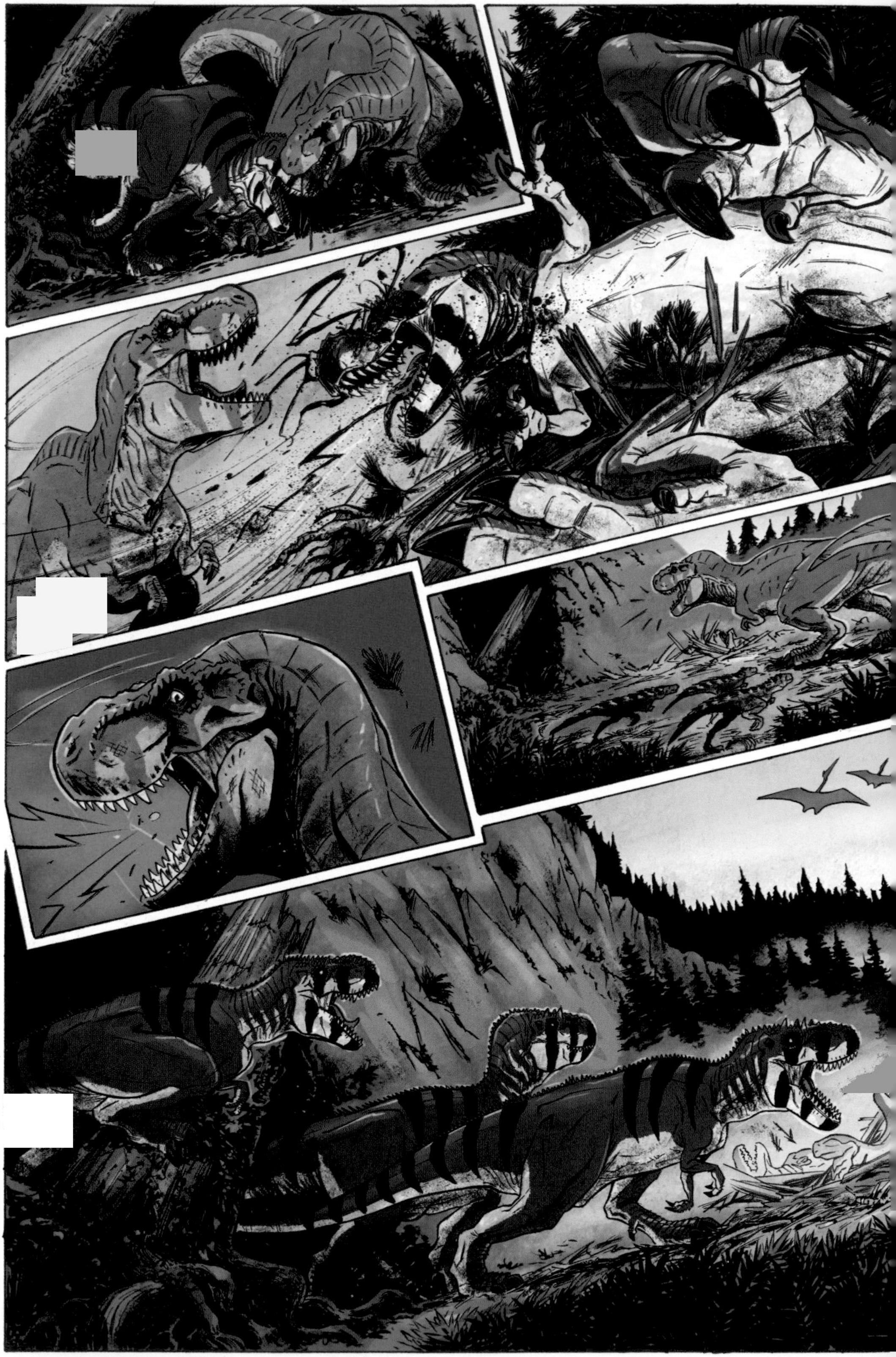

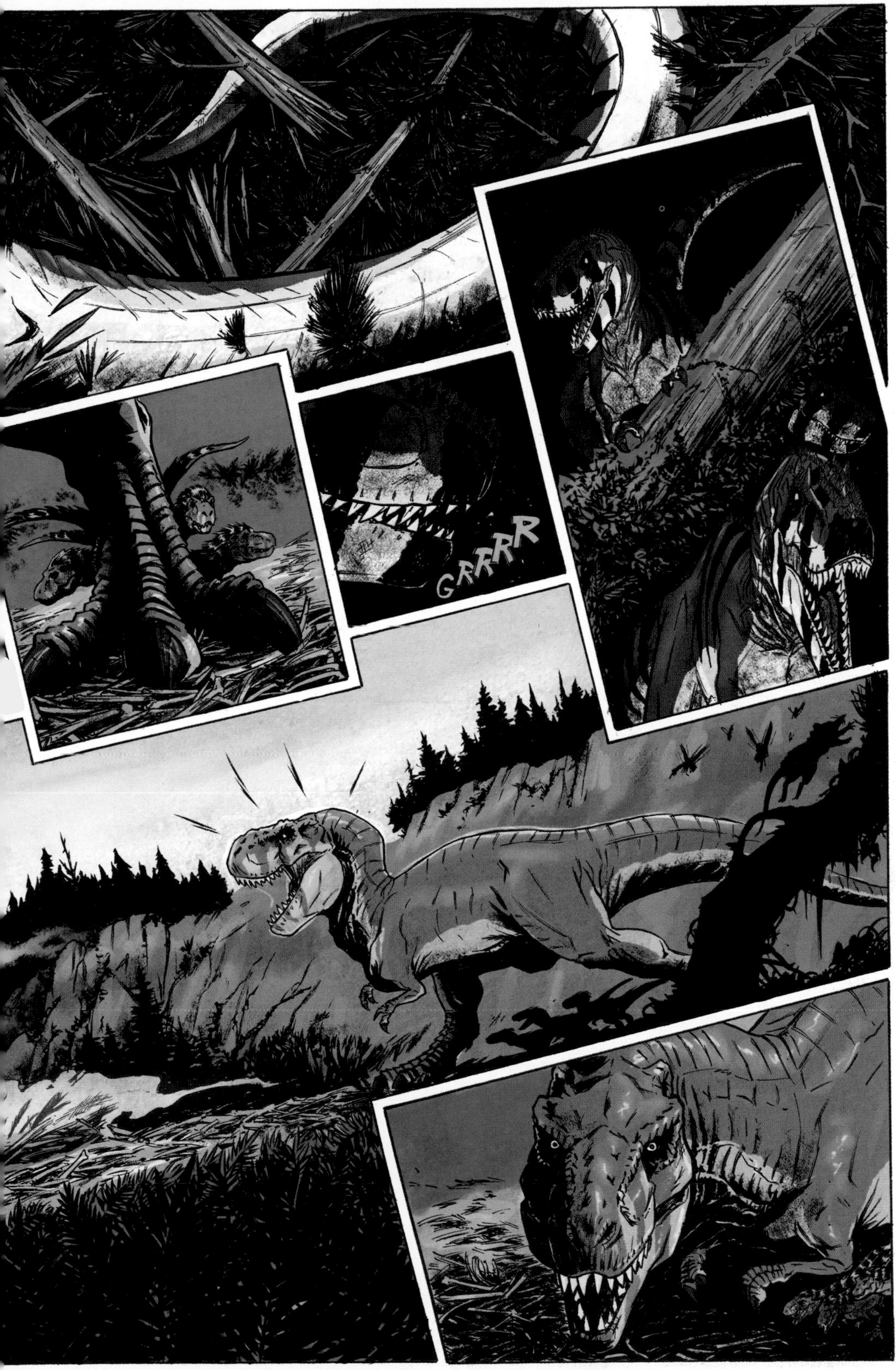
GRRRRR

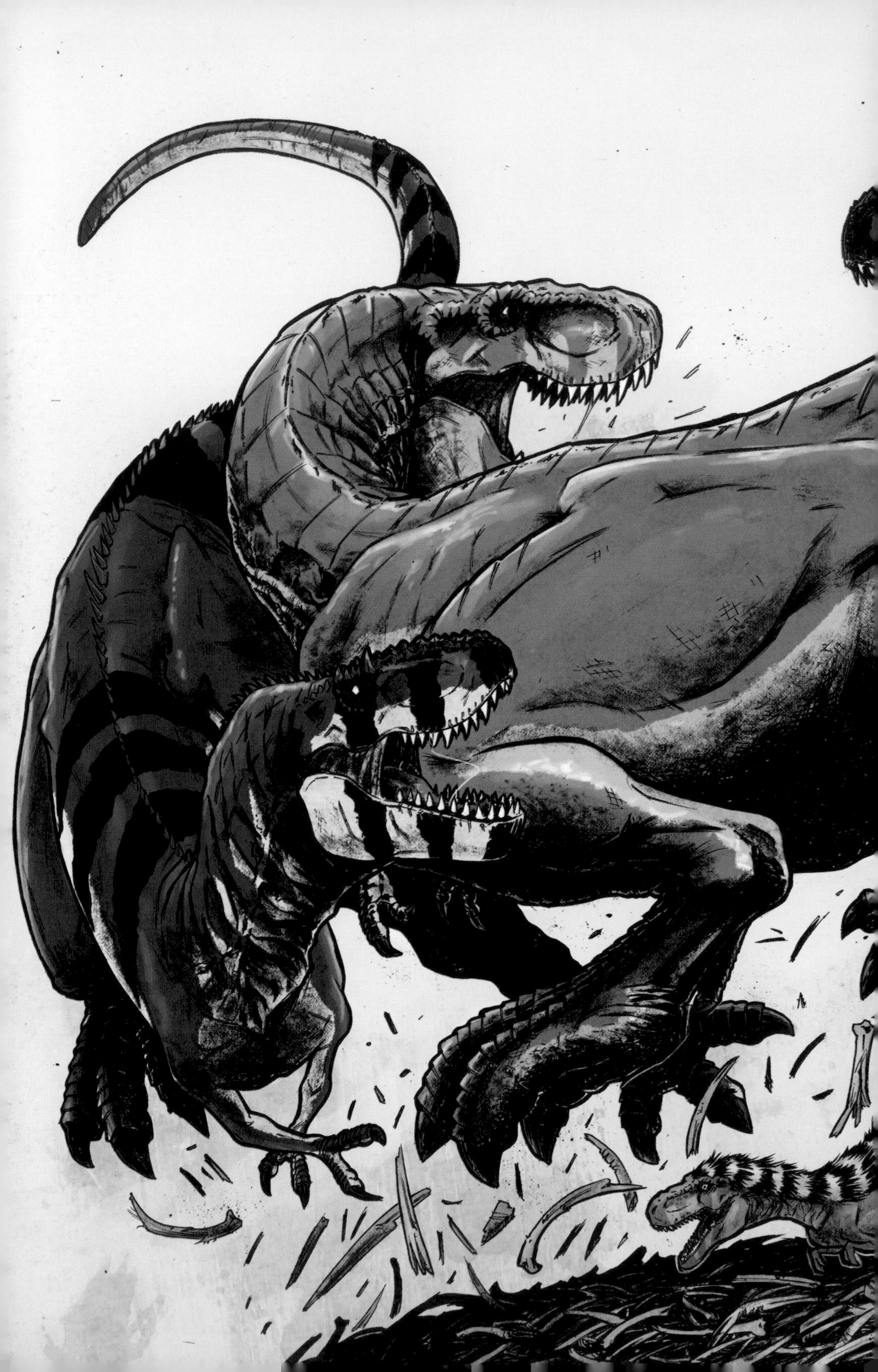

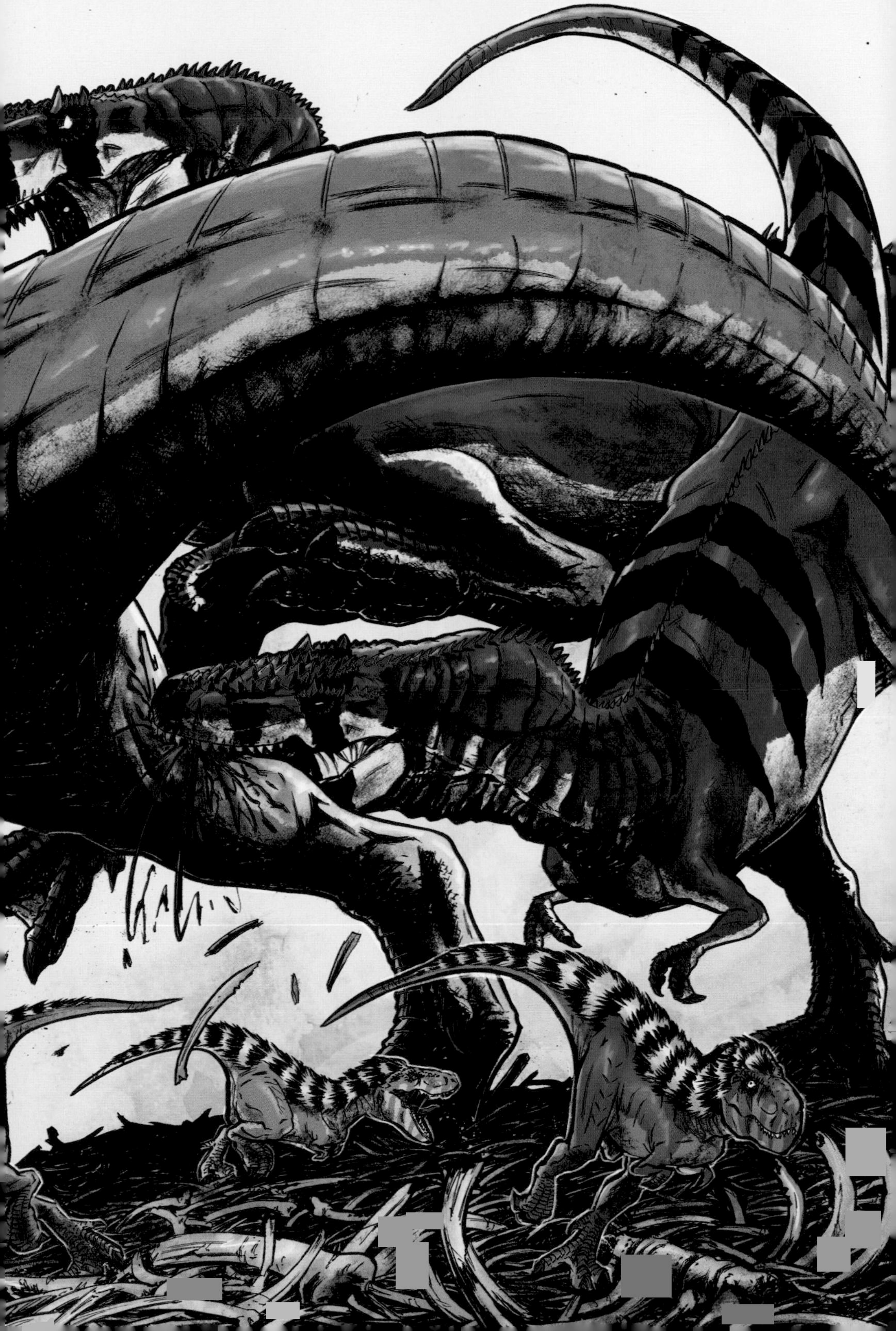

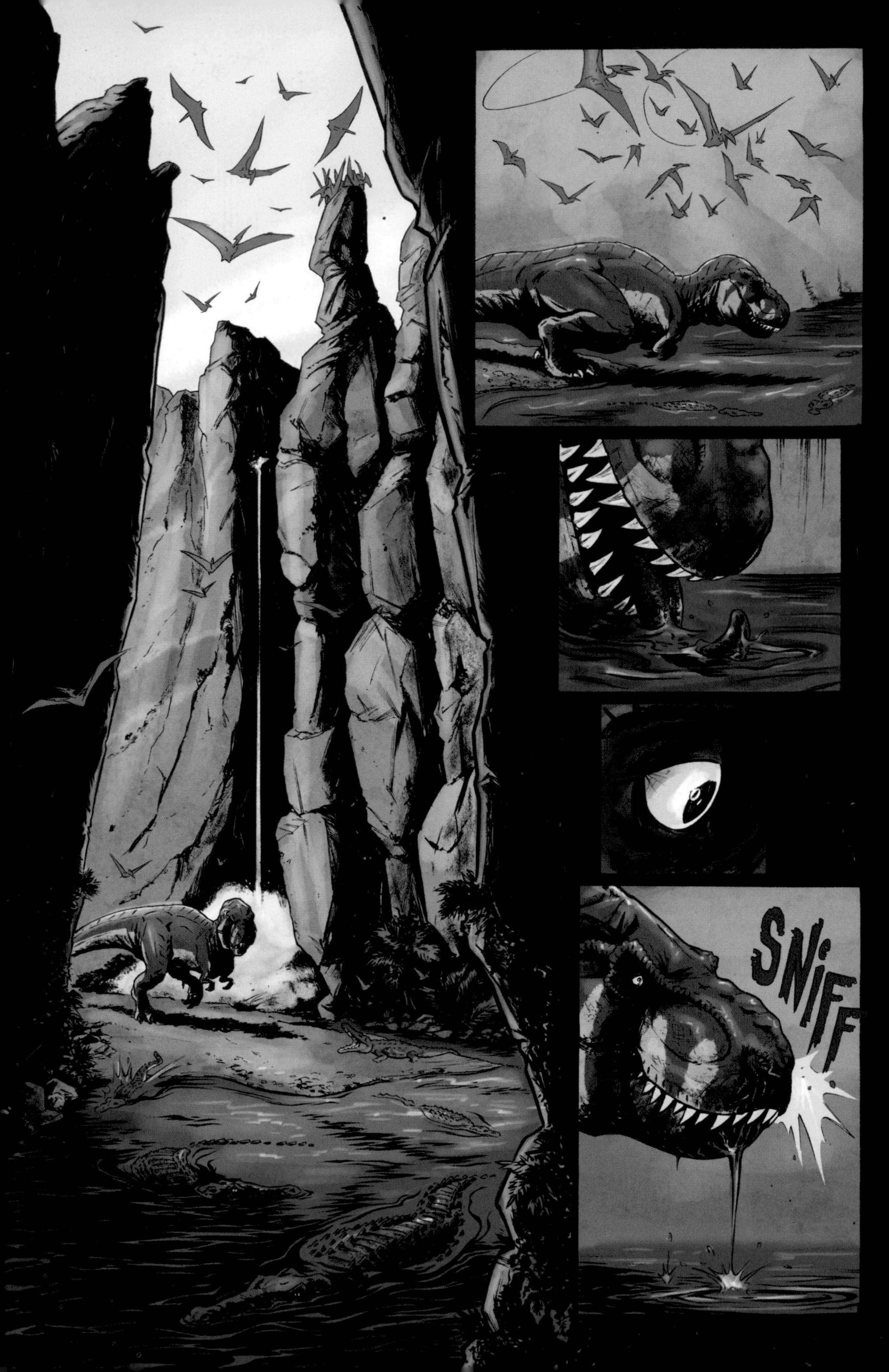
SNIFF

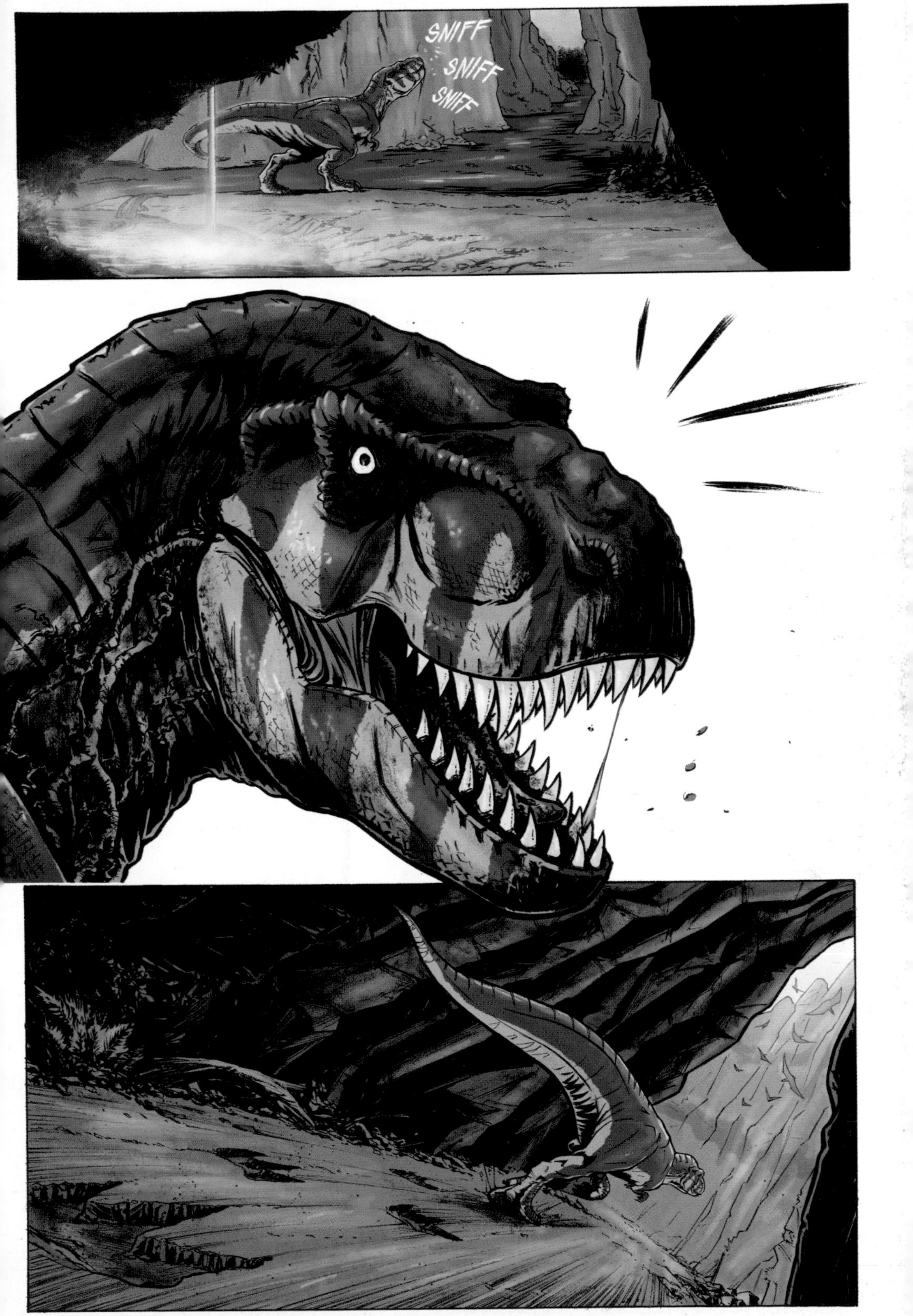
SNIFF
SNIFF
SNIFF

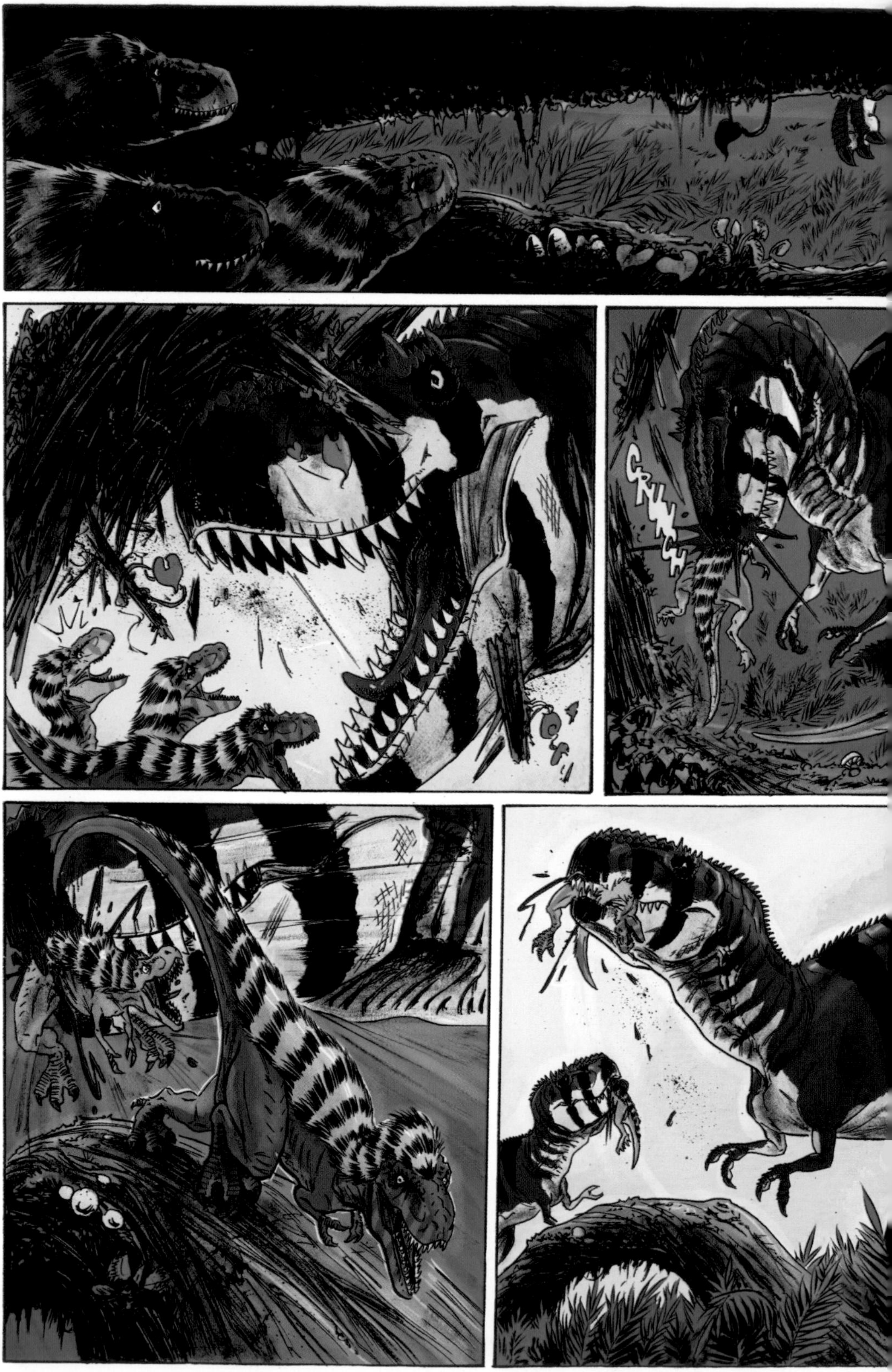
CRUNCH

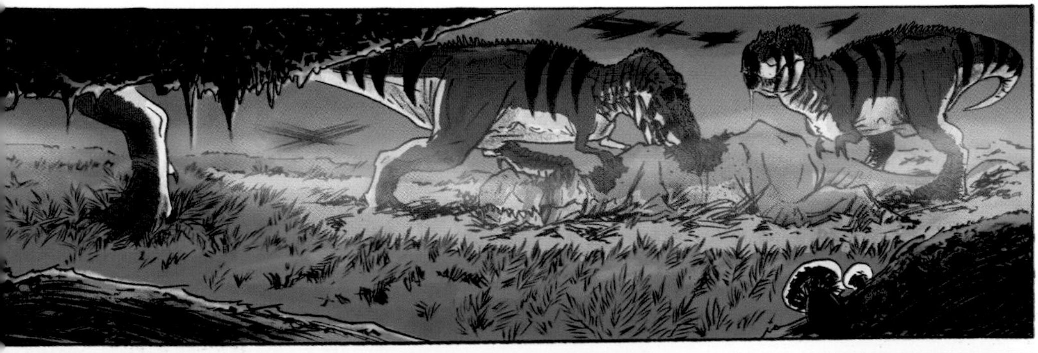

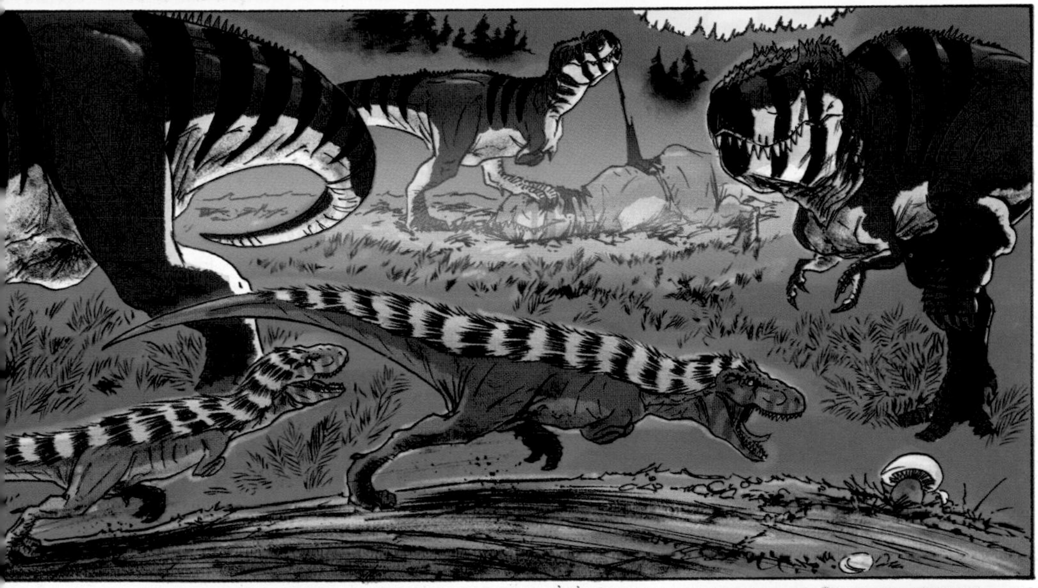

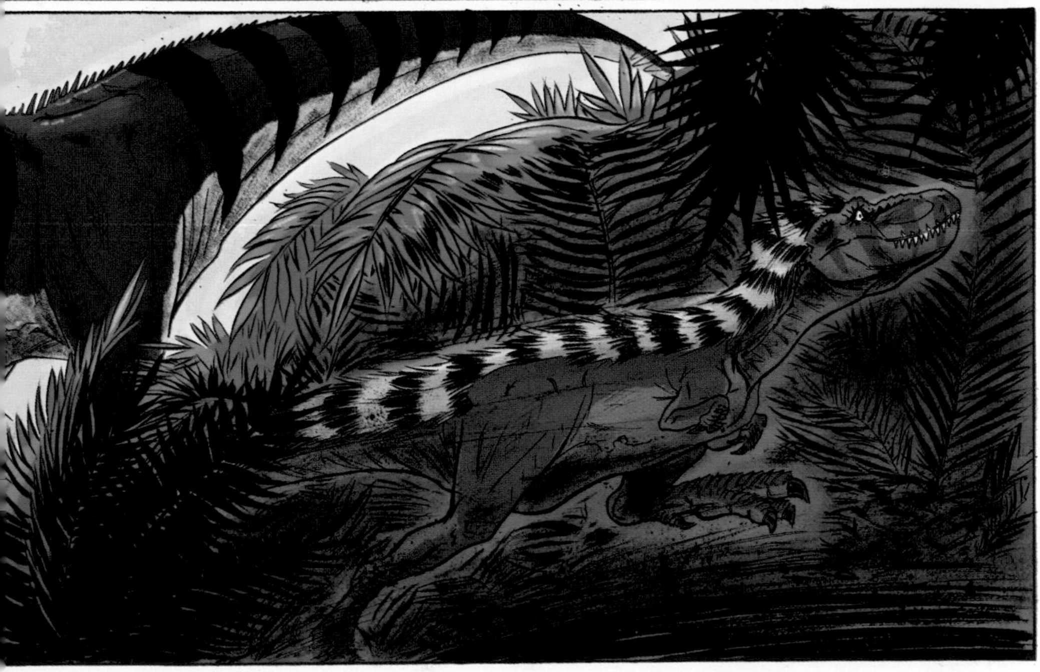

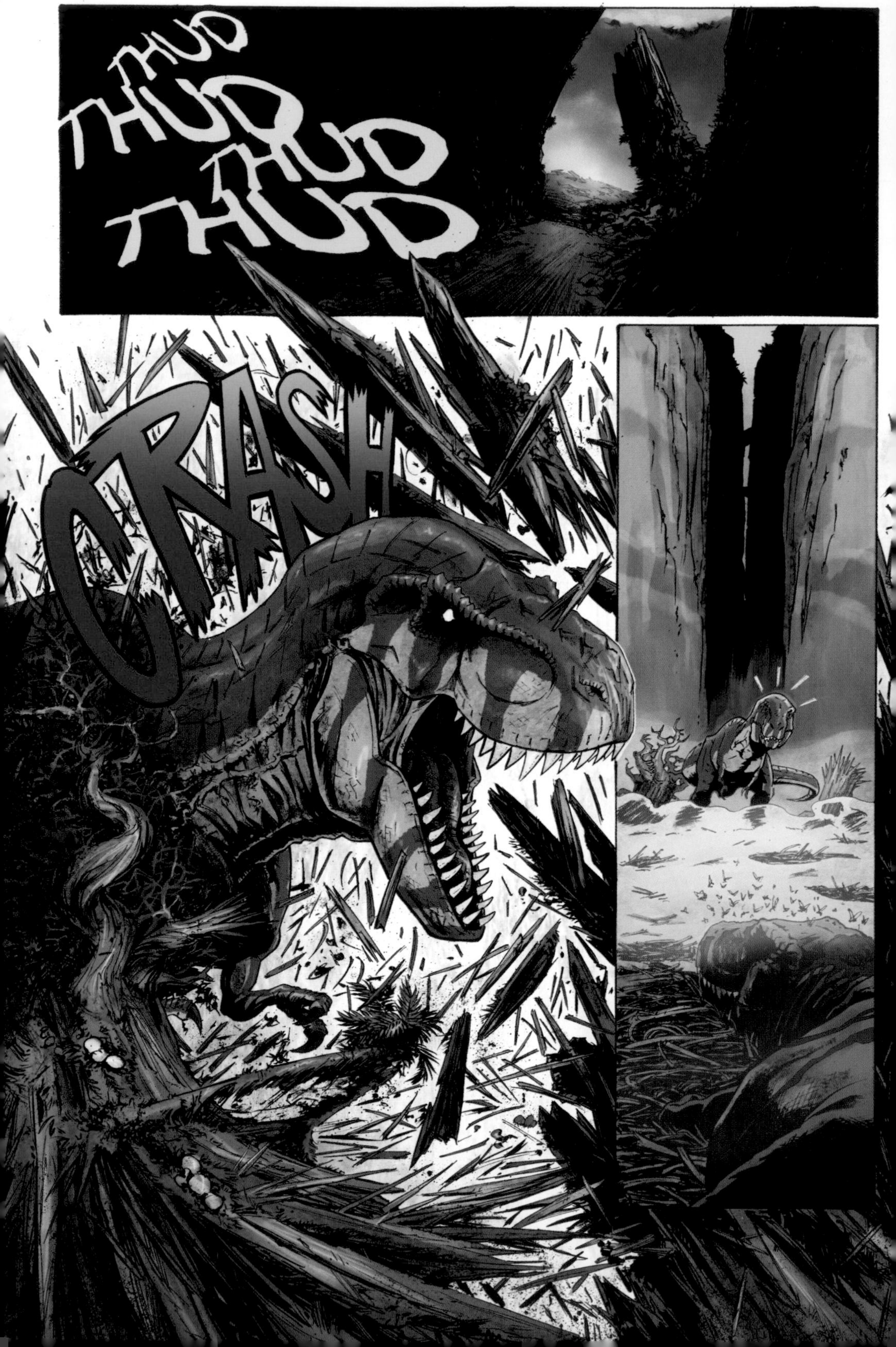
THUD
THUD
THUD
THUD
CRASH

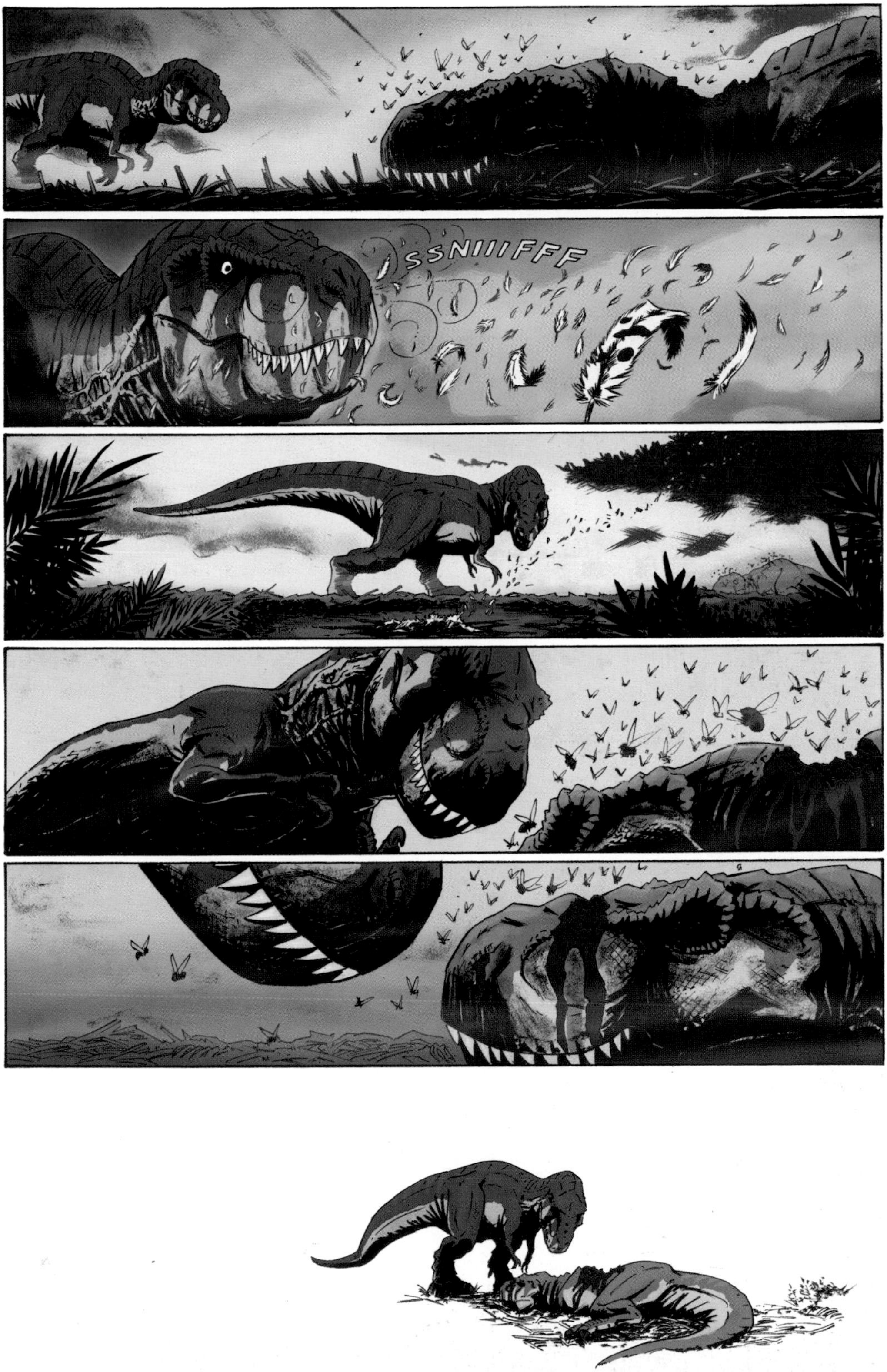
SSNIIIFFF

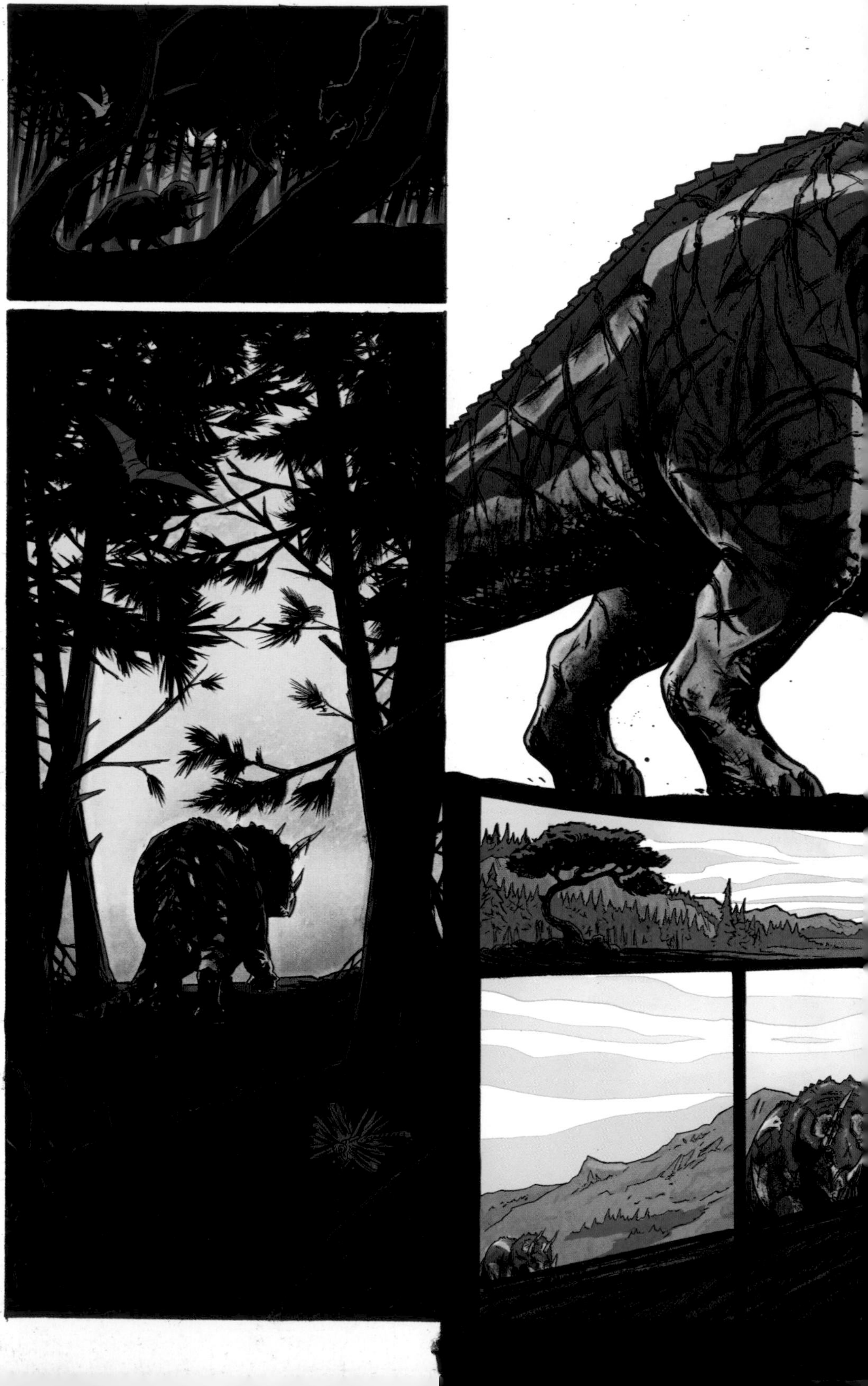

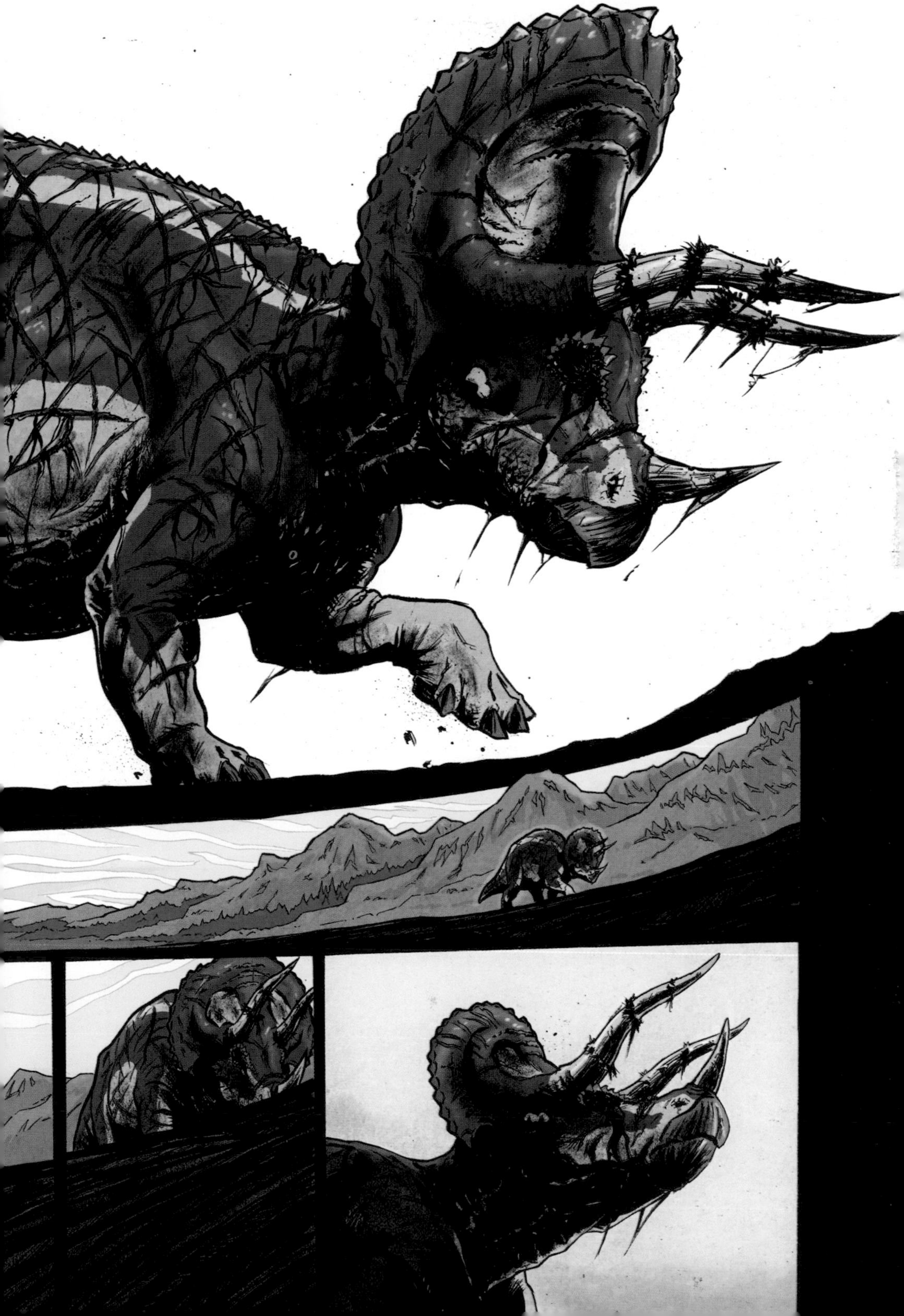

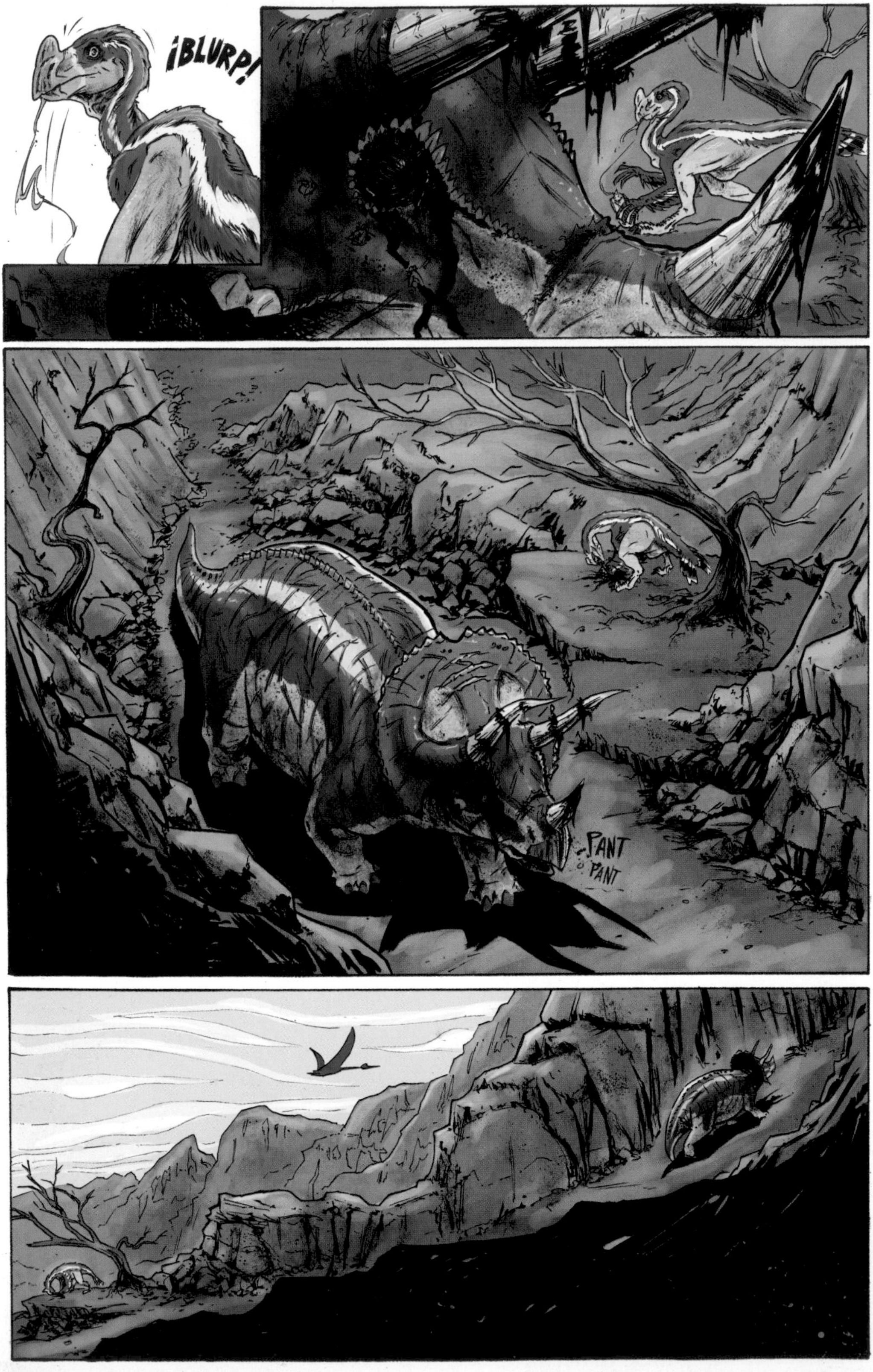
¡BLURP!
PANT
PANT

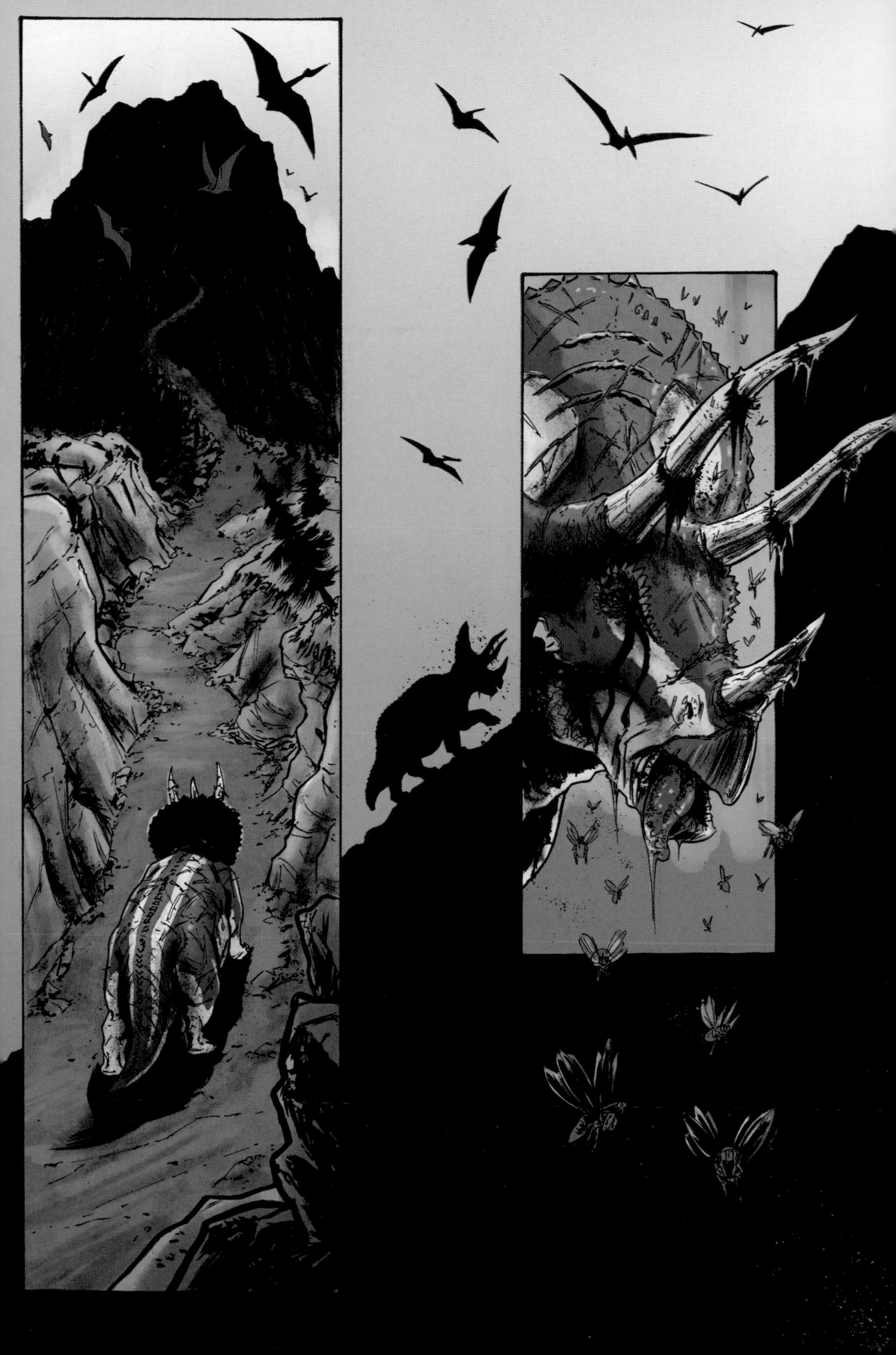

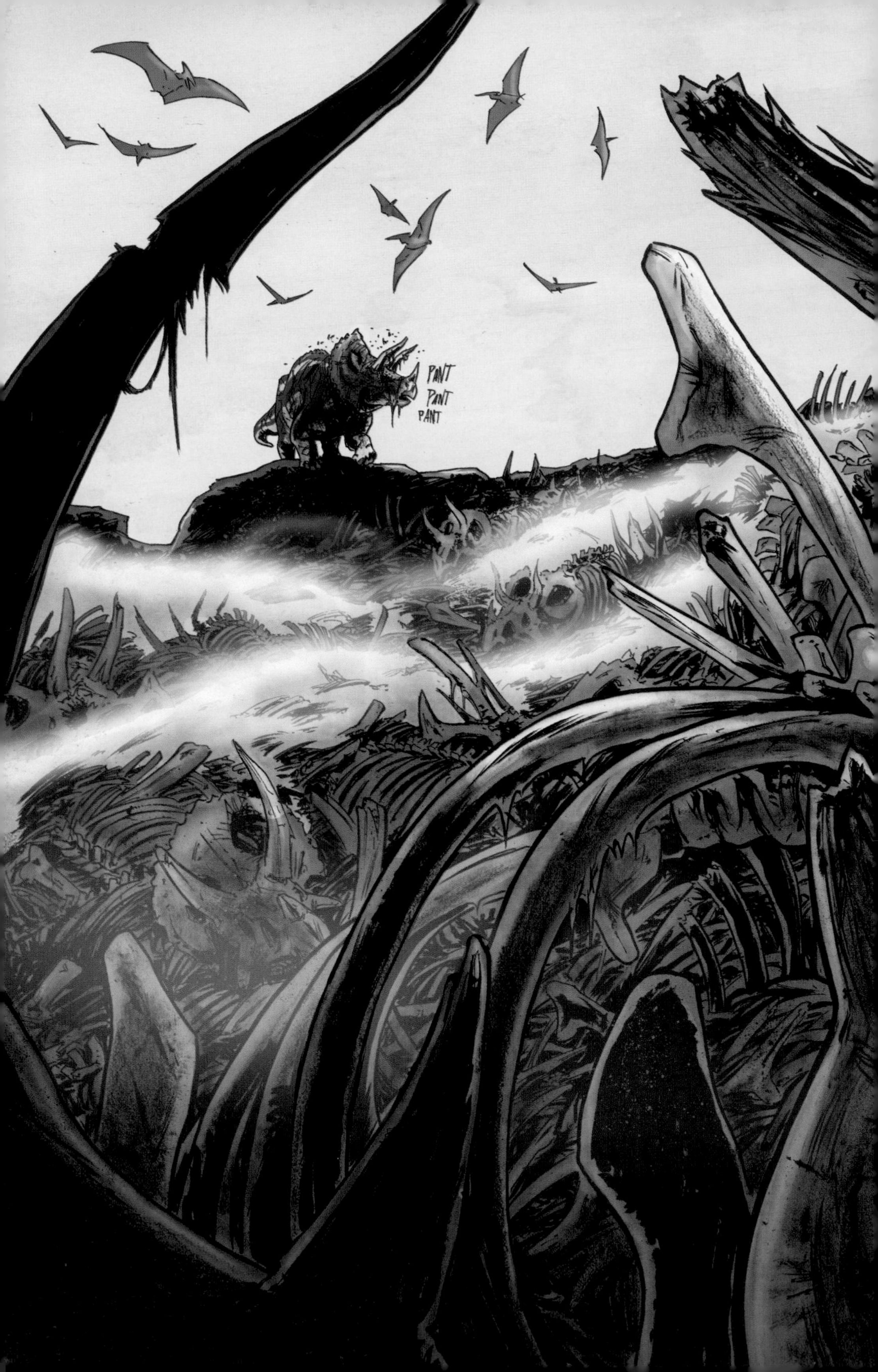
PANT
PANT
PANT

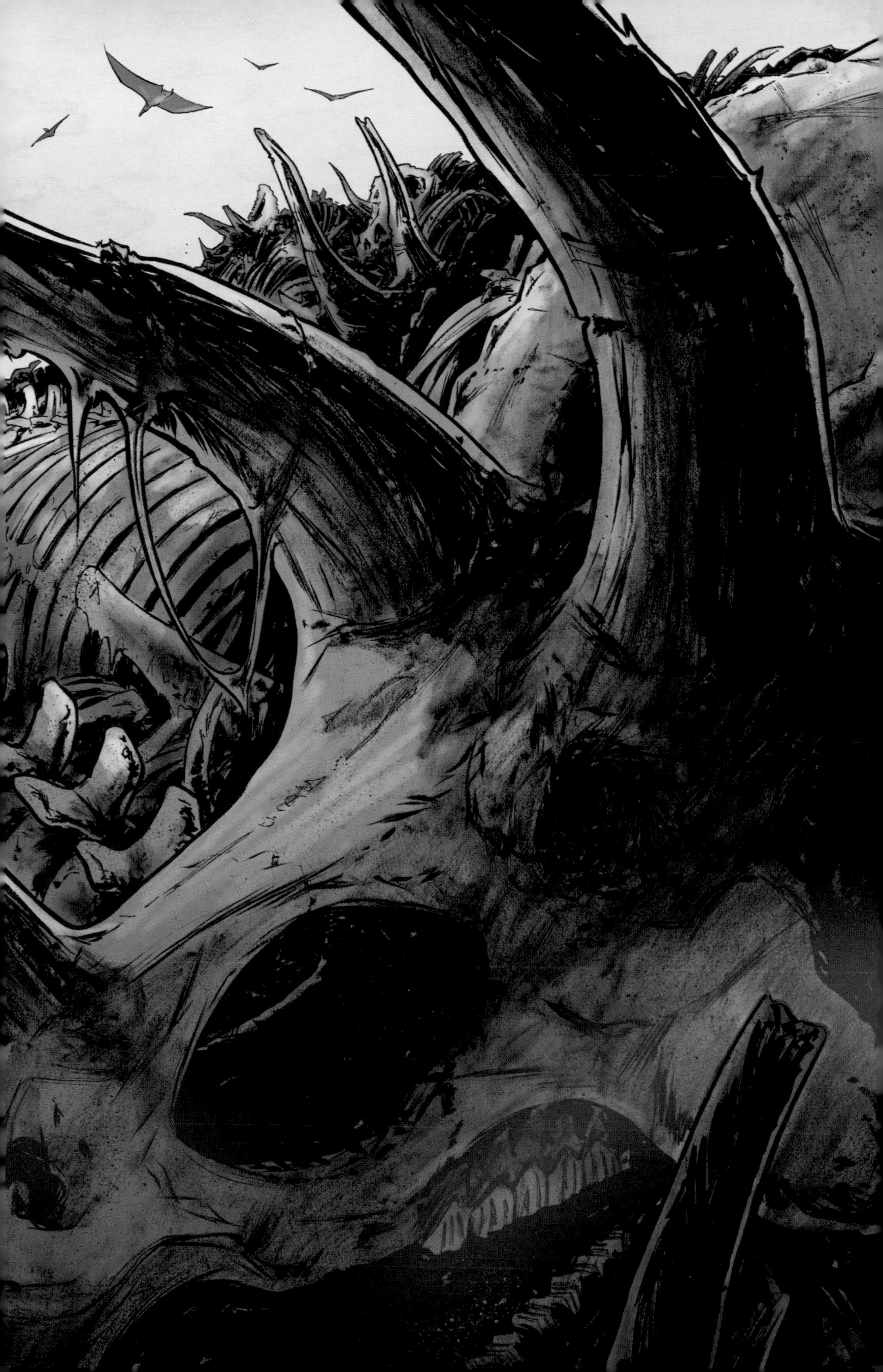

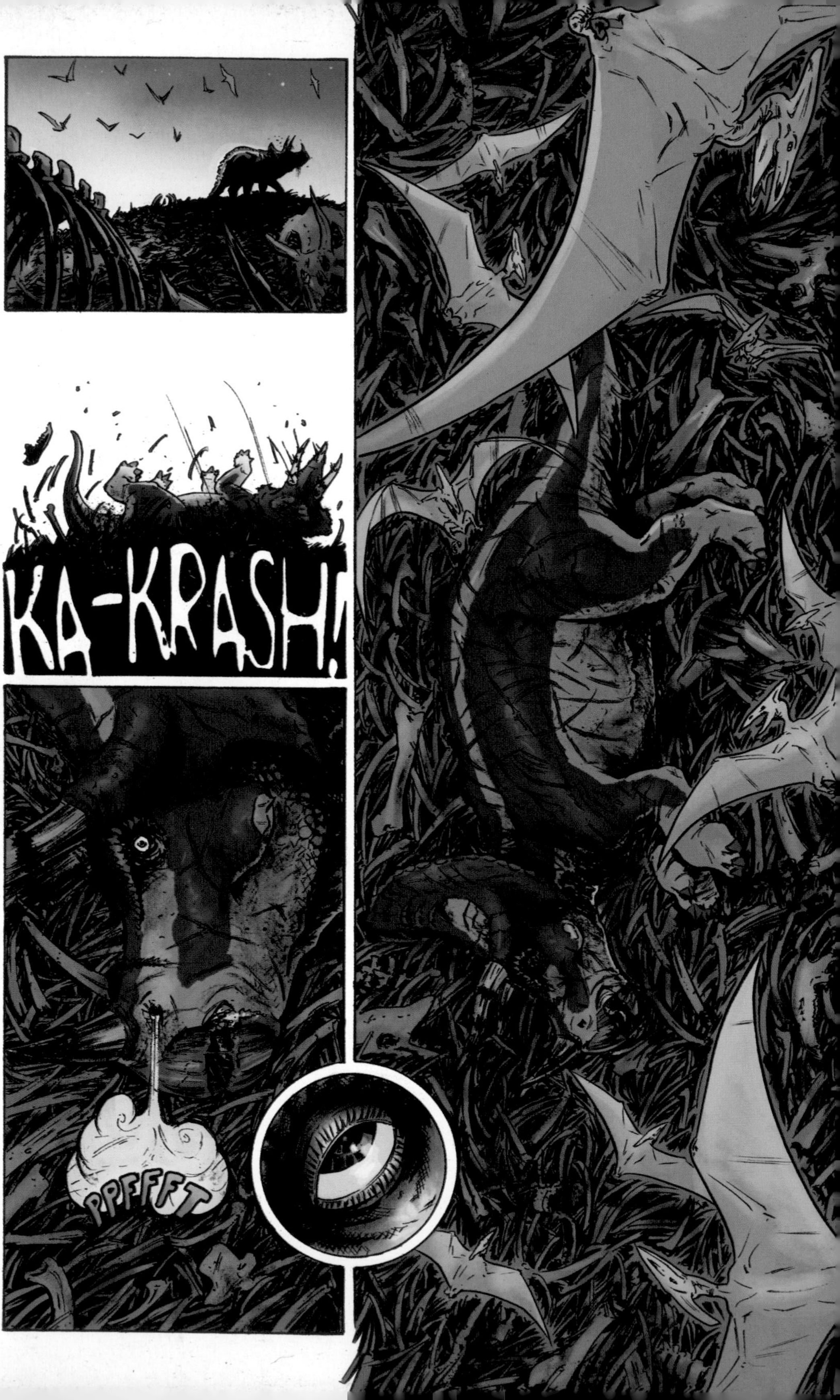
KA-KRASH!
PPFFFT

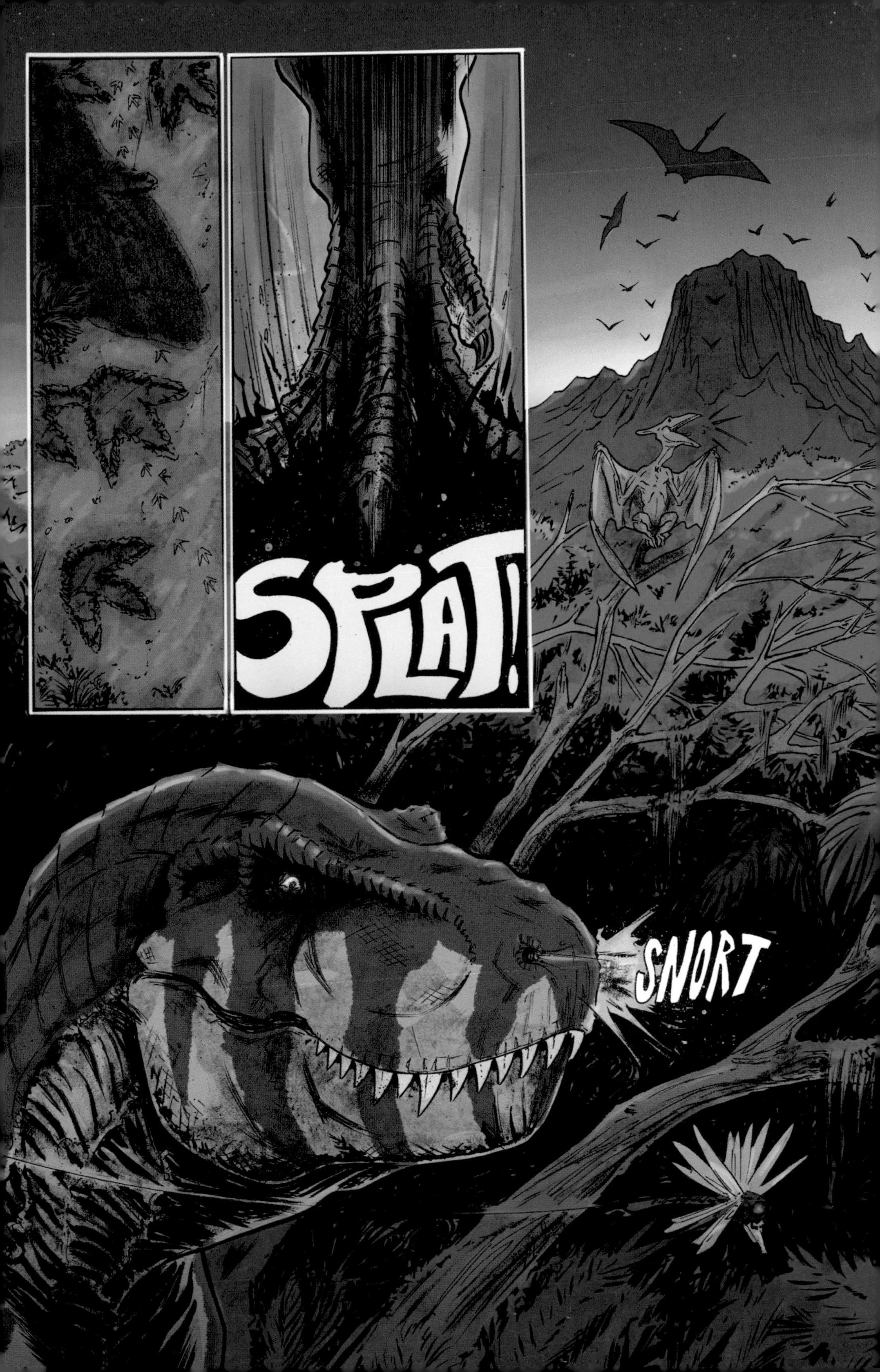
SPLAT!
SNORT

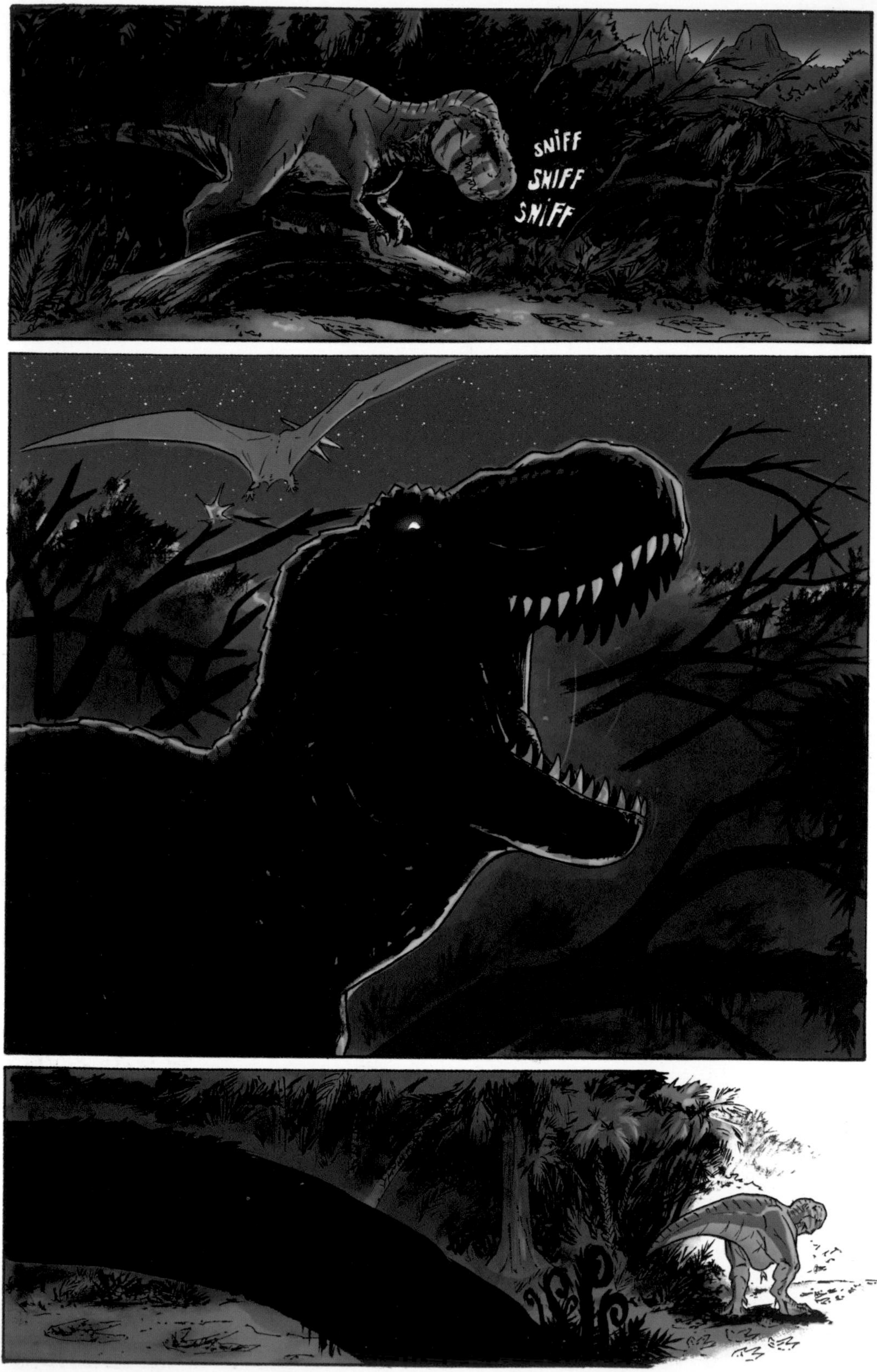
SNIFF
SNIFF
SNIFF

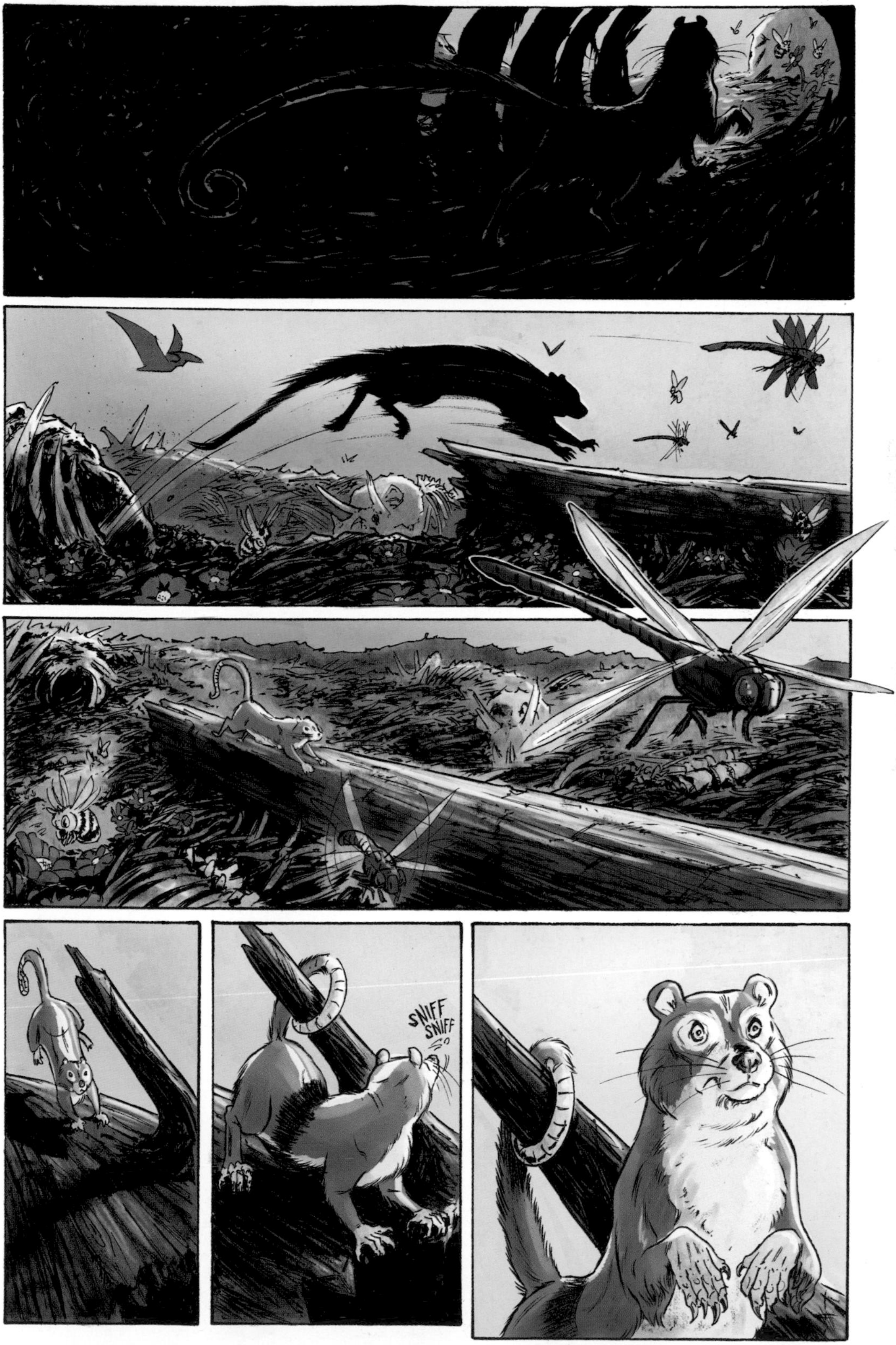
SNIFF
SNIFF

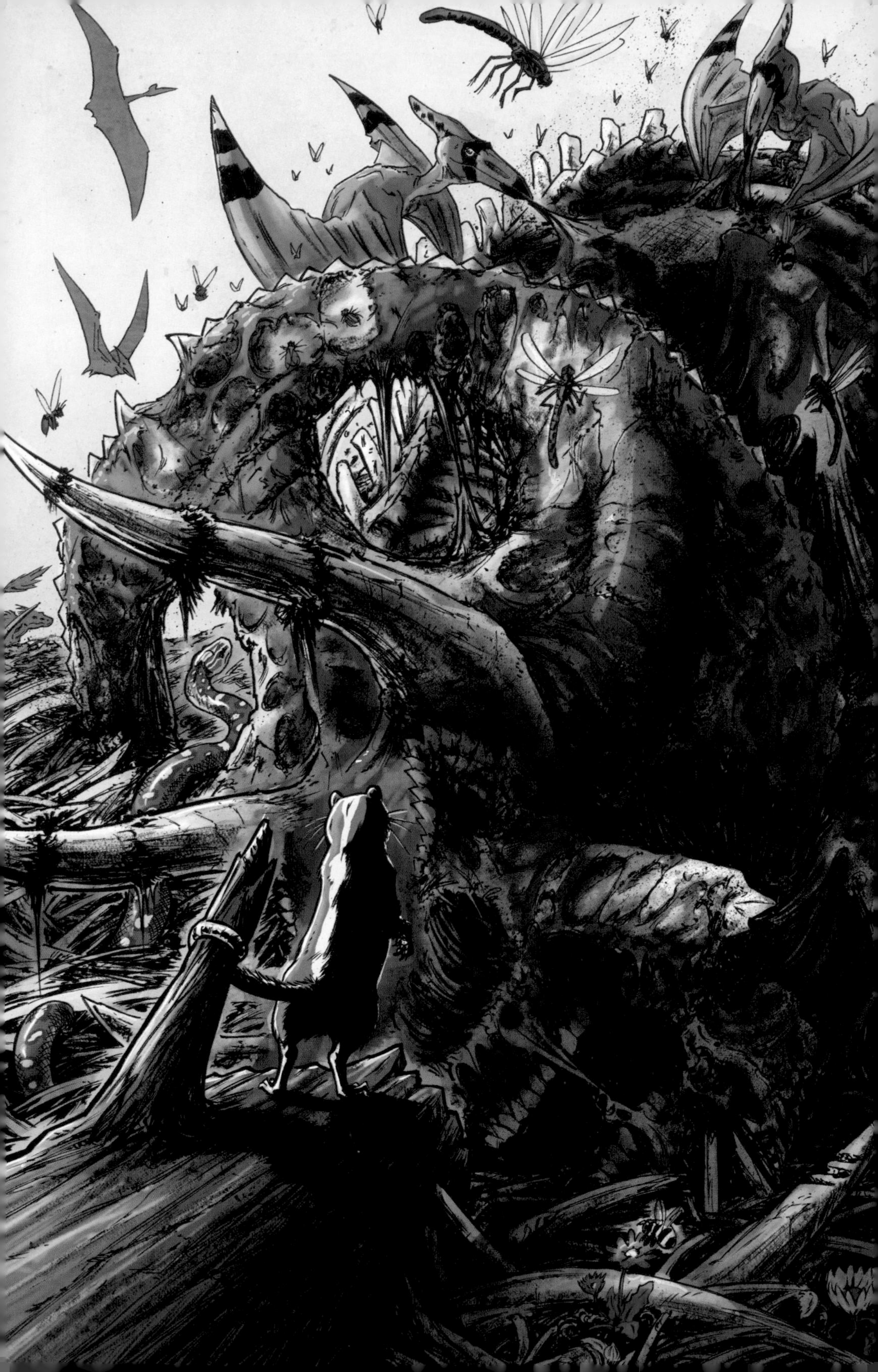

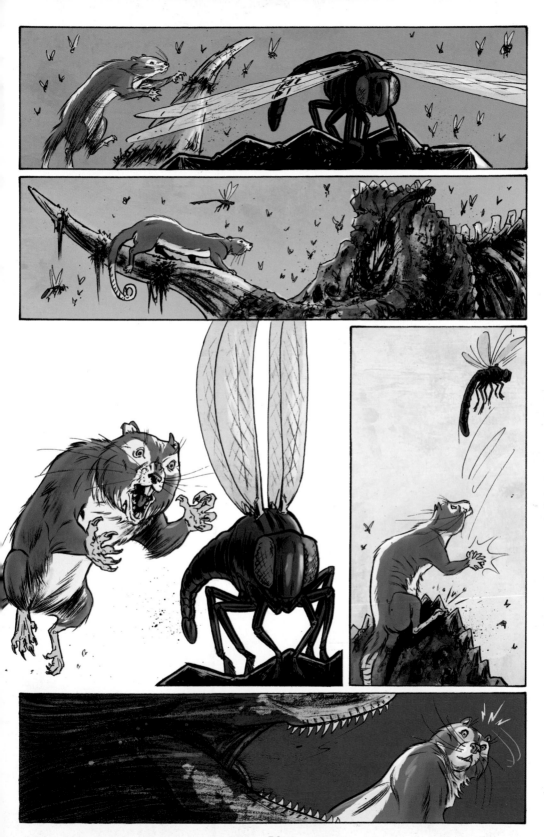

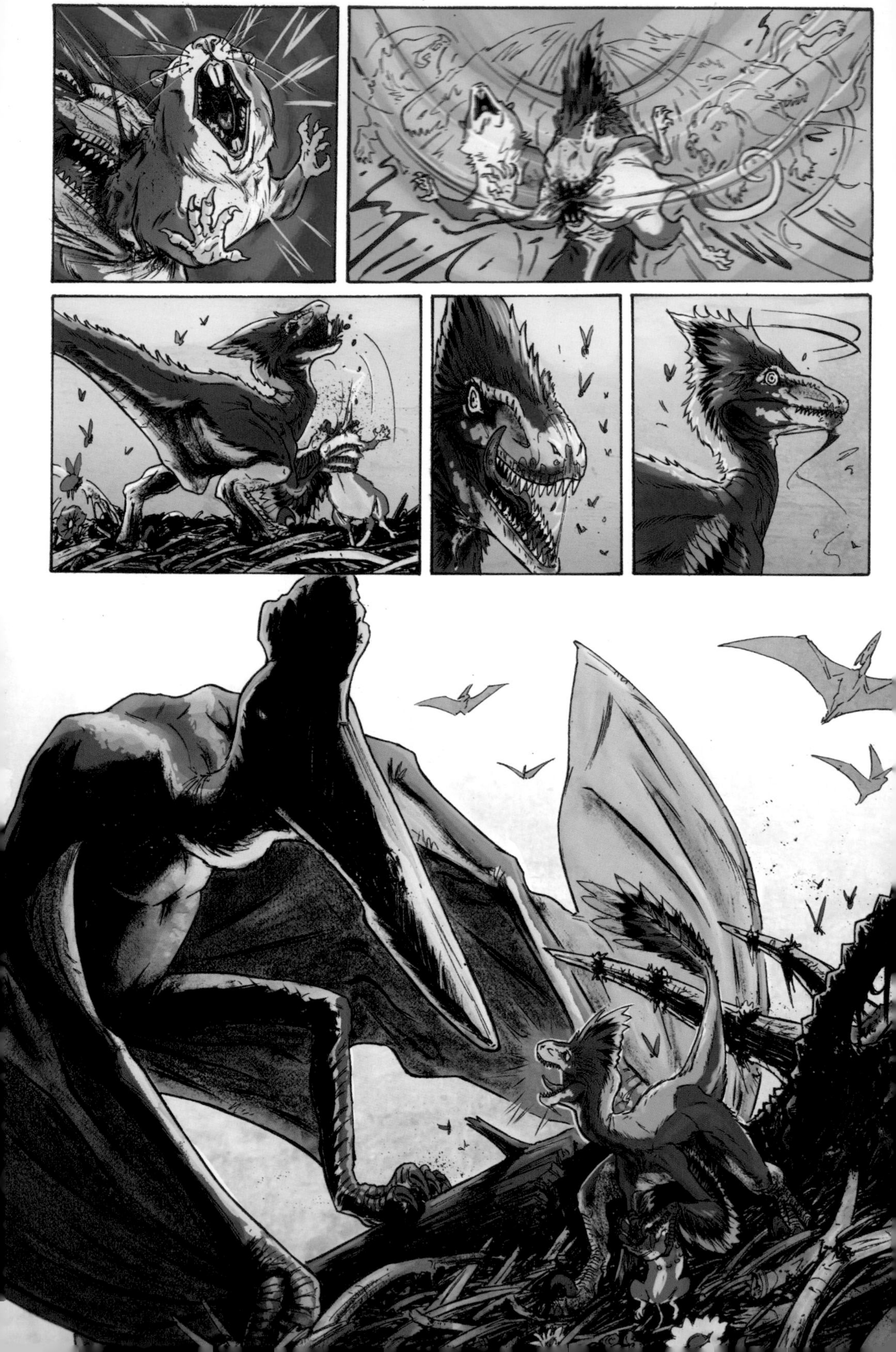

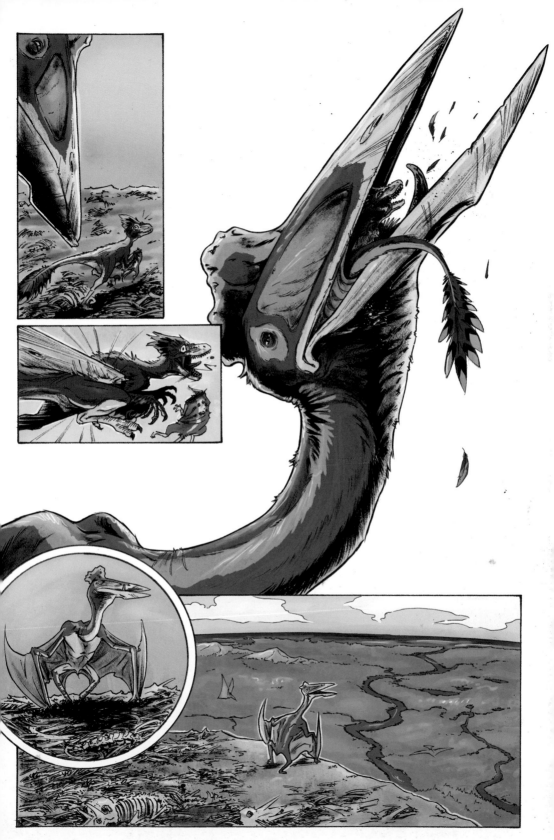

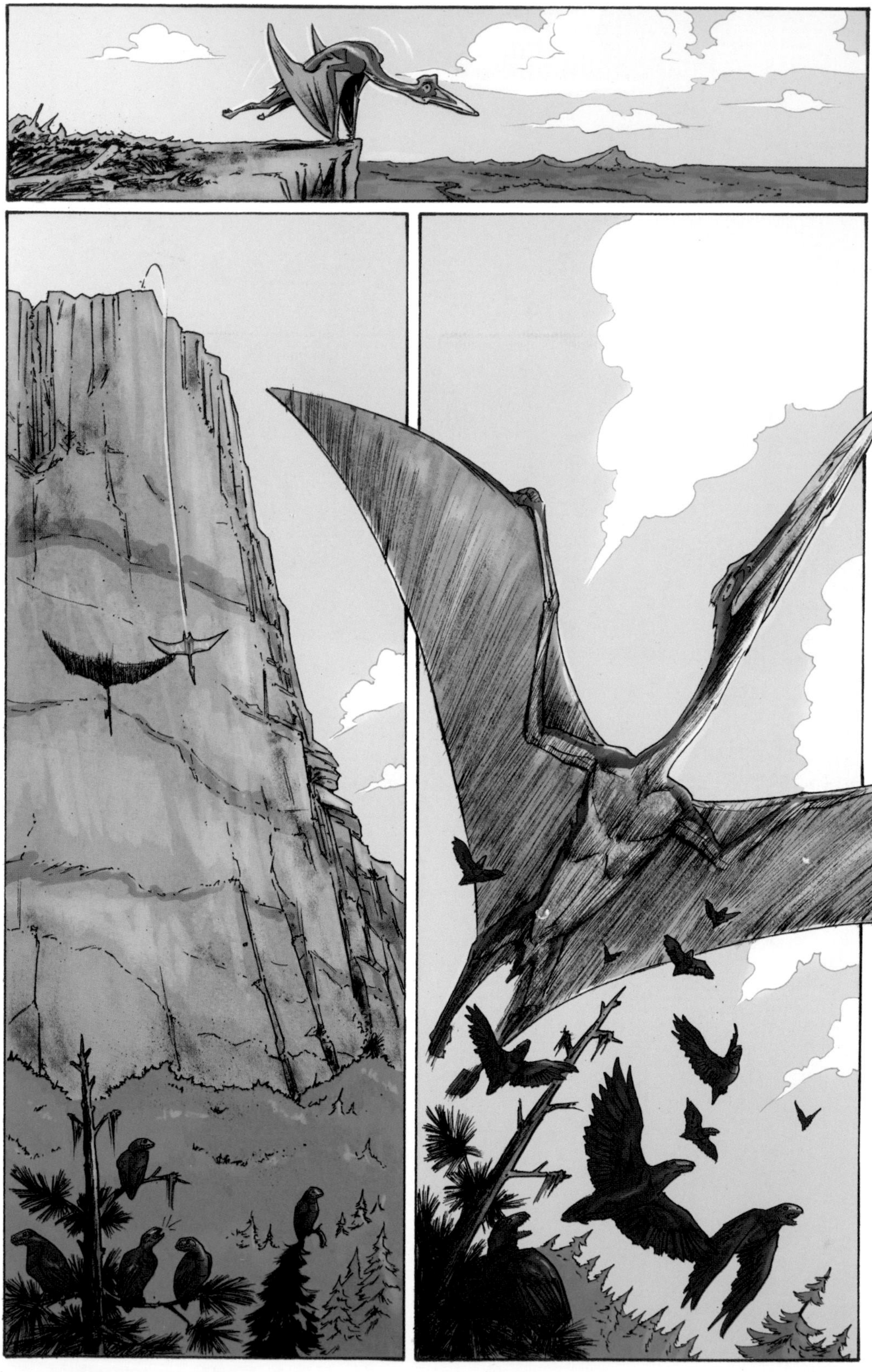

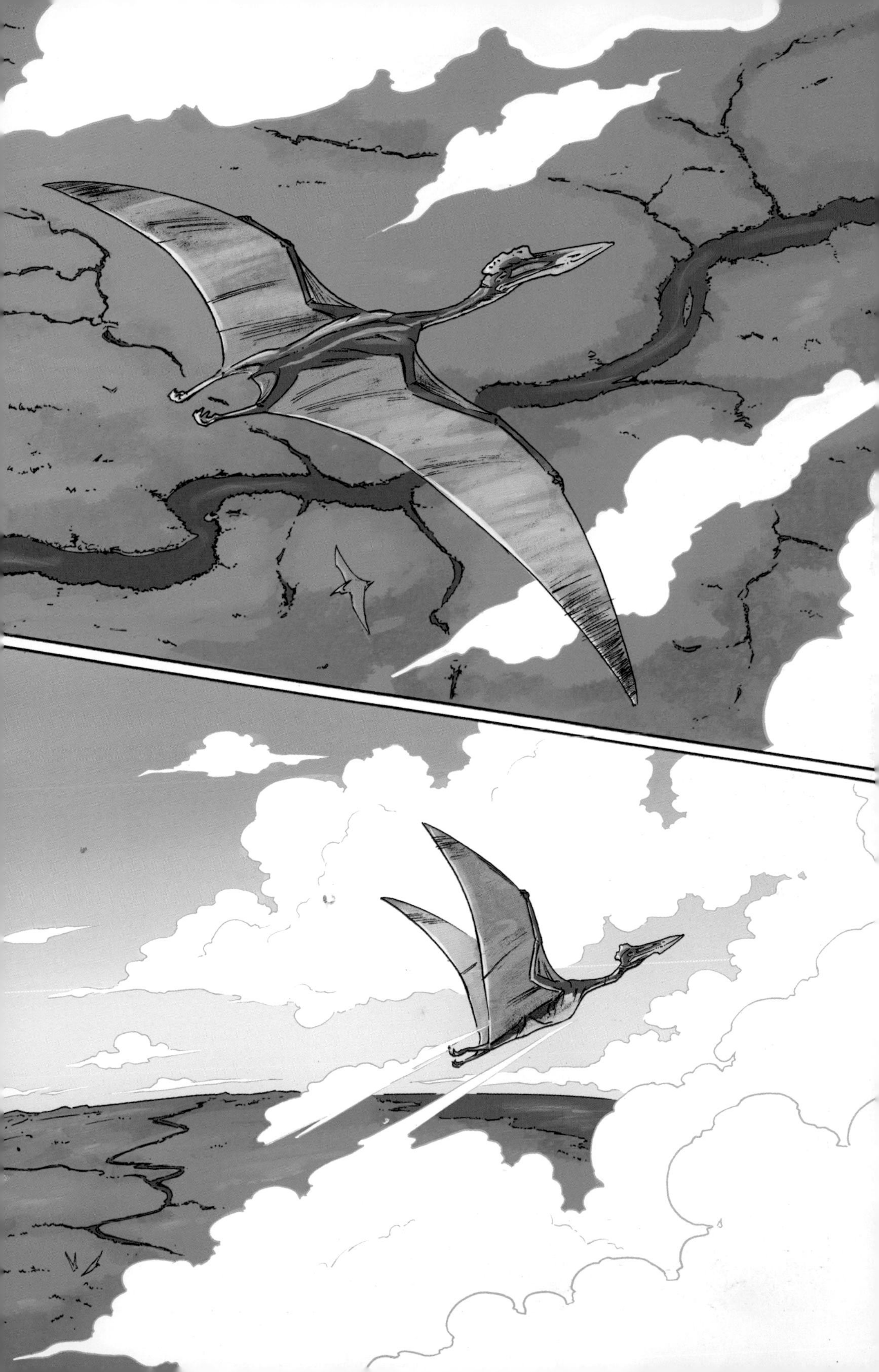

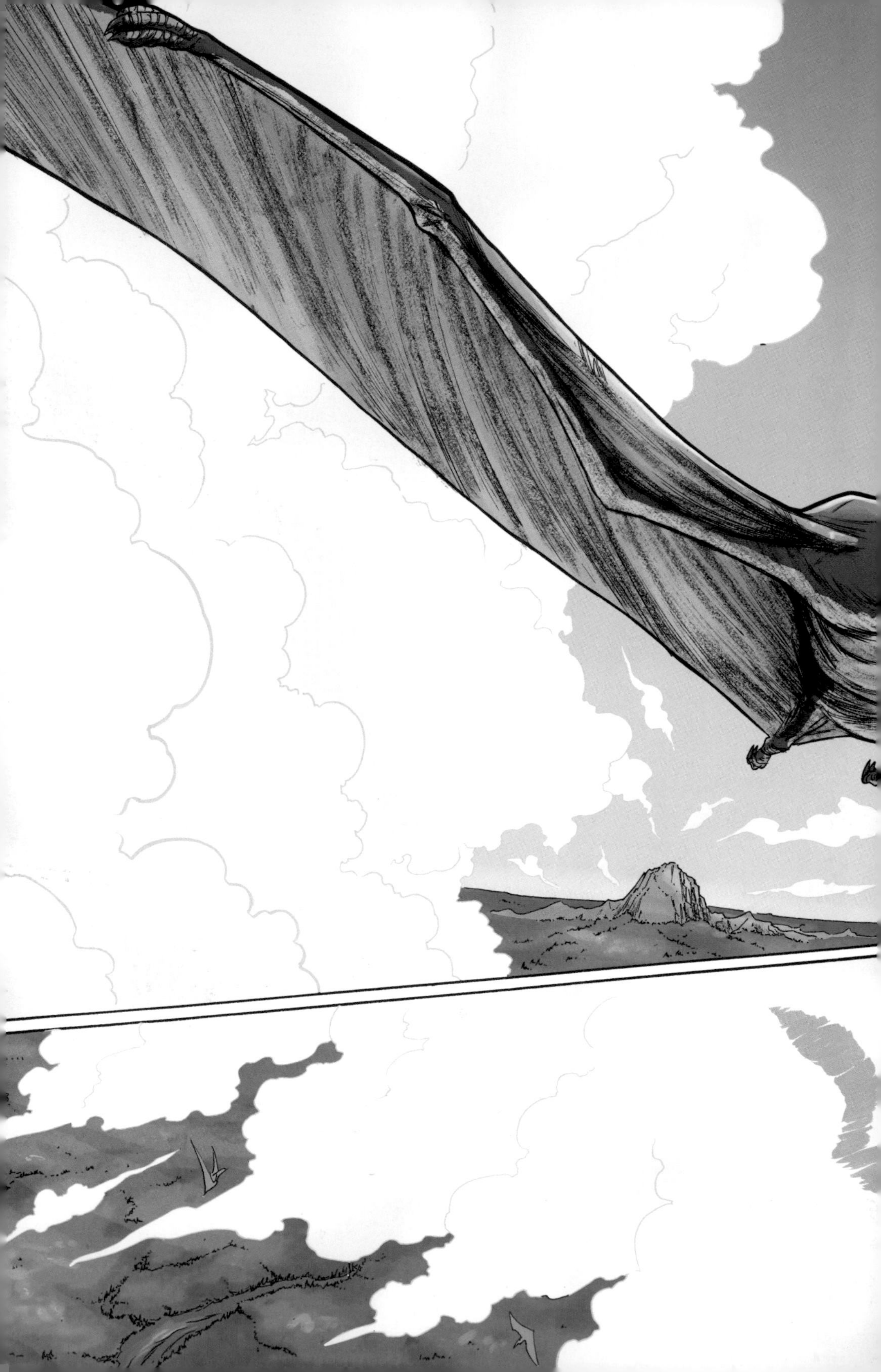

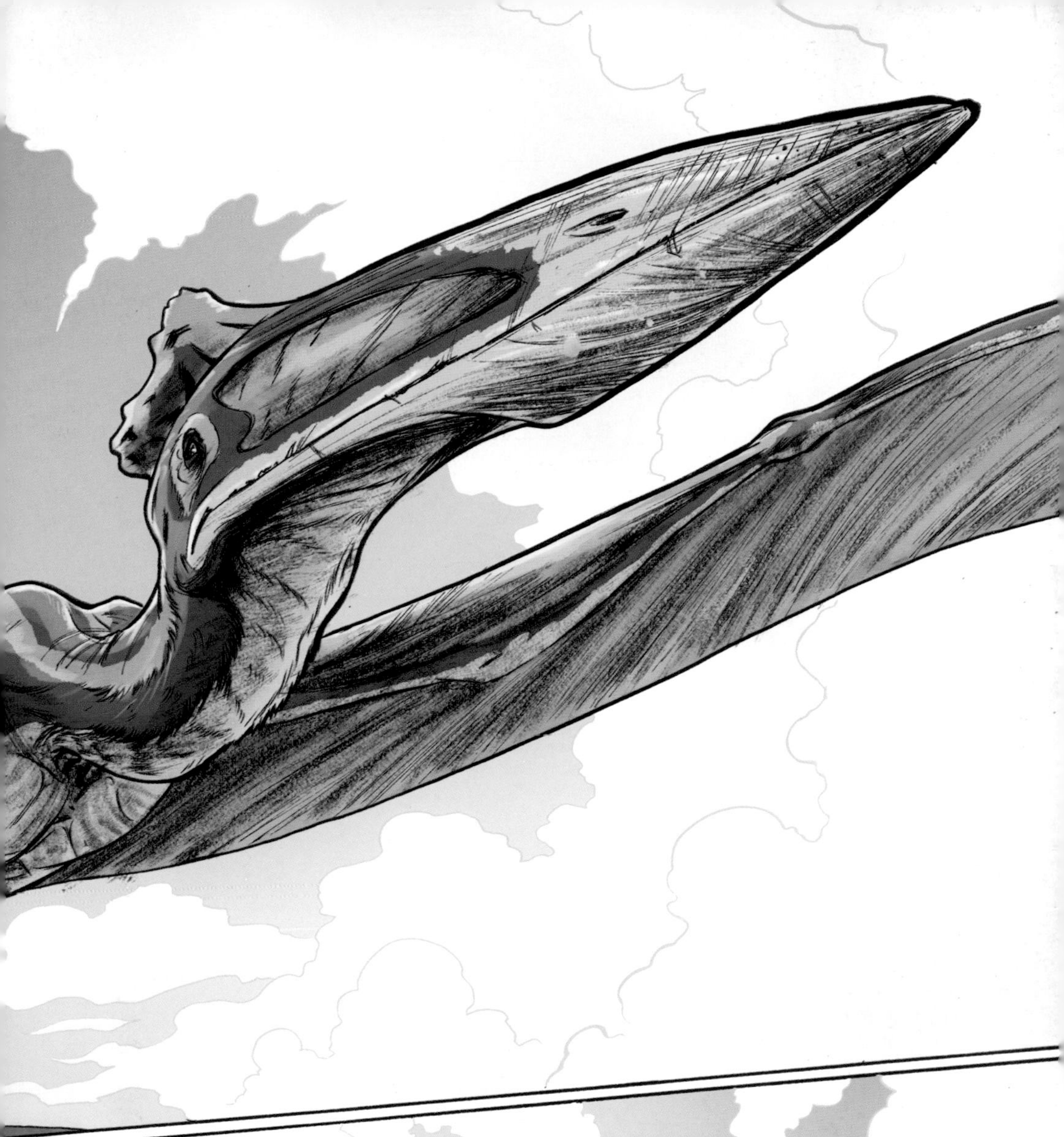

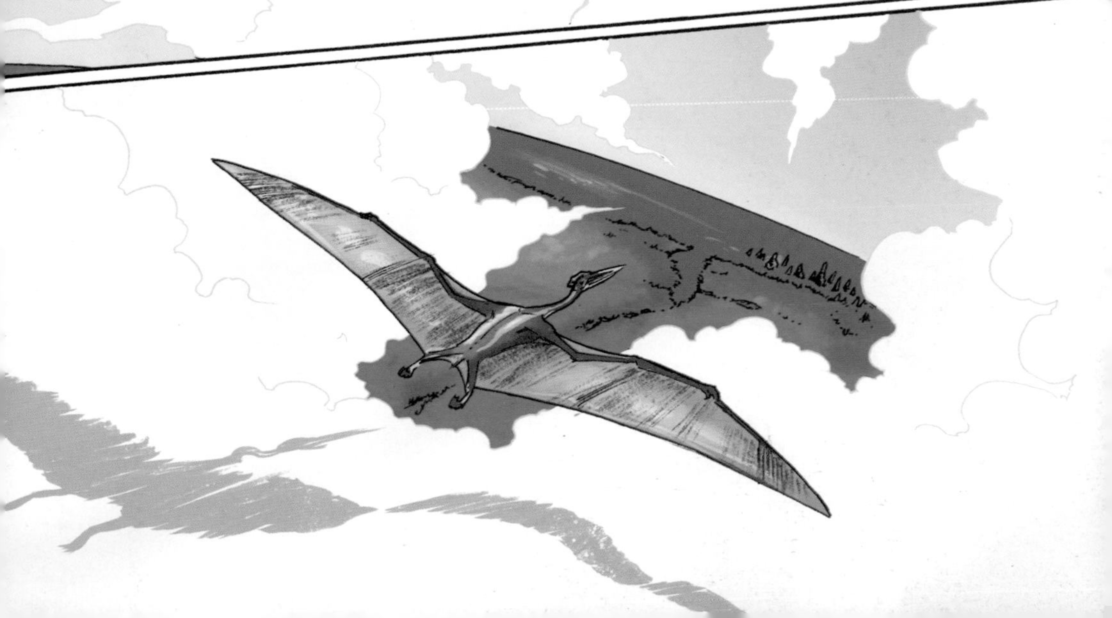

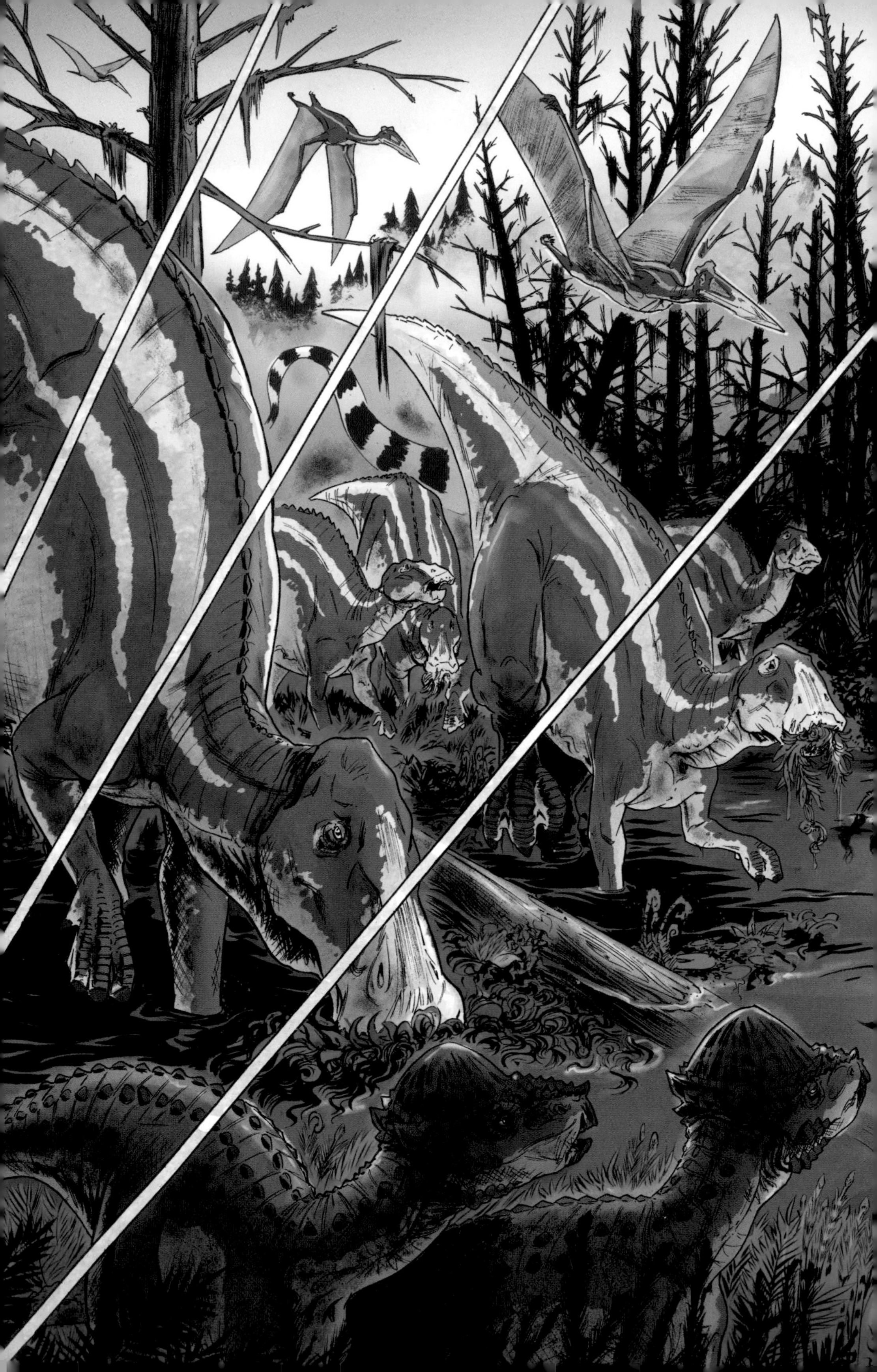

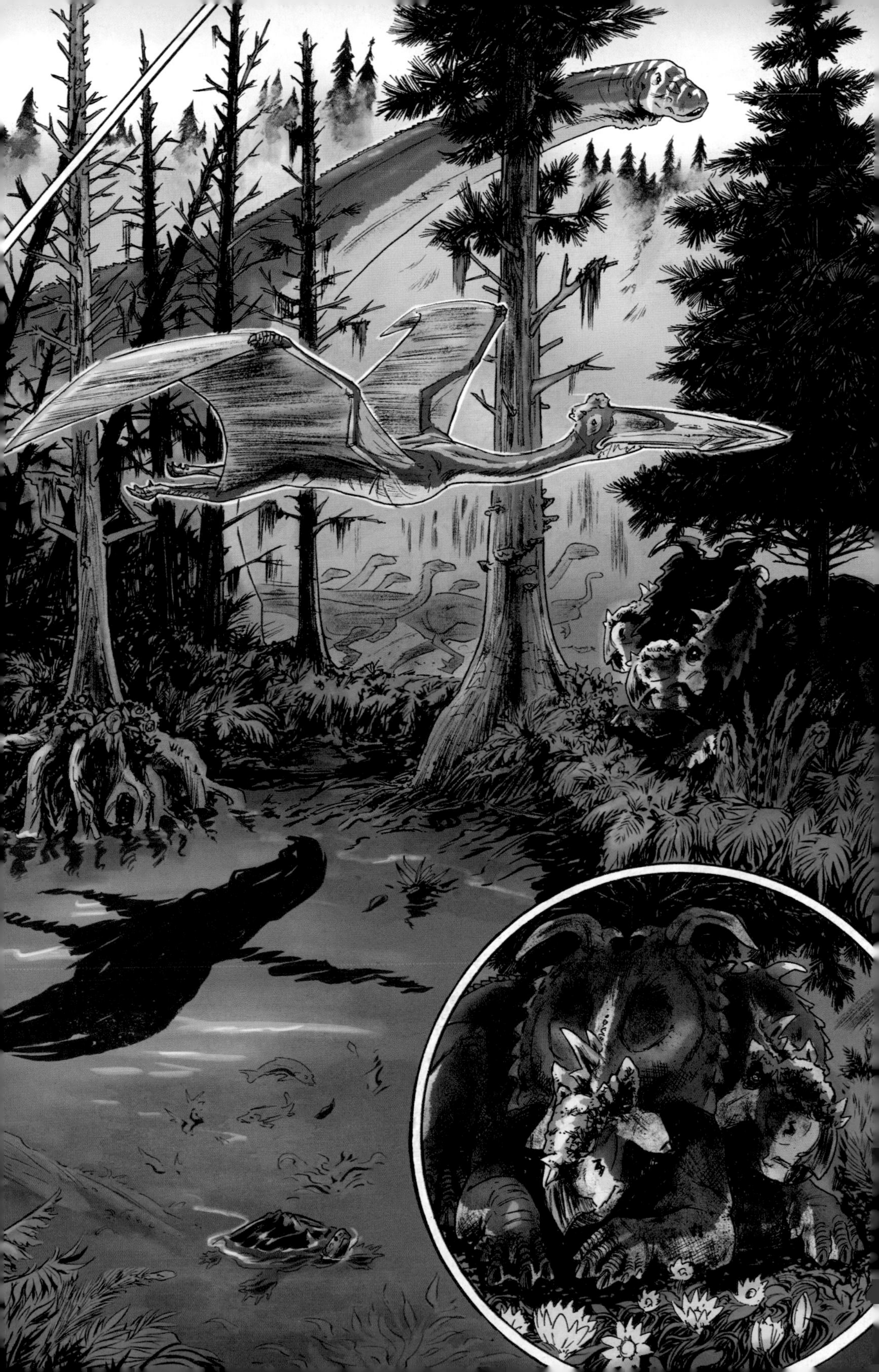

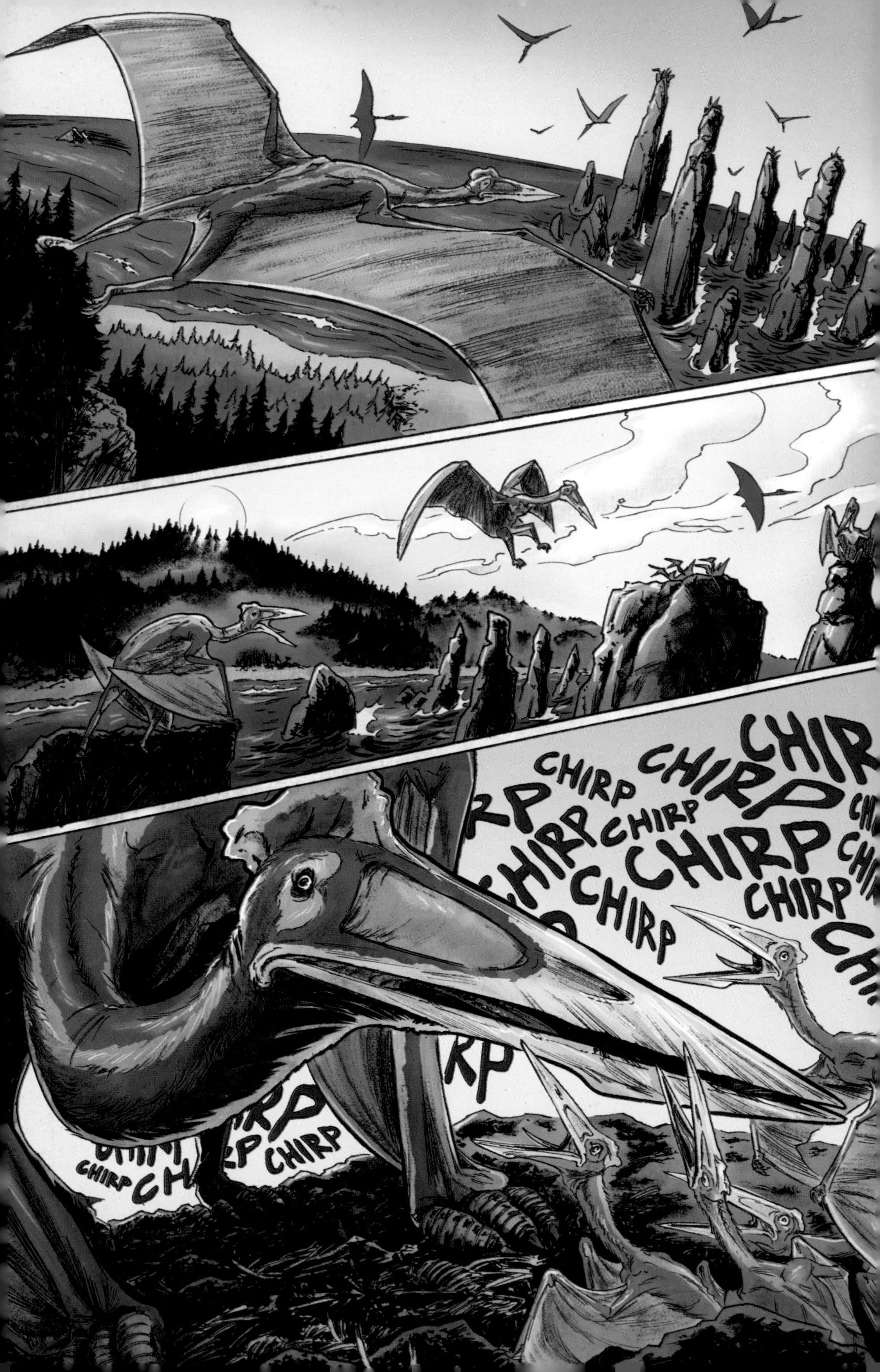
CHIRP
CHIRP
CHIRP
CHIRP
CHIRP
CHIRP
CHIRP
CHIRP
CHIRP

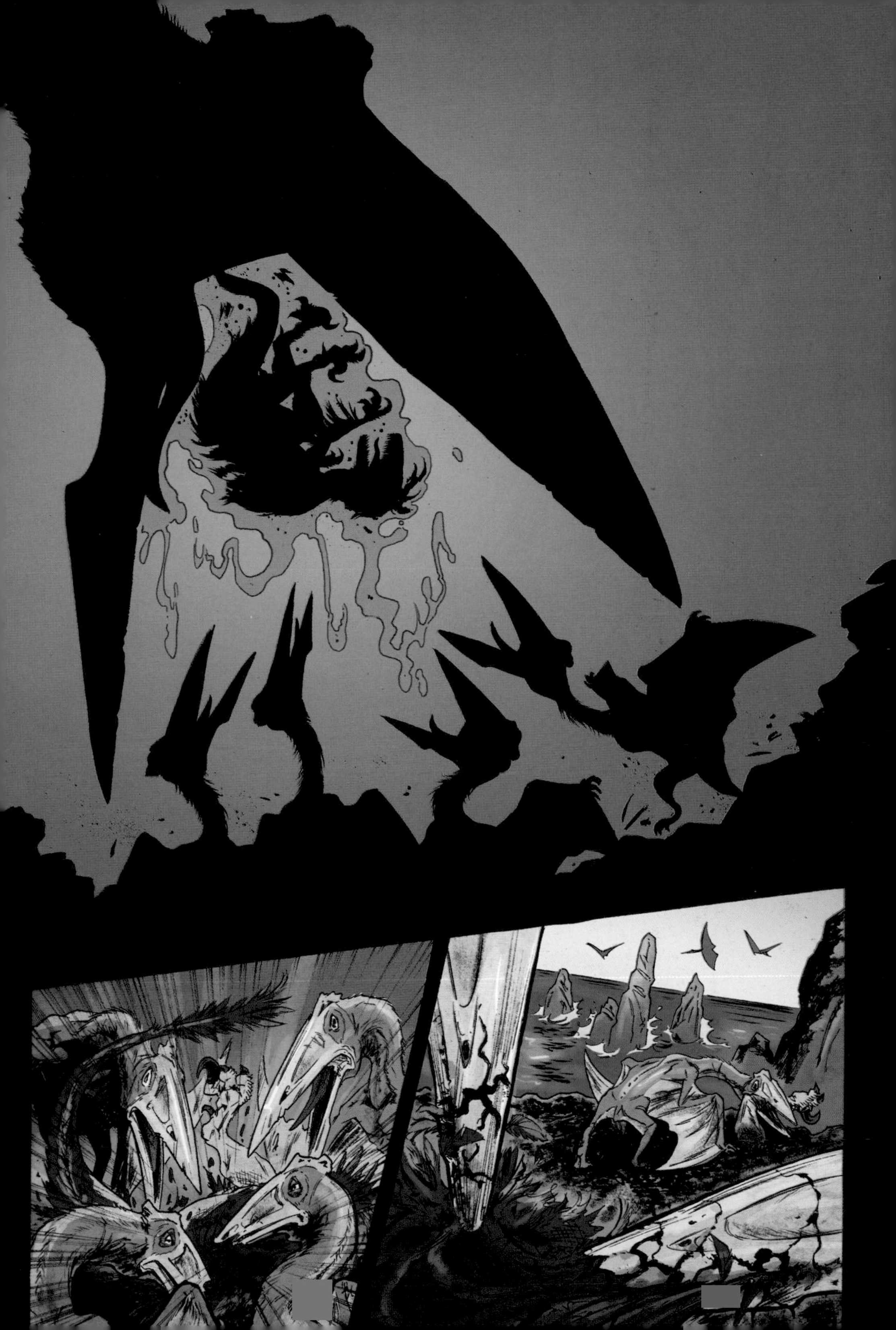

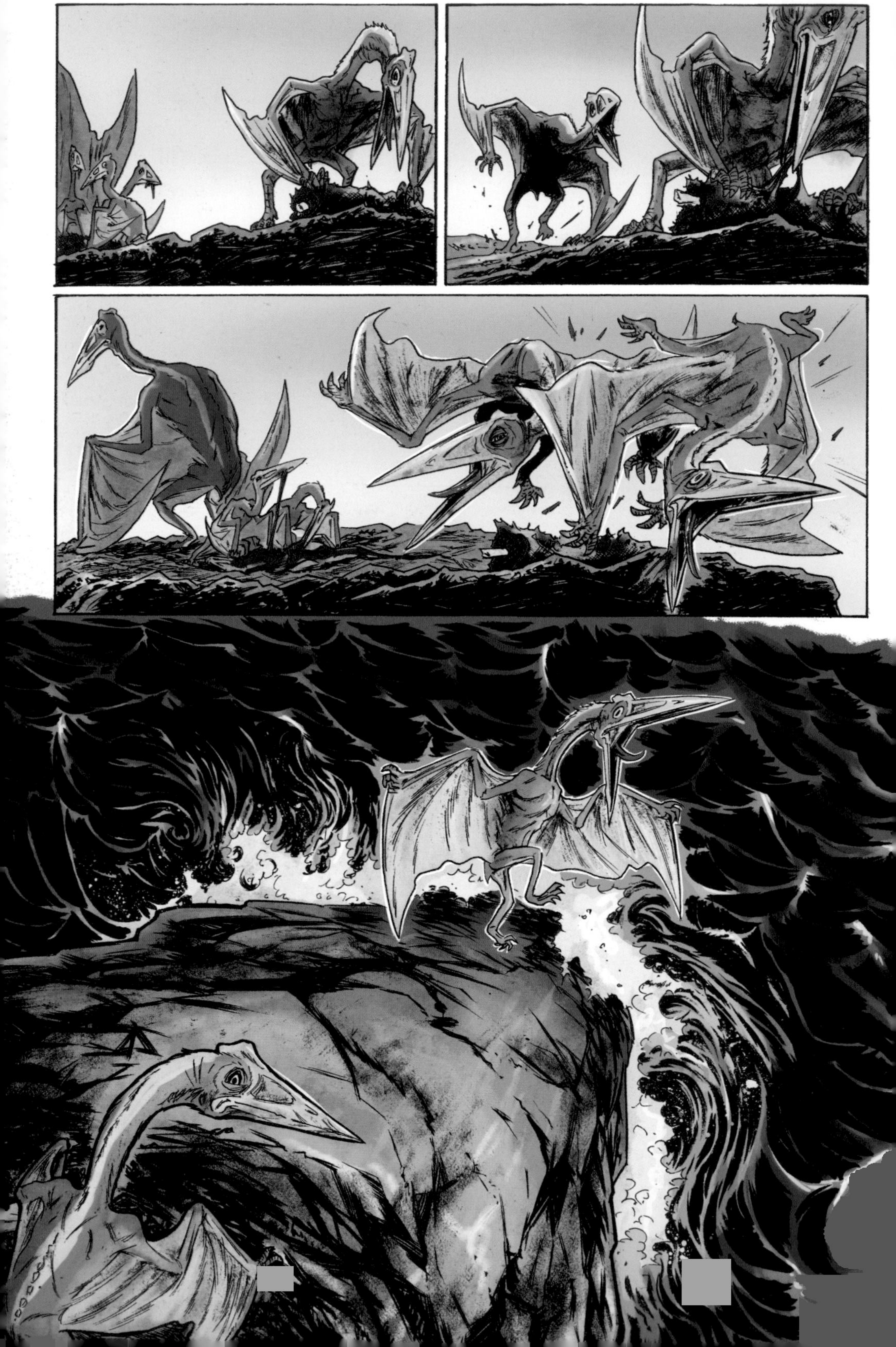

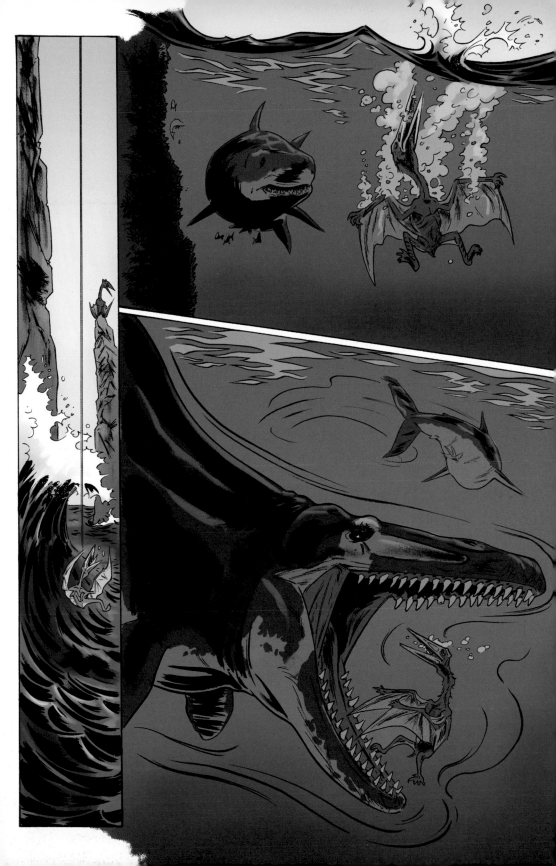

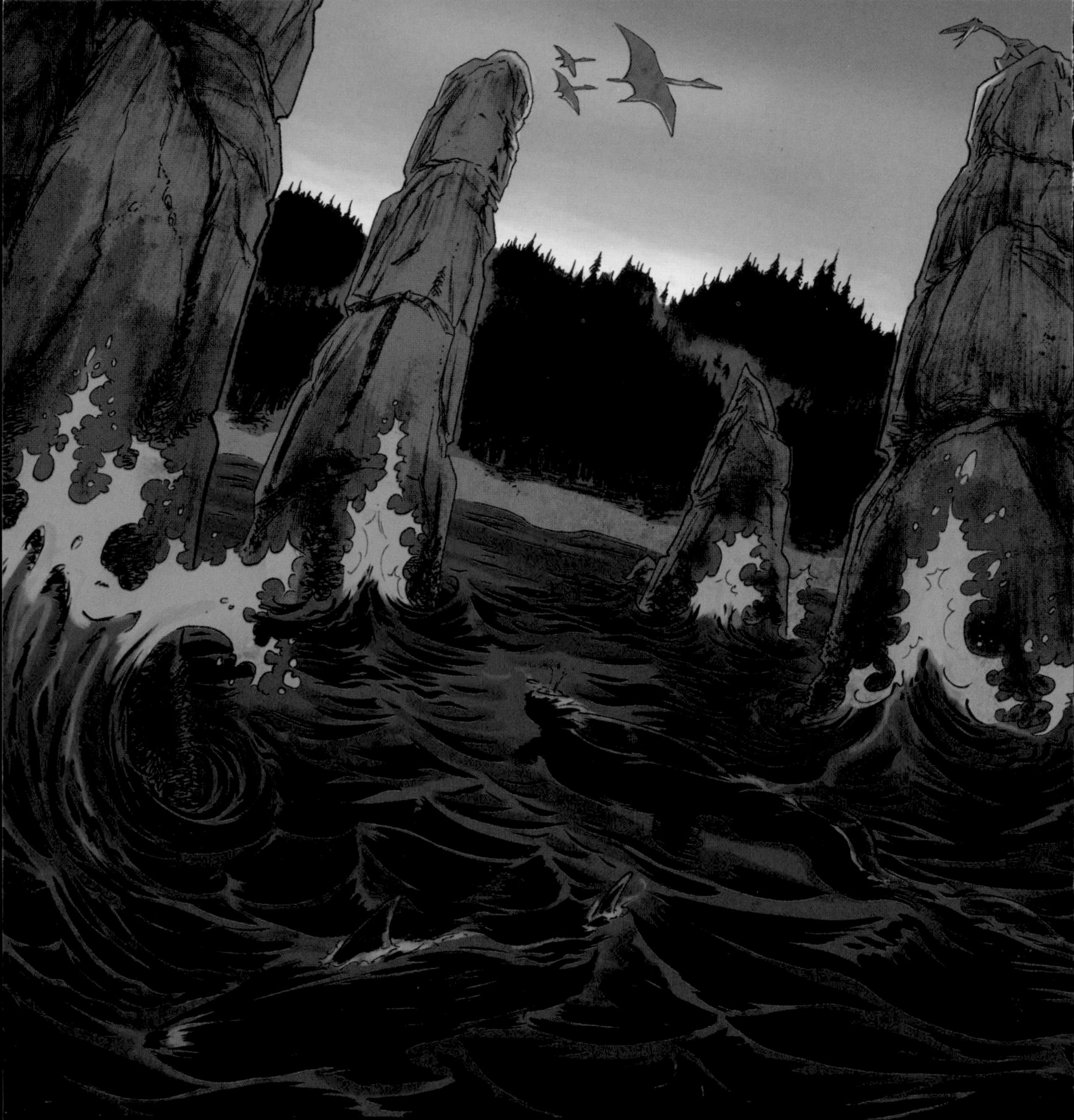
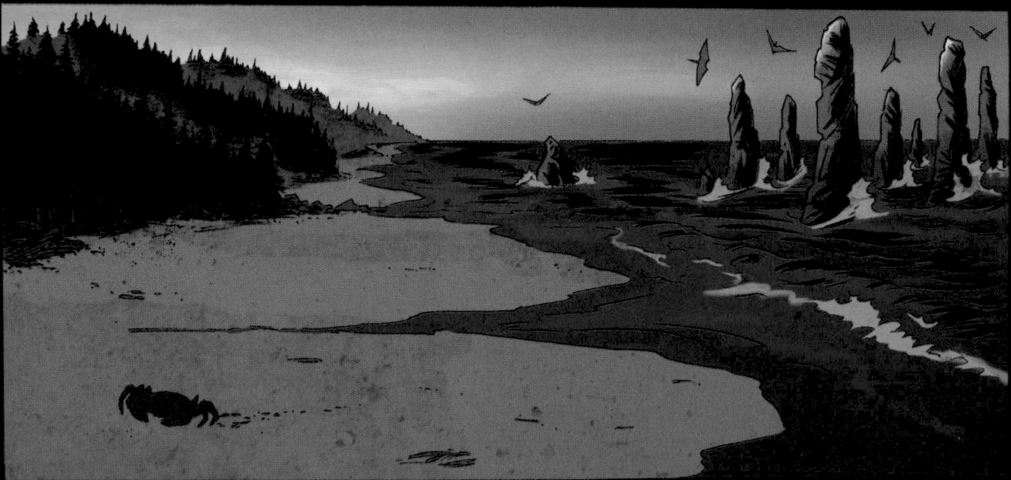

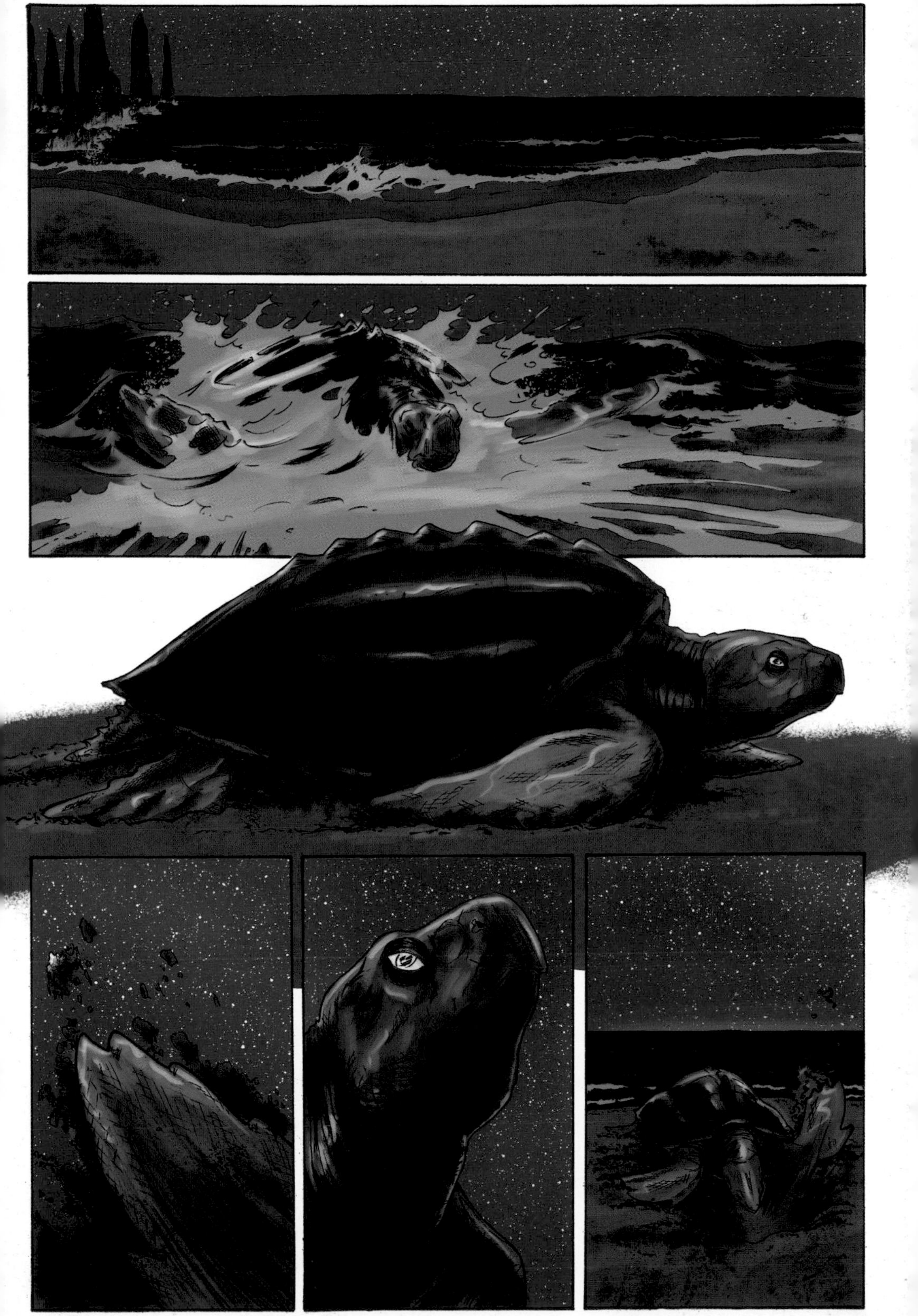

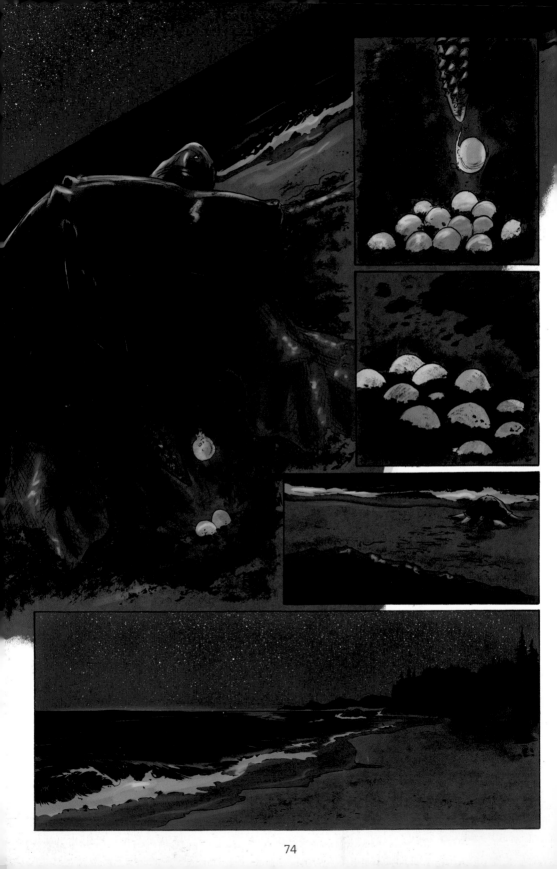

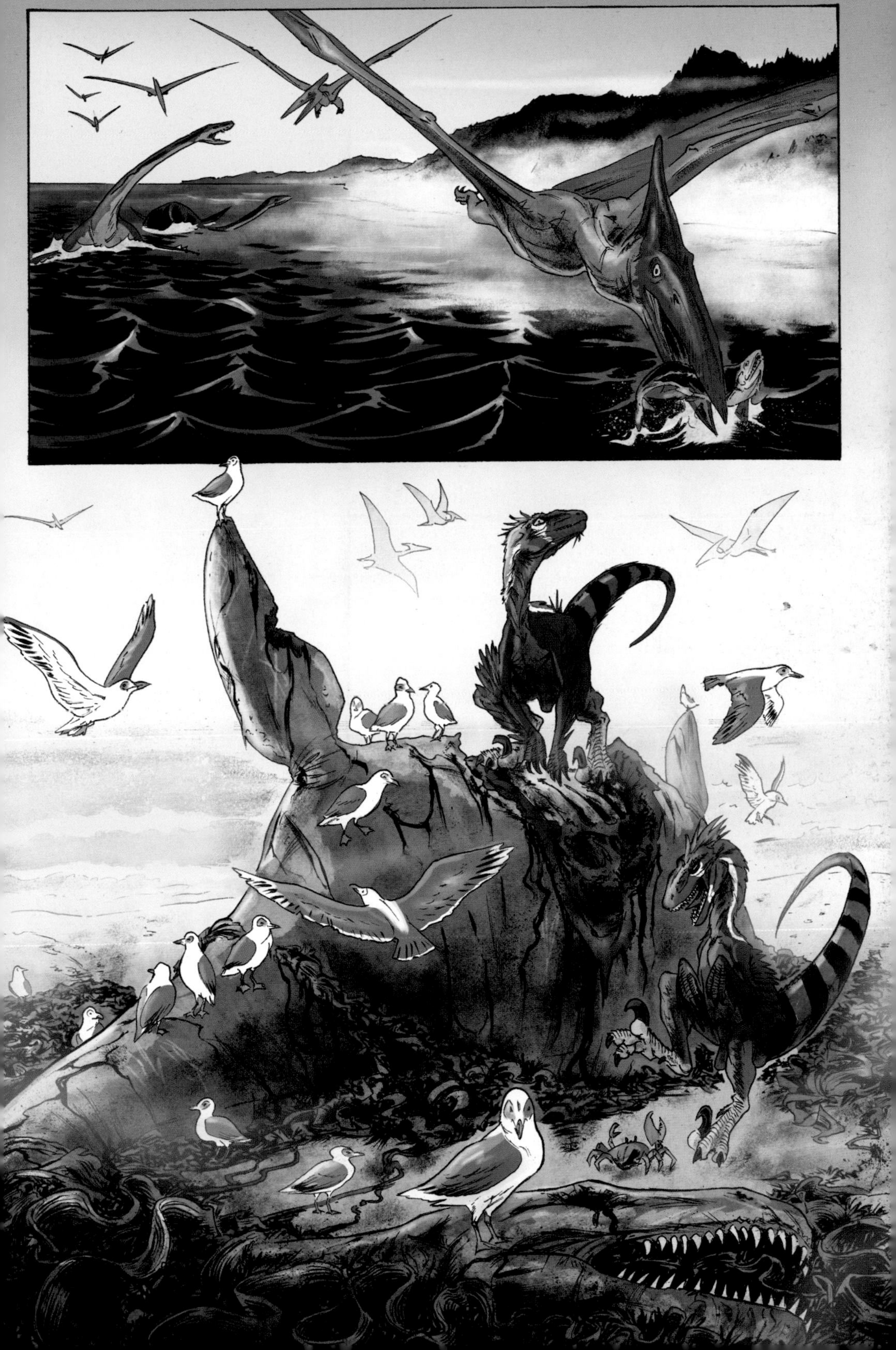

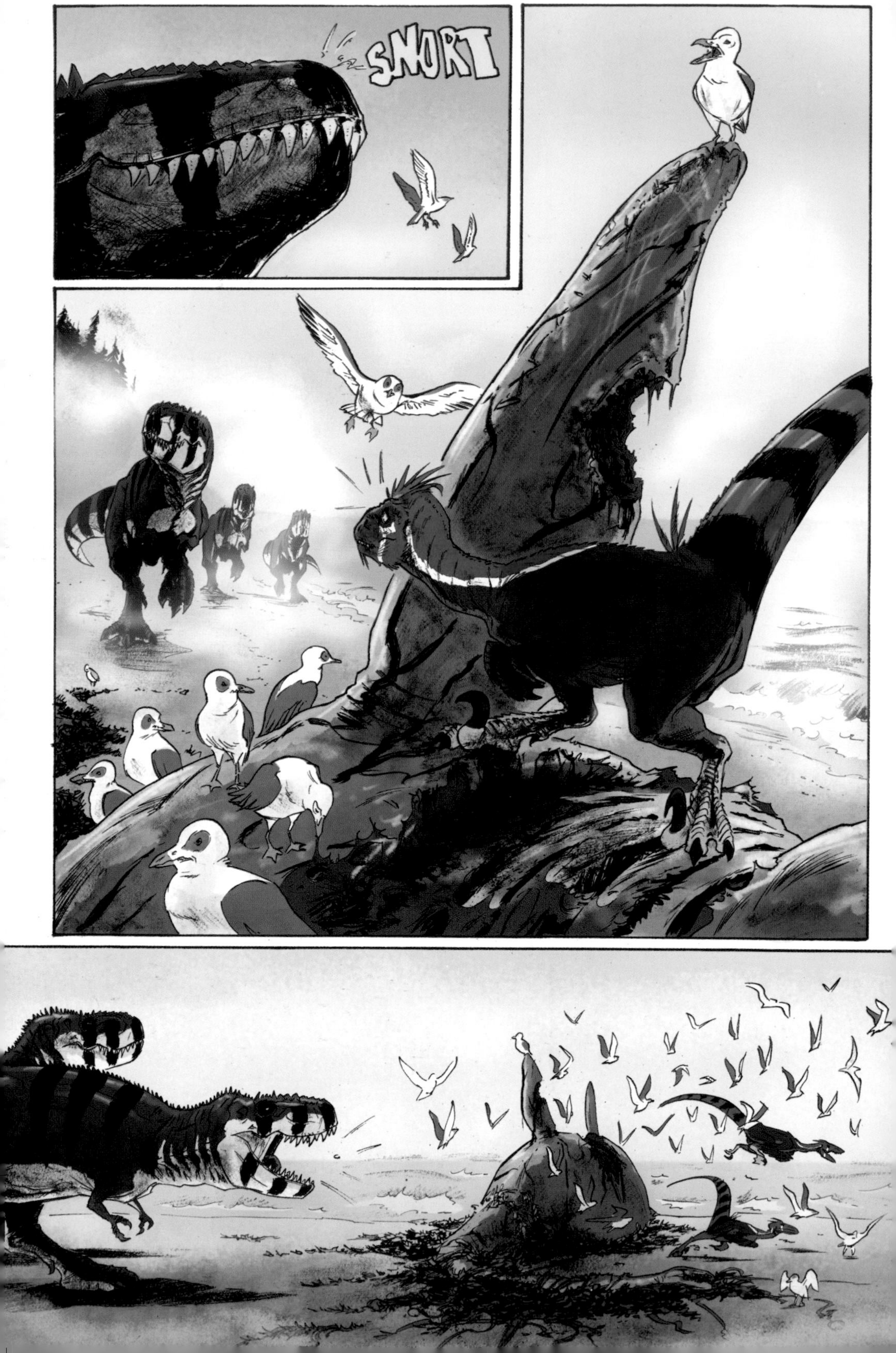
SNORT

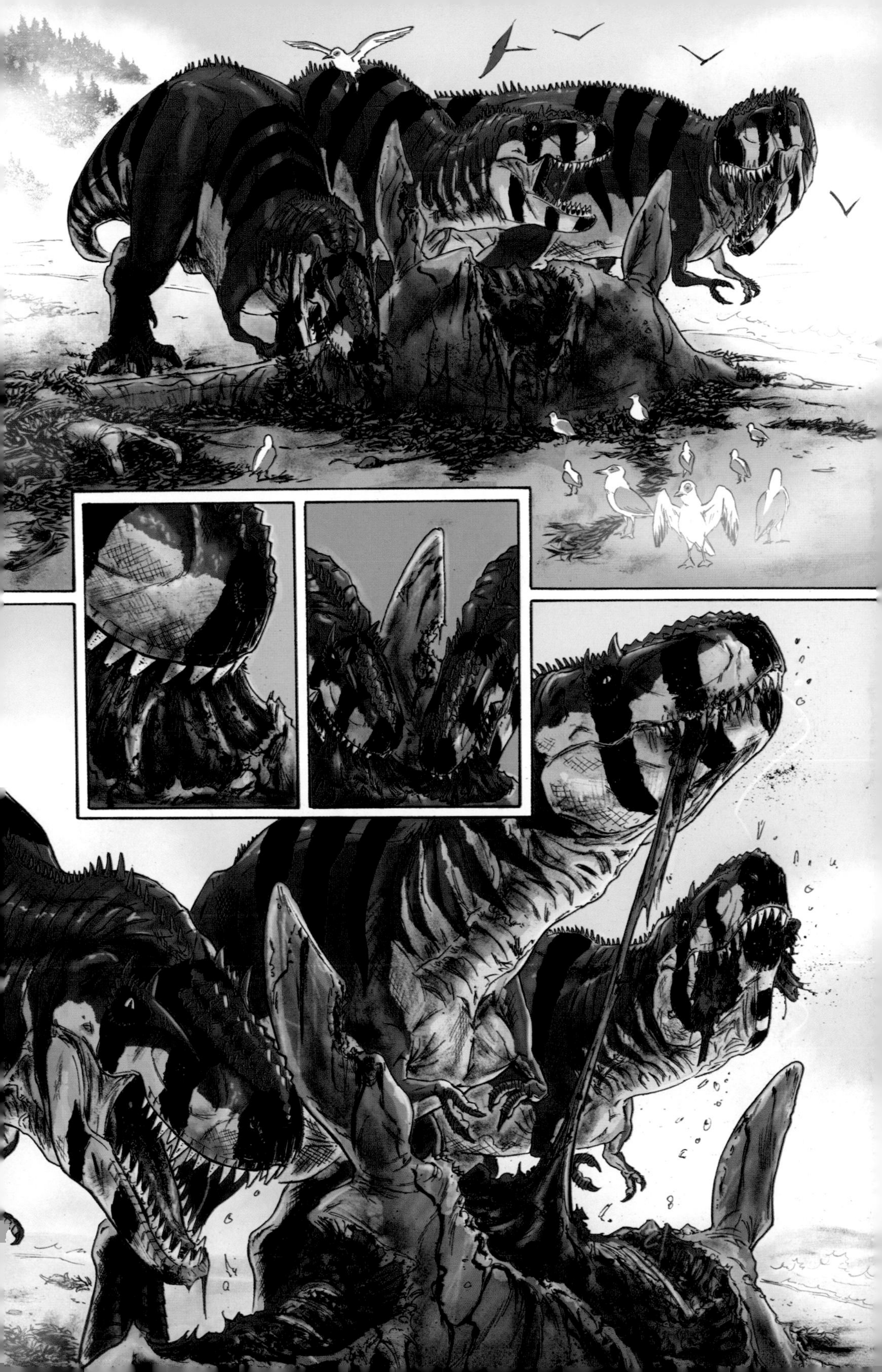

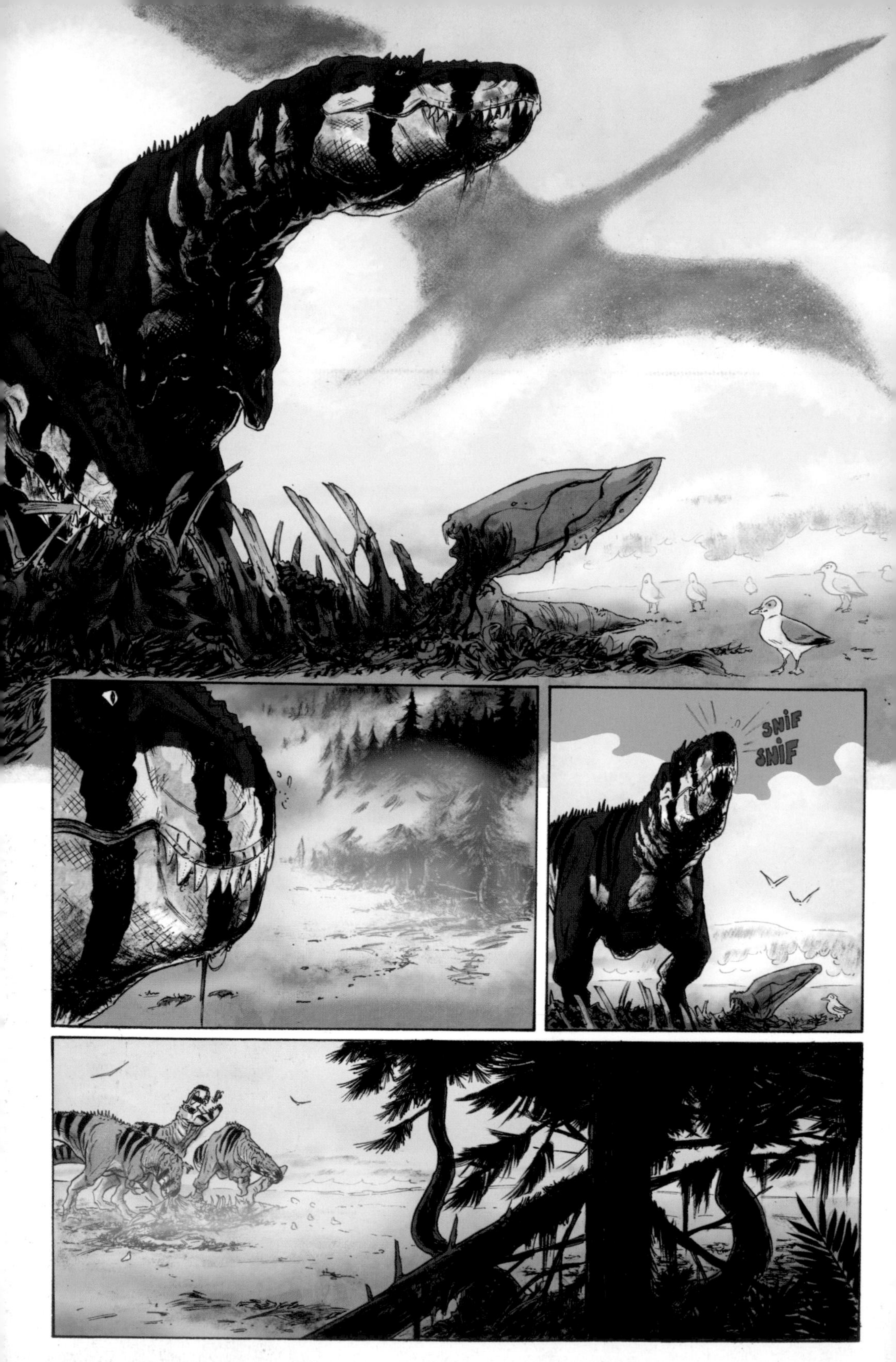
SNIF
SNIF

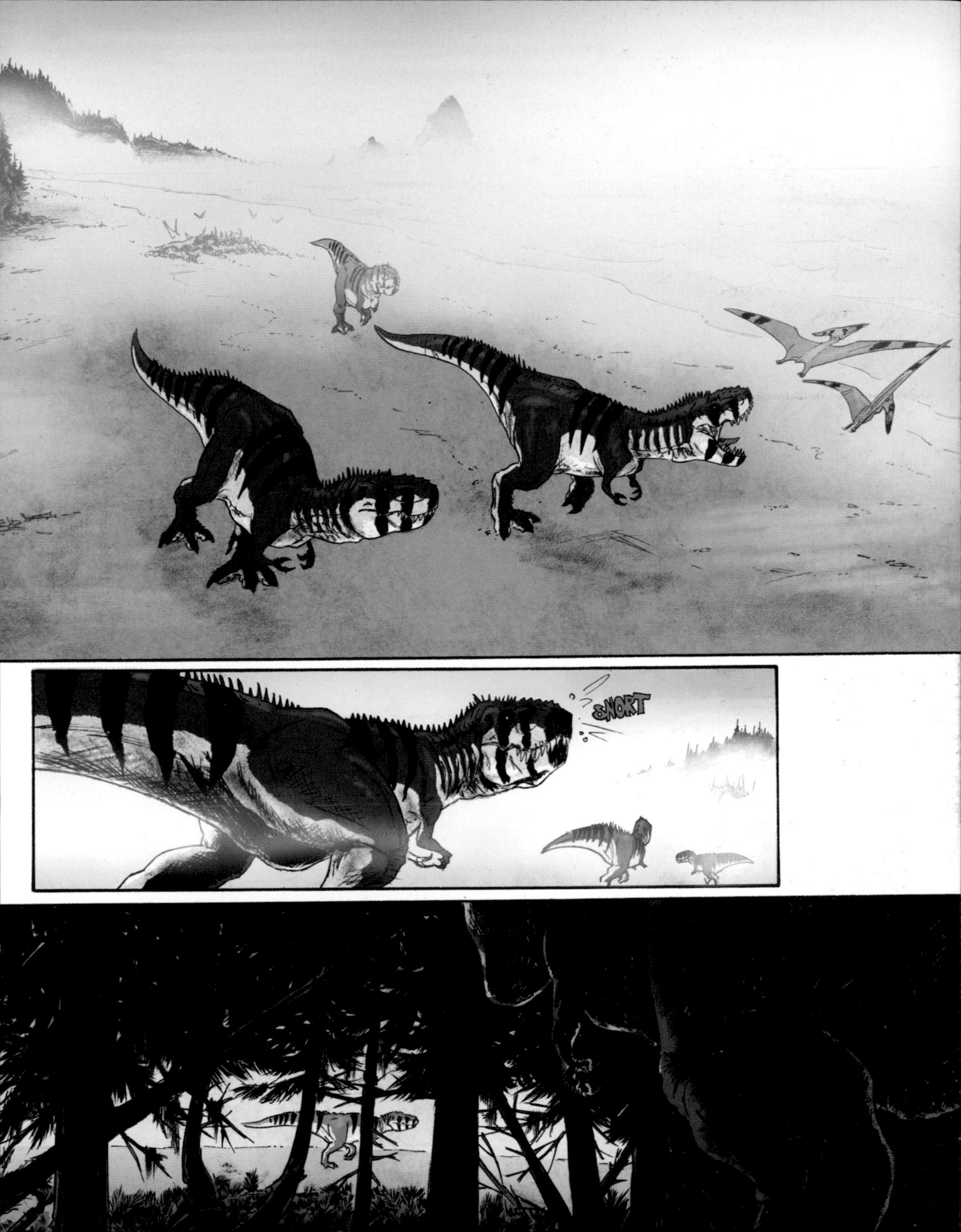
SNORT

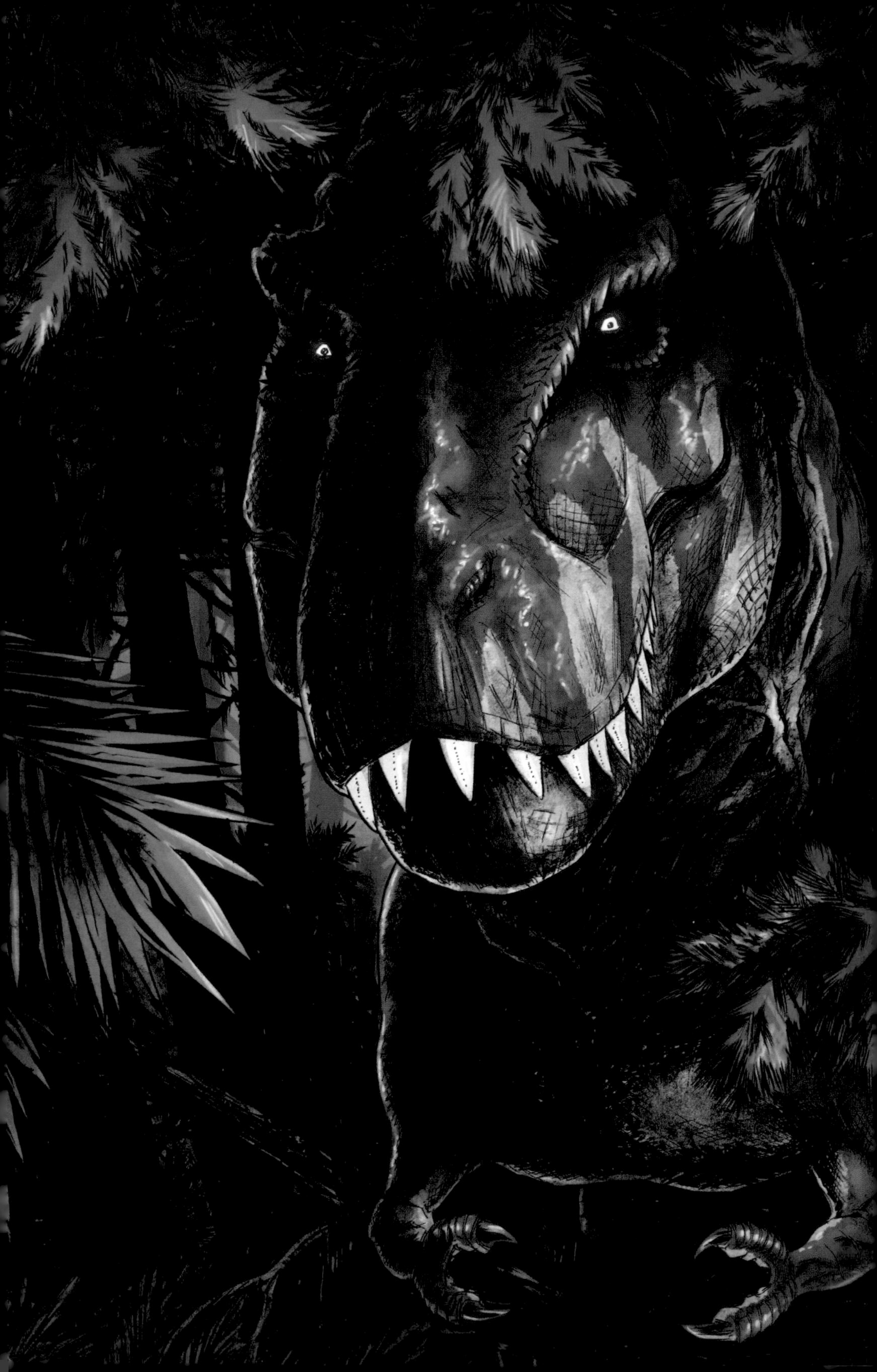

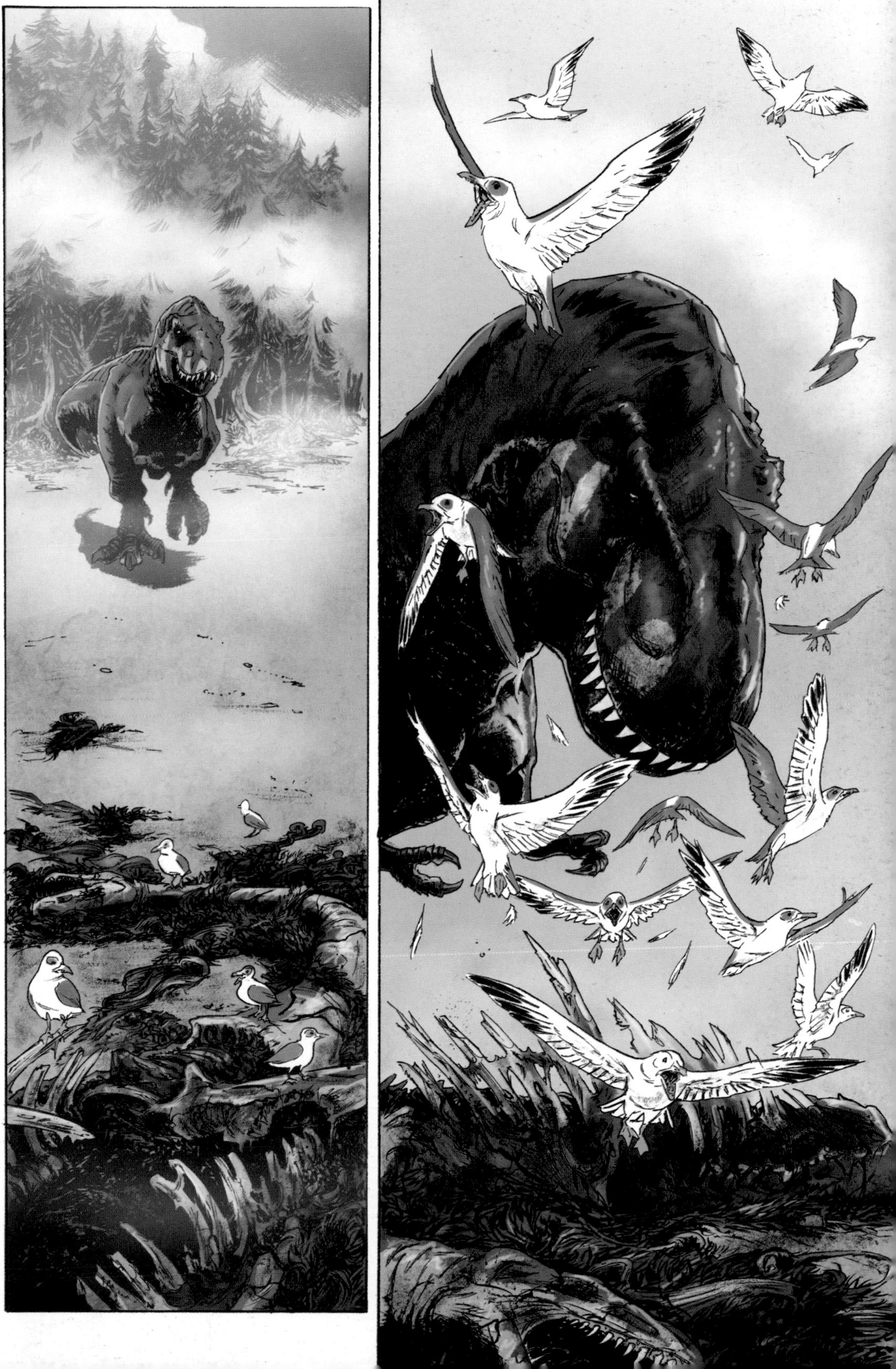

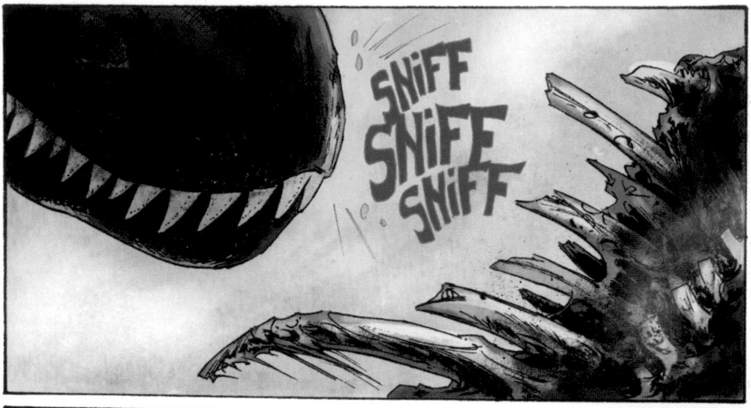
SNIFF
SNIFF
SNIFF

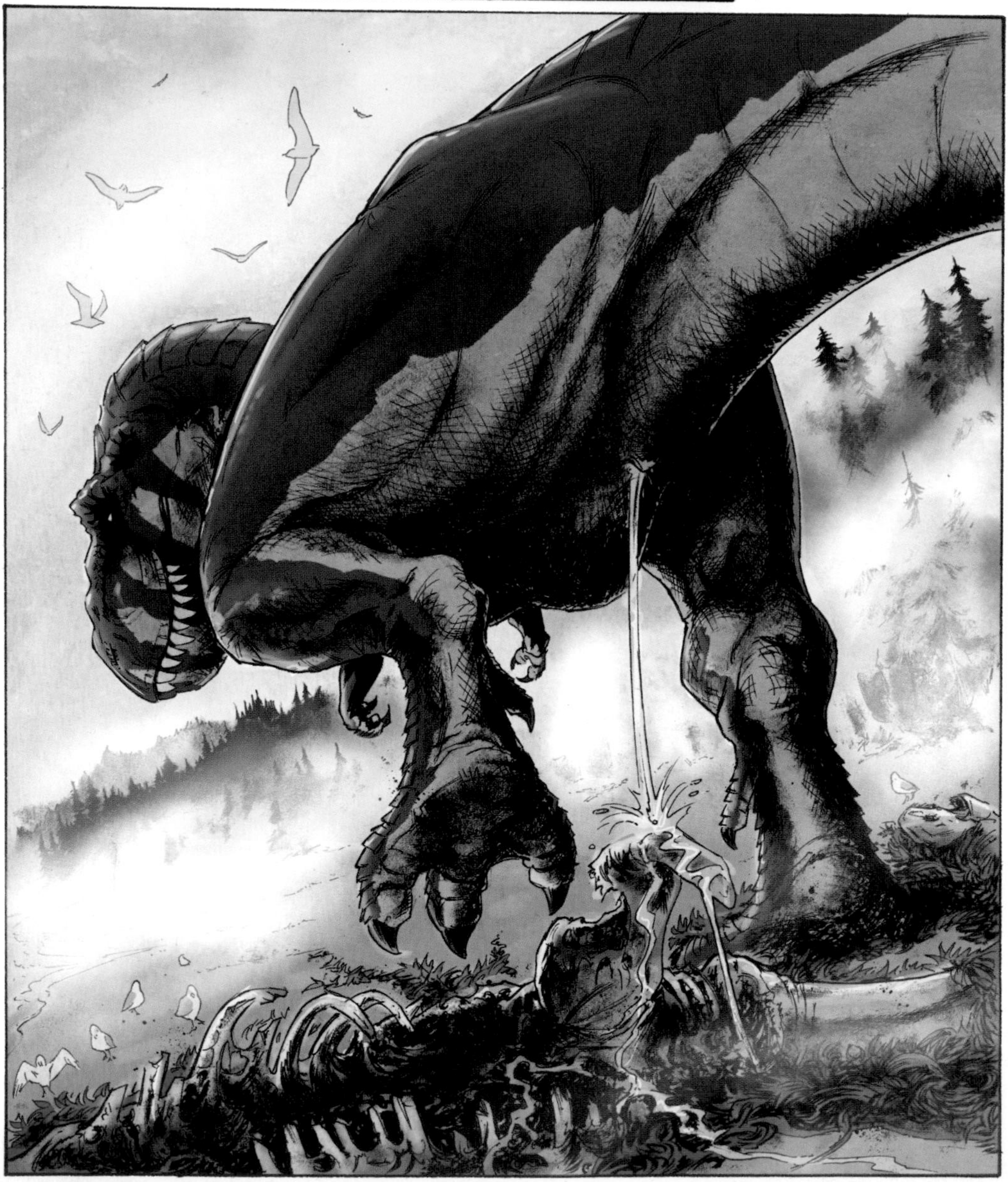

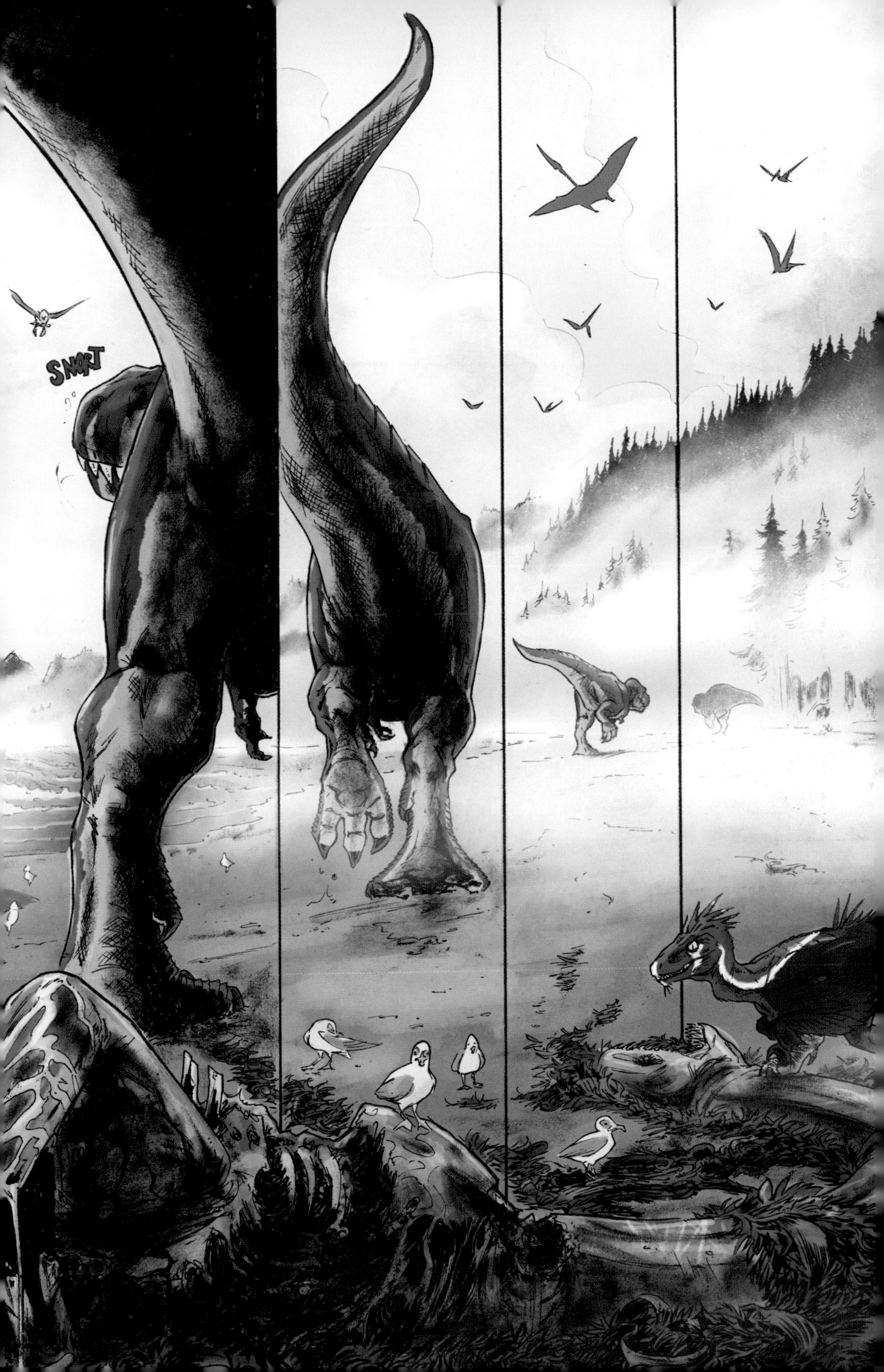
SNORT

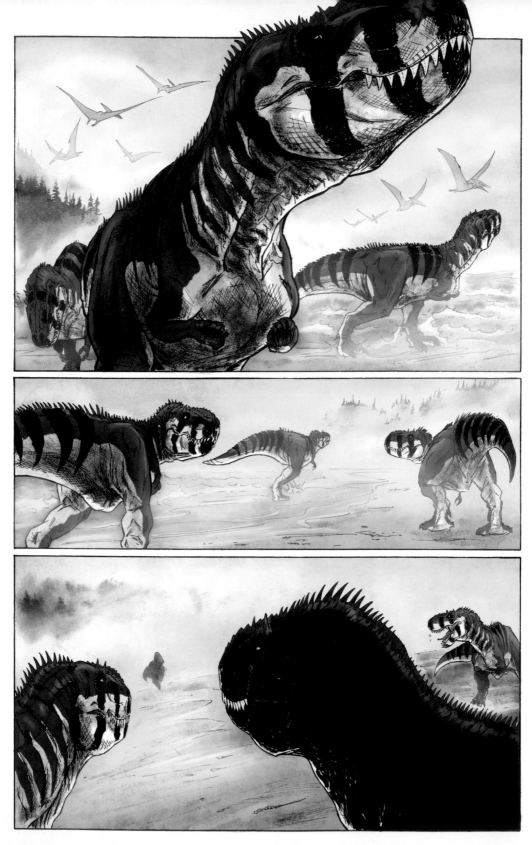

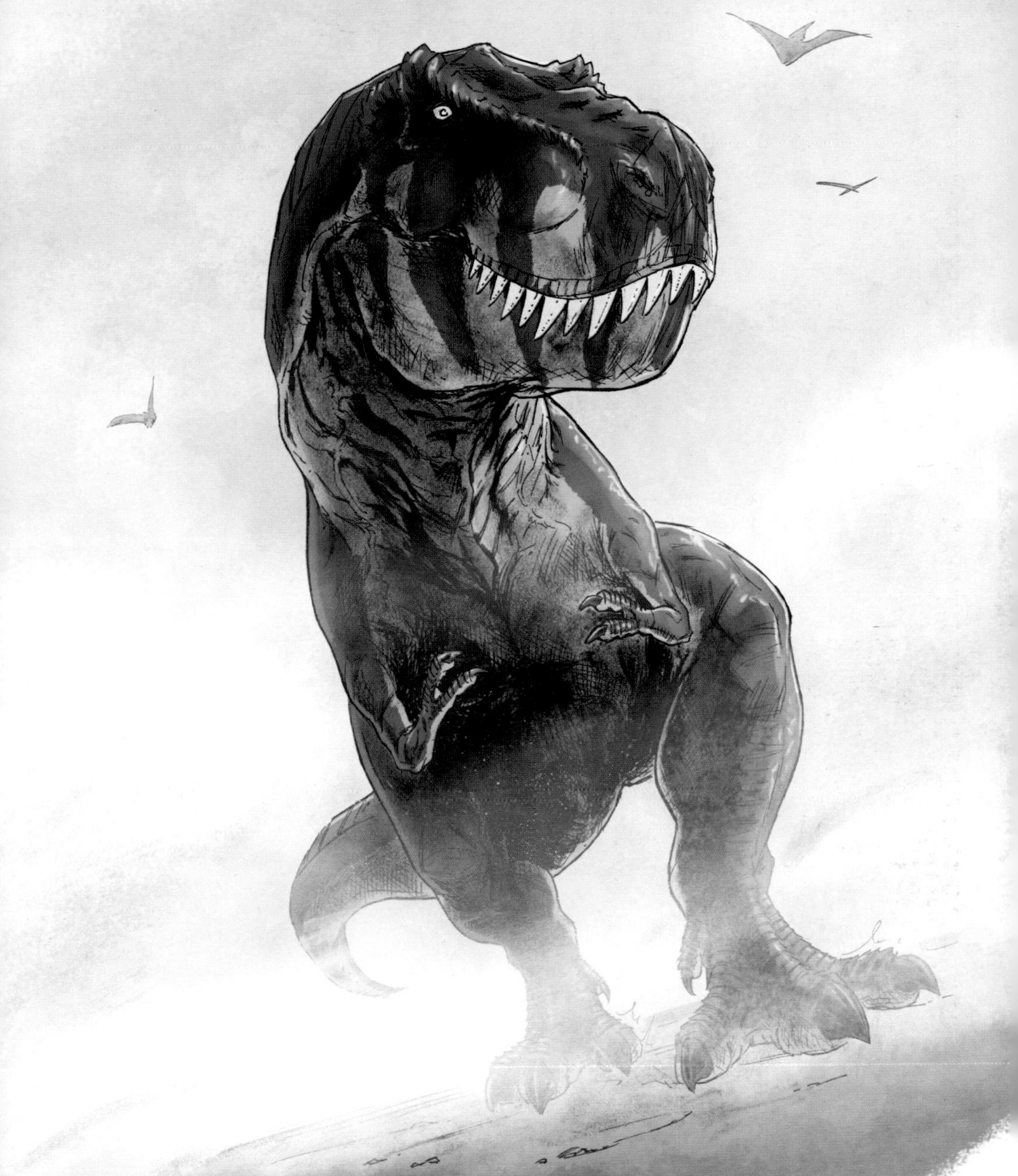

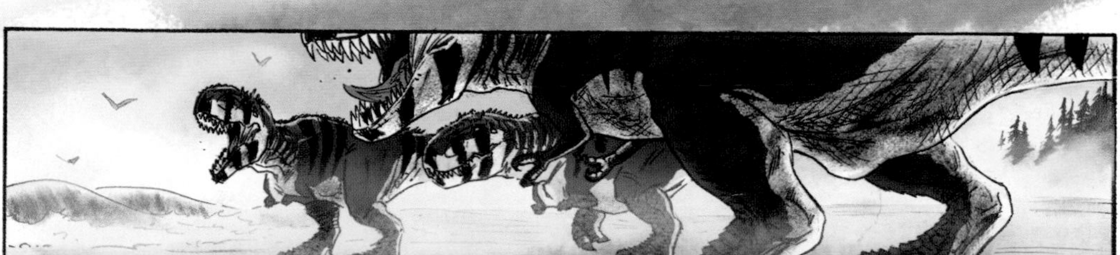

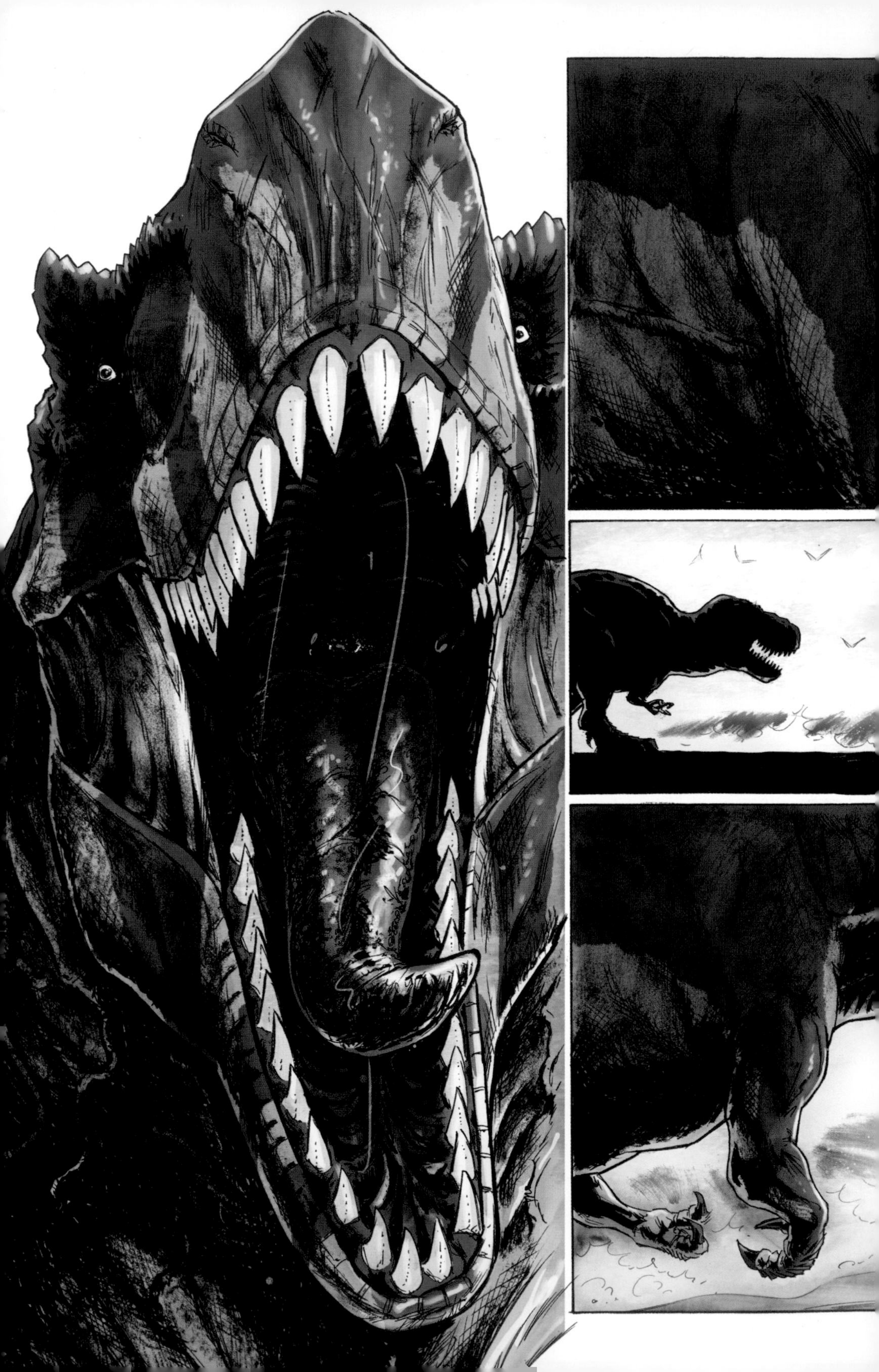

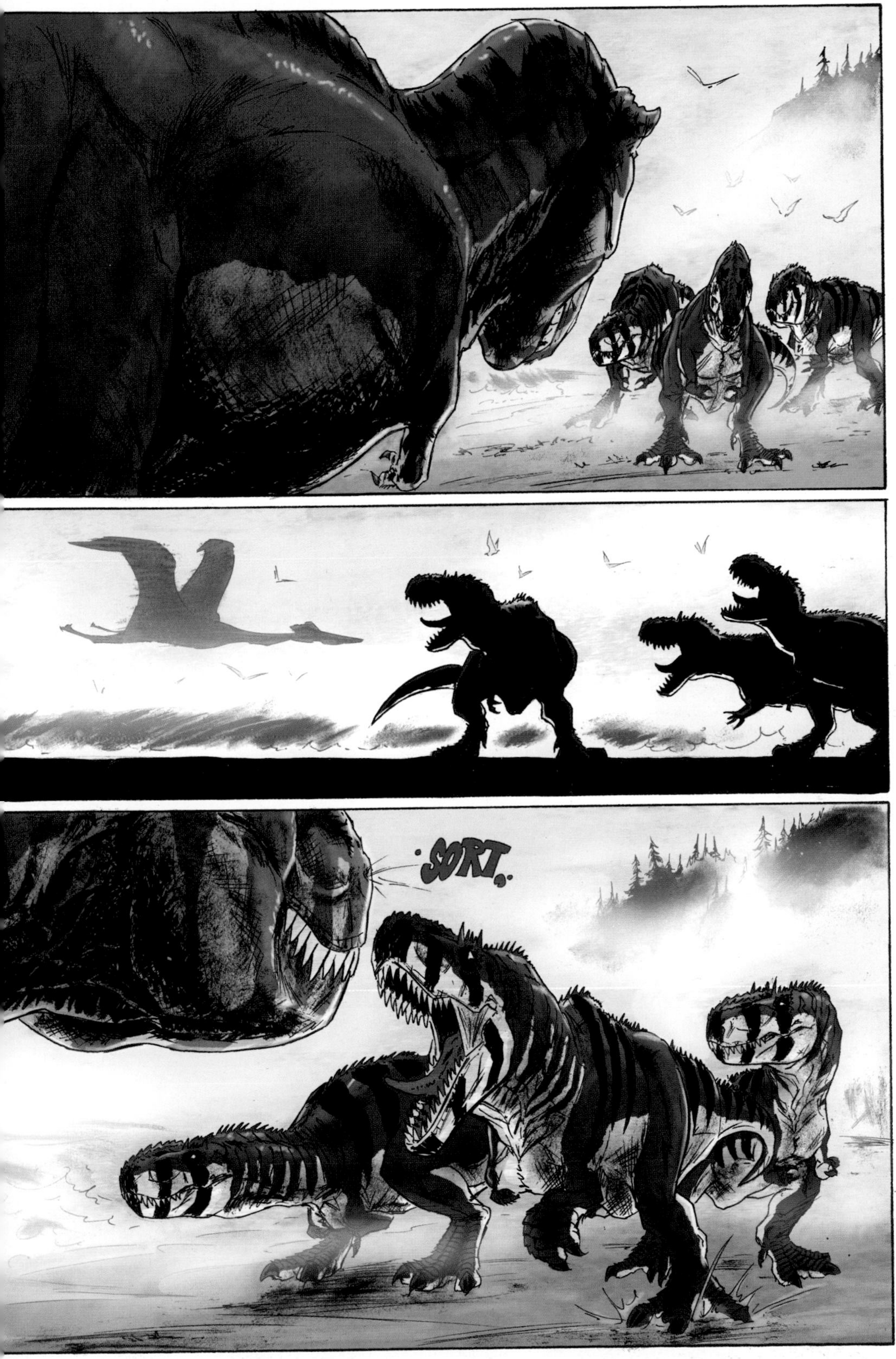
SORT.

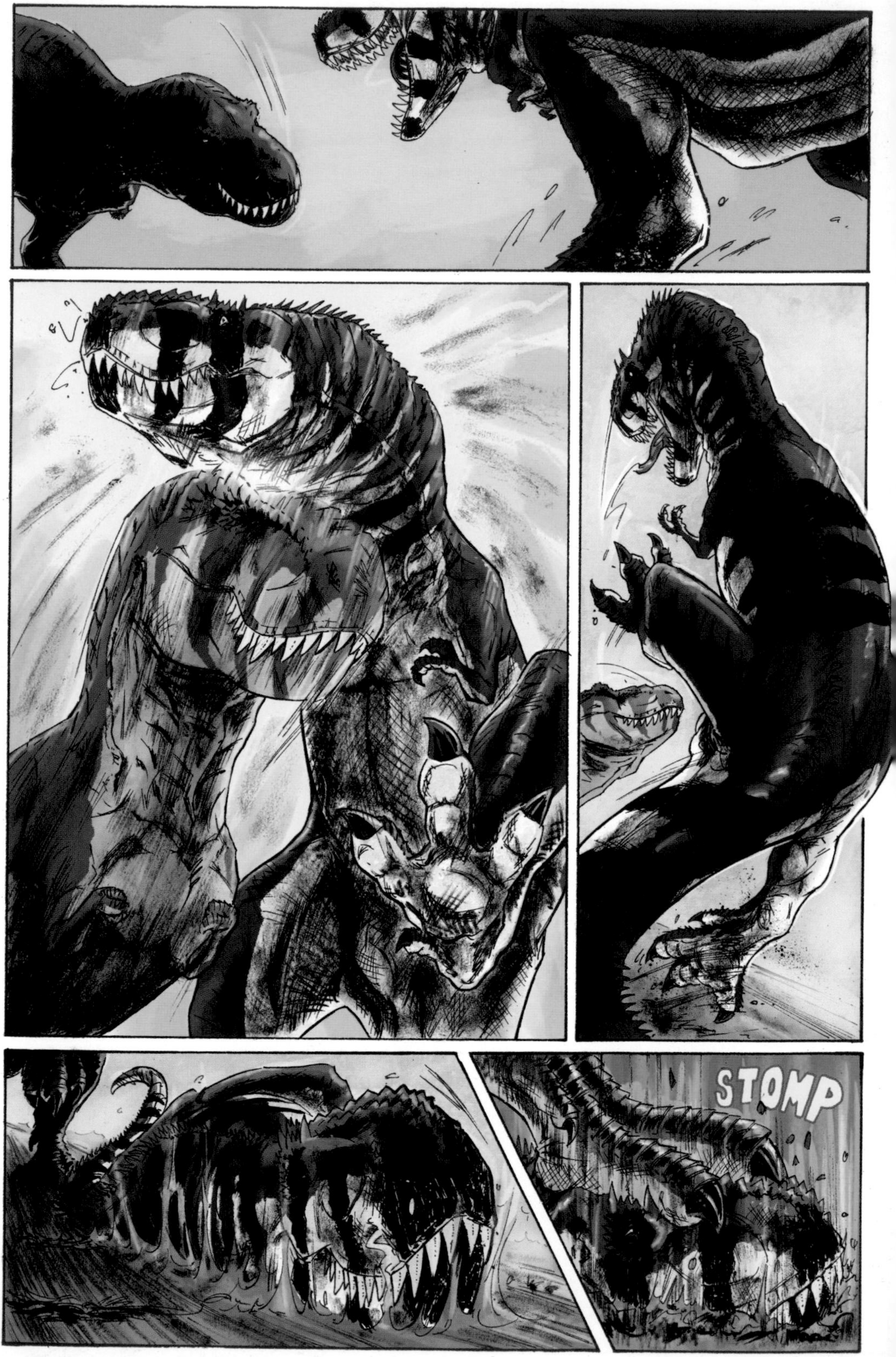
STOMP

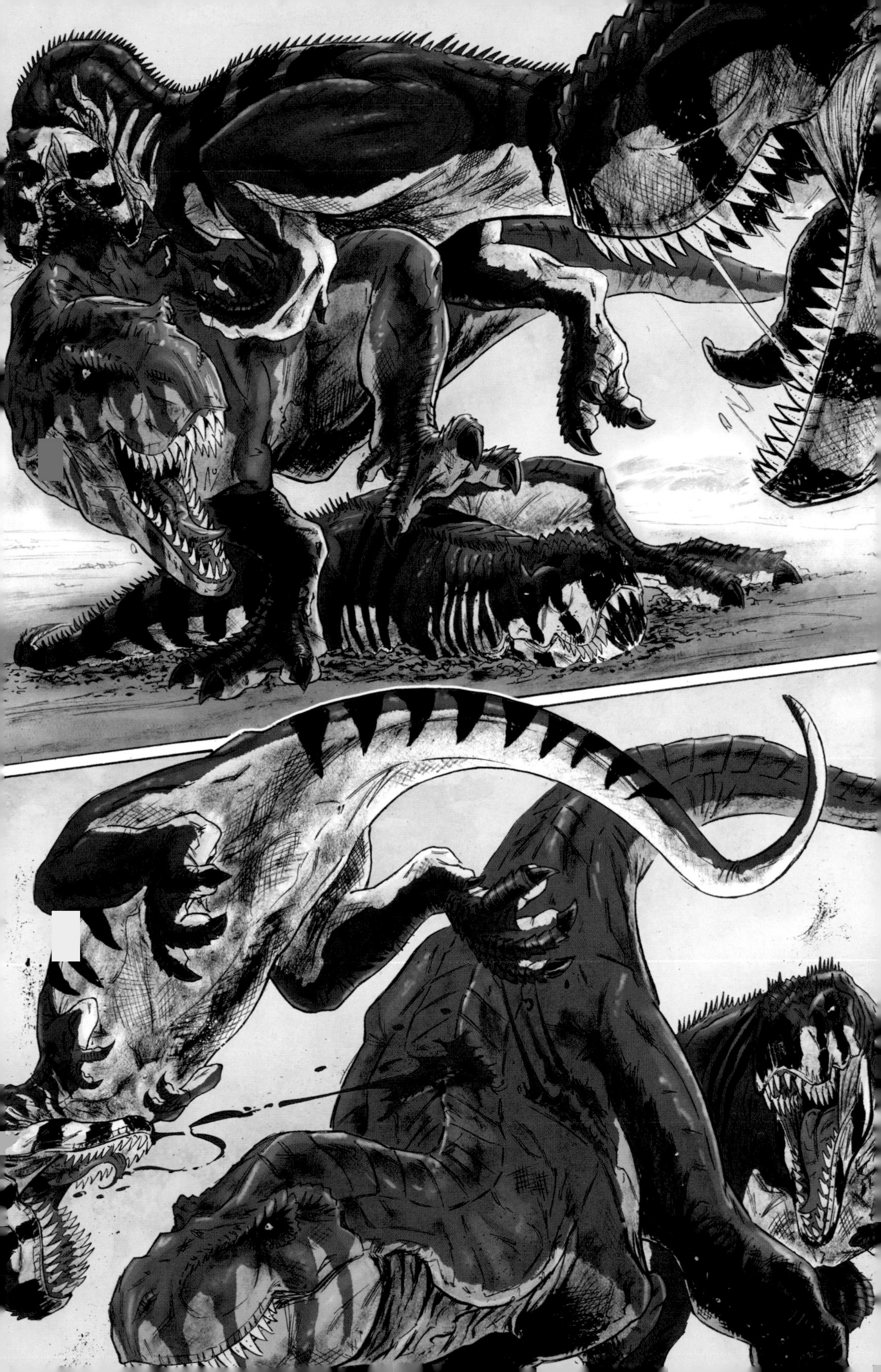

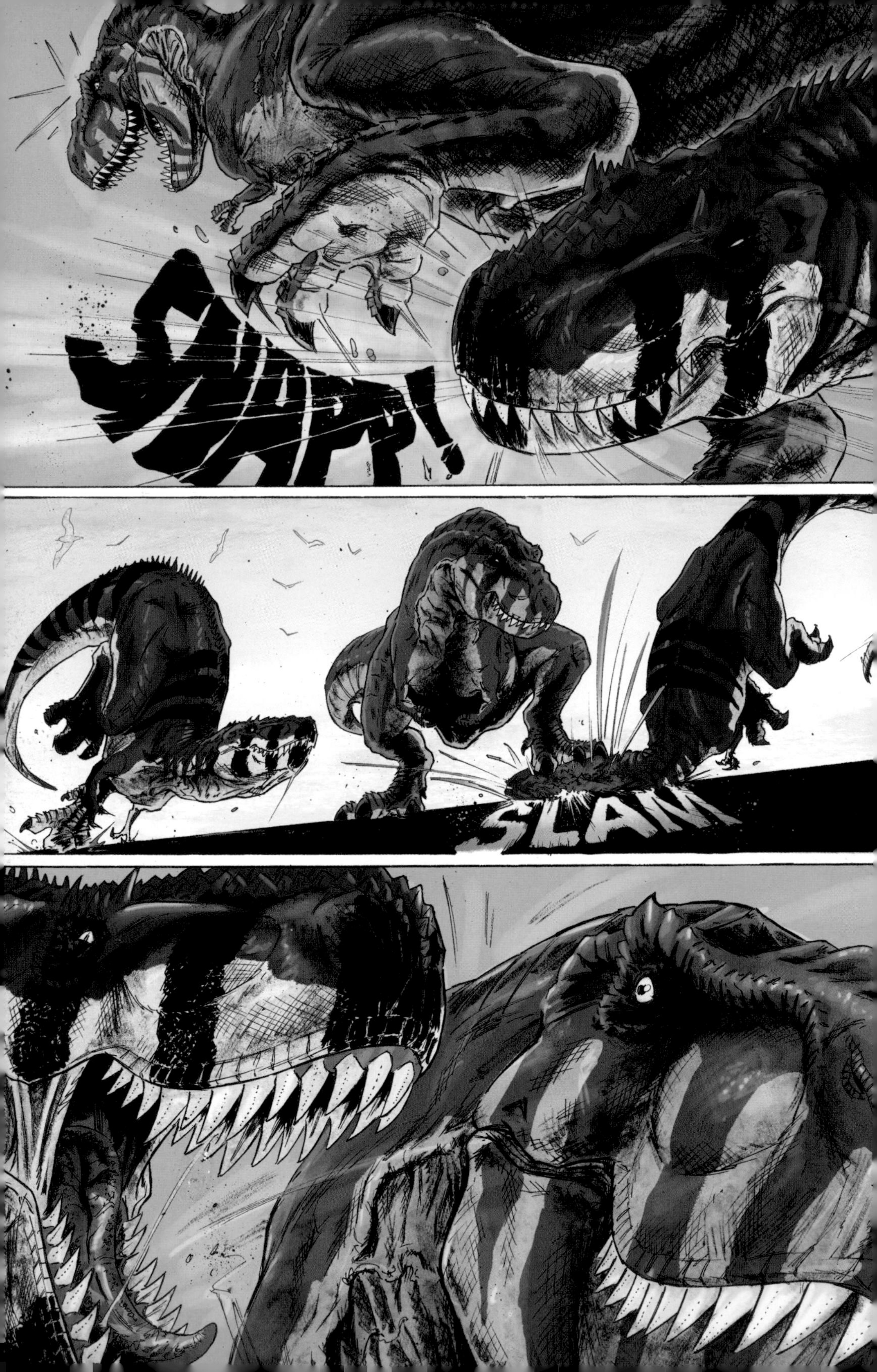
SWAPP!
SLAM

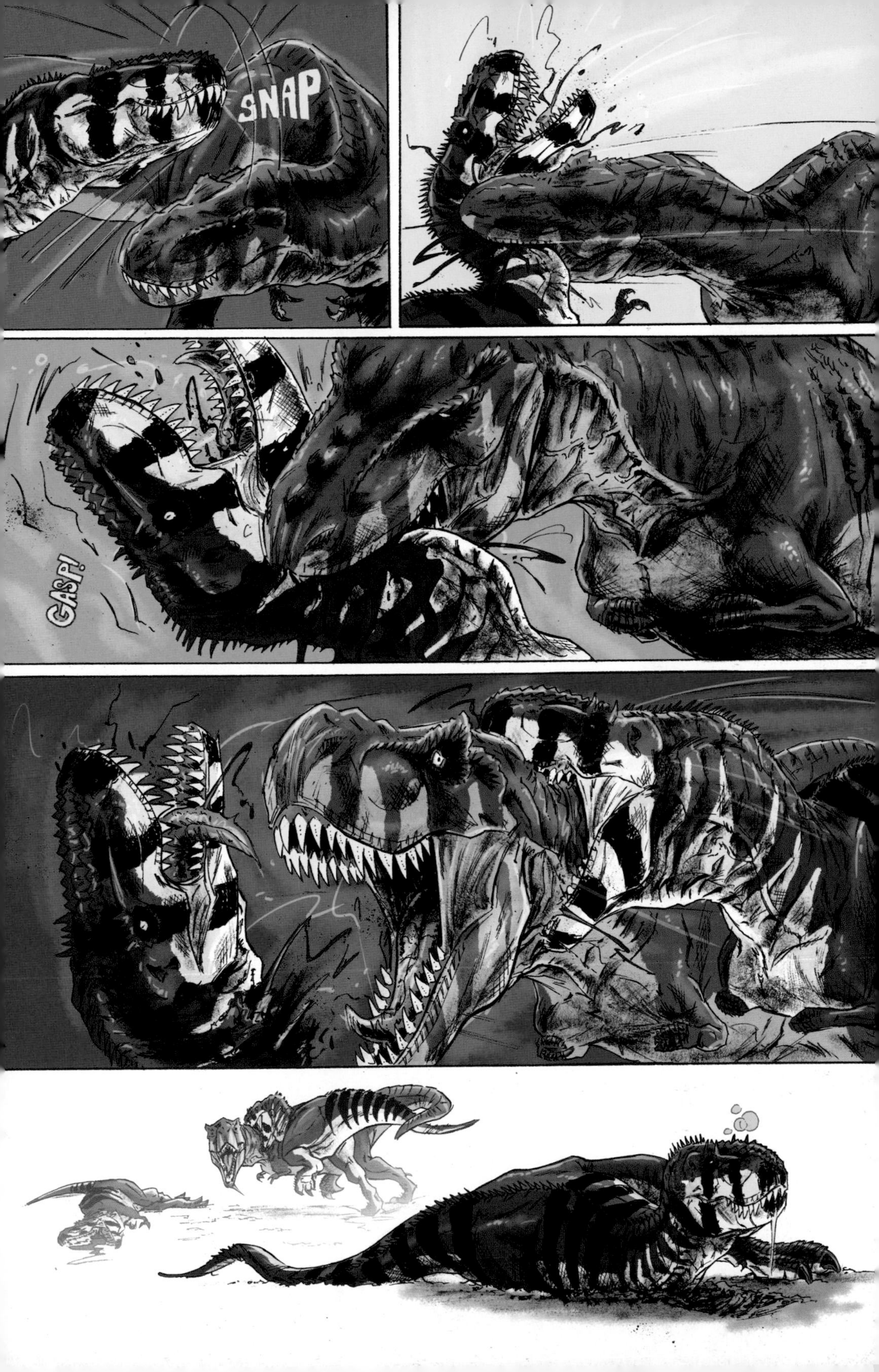
SNAP
GASP!

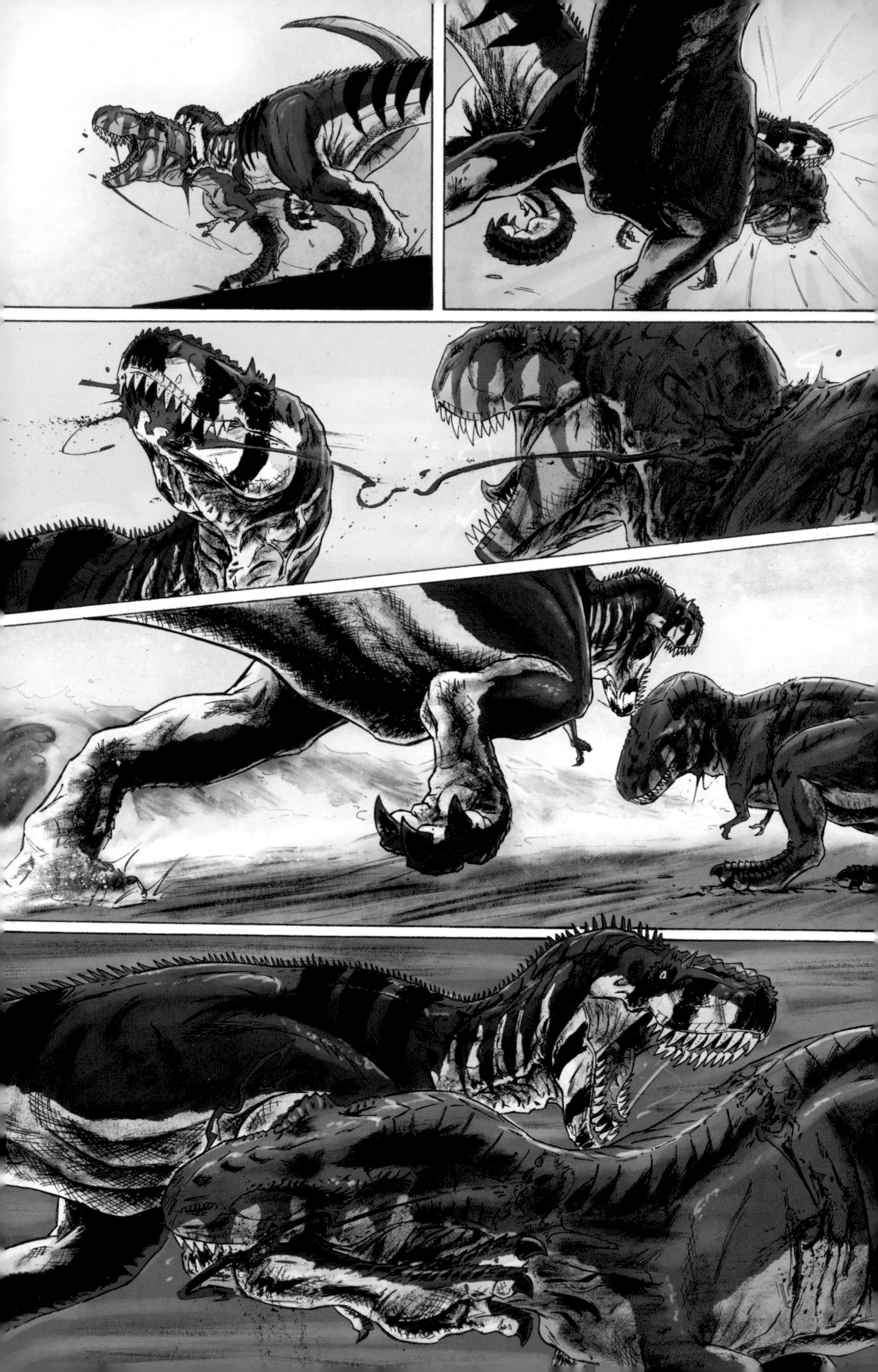

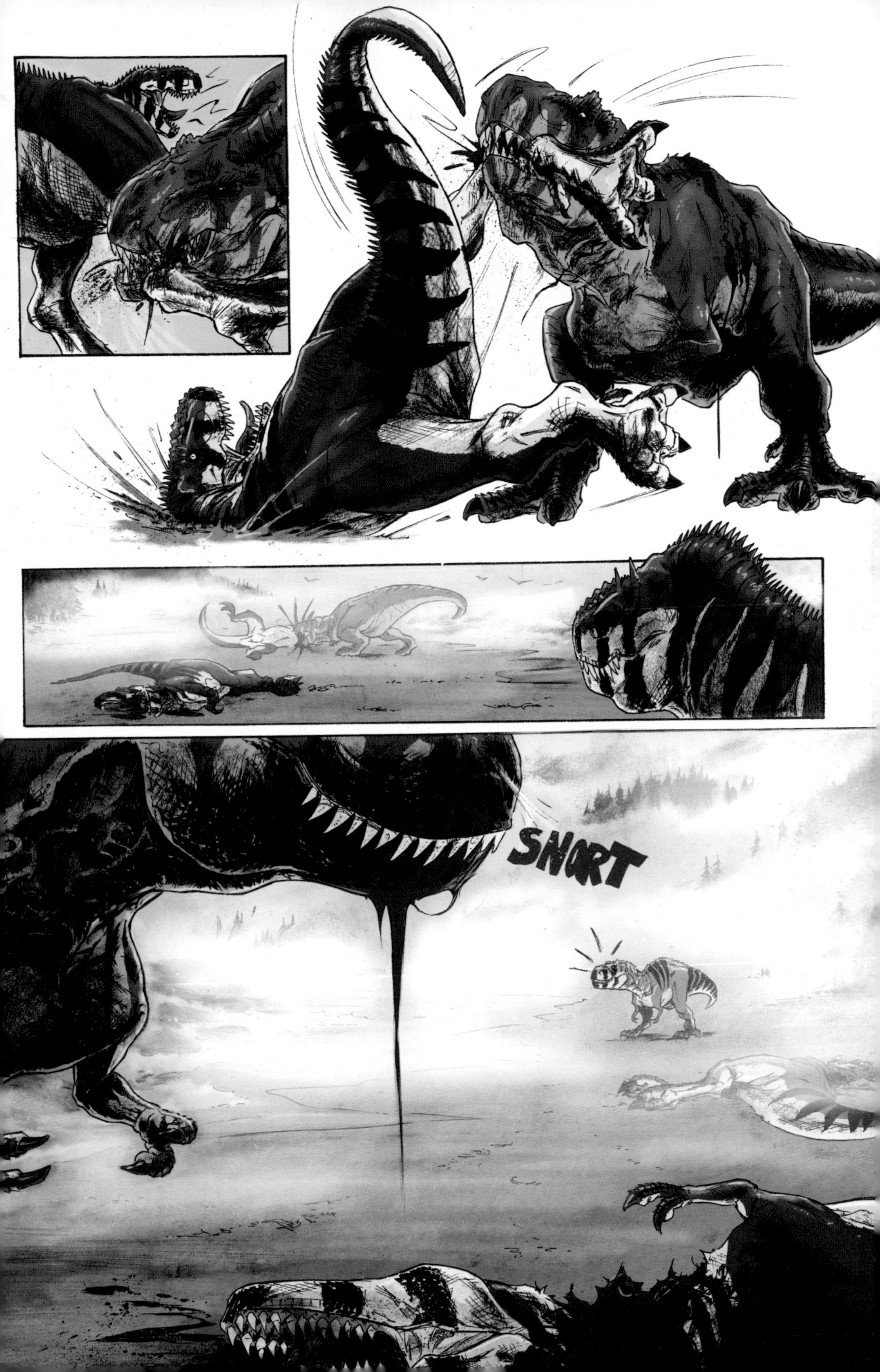
SNORT

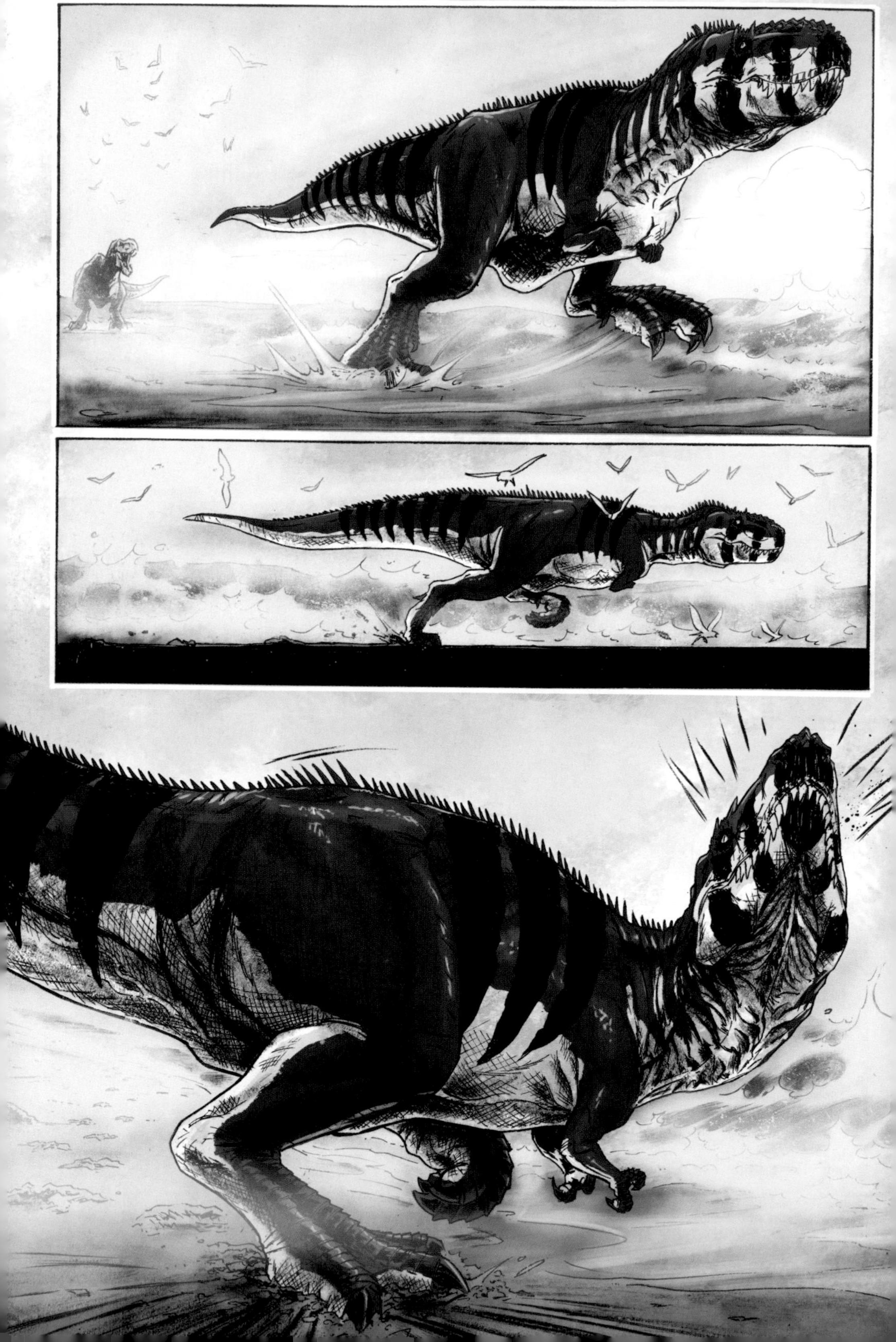

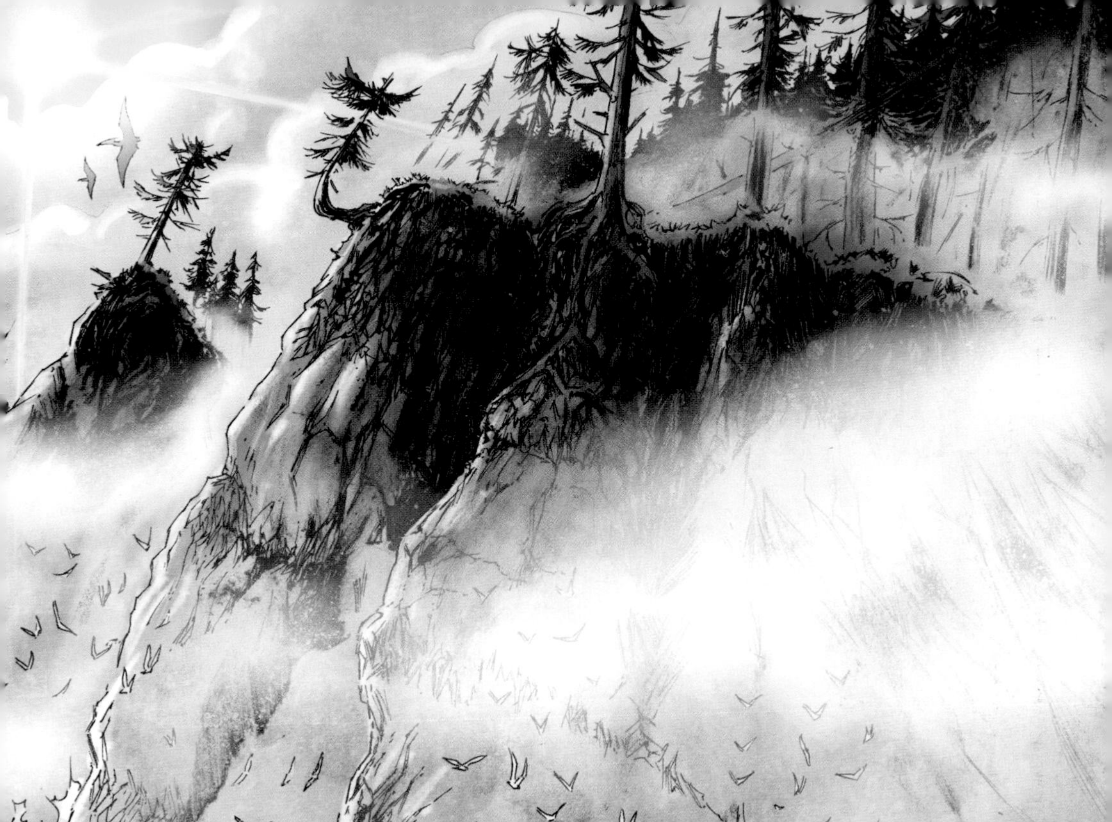

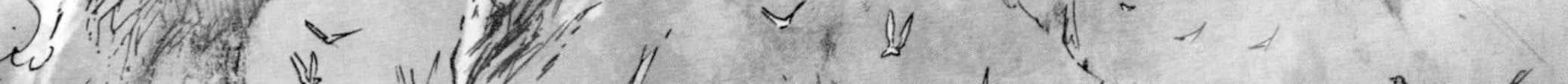
¡HURK!

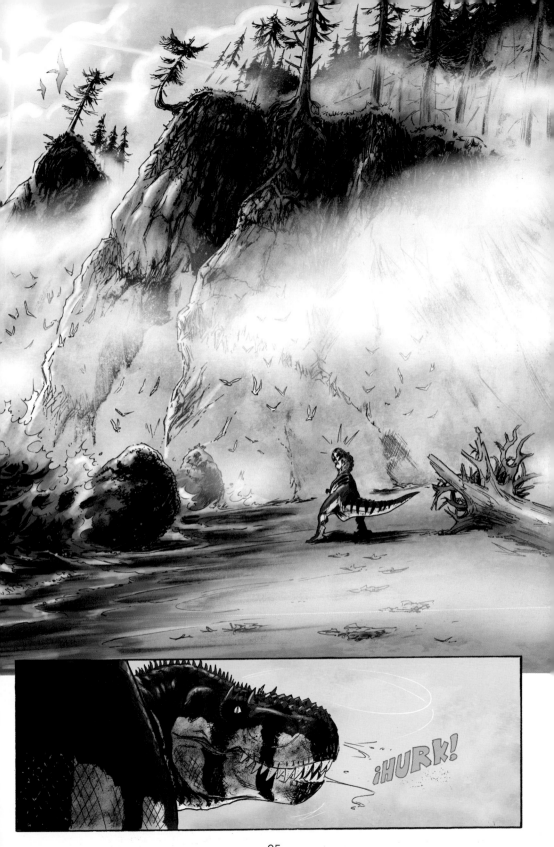

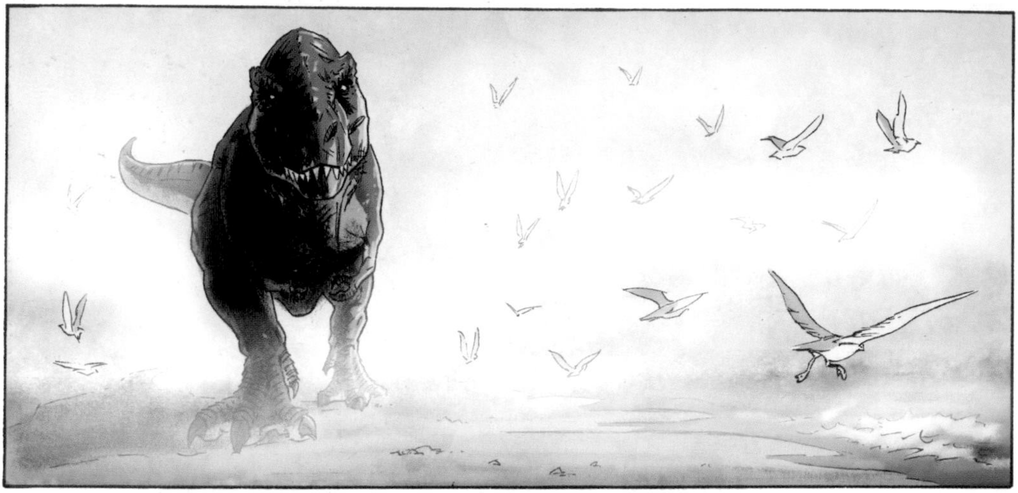

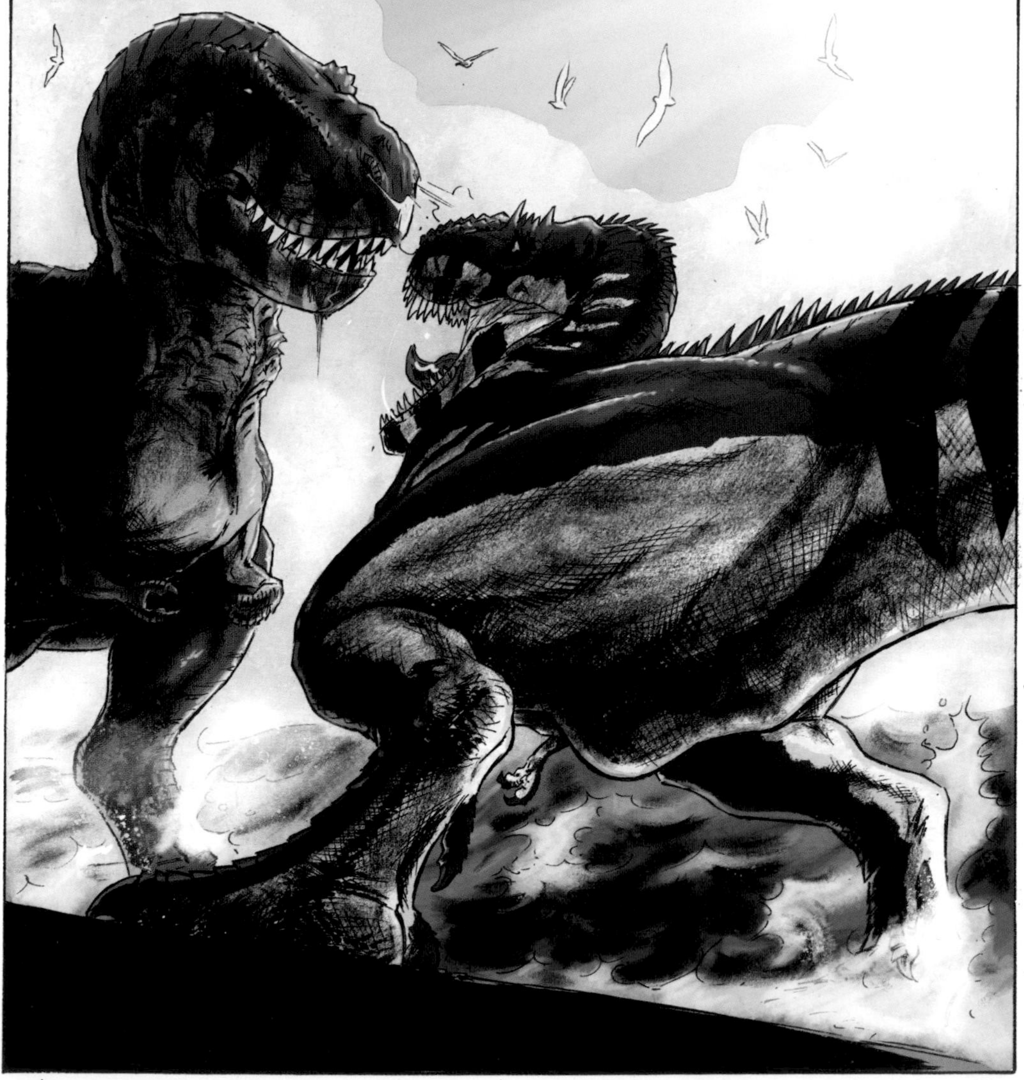

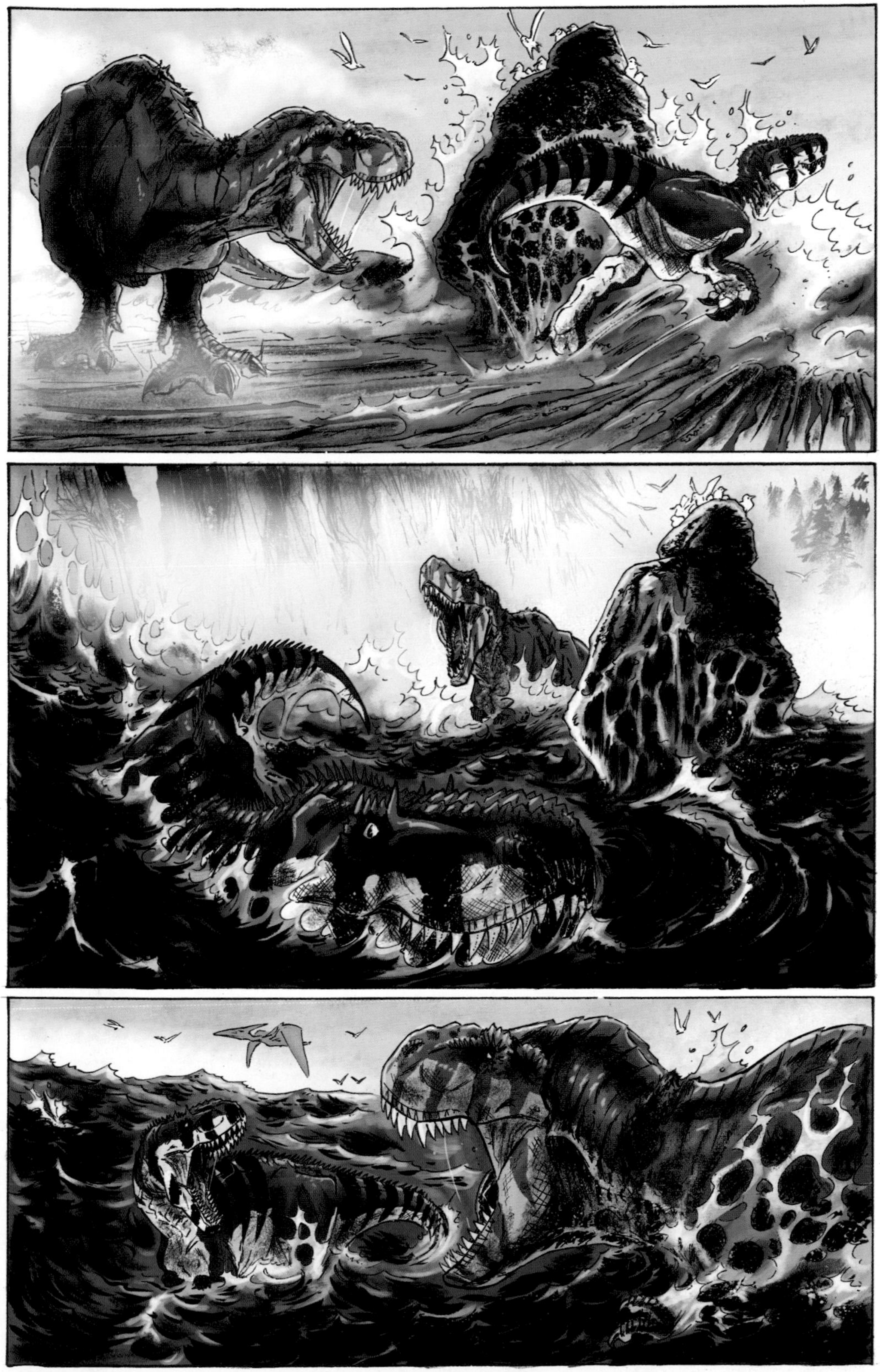

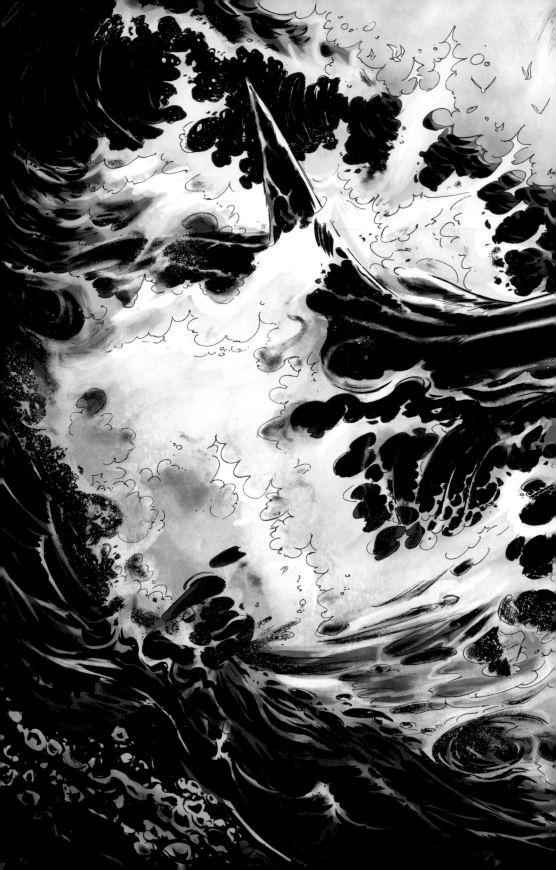

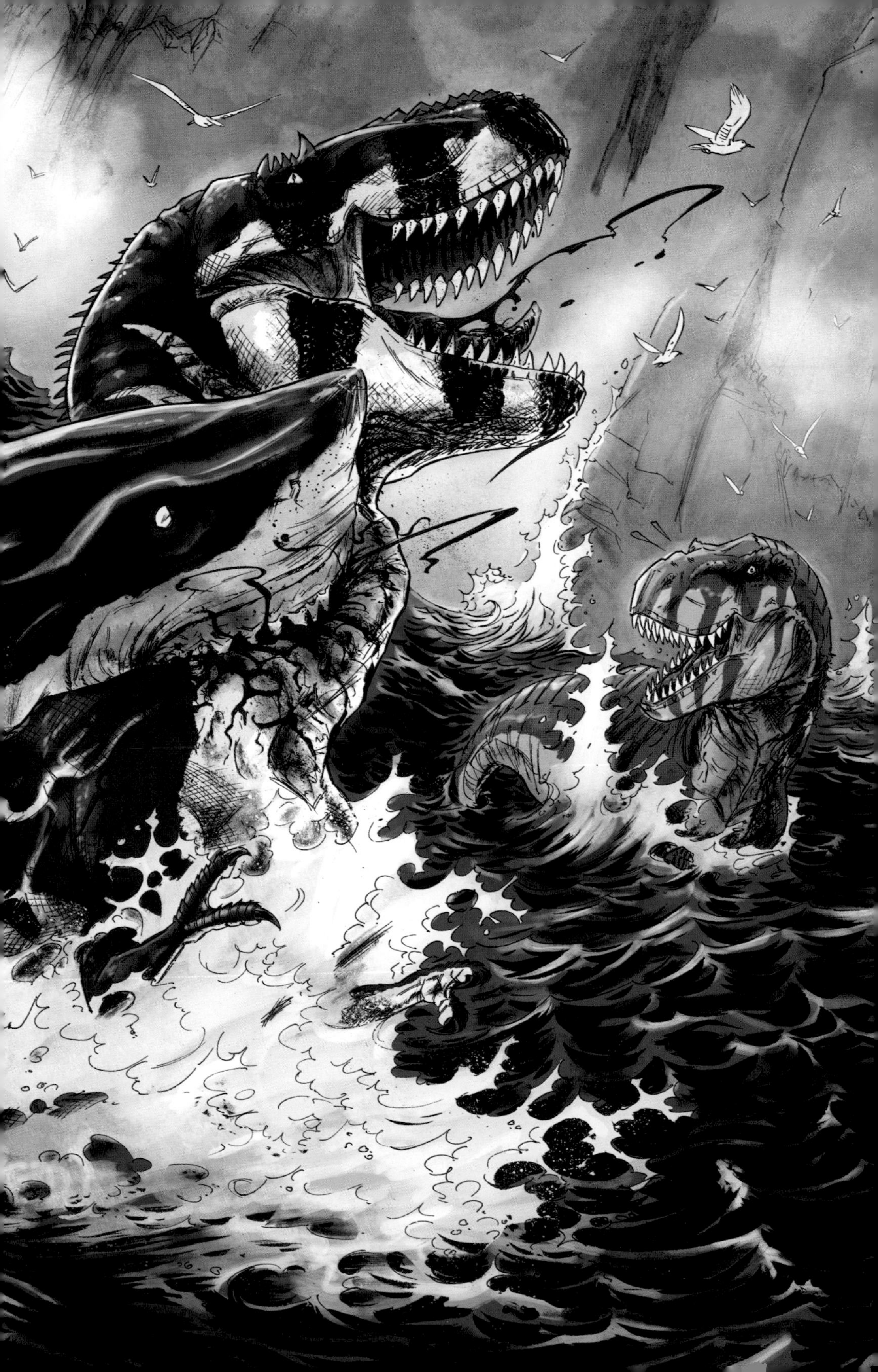

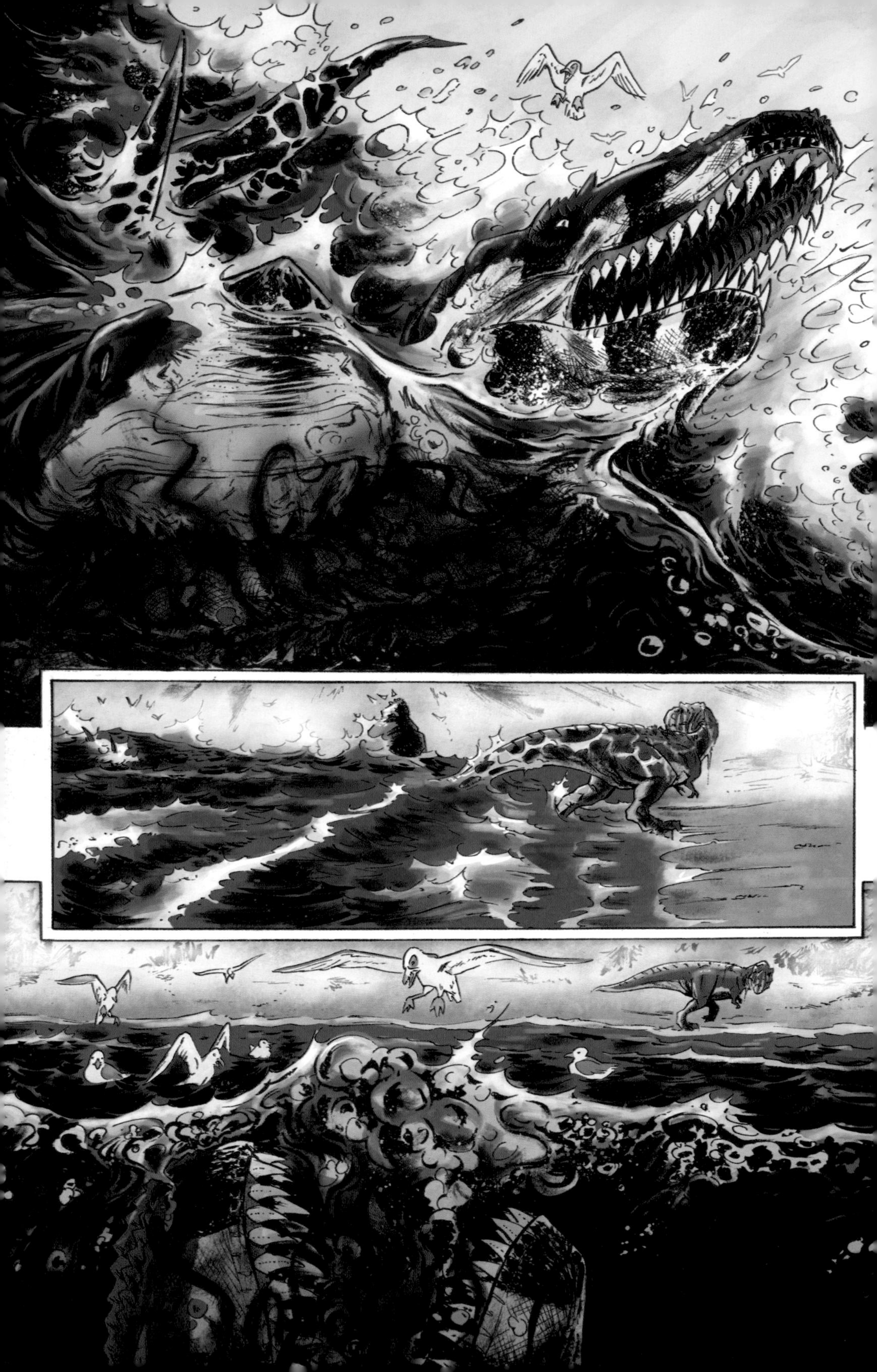

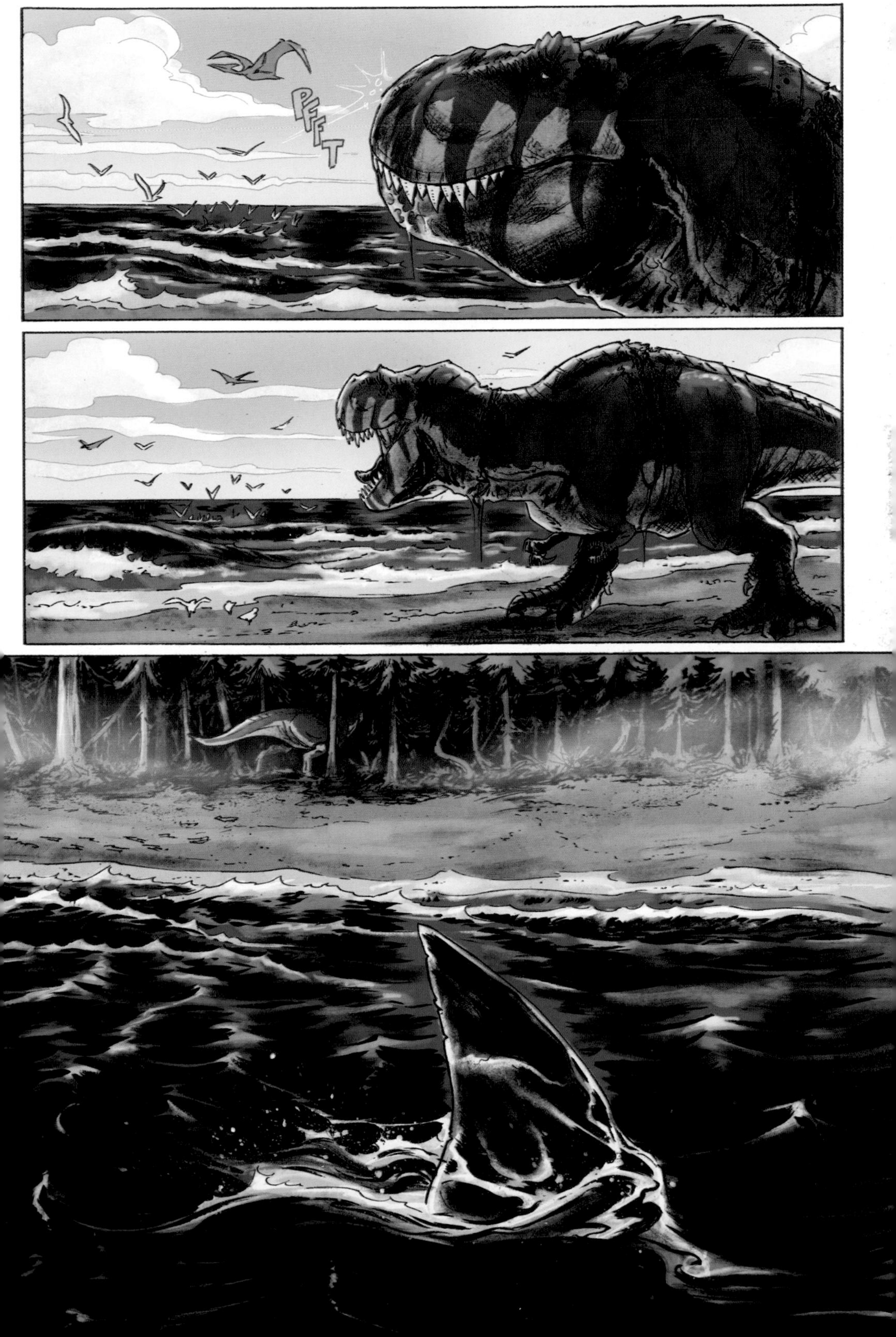
PFFFT

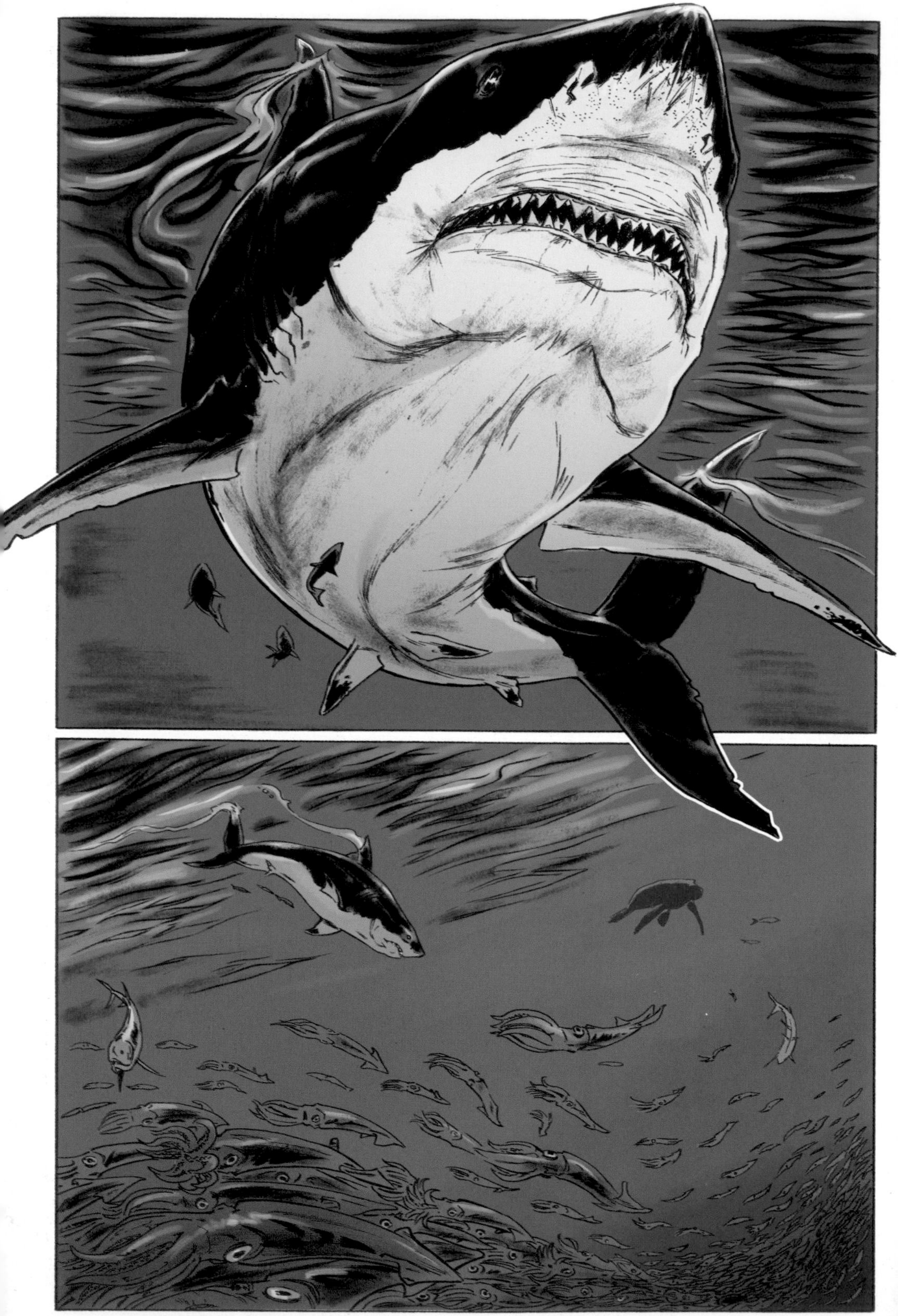

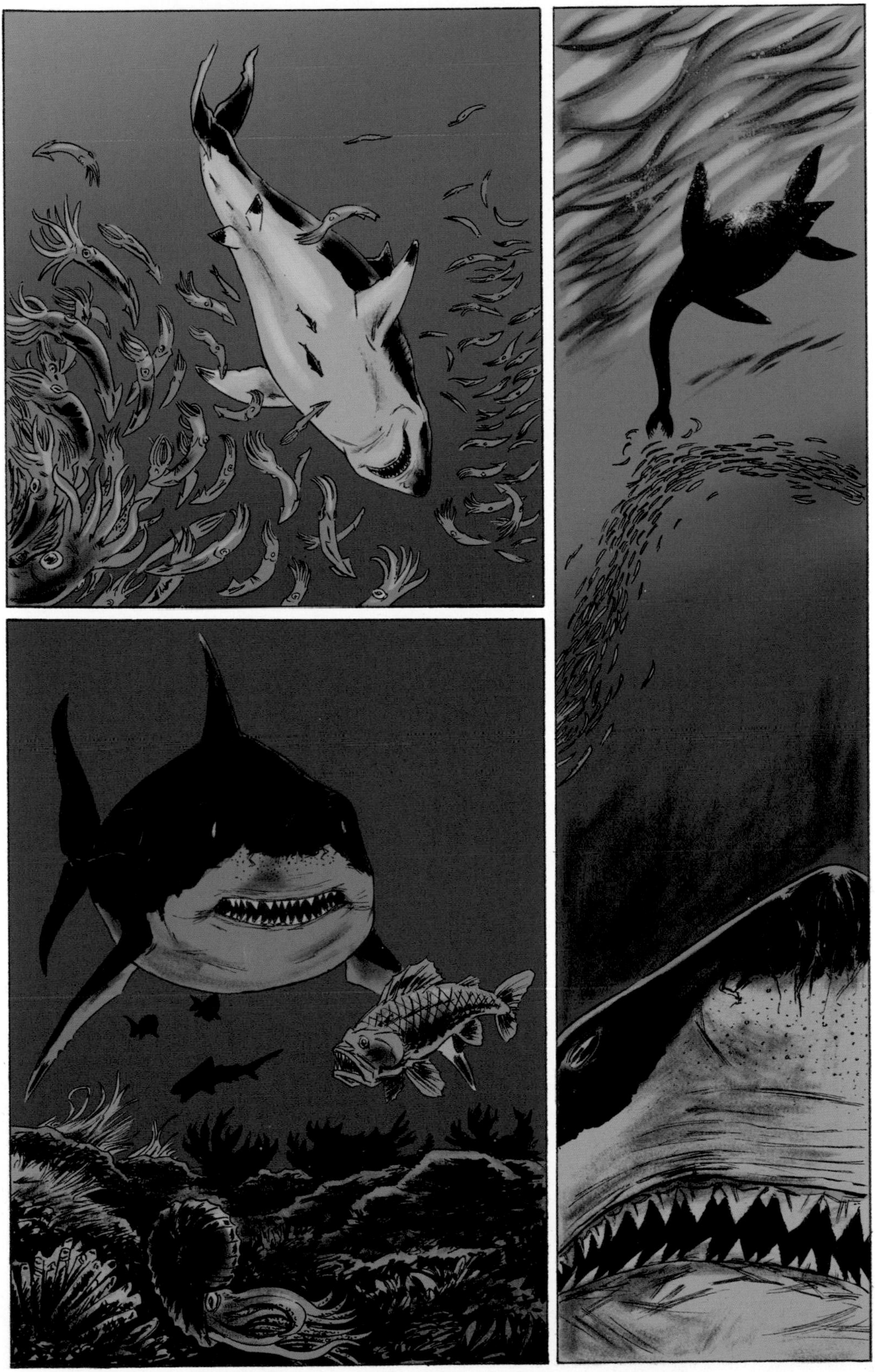

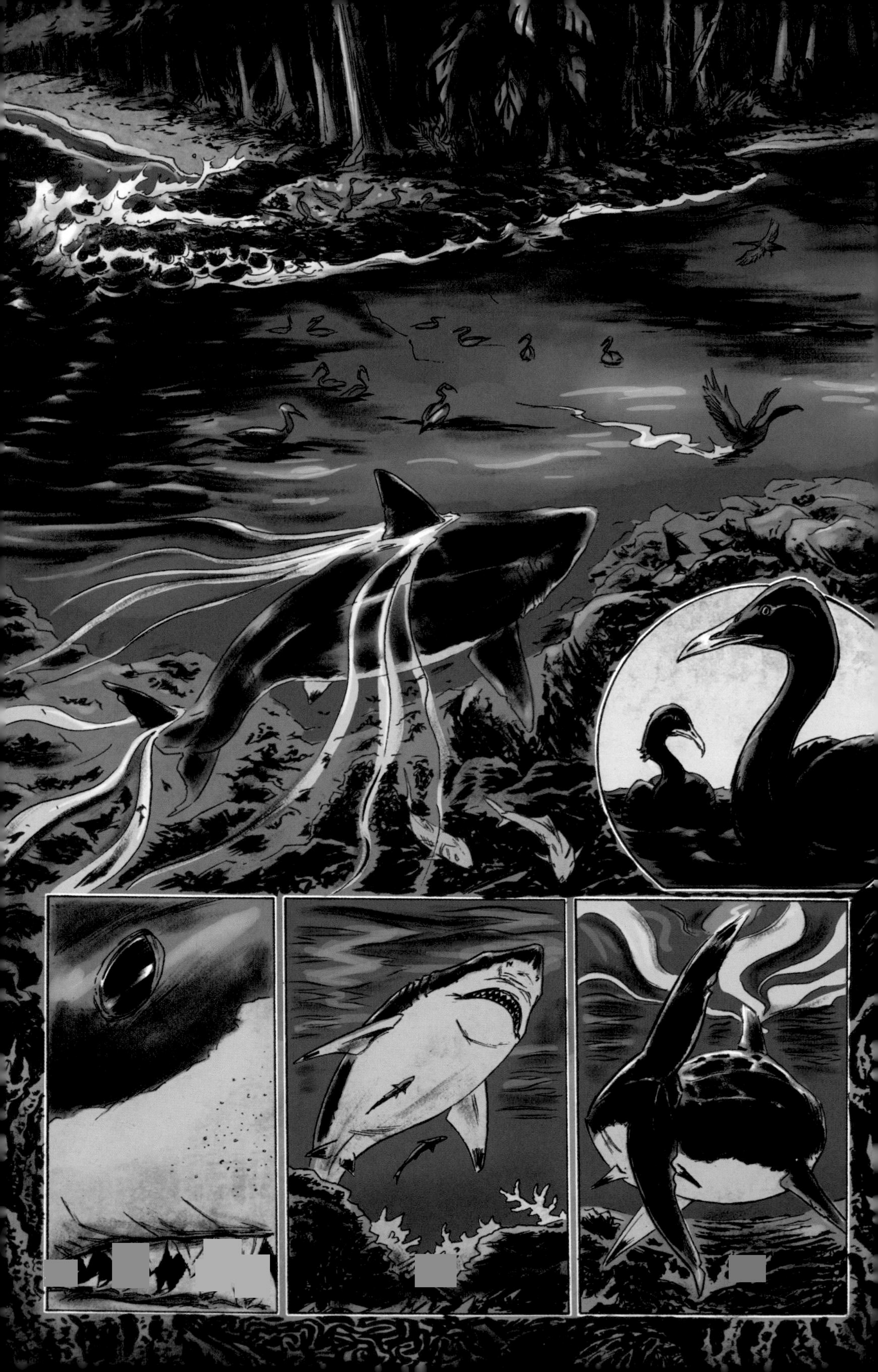

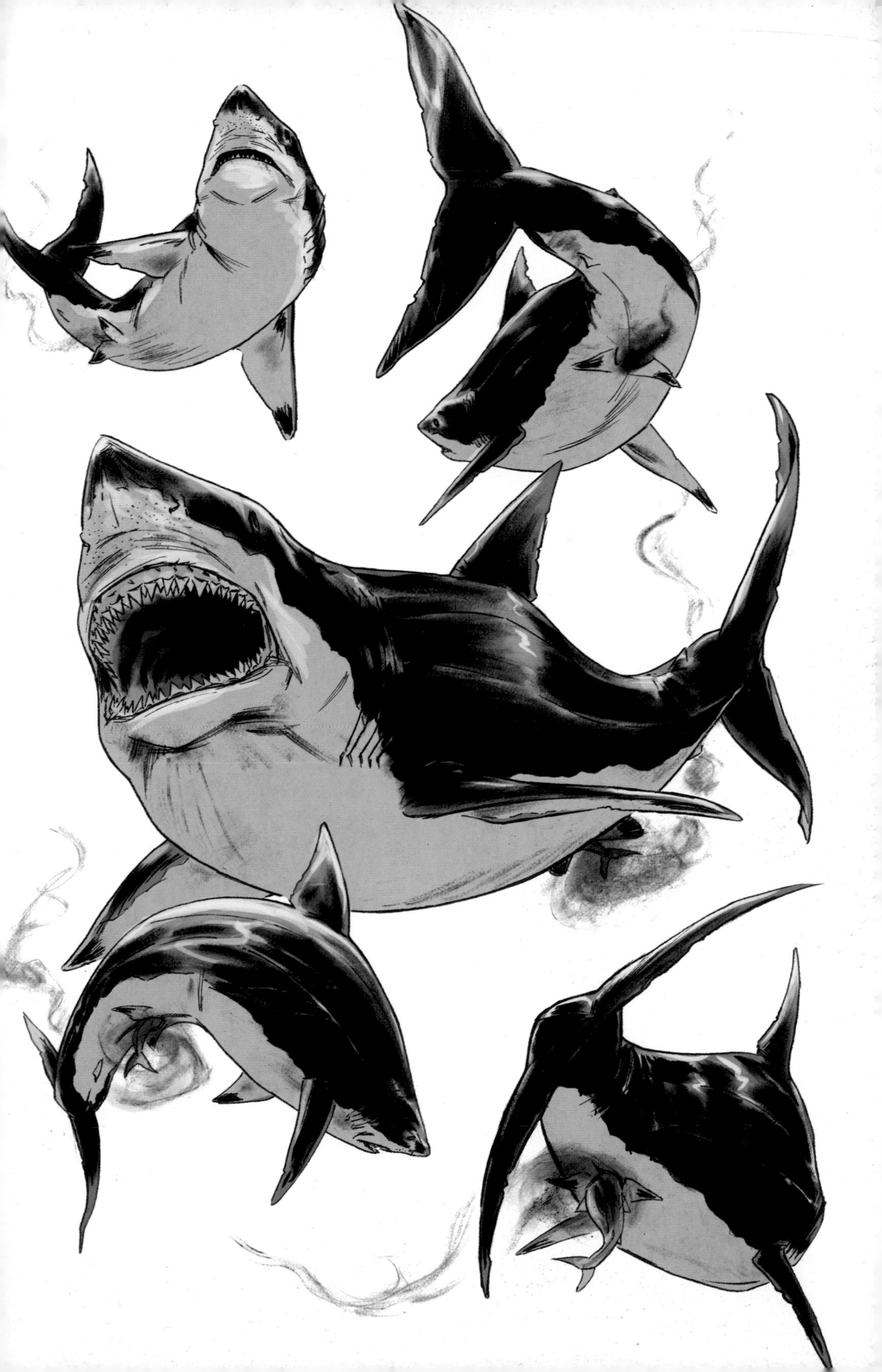

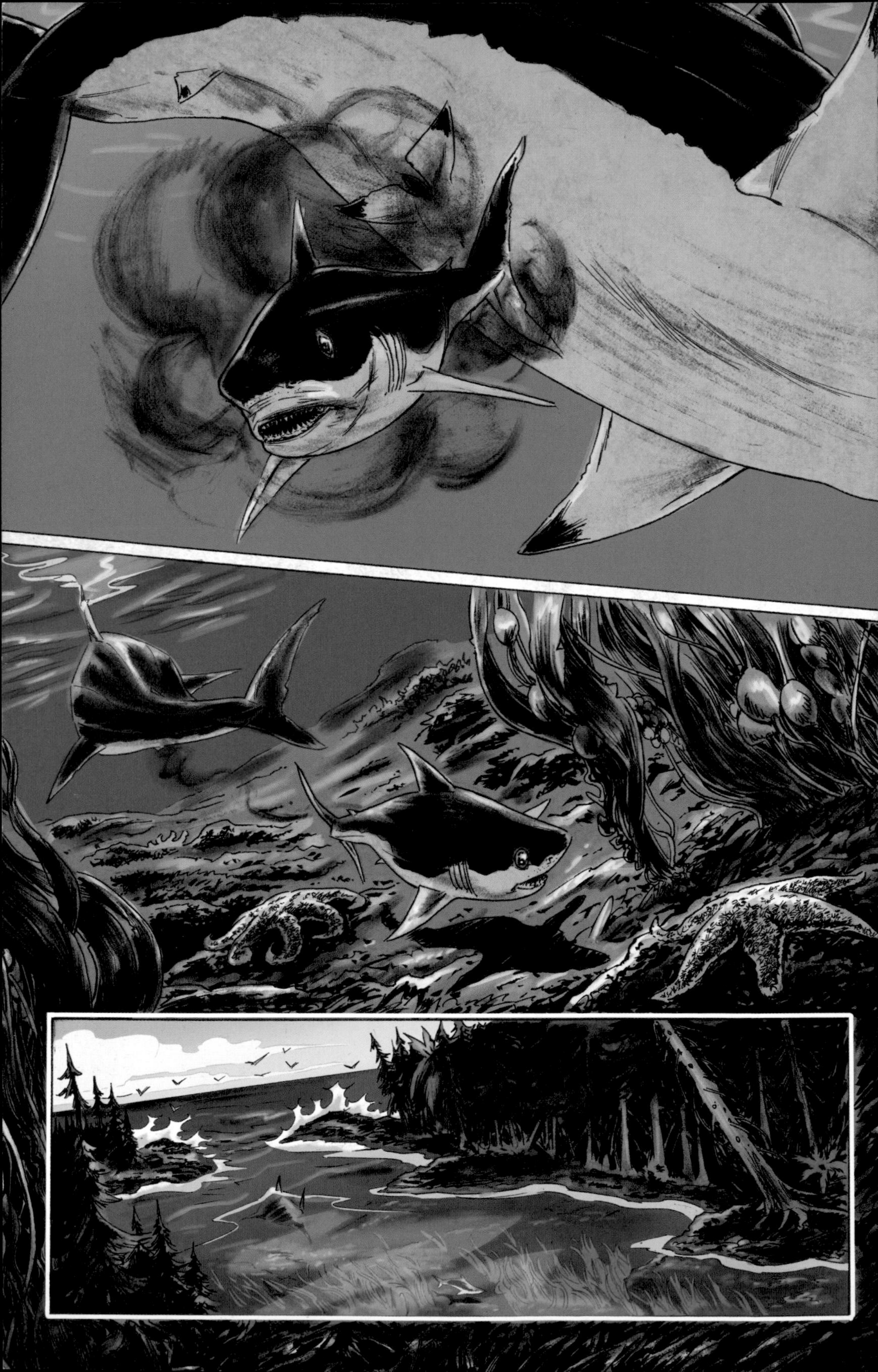

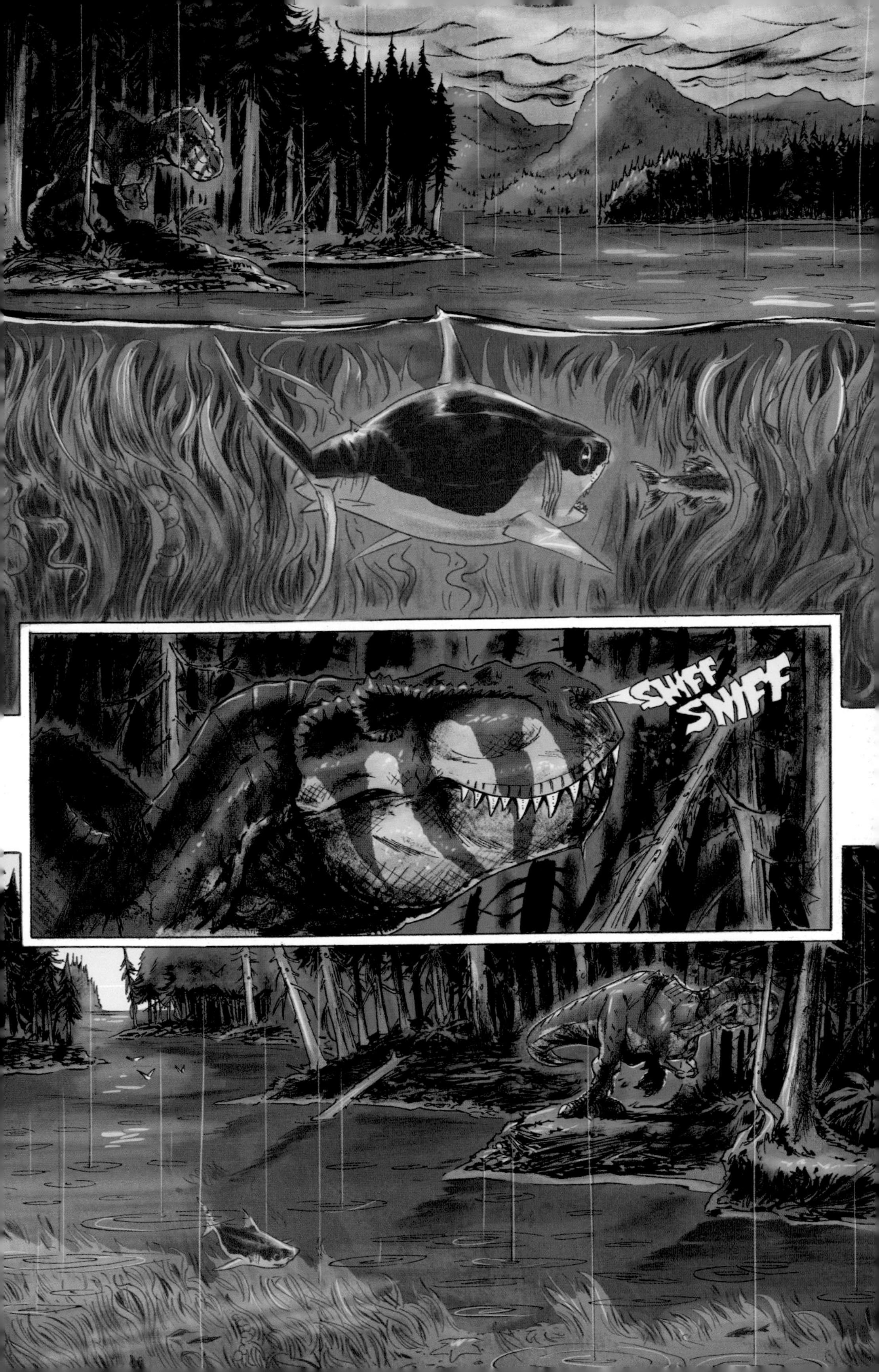
SNIFF SNIFF

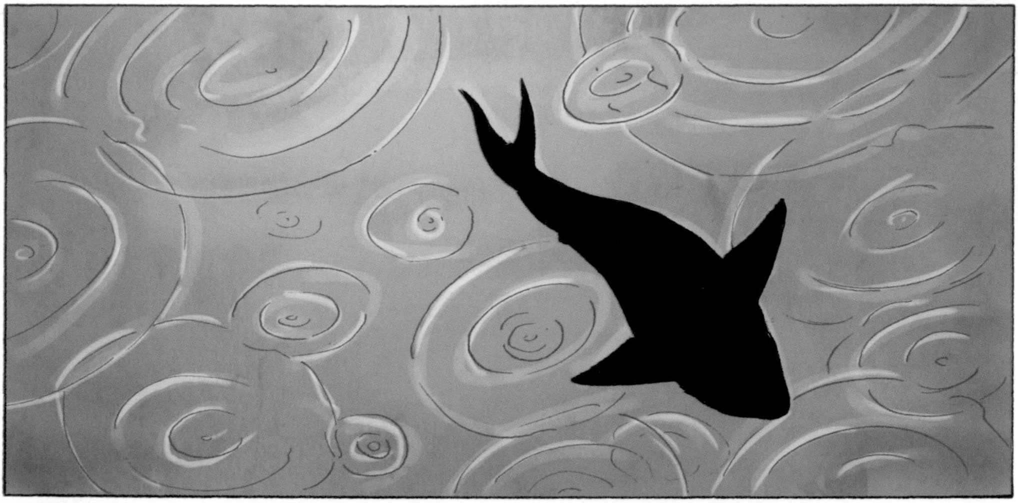

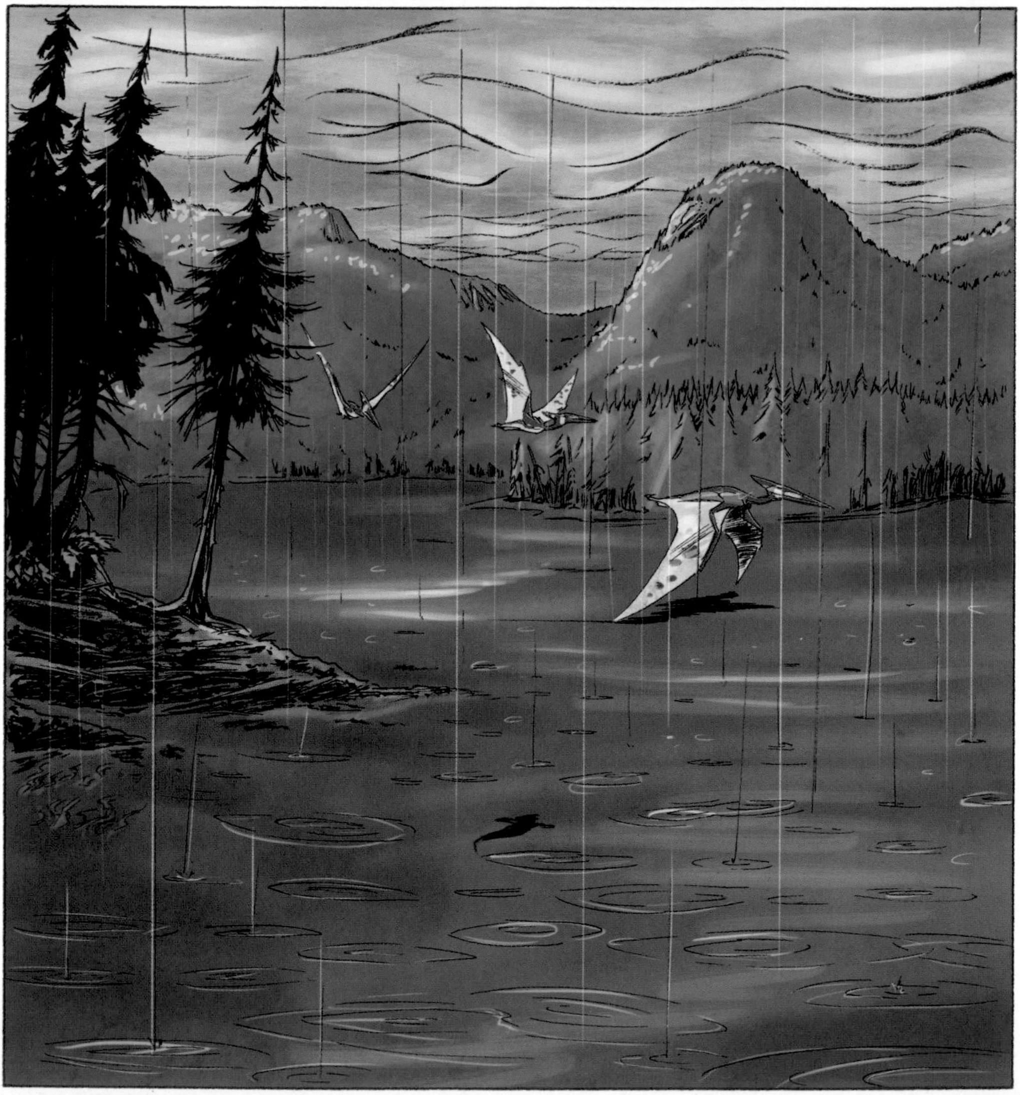

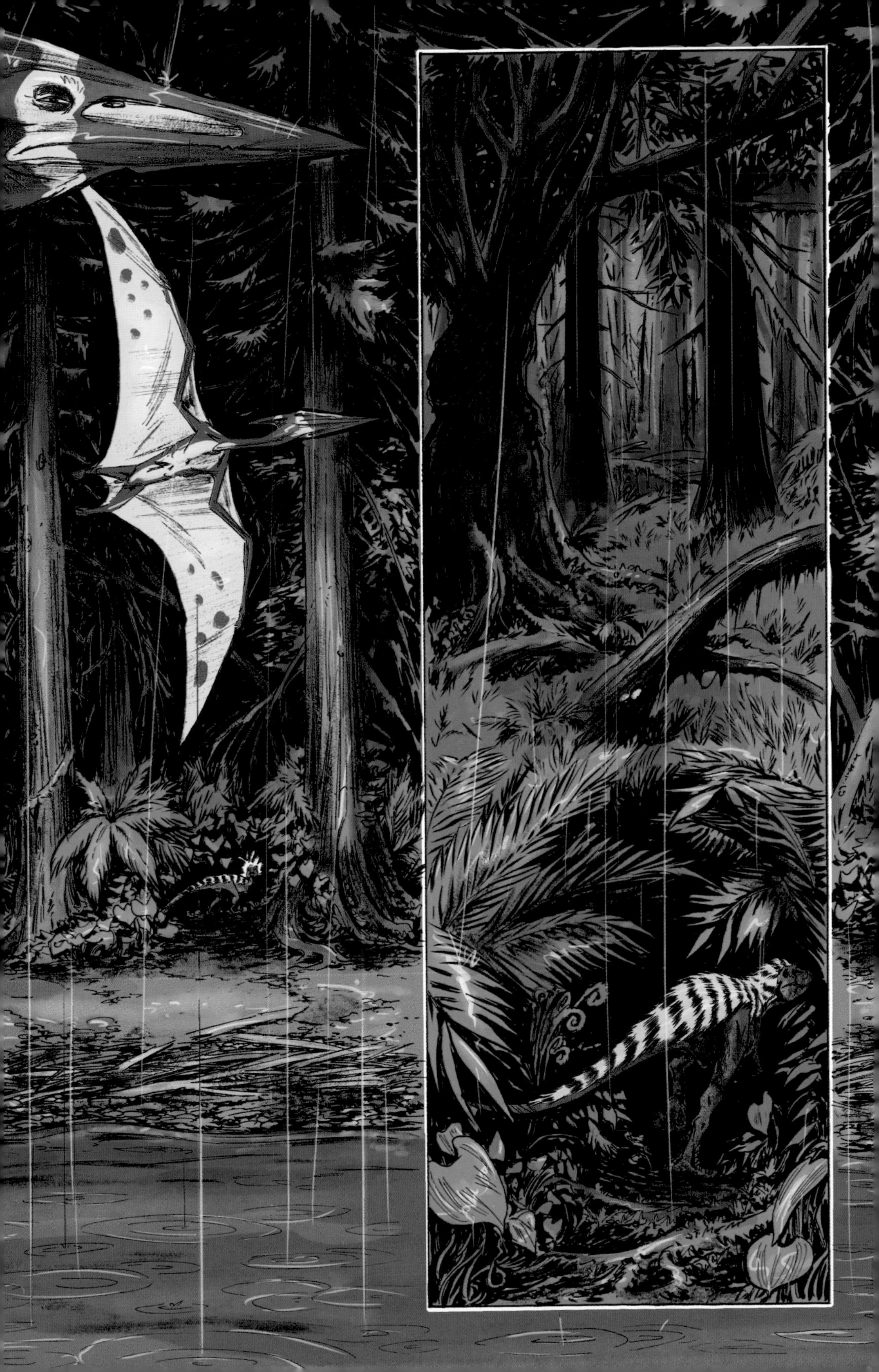

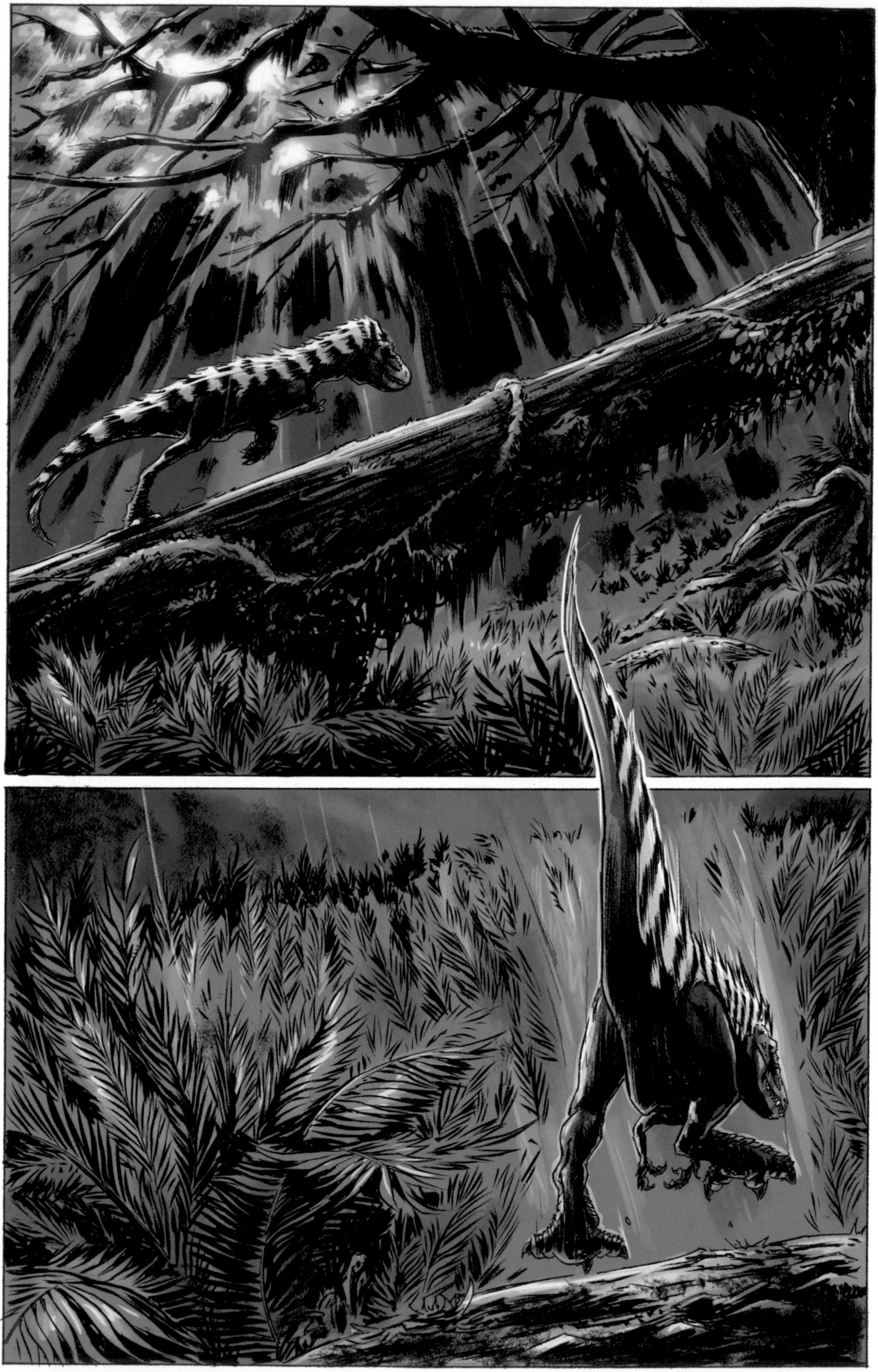

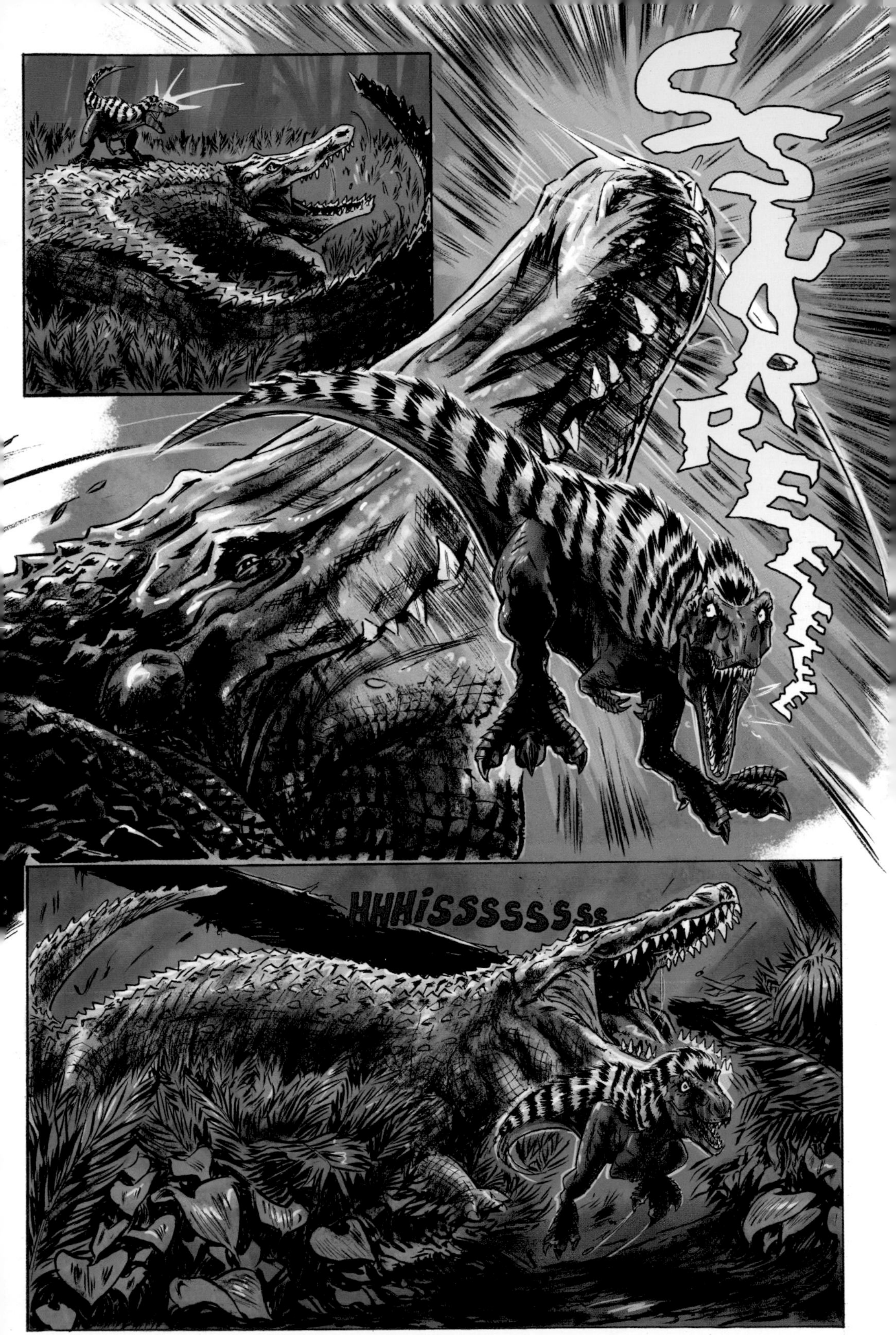
SKRREEEEEEE
HHHiSSSSSSSss

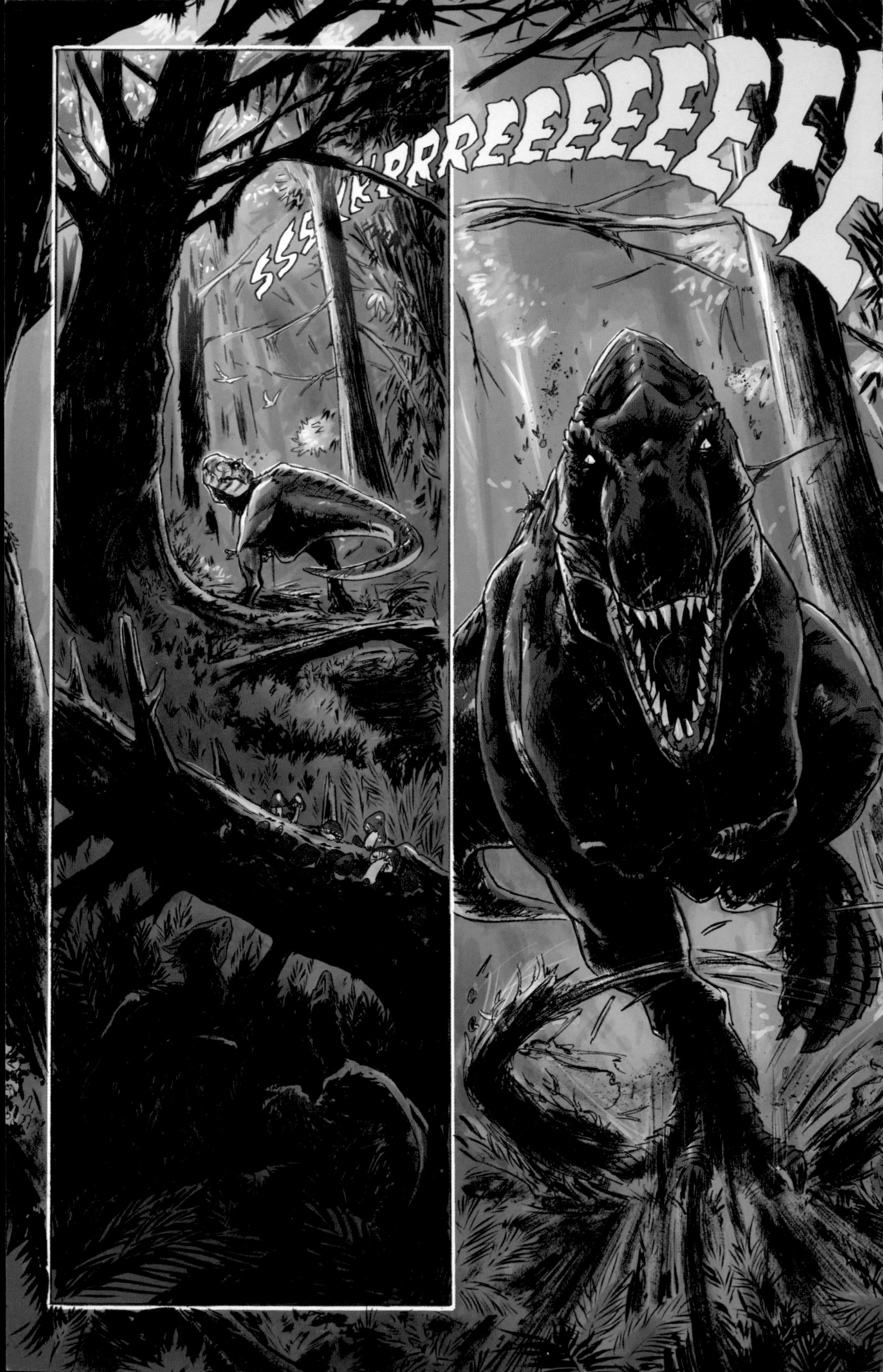
SSSKRRREEEEEEEEE

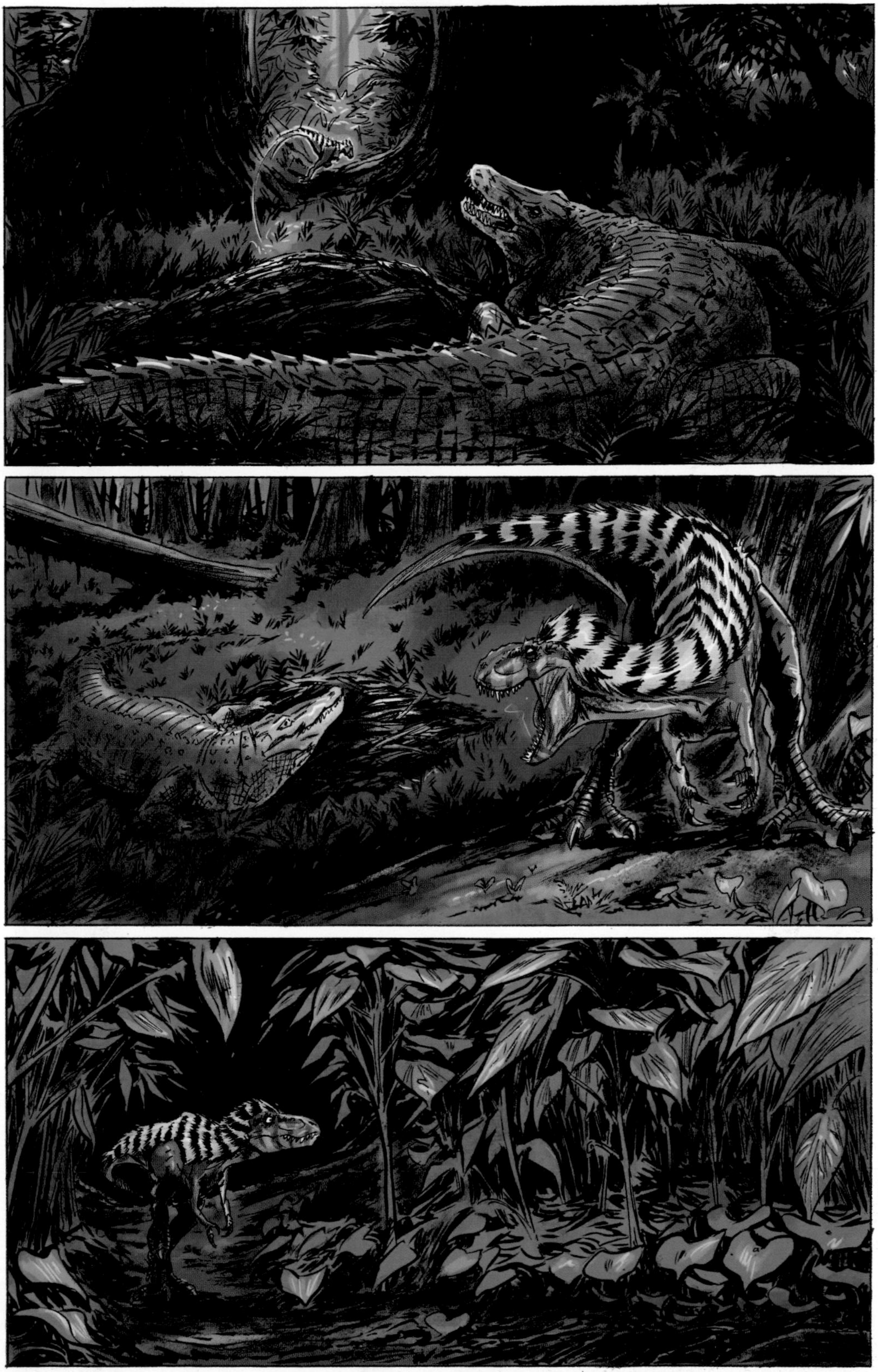

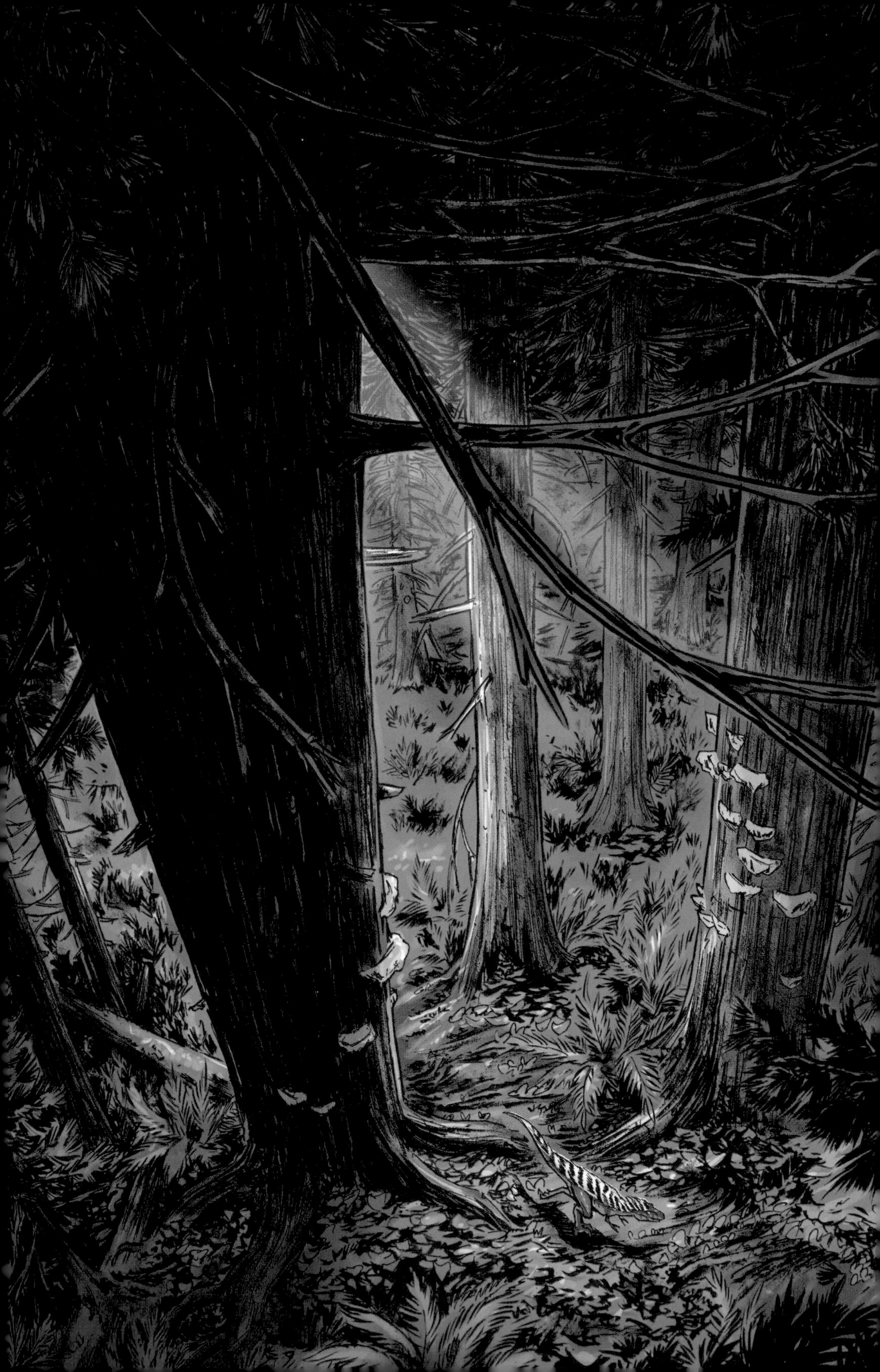

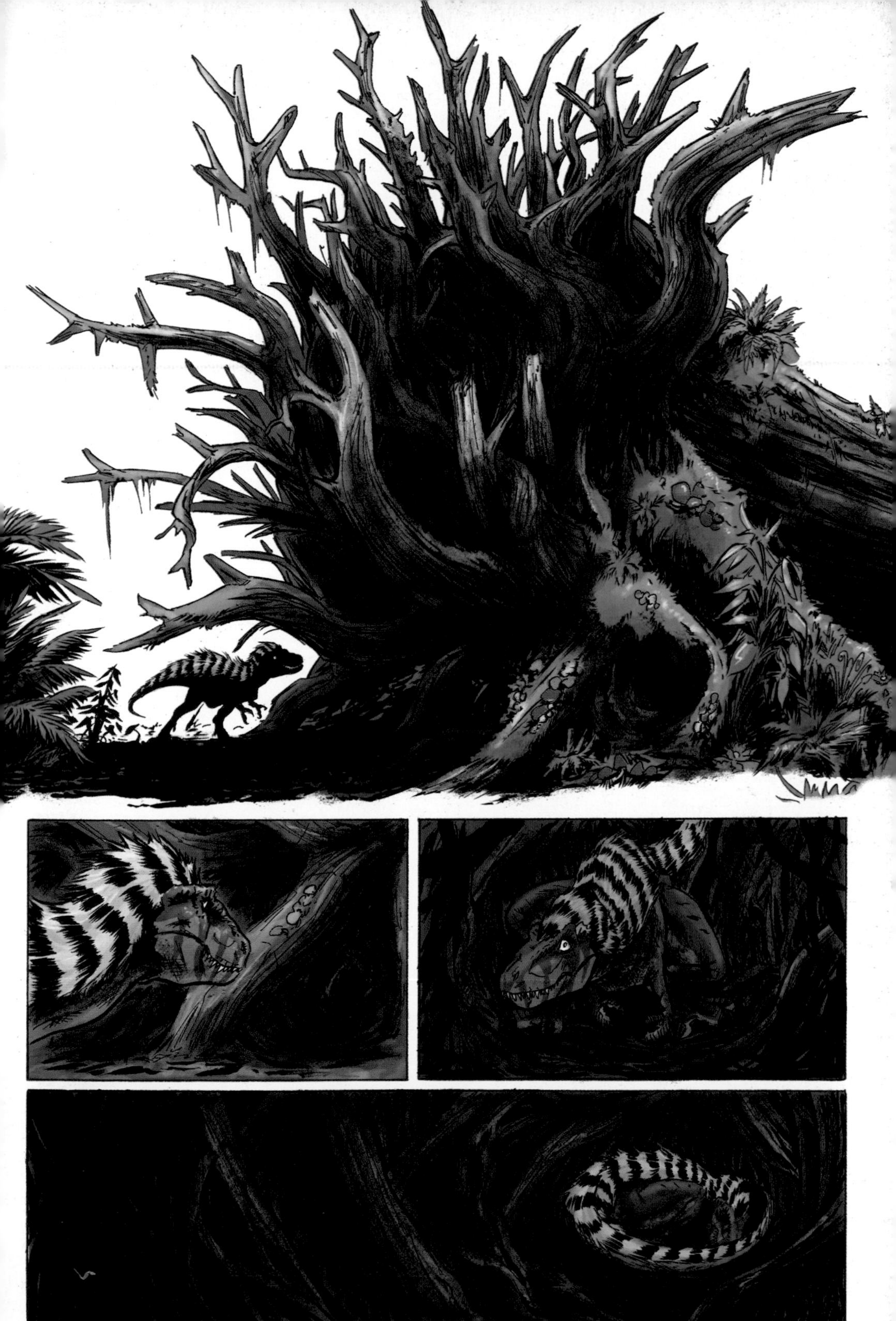

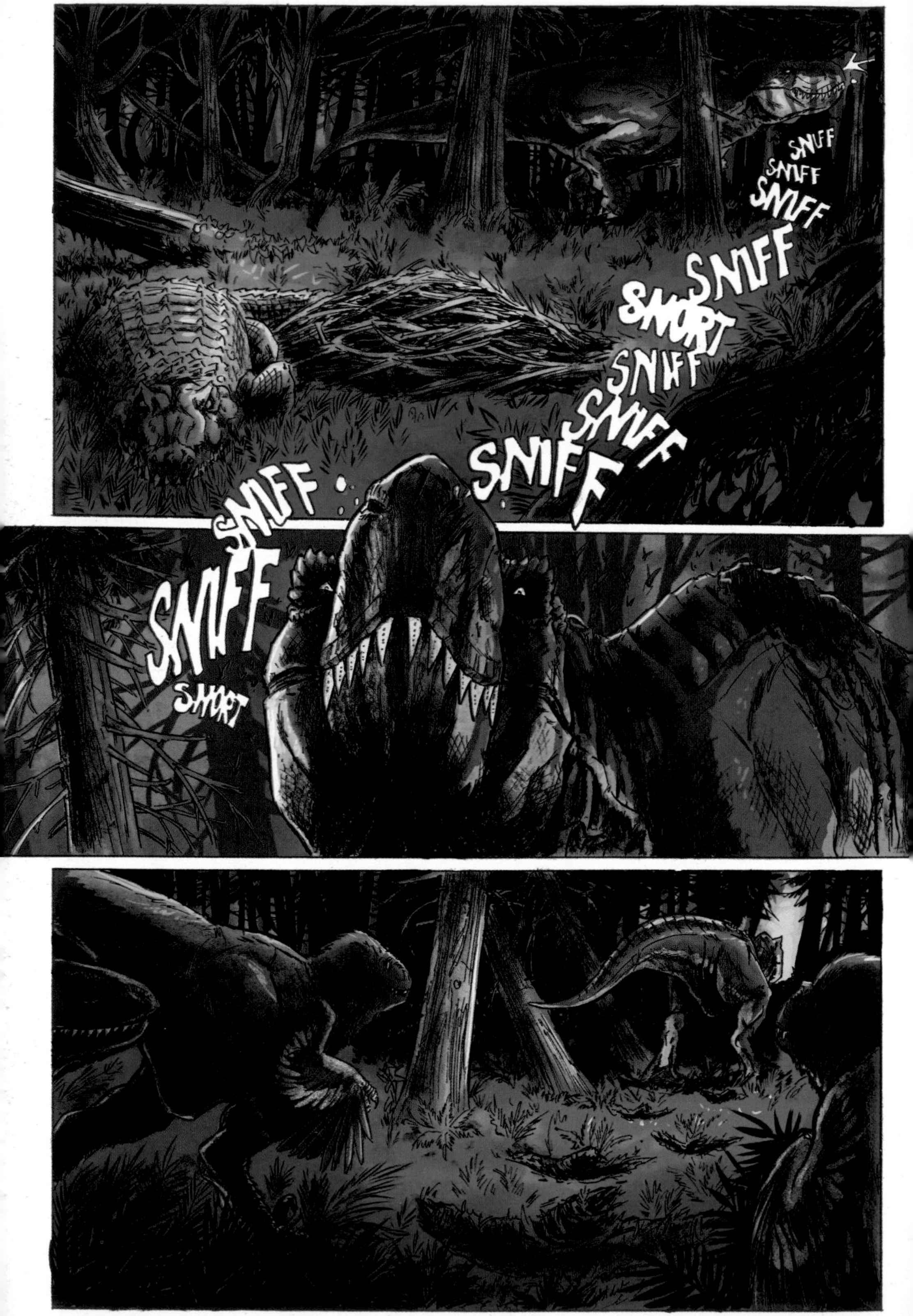
SNIFF
SNIFF
SNIFF
SNIFF
SNORT
SNIFF
SNIFF
SNIFF
SNIFF
SNIFF
SNORT

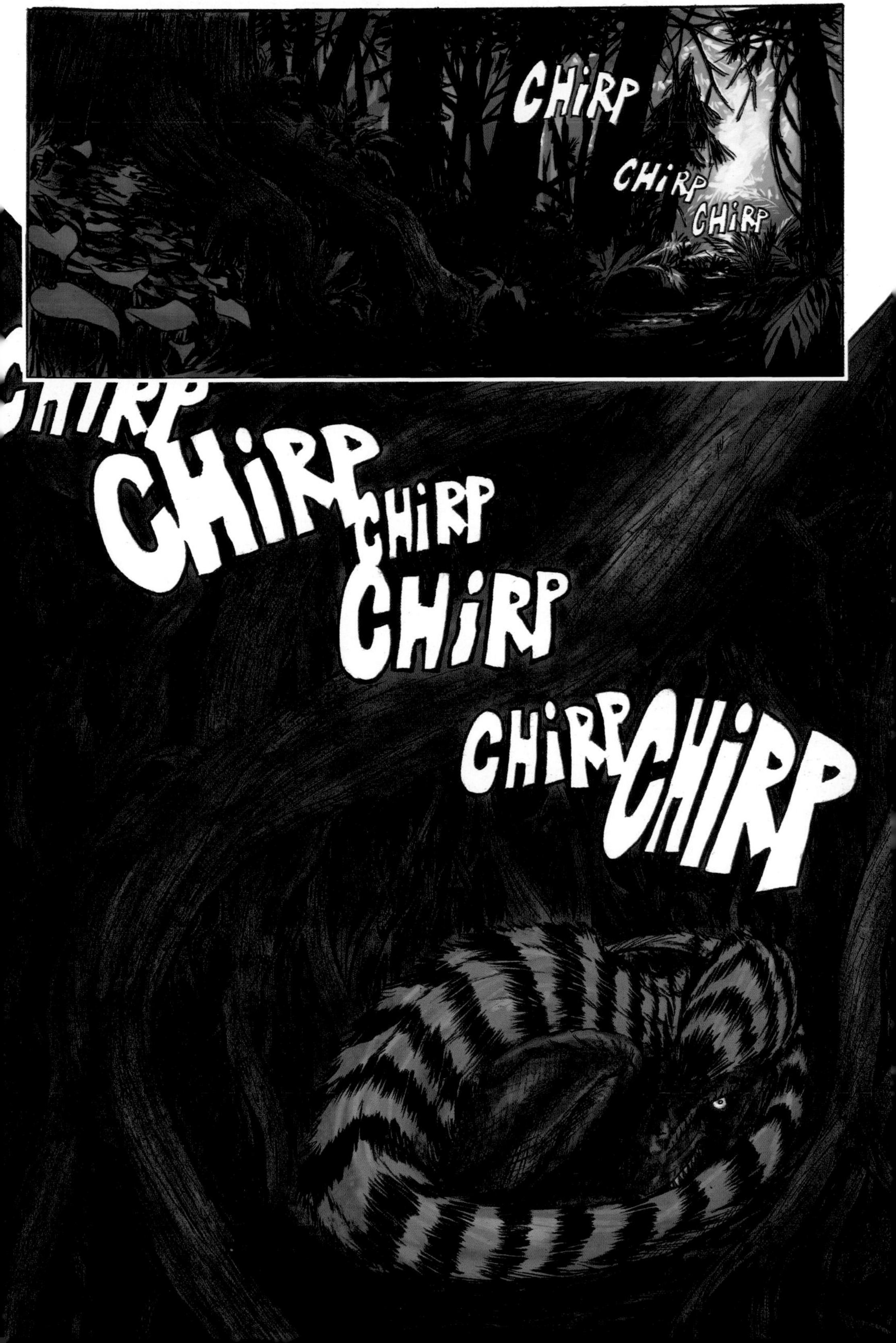
CHIRP
CHIRP
CHIRP
CHIRP
CHIRP
CHIRP
CHIRP
CHIRP

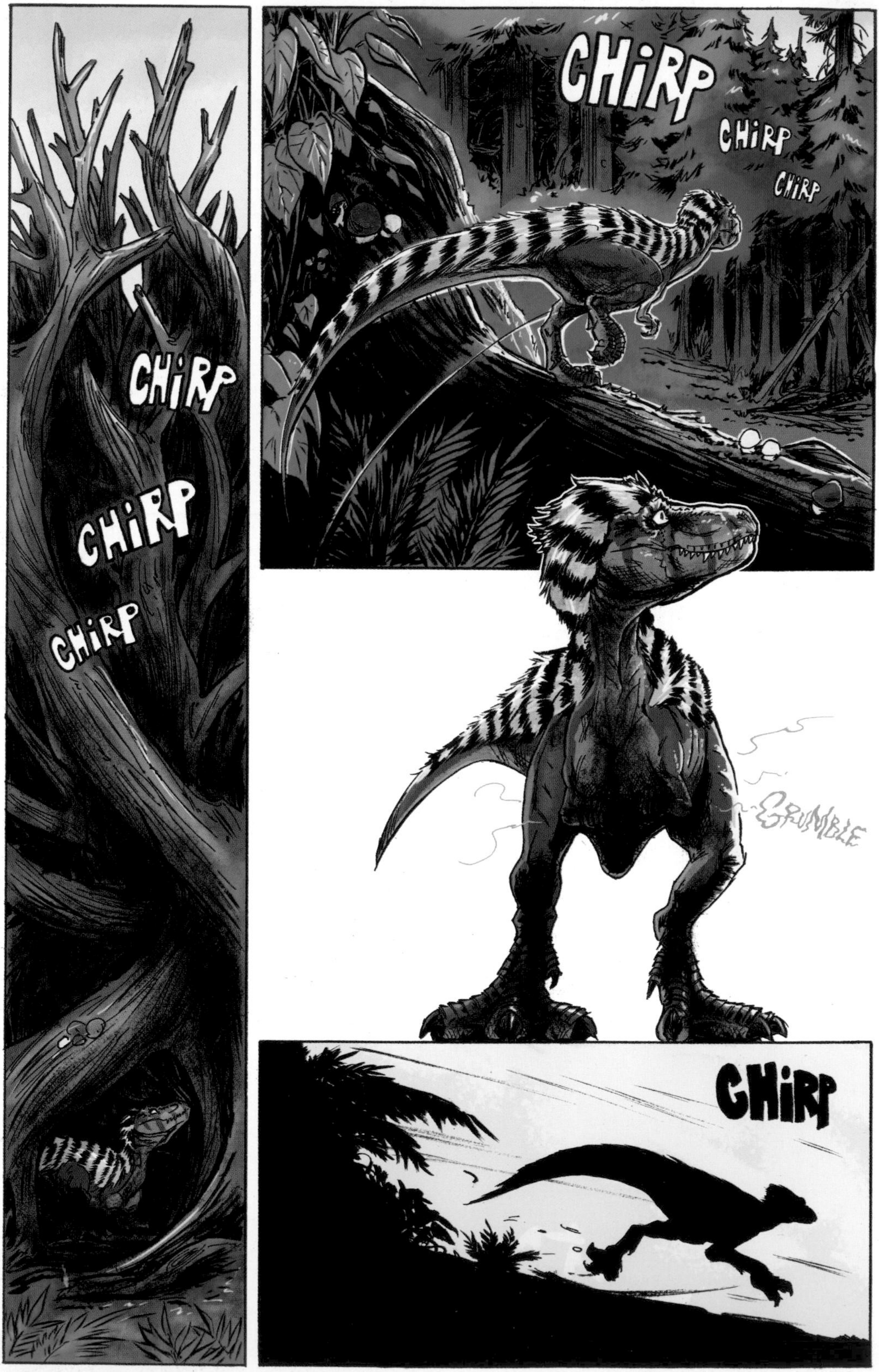
CHIRP
CHIRP
CHIRP
CHIRP
CHIRP
CHIRP
GRUMBLE
CHIRP

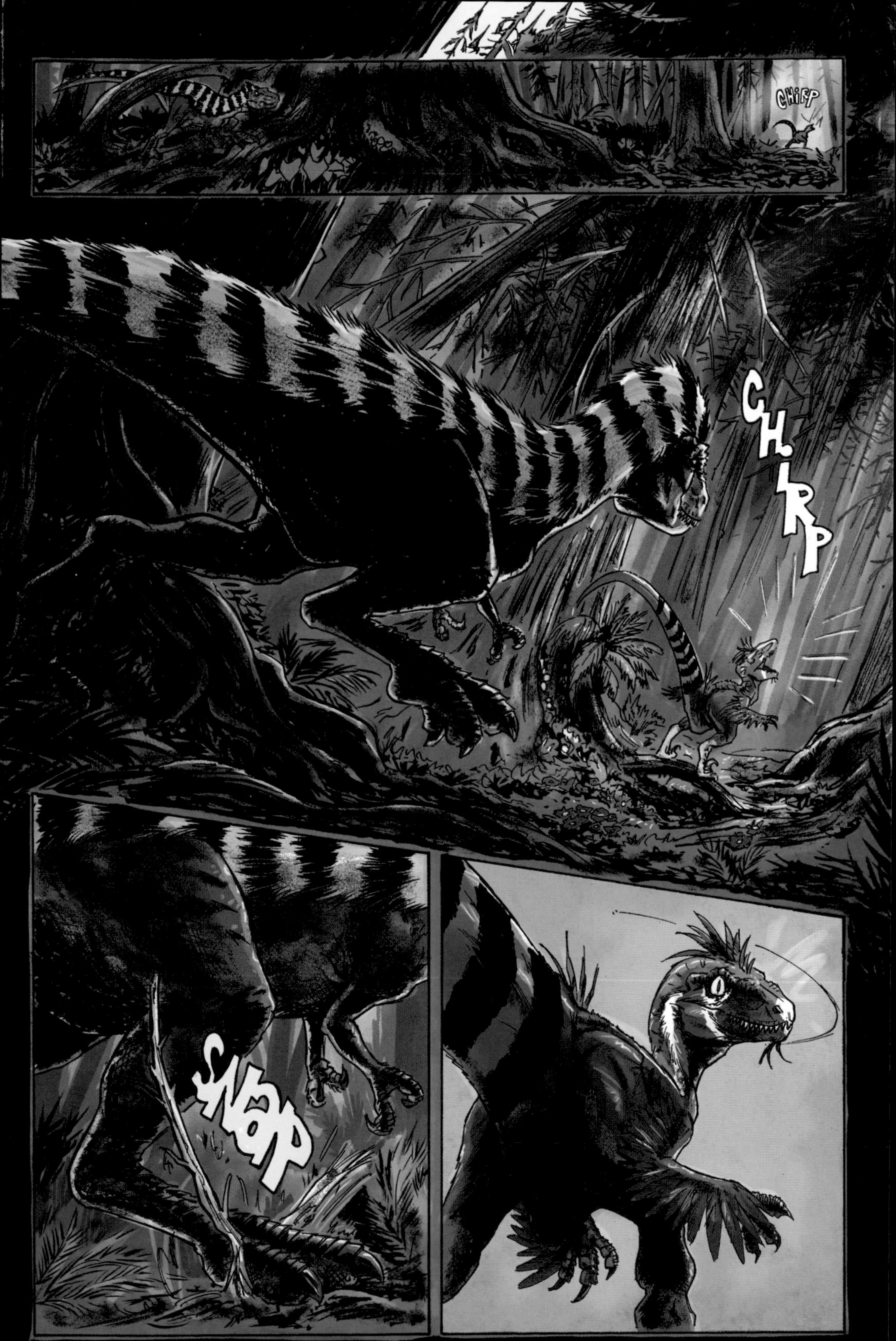
CHIRP
CHIRP
SNAP

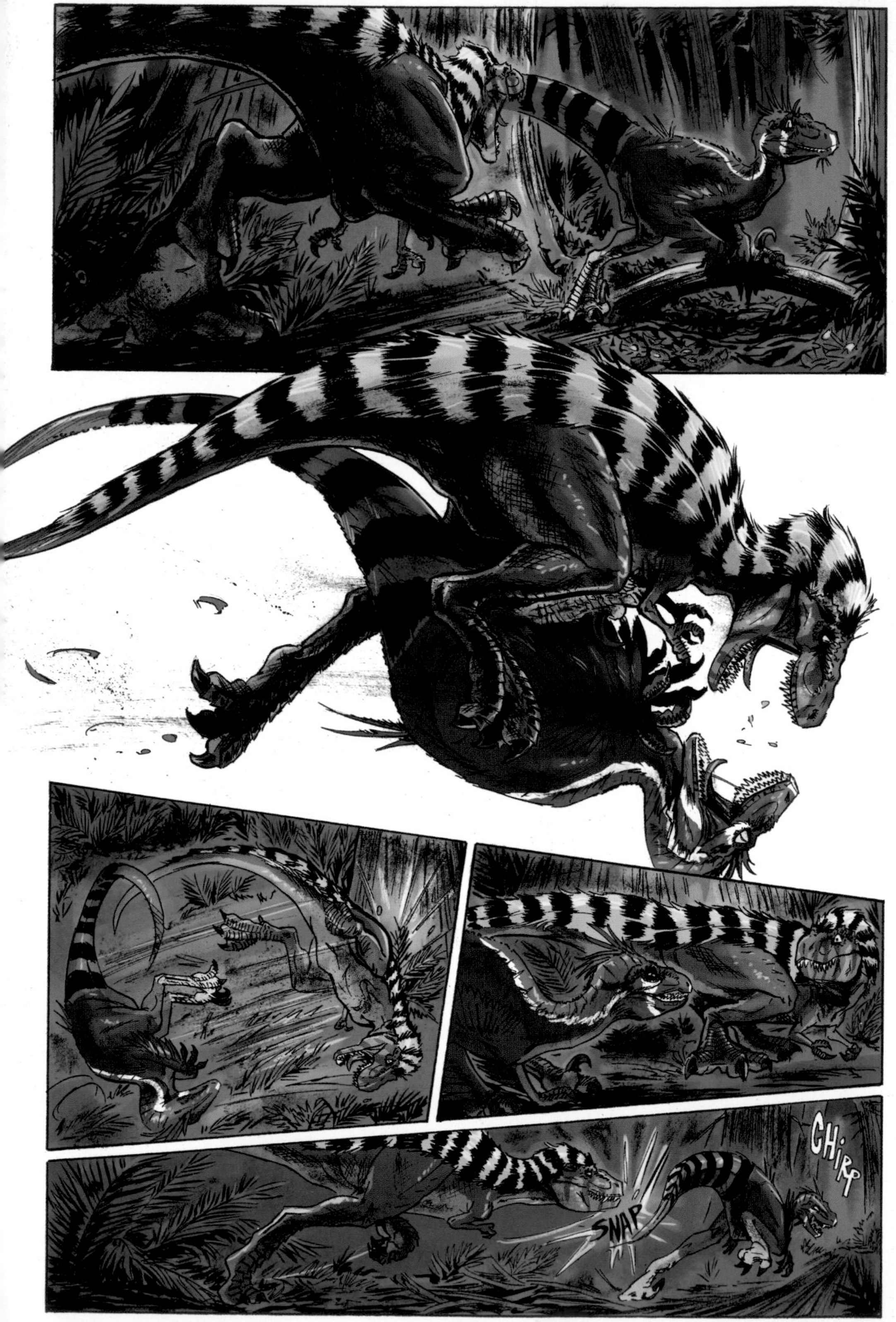
SNAP
CHIRP

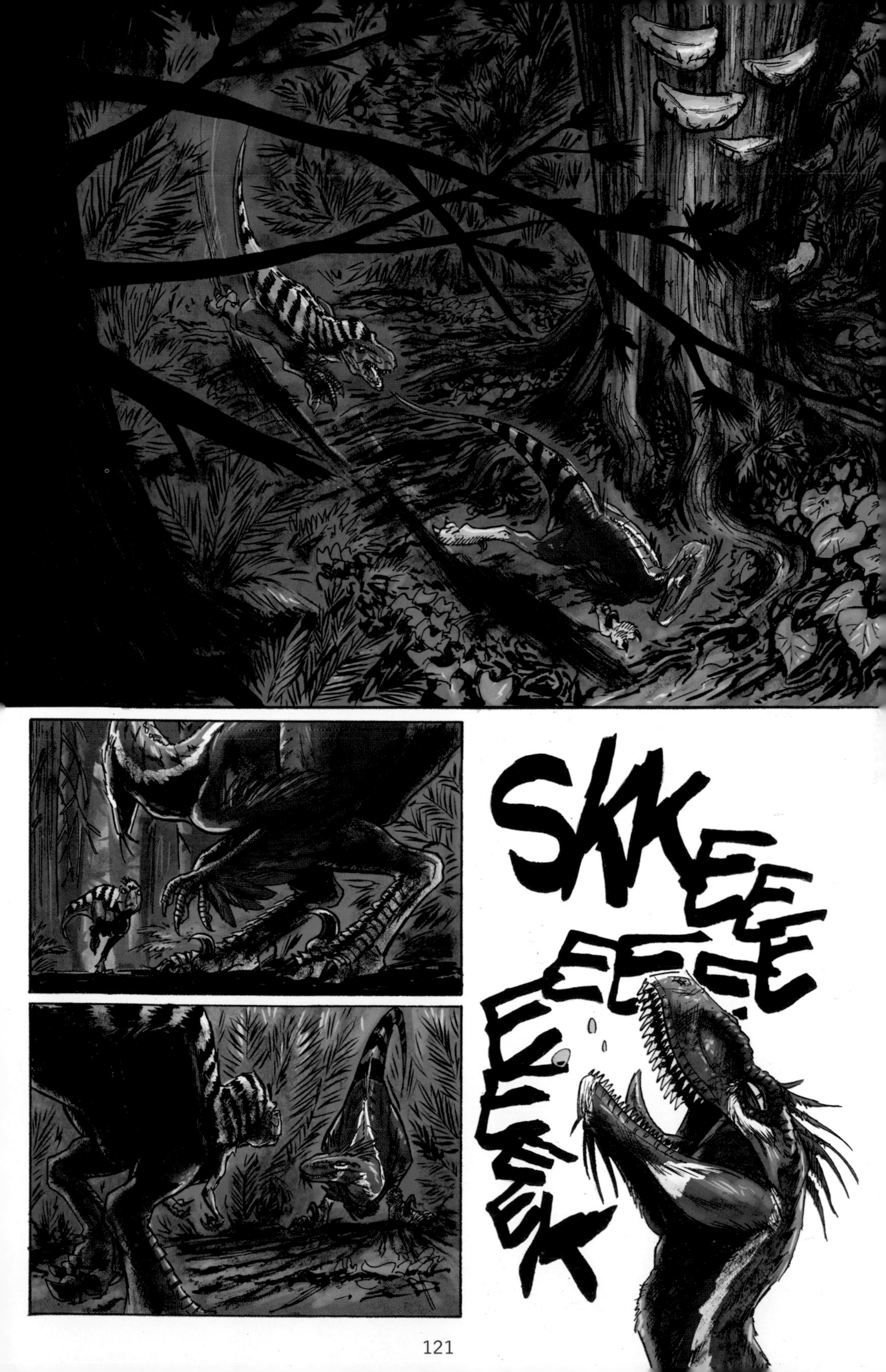
SKKEEEEEEEEEEEEEK

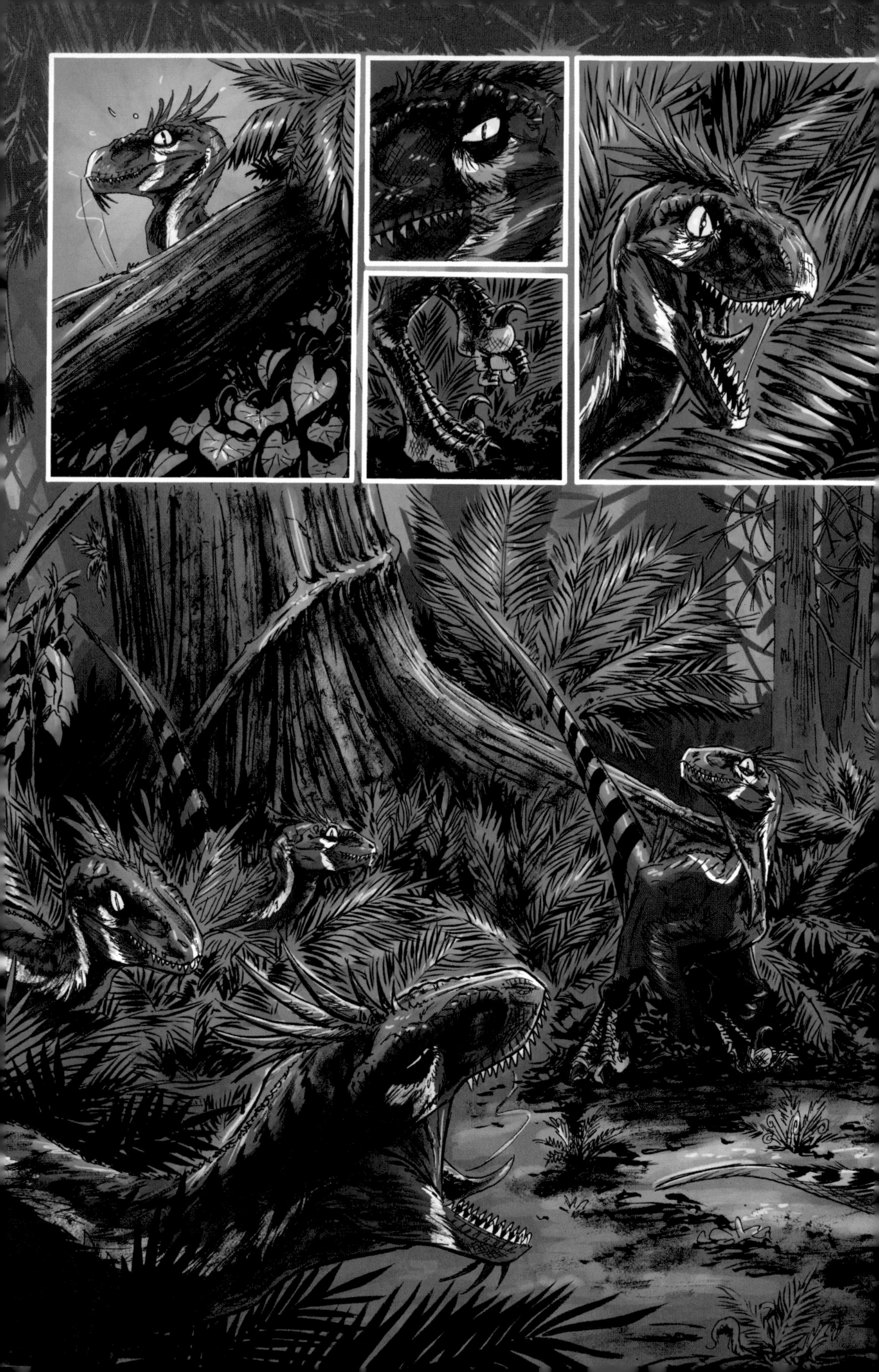

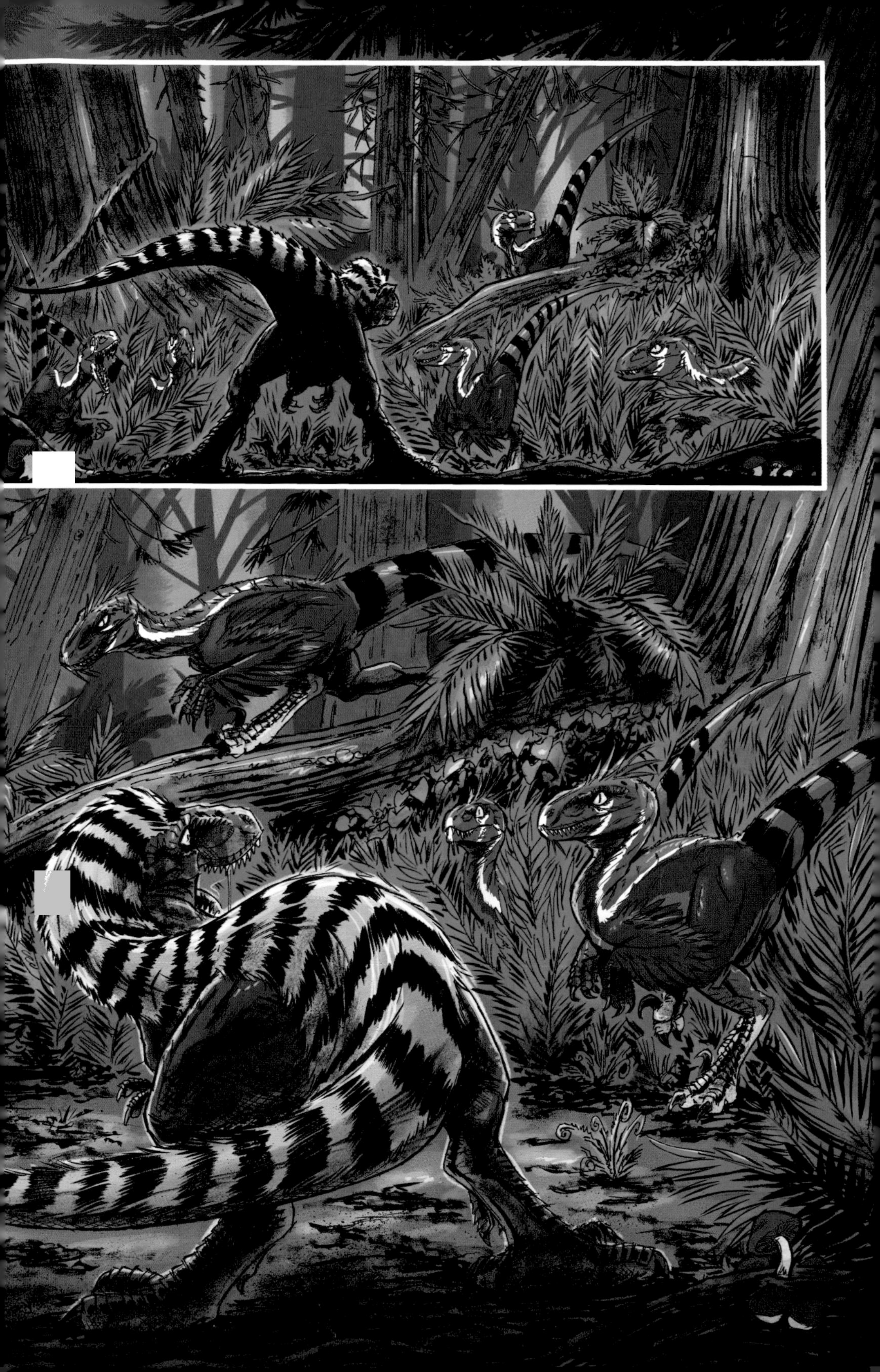

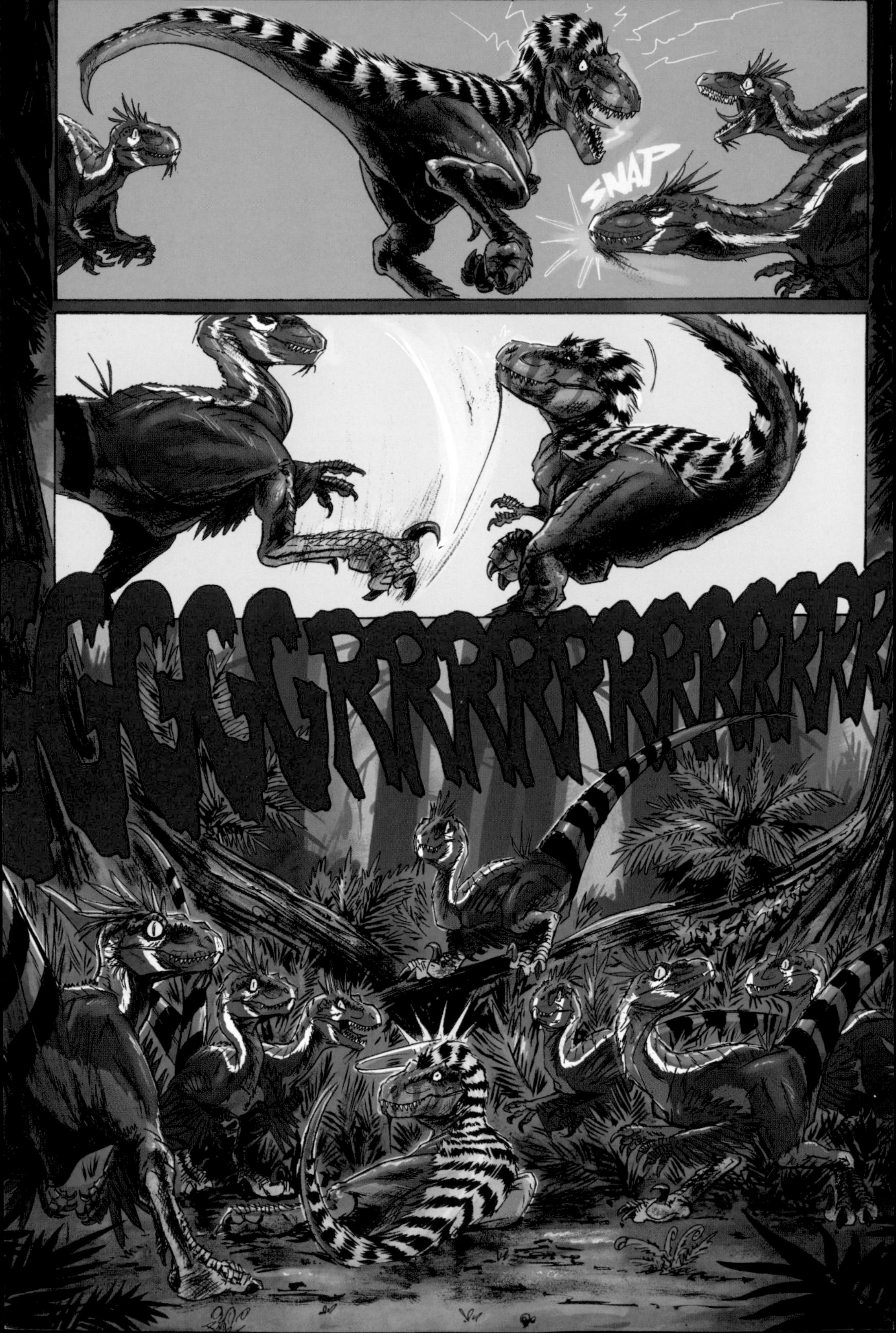
SNAP
GRRRRRRRRRRRRRRR

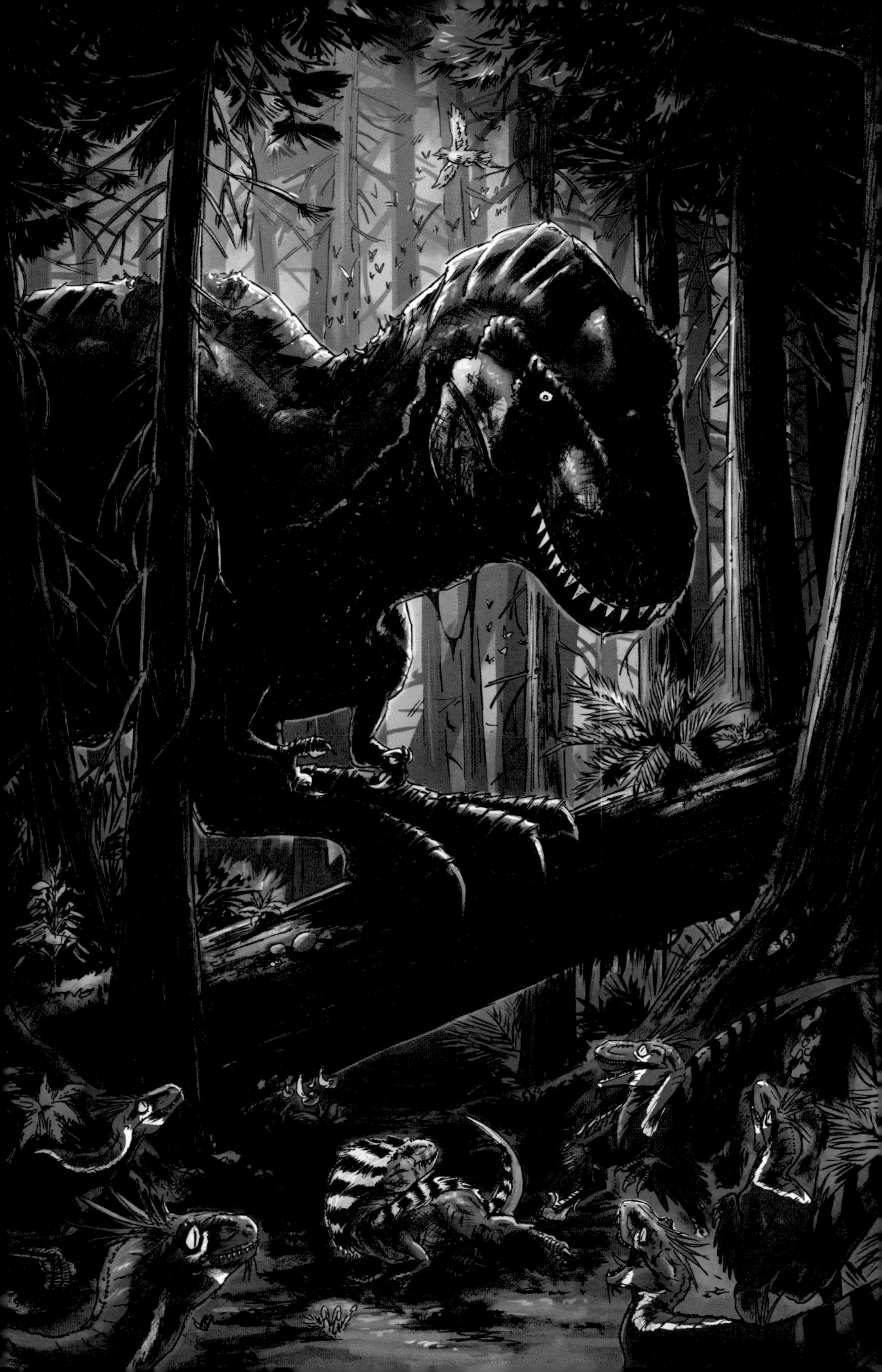

SSSSSSSSS

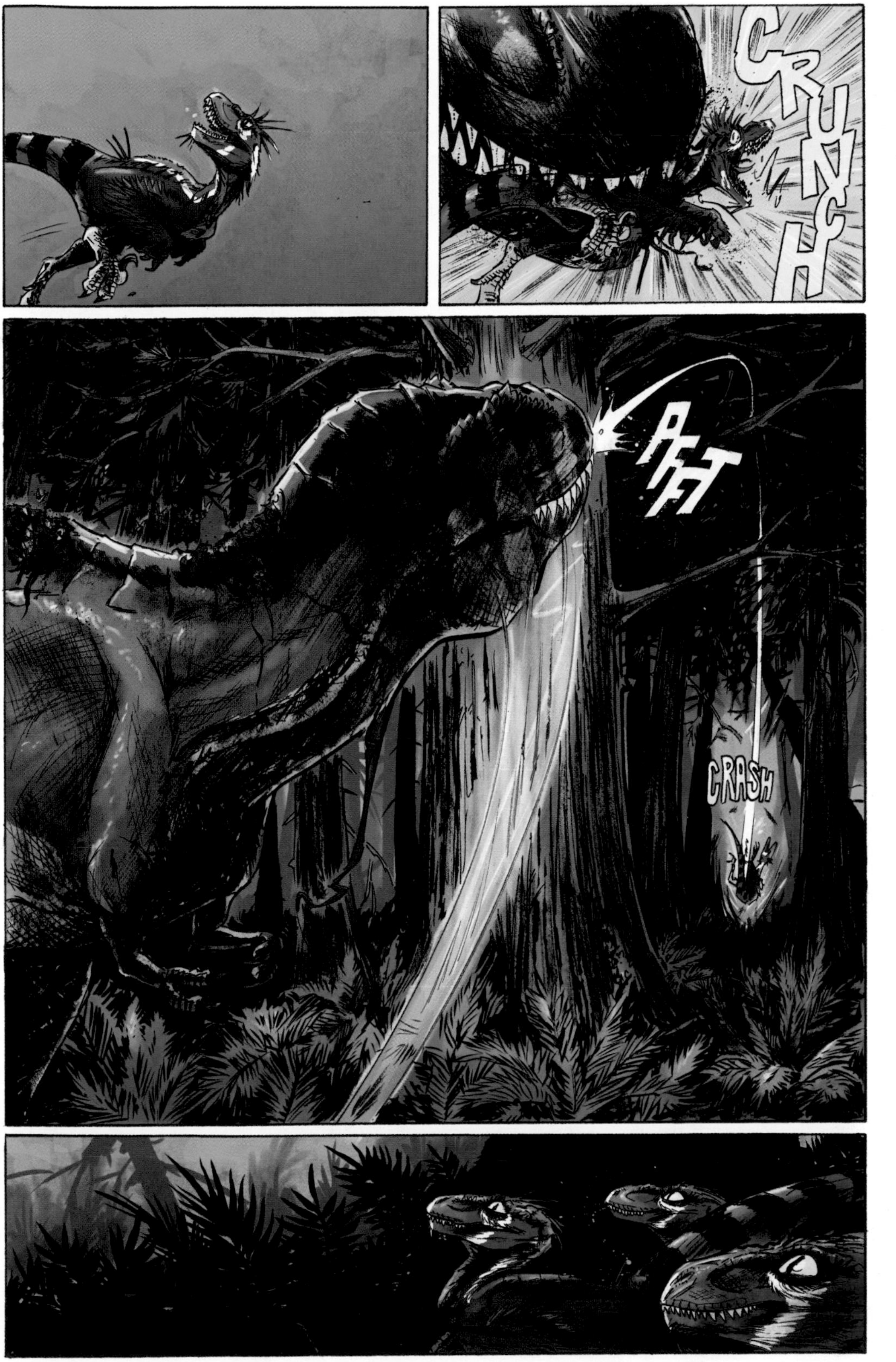
CRUNCH
CRASH

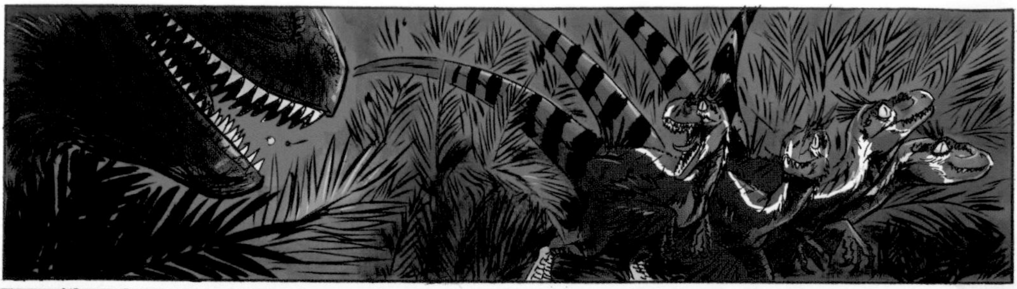
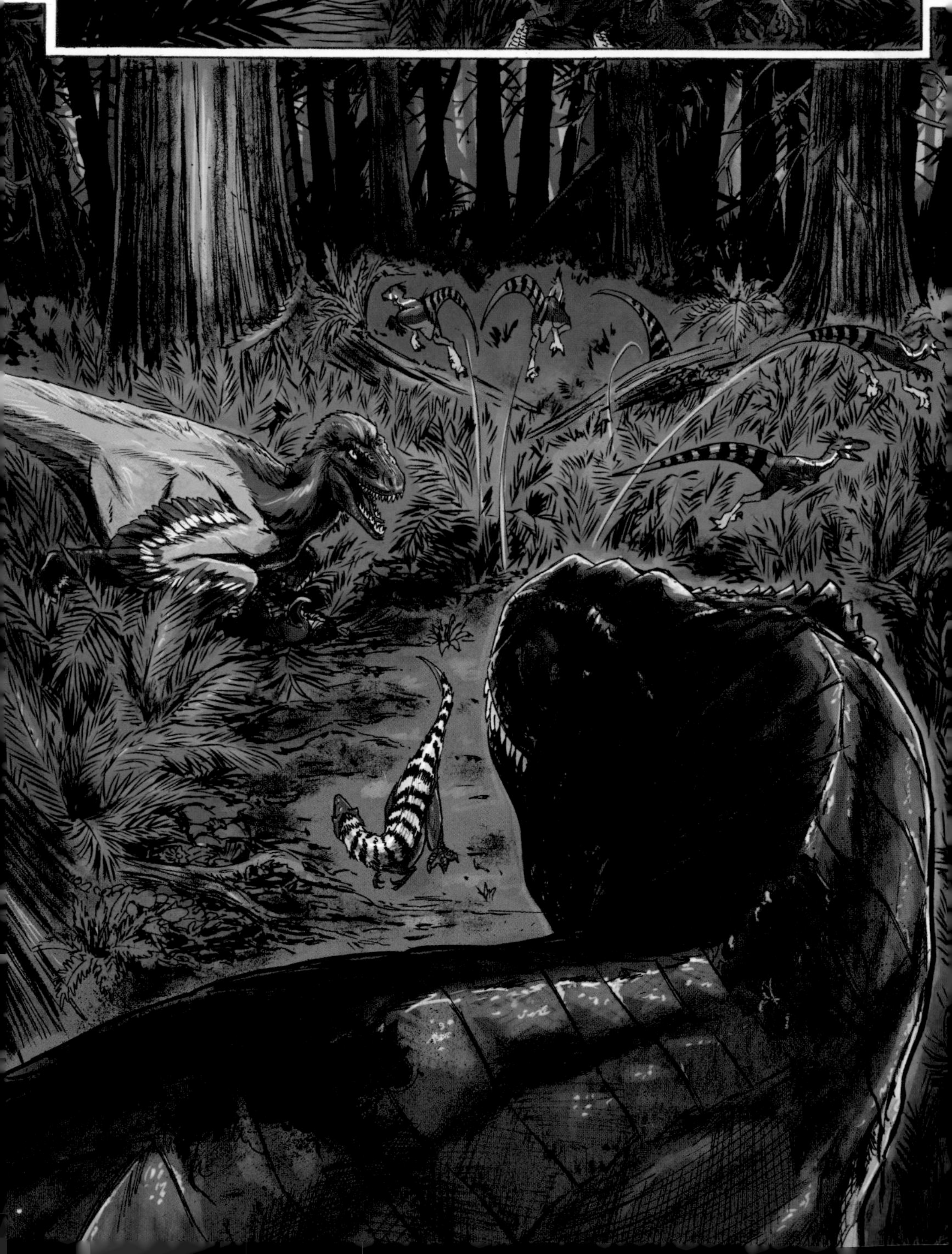

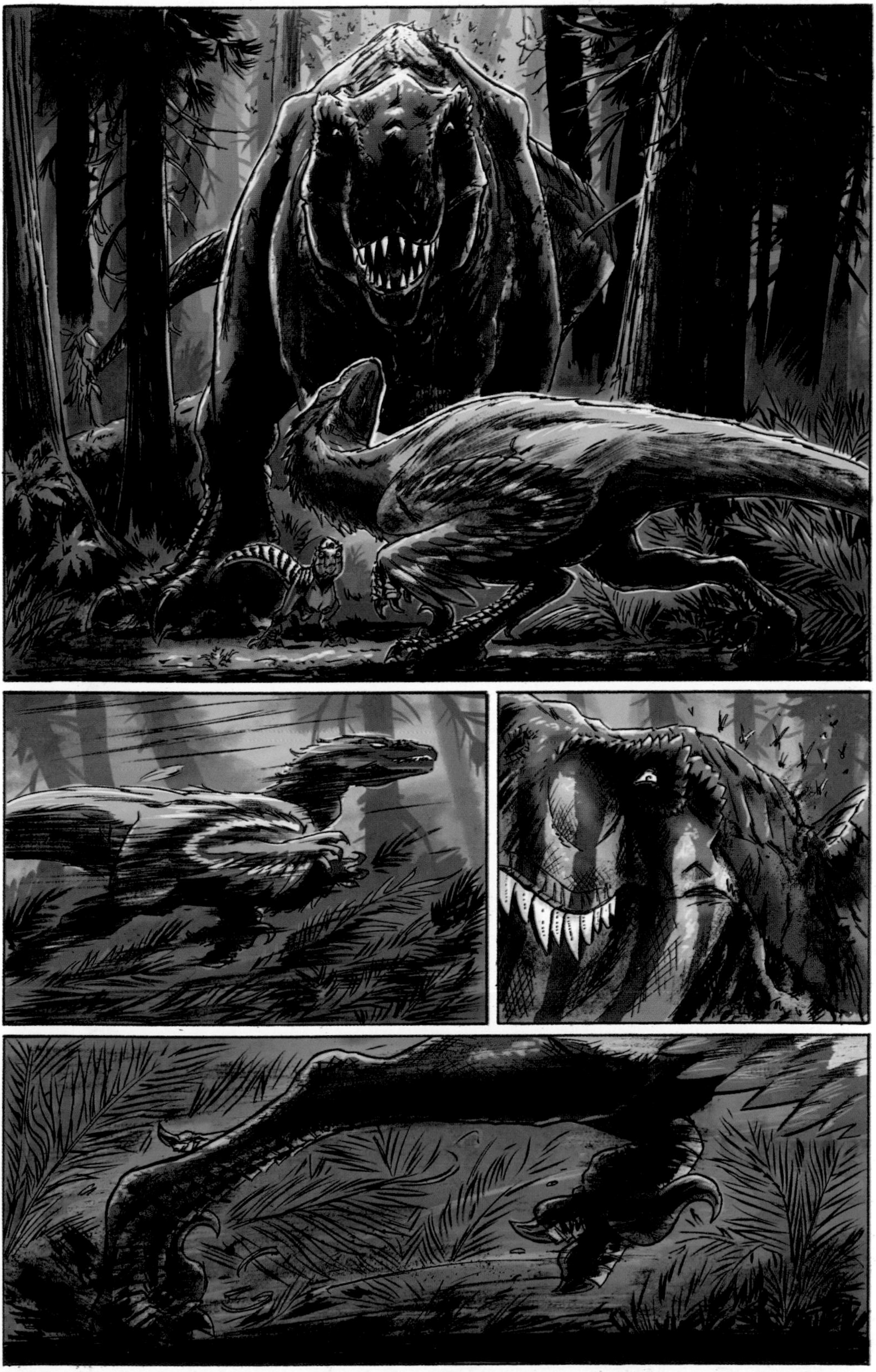

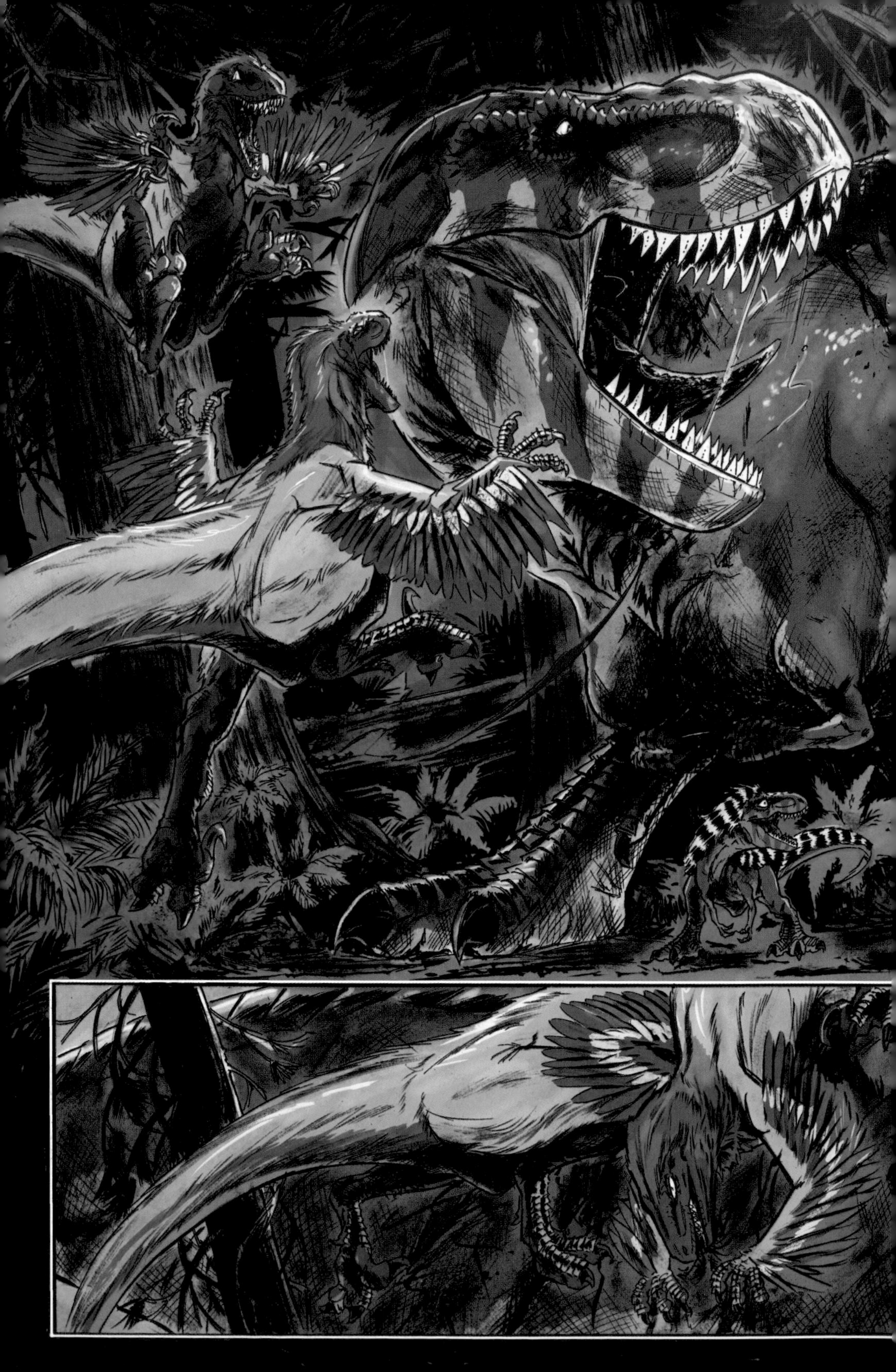

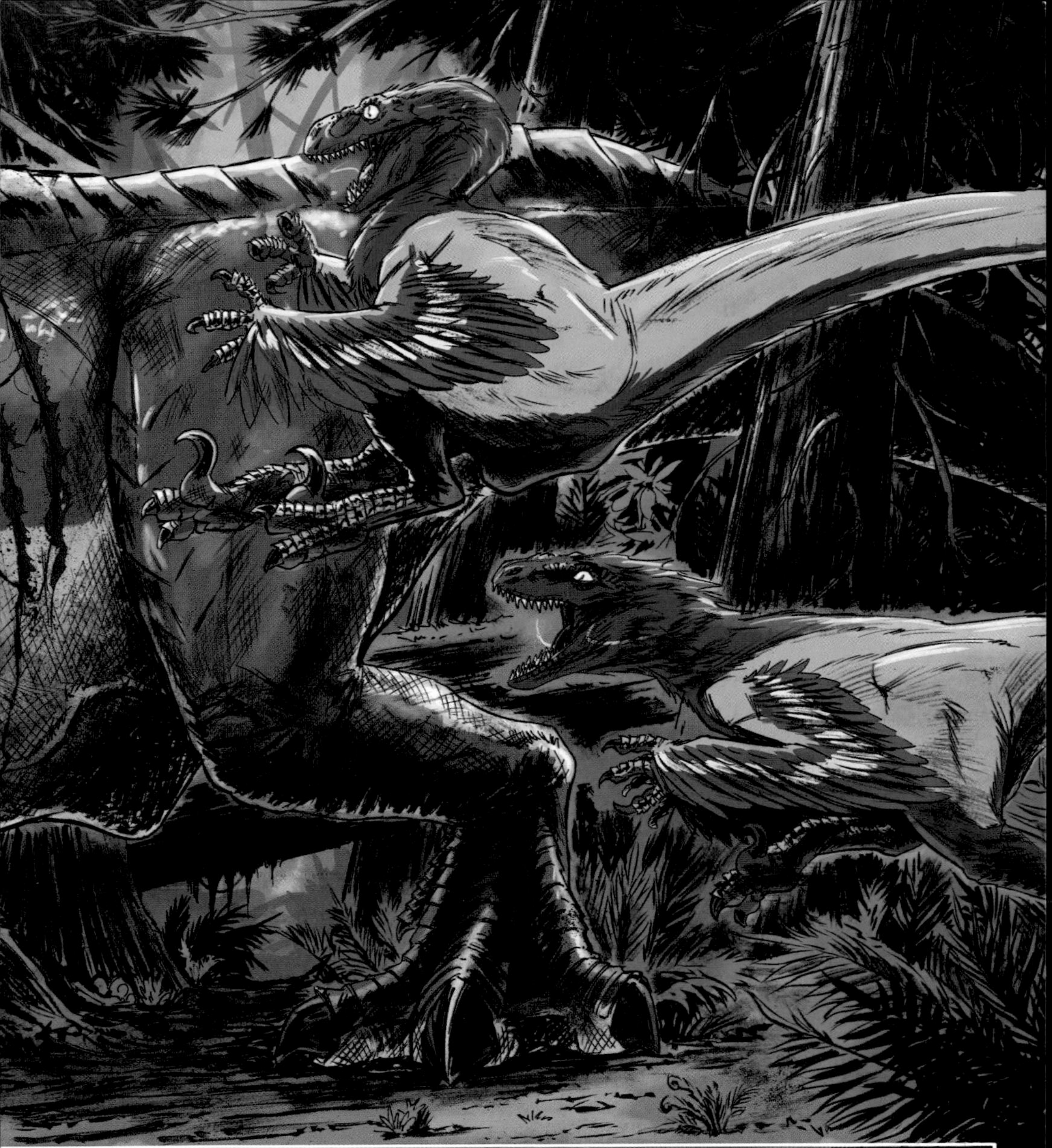
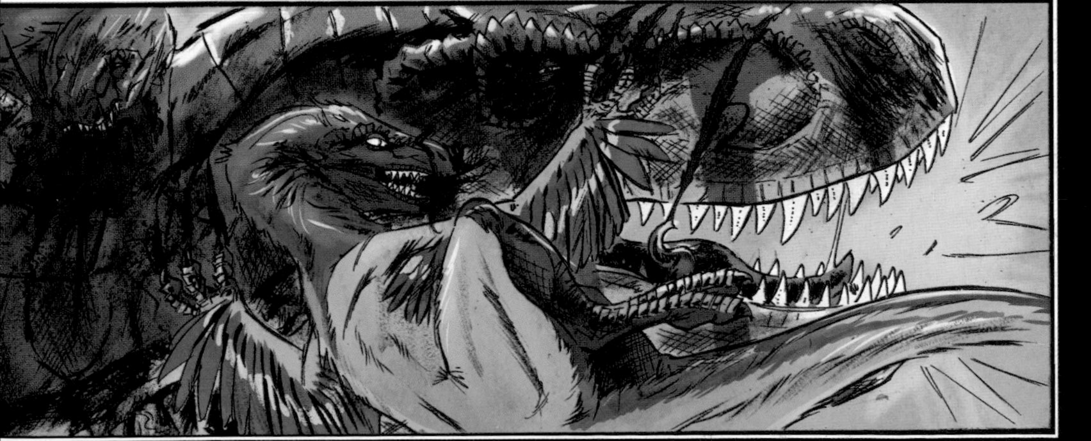

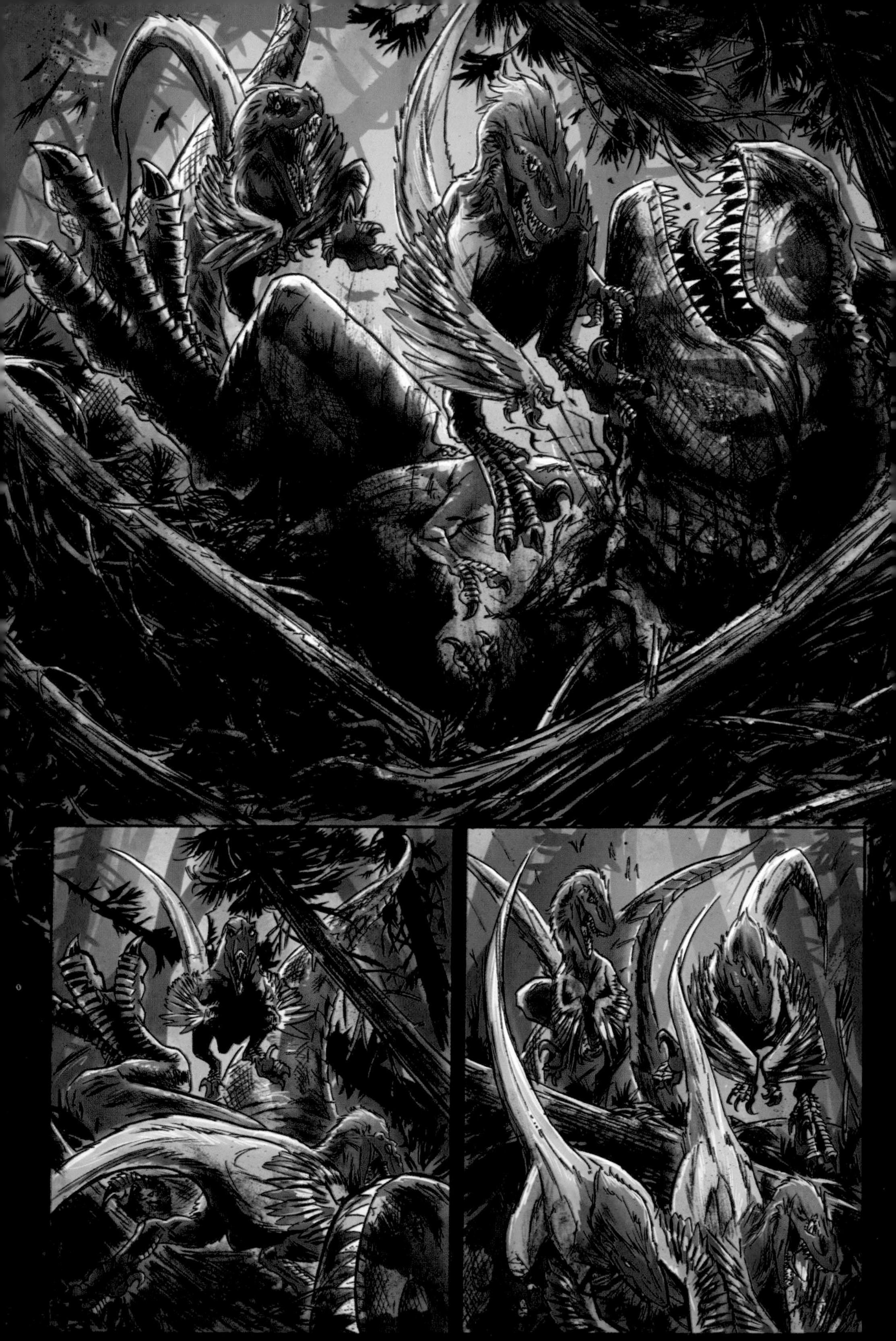

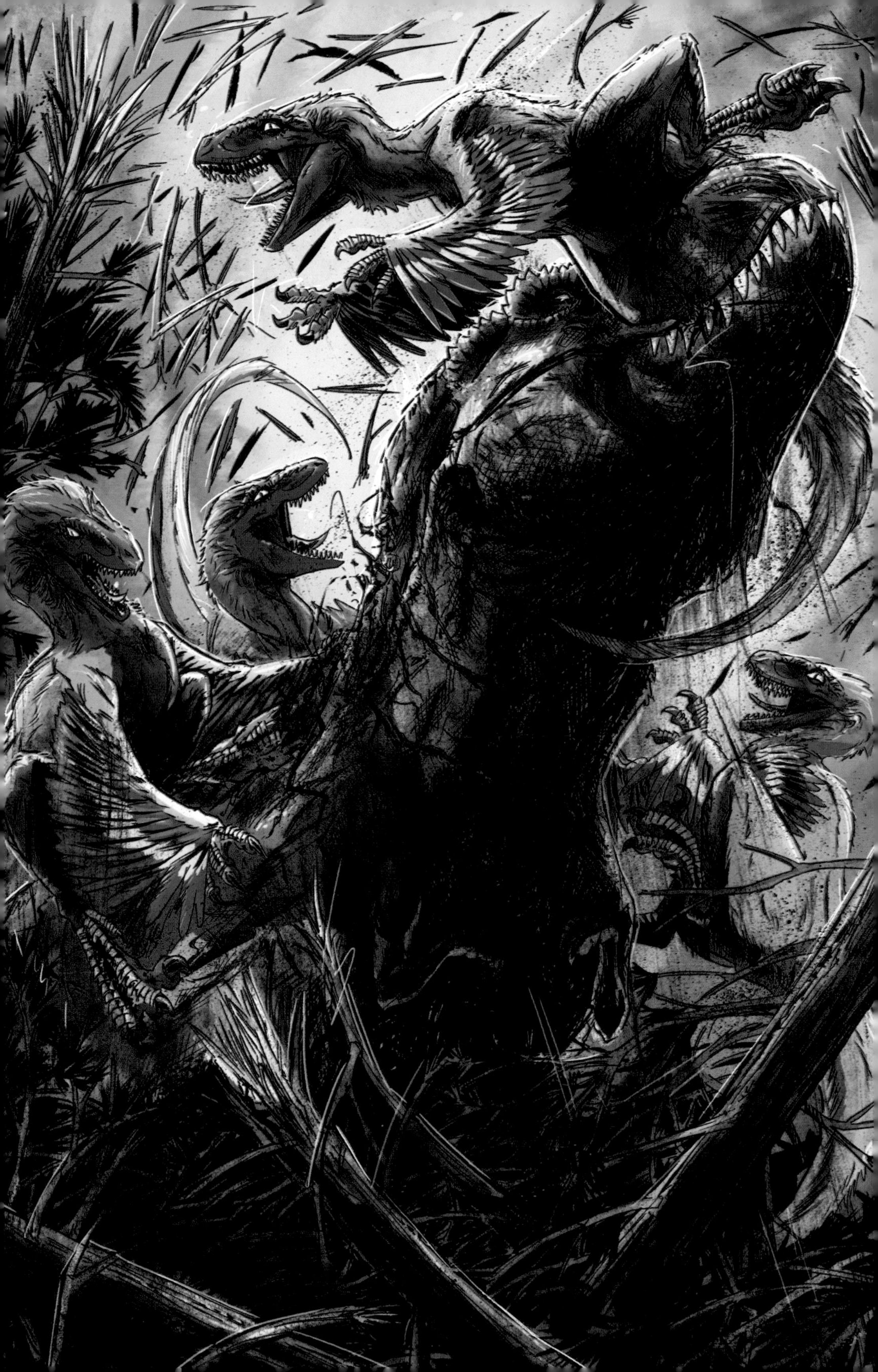

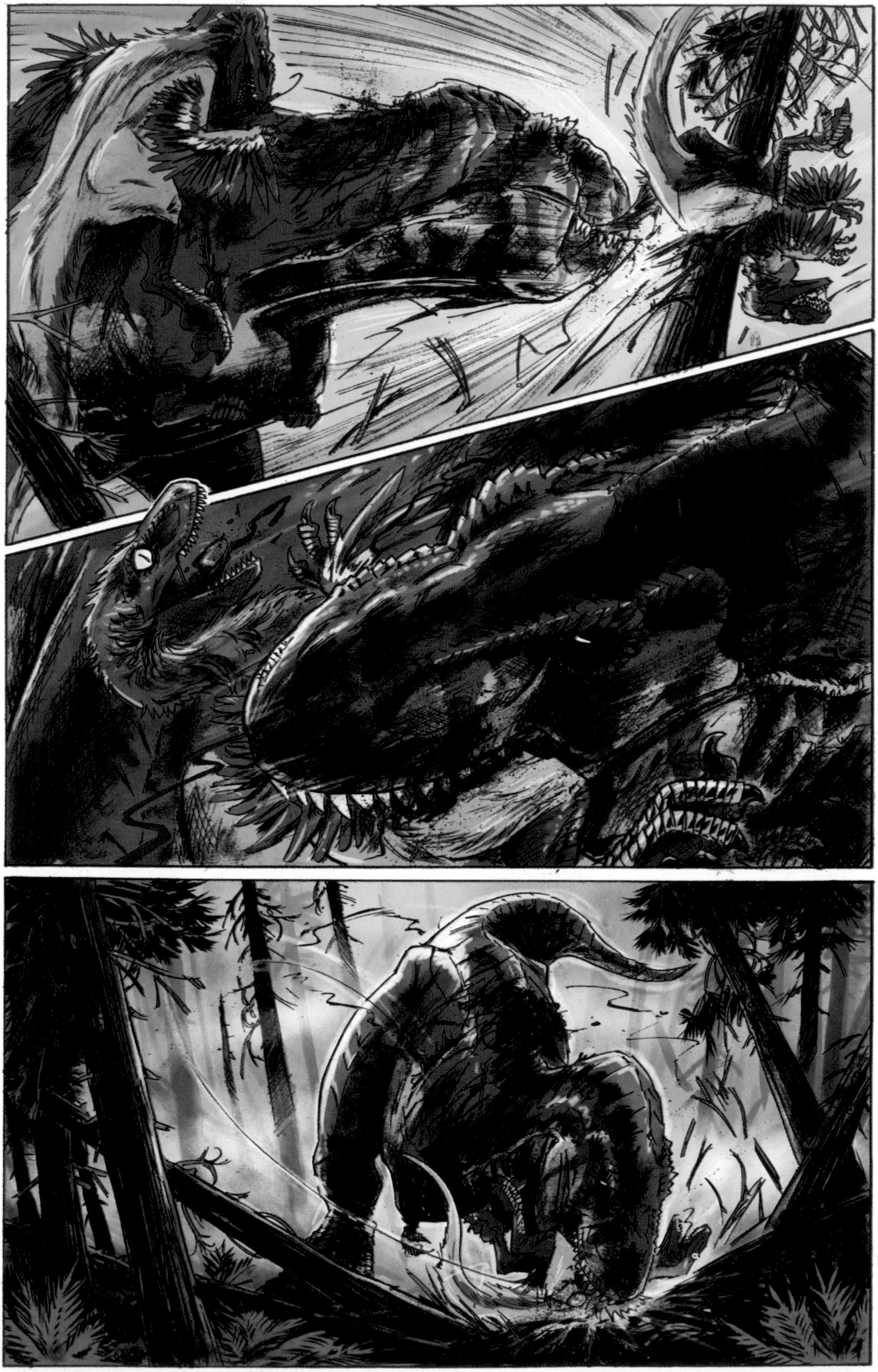

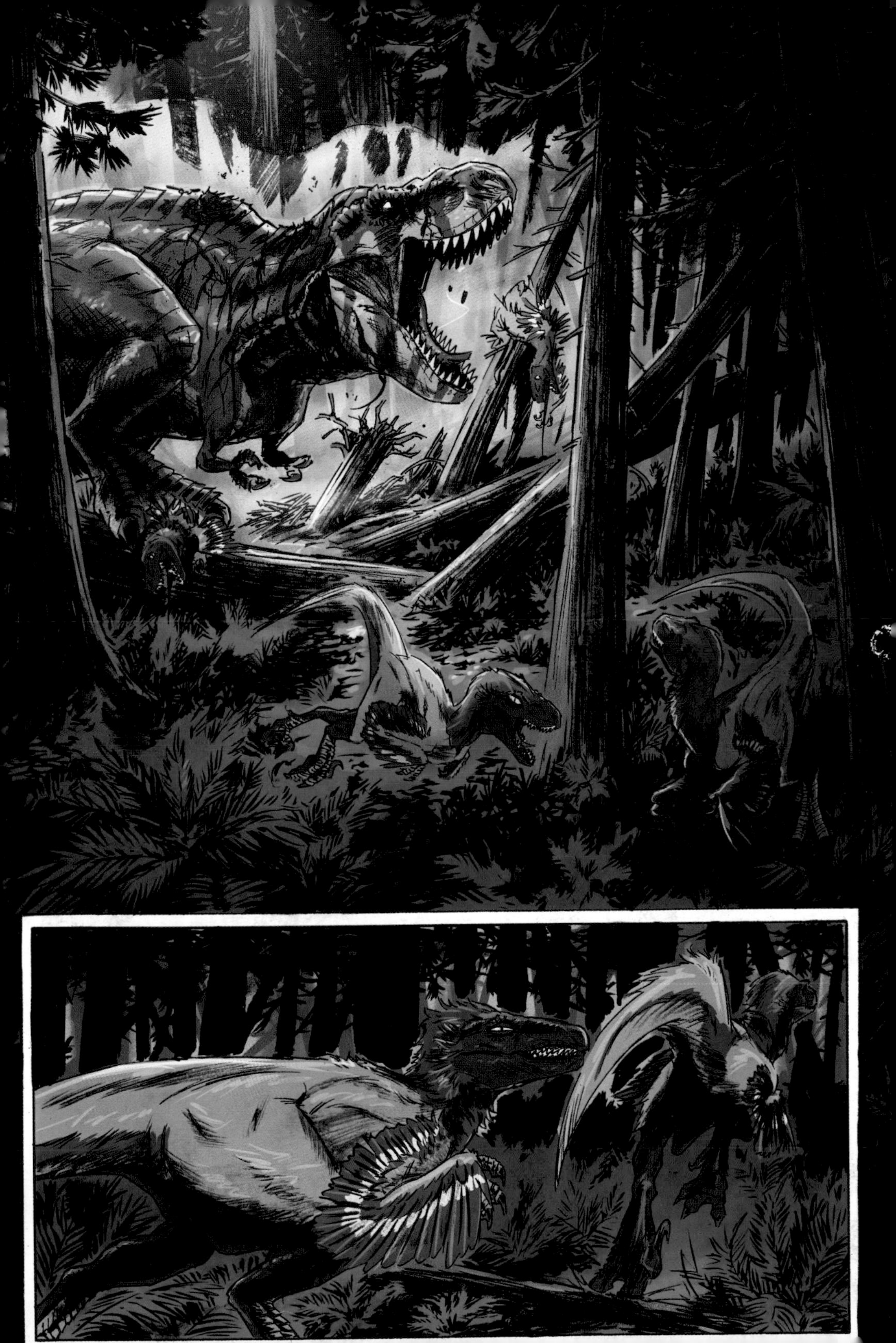

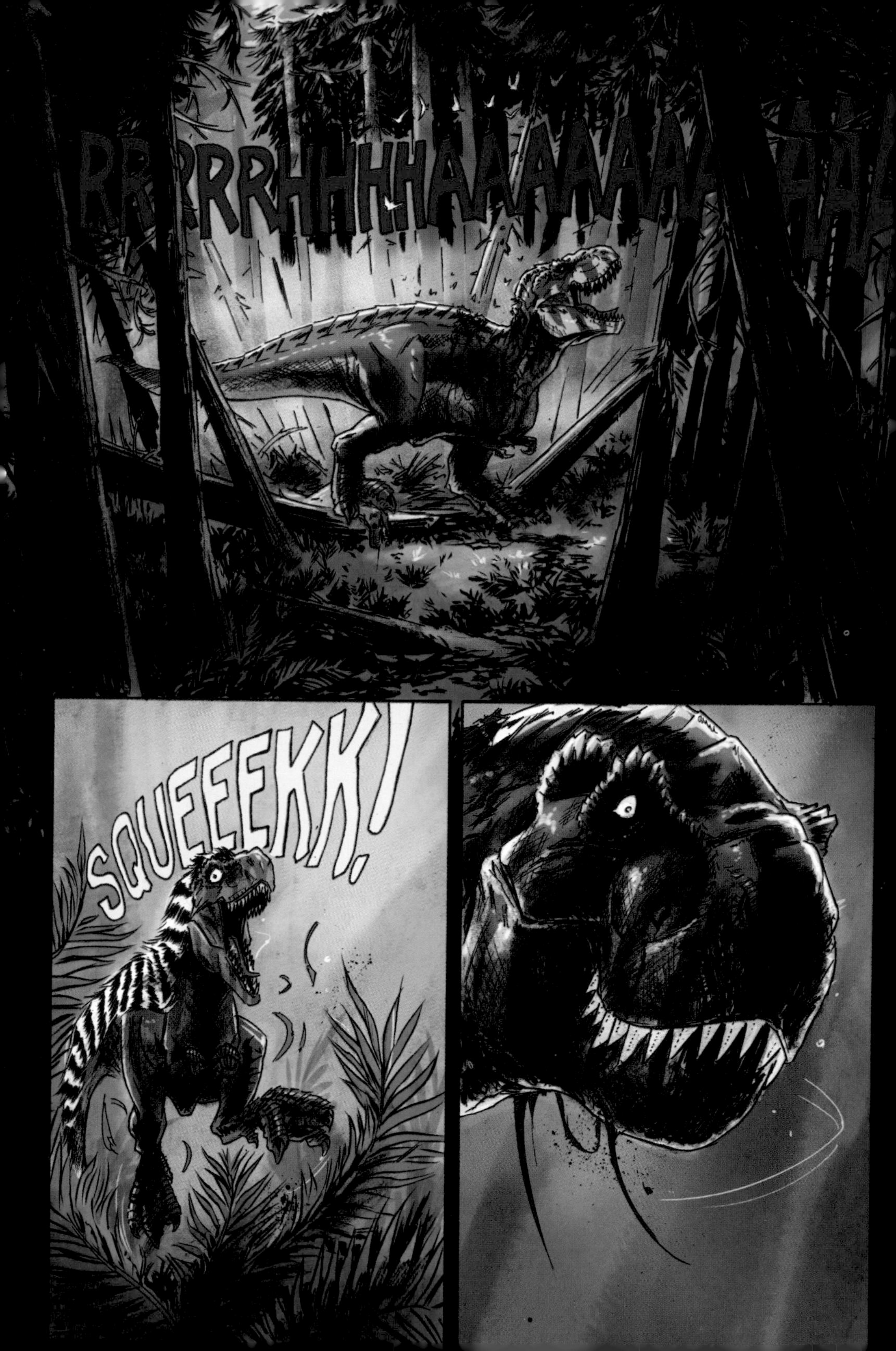
RRRRRHHHHAAAAAAAAAHH
SQUEEEKK!

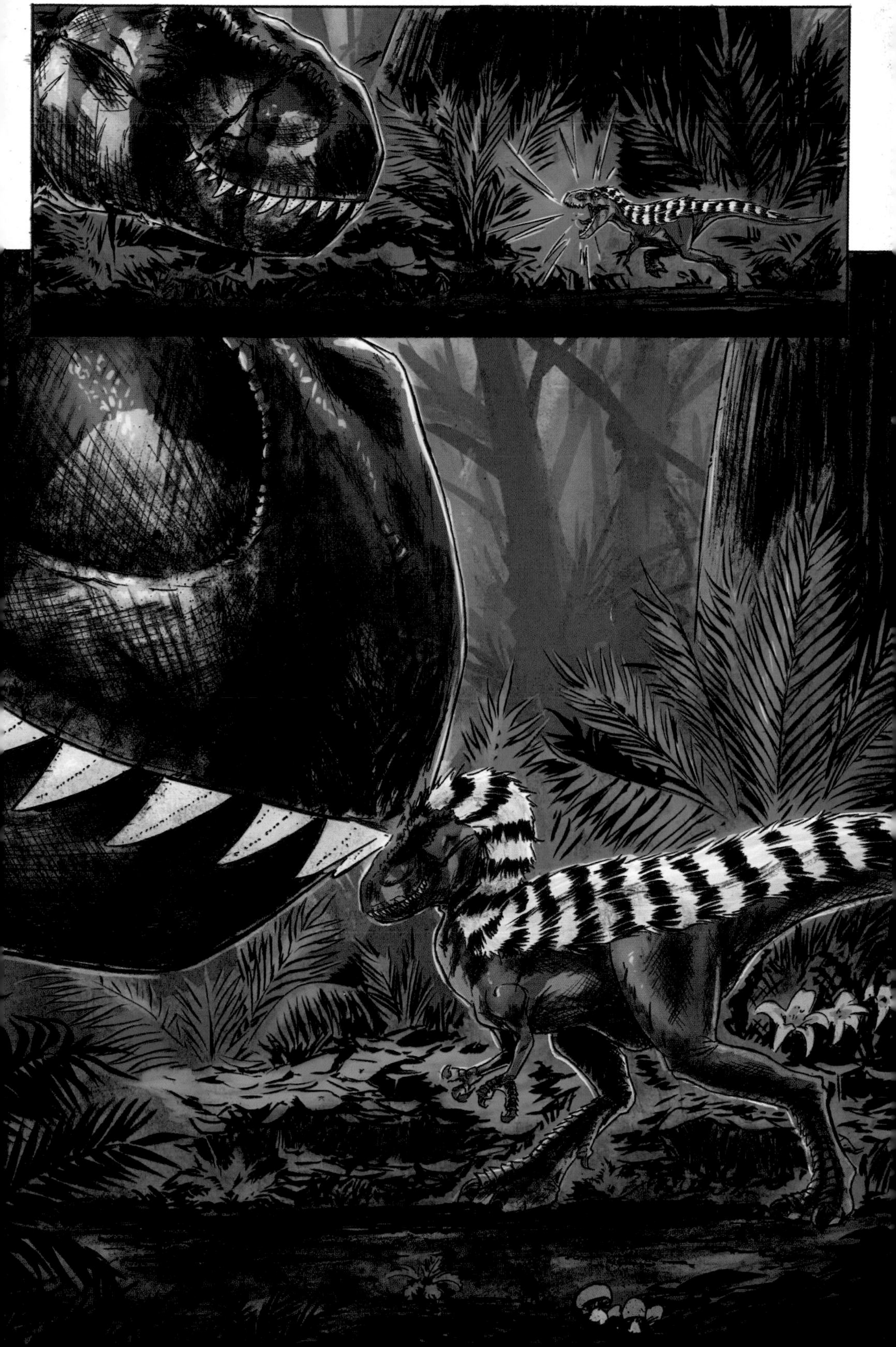

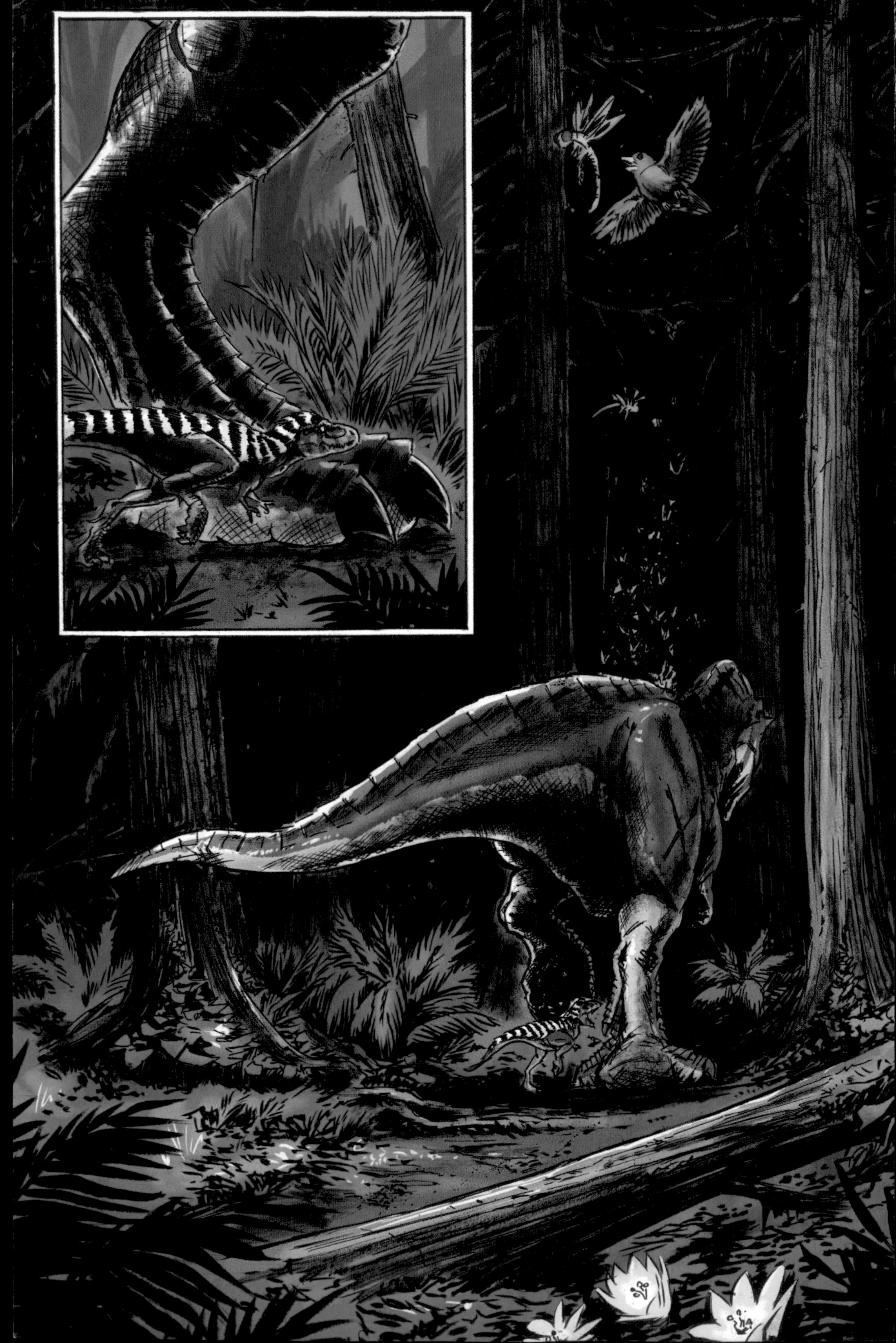

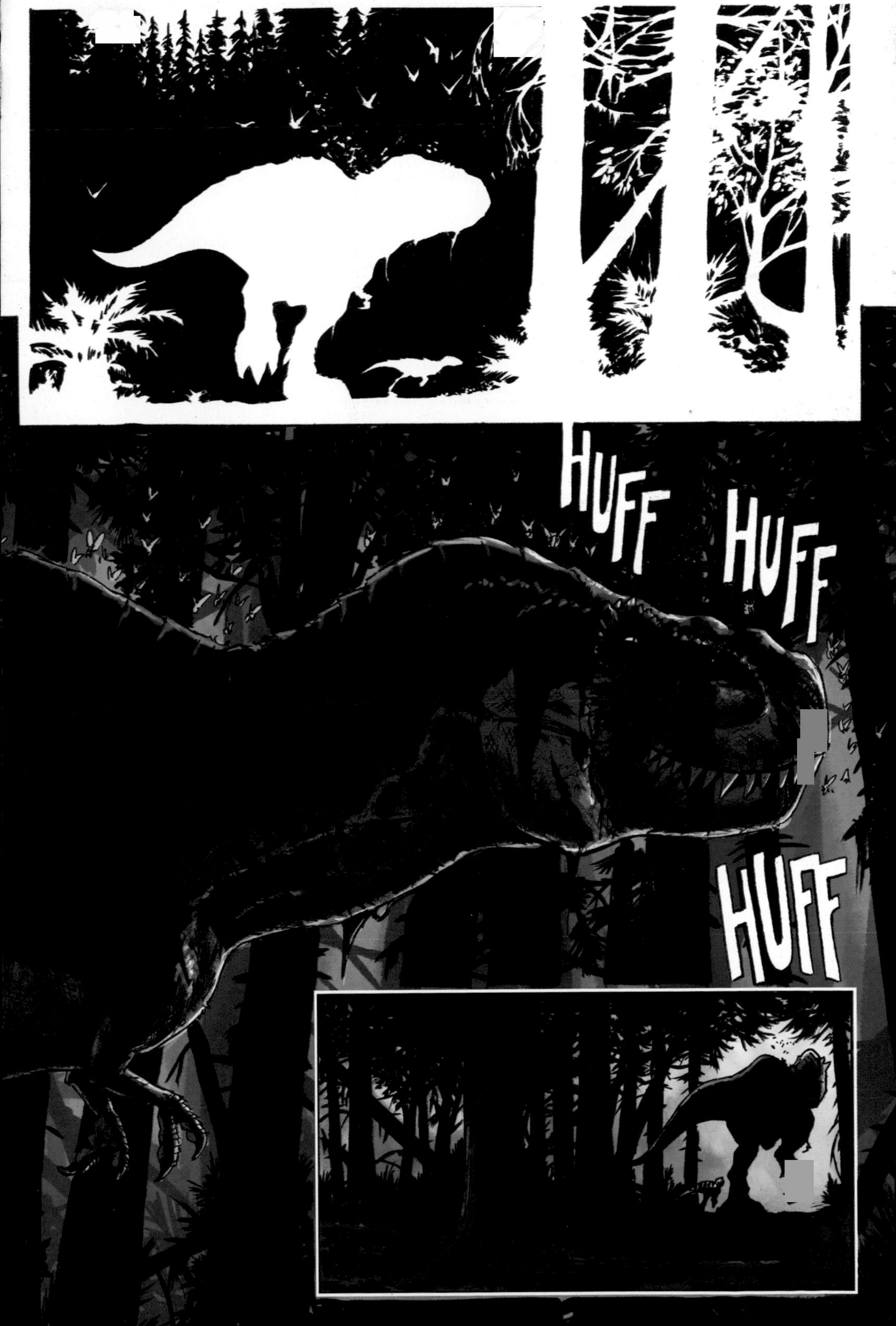
HUFF HUFF
HUFF

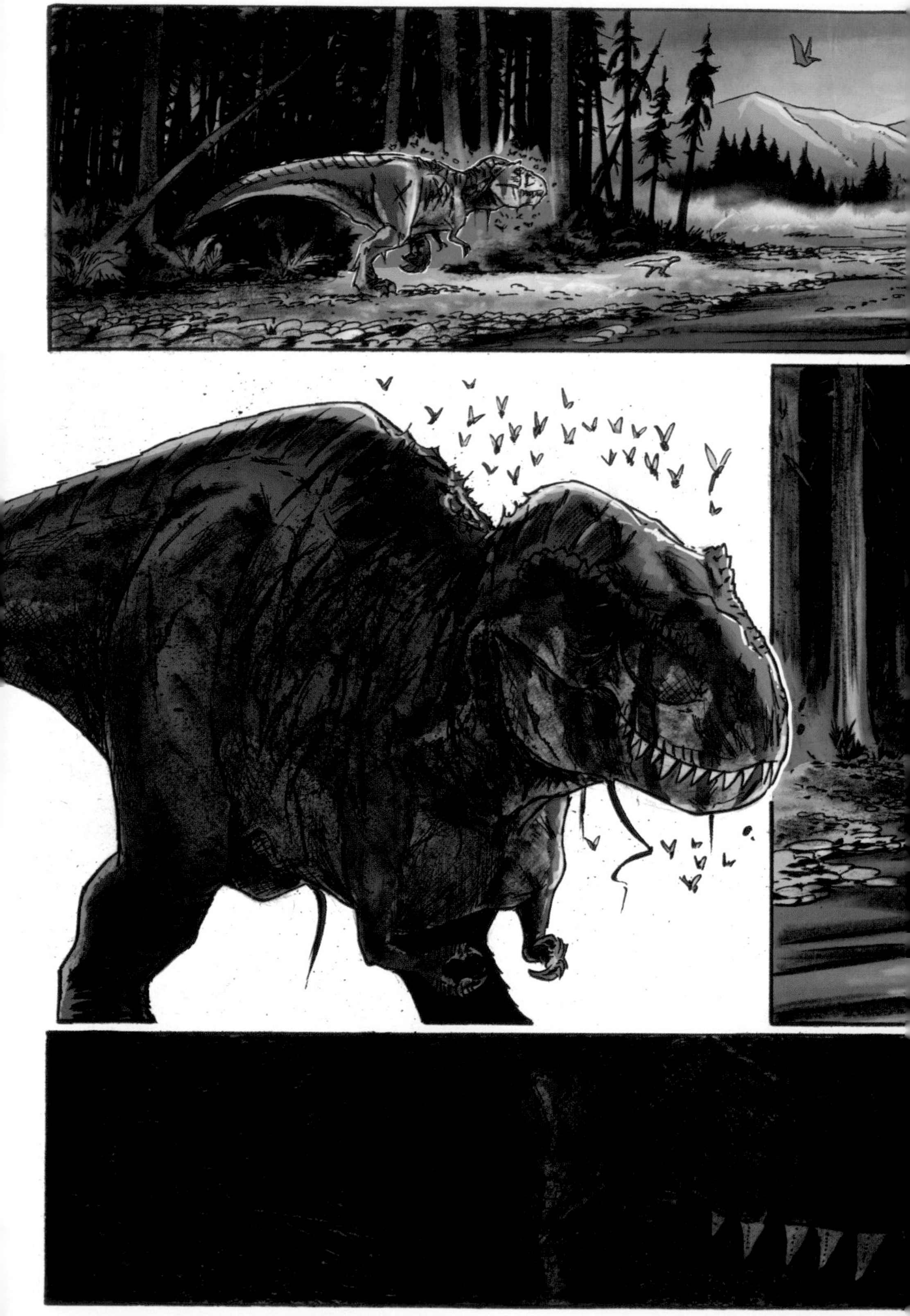

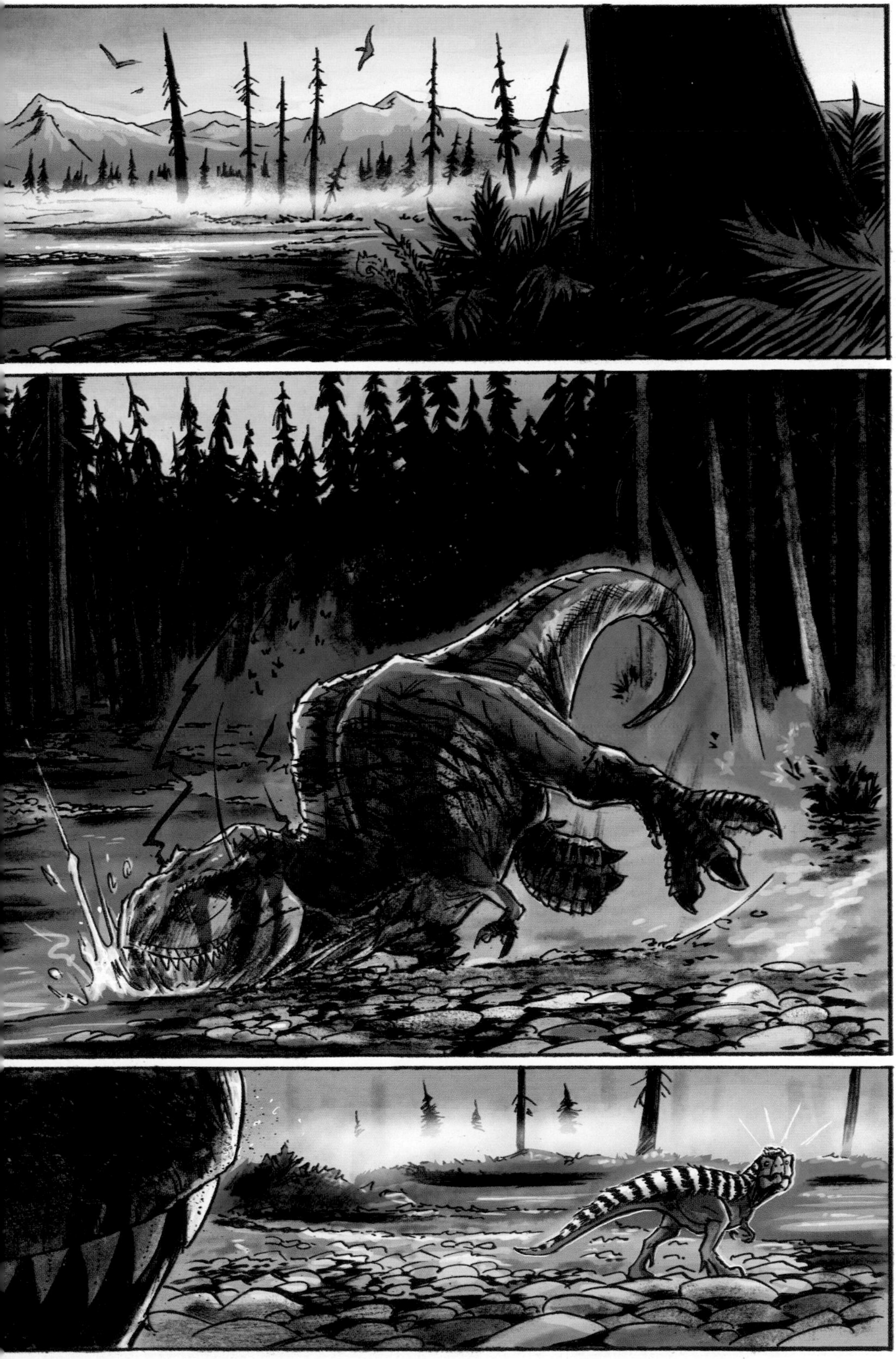

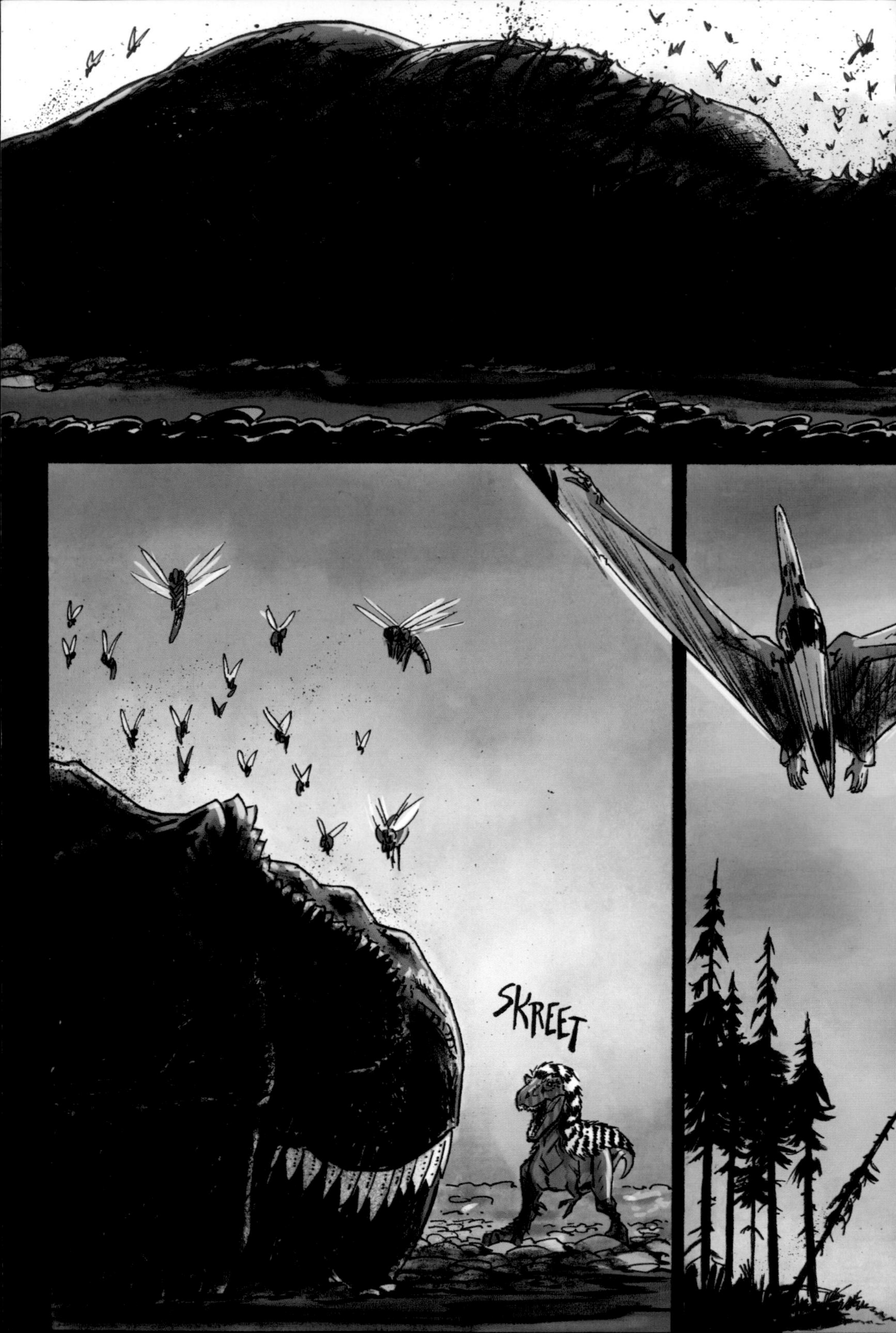
SKREET

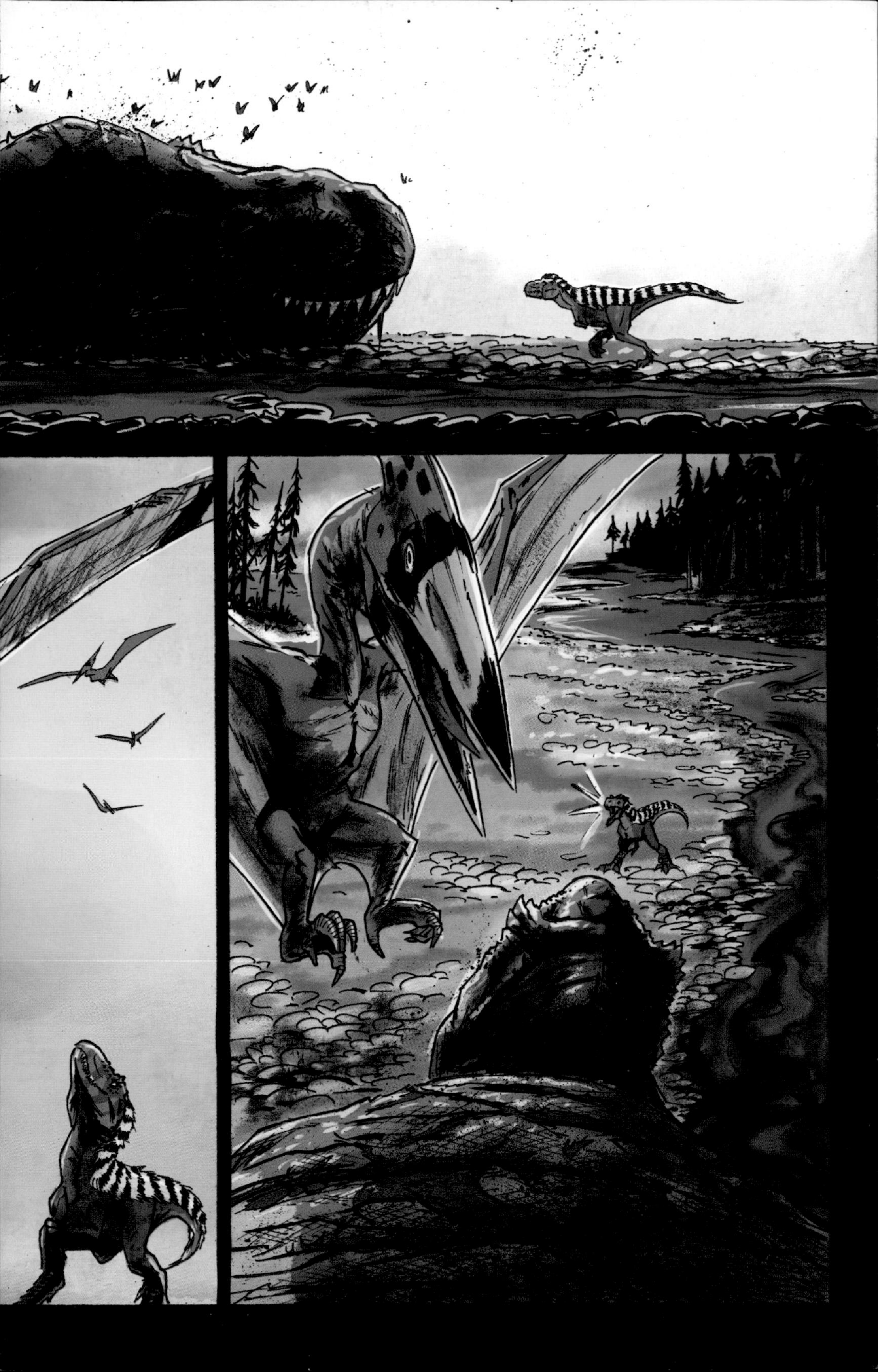

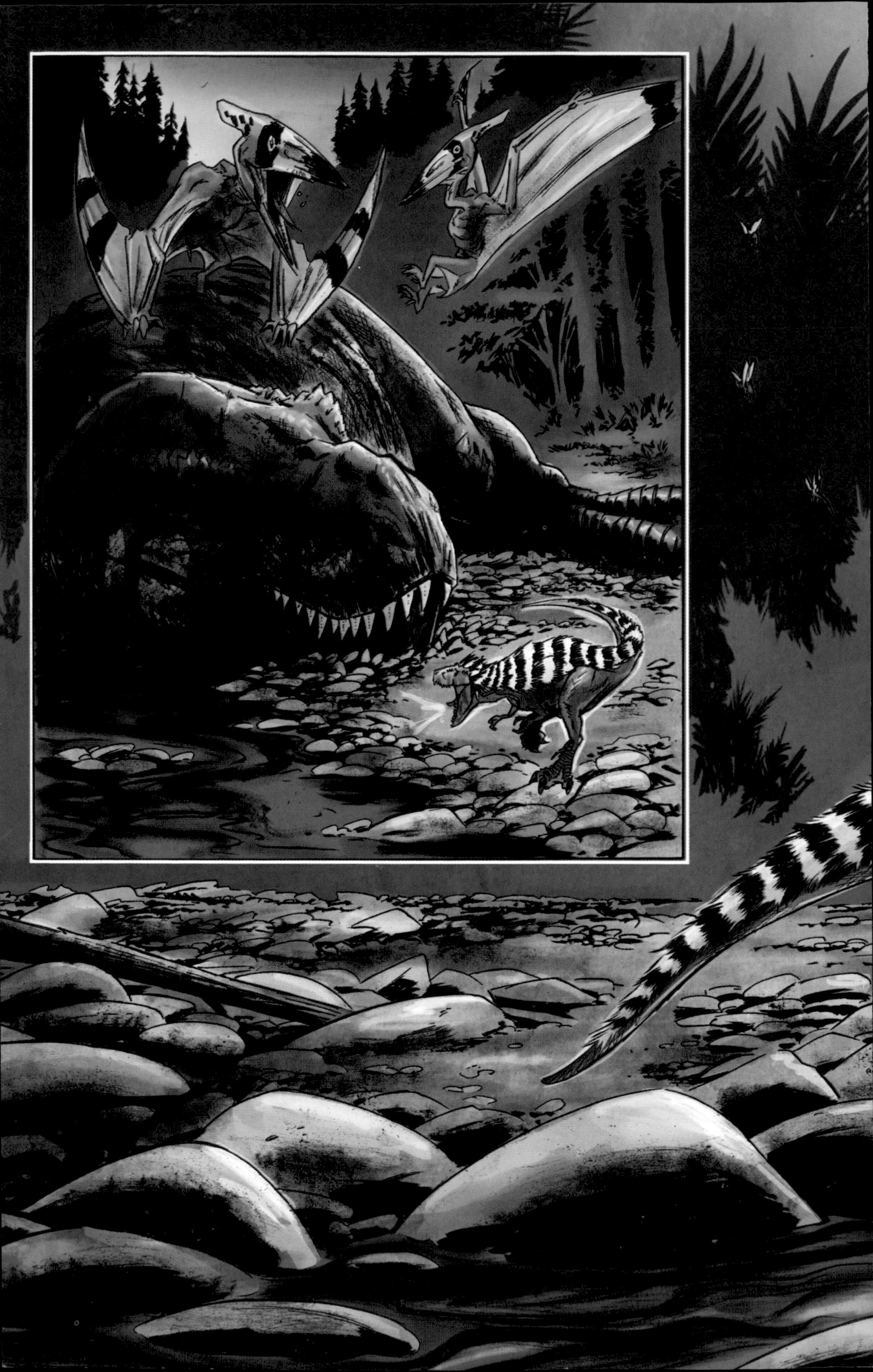

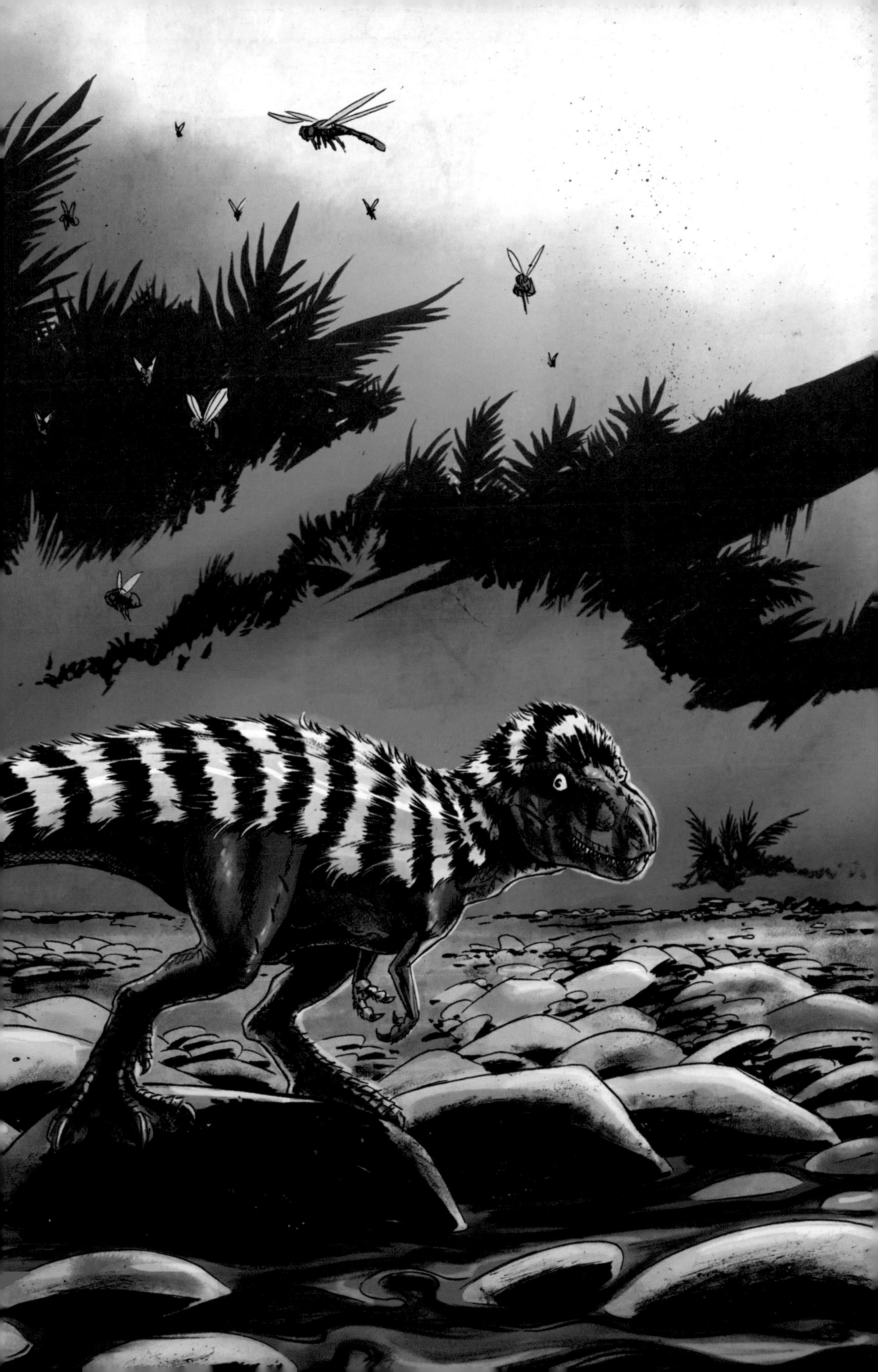

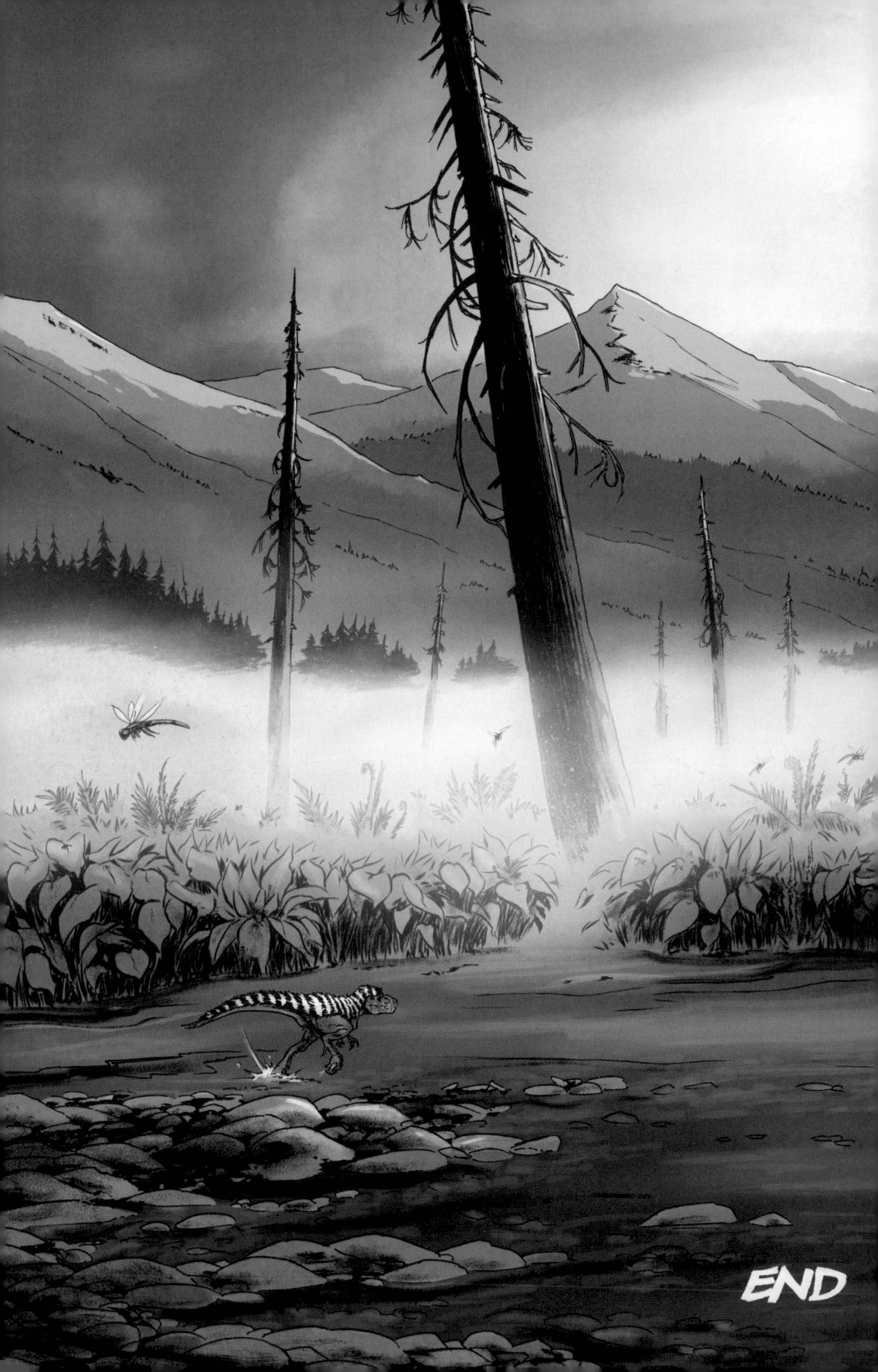
END

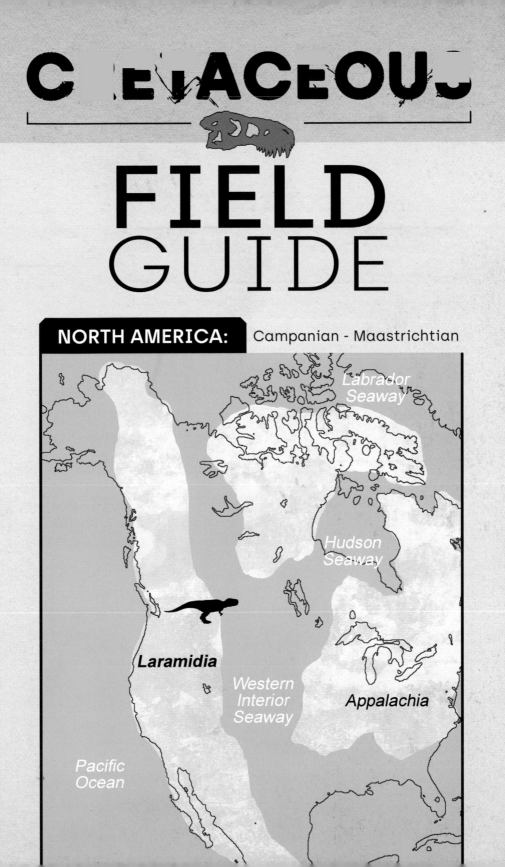

CRETACEOUS

FIELD
GUIDE

NORTH AMERICA: Campanian - Maastrichtian

Labrador
Seaway

Hudson
Seaway

Laramidia

Western
Interior
Seaway

Appalachia

Pacific
Ocean

DROMAEOSAURUS ALBERTENSIS

DINOSAUR: carnivore
LENGTH: 2 m (6.6 ft)
WEIGHT: 15 kg (33 lb)

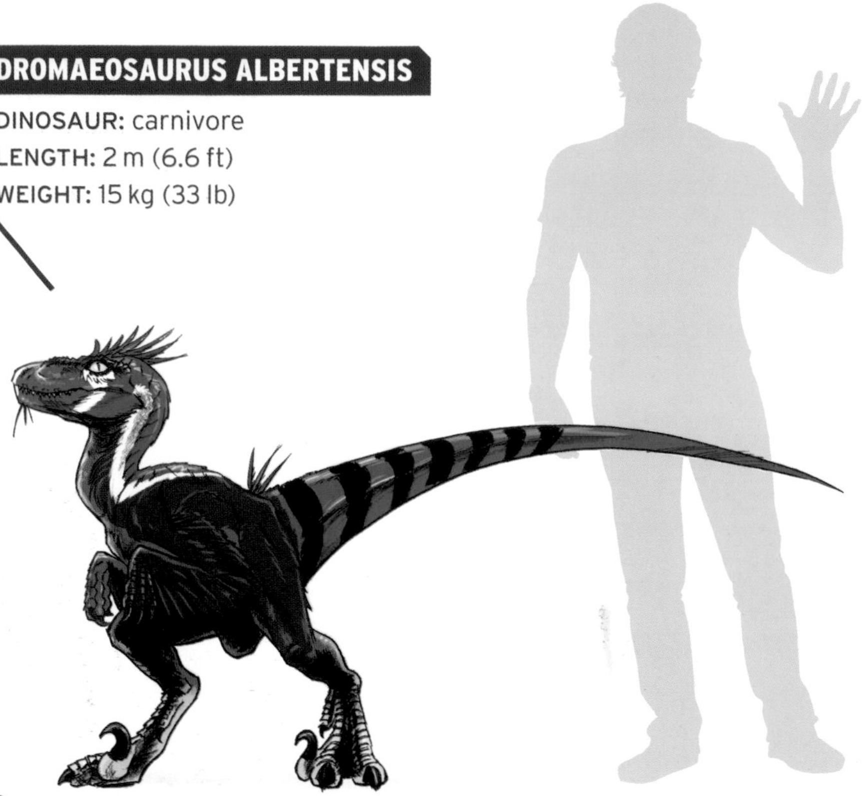

DAKOTARAPTOR STEINI

DINOSAUR: carnivore
LENGTH: 5.5 m (19.6 ft)
WEIGHT: 453 kg (1000 lb)

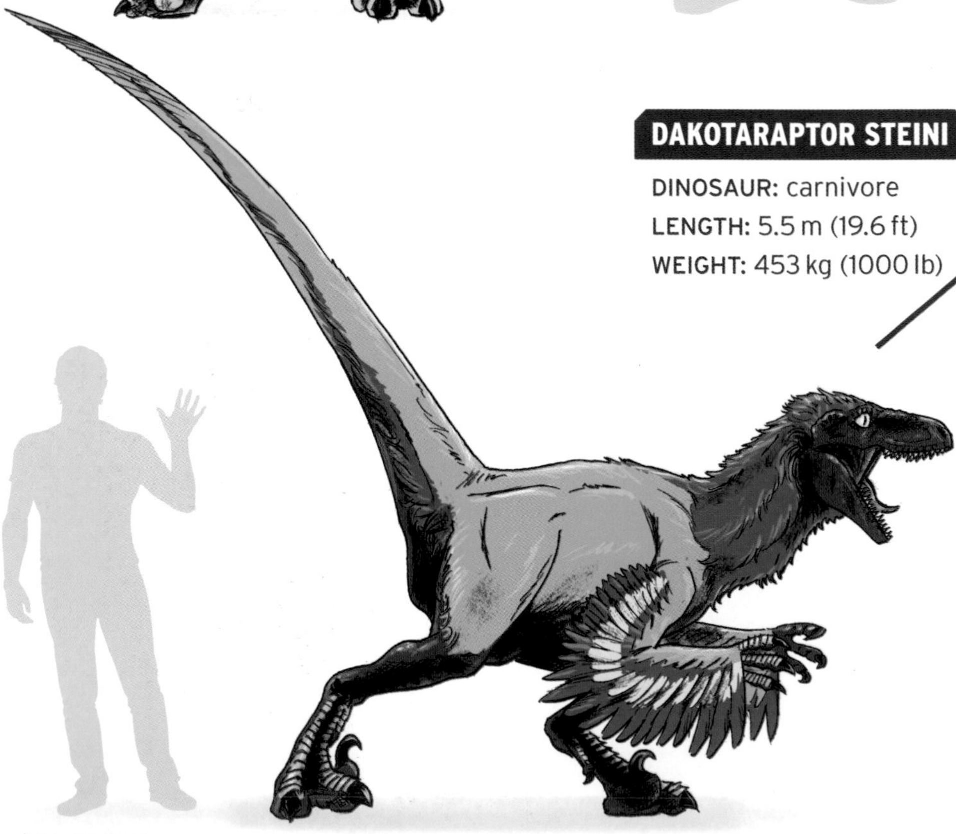

SAURORNITHOLESTES

DINOSAUR: carnivore
LENGTH: 1.8 m (5.9 ft)
WEIGHT: 10 kg (22 lb)

PTILODUS

MAMMAL: omnivore
LENGTH: 50 cm (20 in)
WEIGHT: 120 g (4.2 oz)

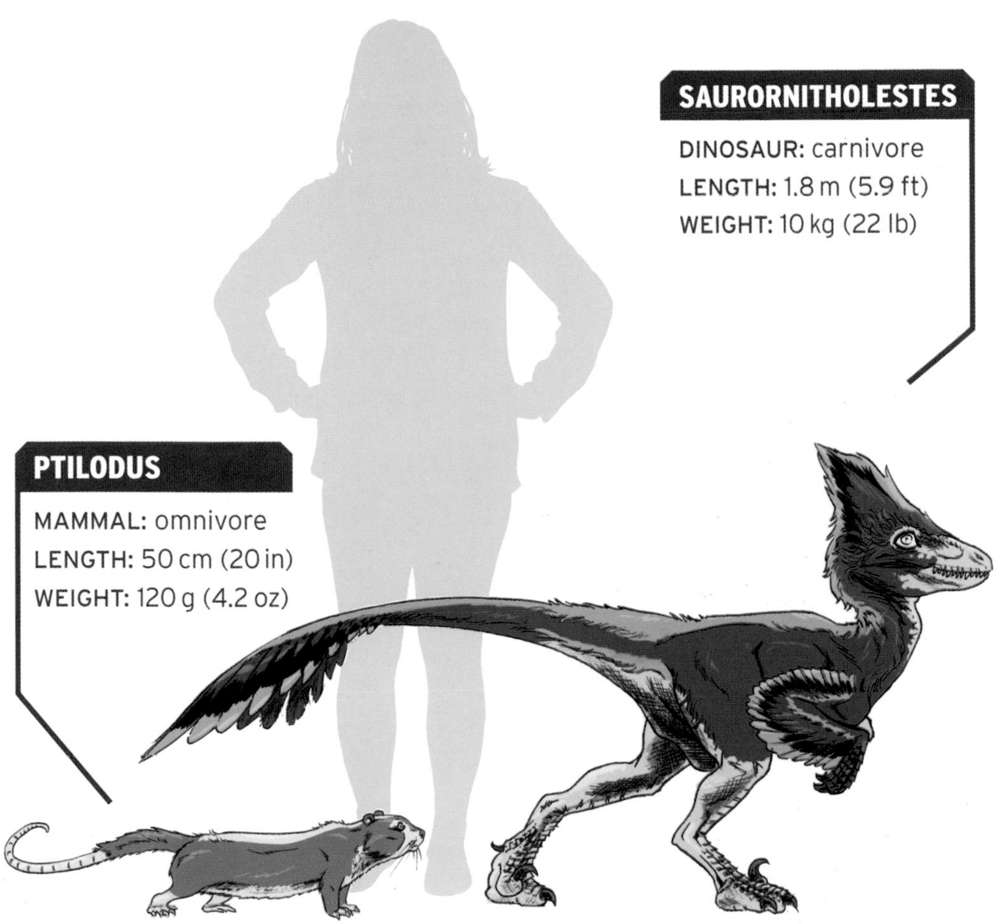

CHIROSTENOTES

DINOSAUR: omnivore
LENGTH: 2 m (6.6 ft)
WEIGHT: 30 kg (66 lb)

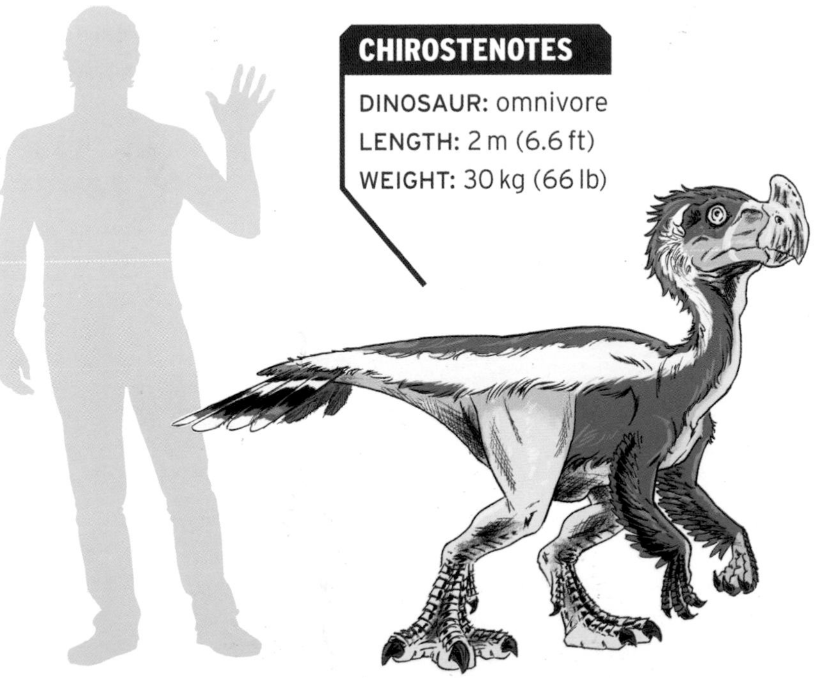

PACHYCEPHALOSAURUS WYOMINGENSIS

DINOSAUR: herbivore
LENGTH: 4.5 m (15 ft)
WEIGHT: 450 kg (1000 lb)

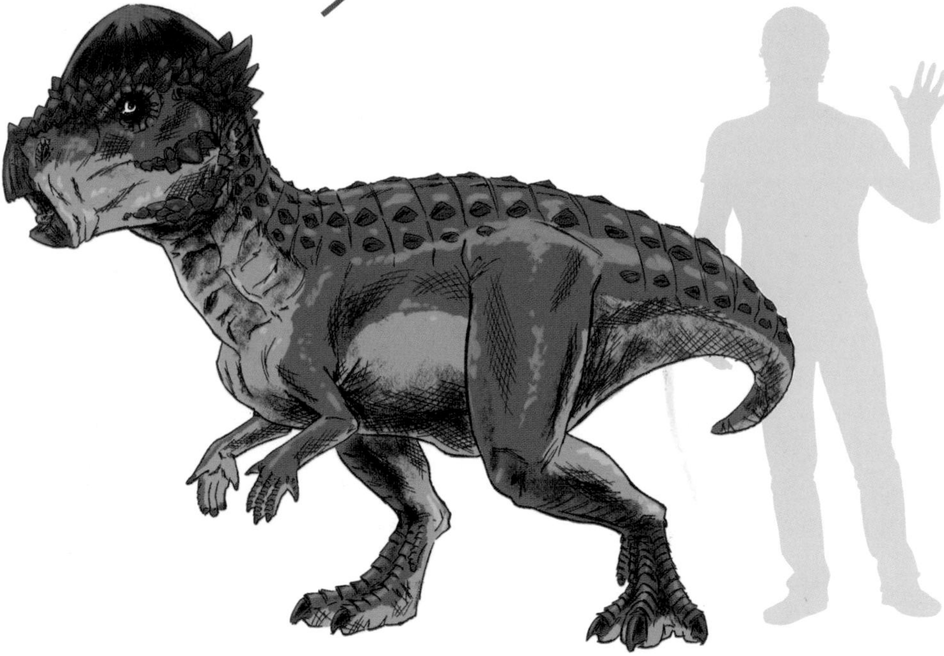

PARASAUROLOPHUS

DINOSAUR: herbivore
LENGTH: 10 m (23 ft)
WEIGHT: 5 tonnes

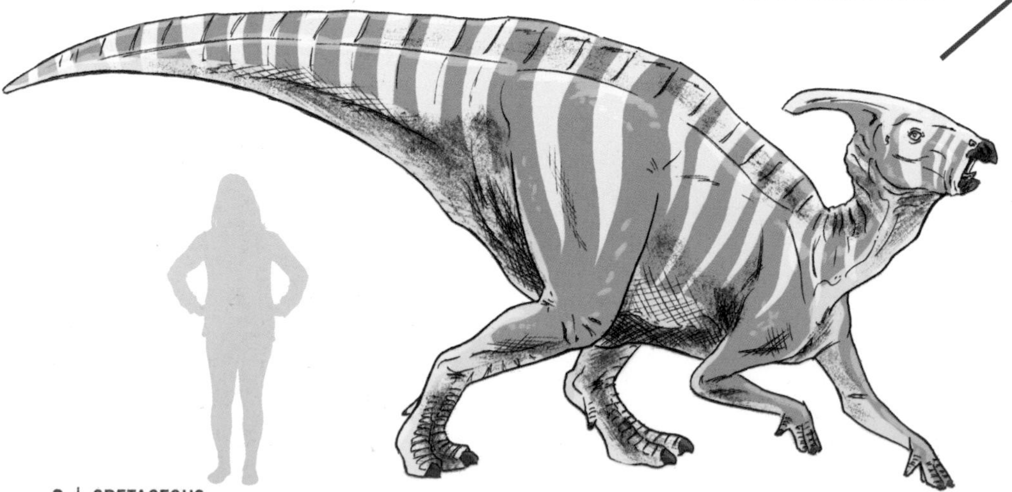

EDMONTOSAURUS REGALIS

DINOSAUR: herbivore
LENGTH: 9 m (30 ft)
WEIGHT: 3.7 tonnes

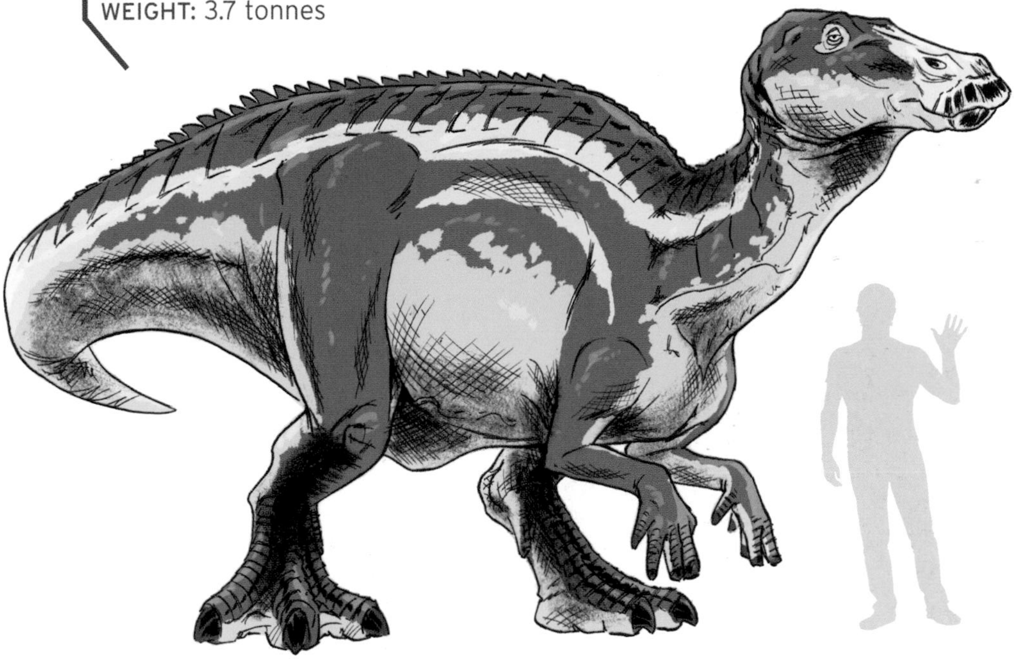

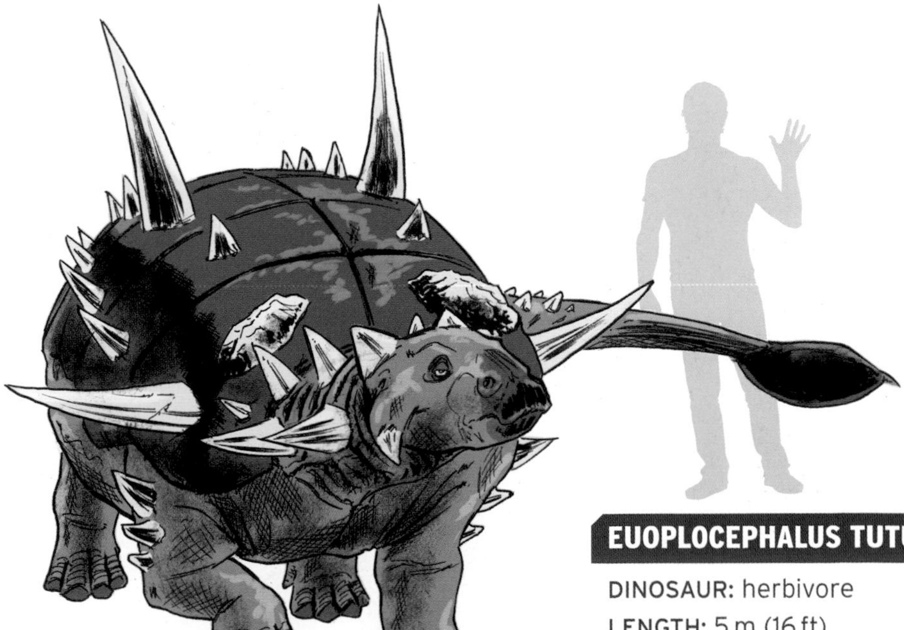

EUOPLOCEPHALUS TUTUS

DINOSAUR: herbivore
LENGTH: 5 m (16 ft)
WEIGHT: 2 tonnes

TRICERATOPS HORRIDUS

DINOSAUR: herbivore
LENGTH: 8 m (25 ft)
WEIGHT: 9 tonnes

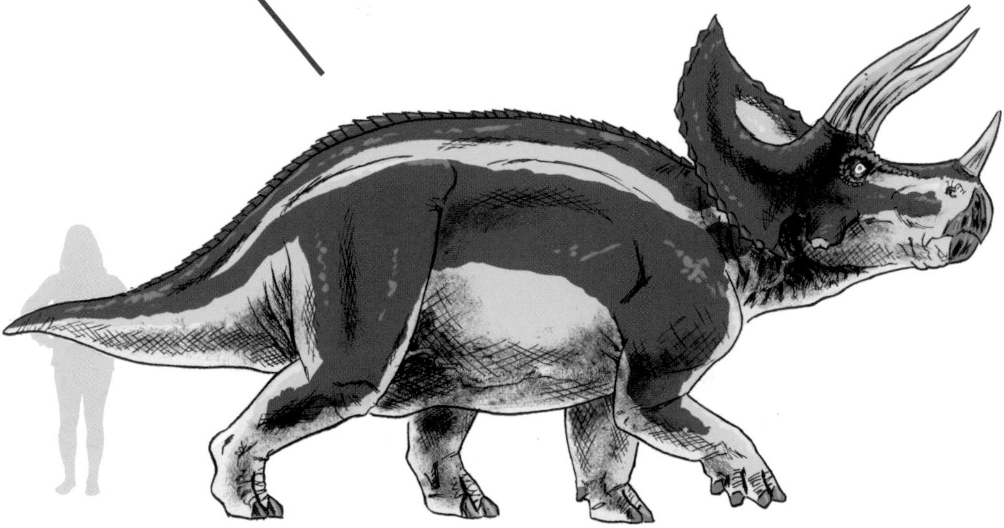

PACHYRHINOSAURUS

DINOSAUR: herbivore
LENGTH: 6 m (20 ft)
WEIGHT: 3 tonnes

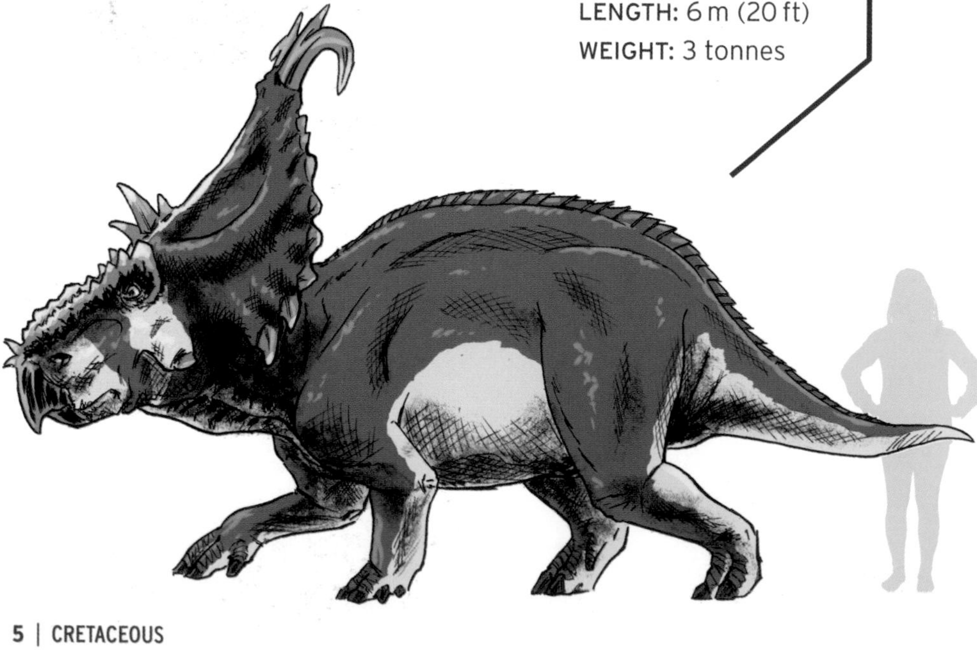

ALAMOSAURUS SANJUANENSIS

DINOSAUR: herbivore
LENGTH: 30 m (98 ft)
WEIGHT: 80 tonnes

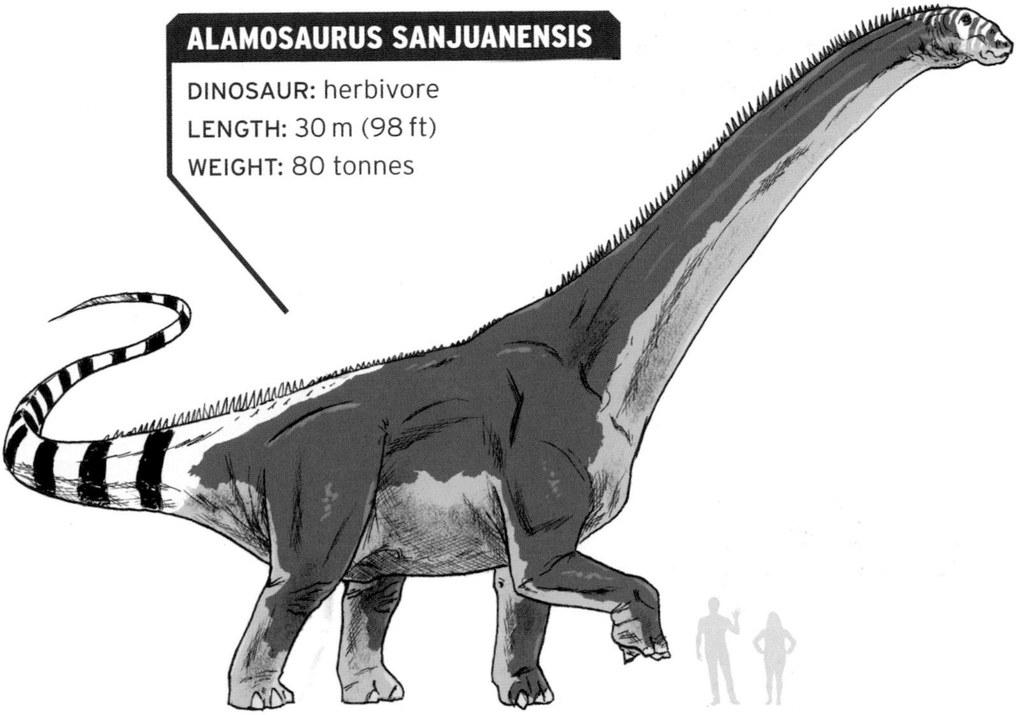

ALBERTOSAURUS SARCOPHAGUS

DINOSAUR: carnivore
LENGTH: 8 m (27 ft)
WEIGHT: 2.5 tonnes

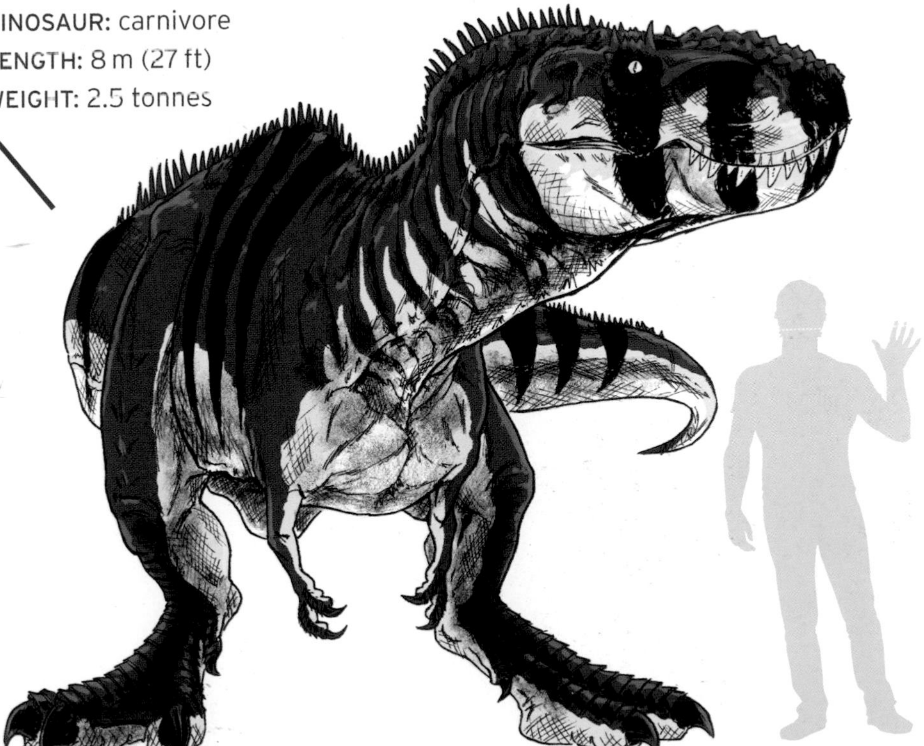

TYRANNOSAURUS REX
DINOSAUR: carnivore
LENGTH: 12 m (40 ft)
WEIGHT: 7 tonnes

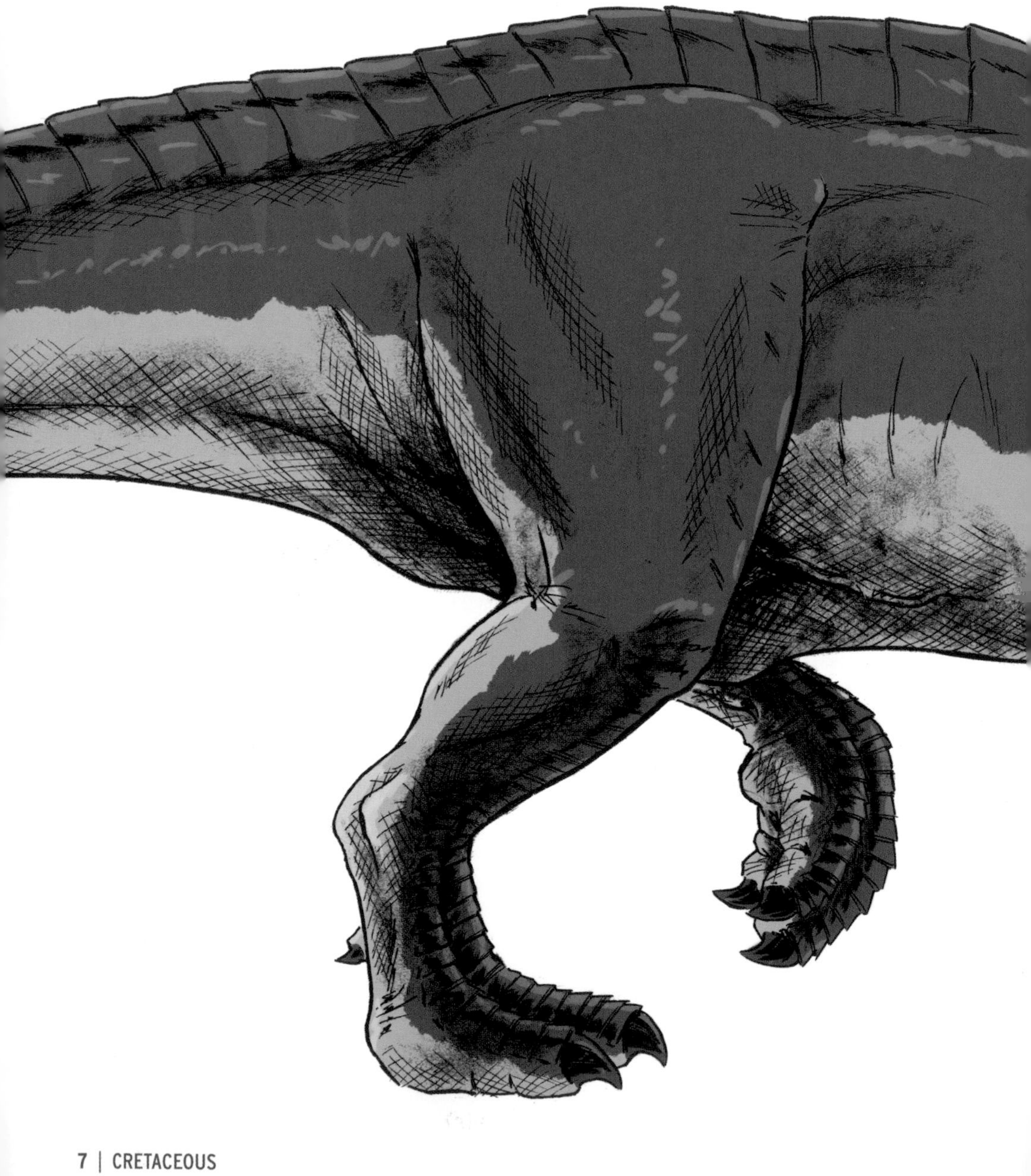

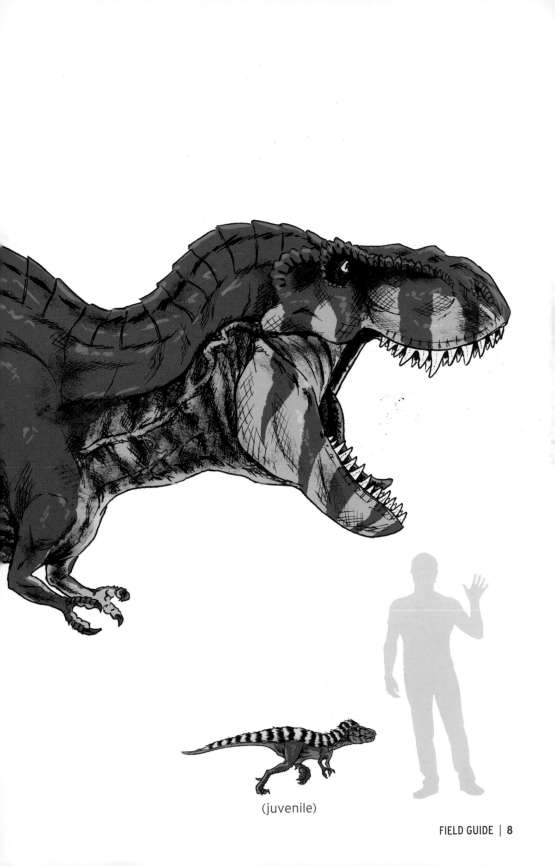

(juvenile)

QUETZALCOATLUS NORTHROPI

REPTILE: carnivore

LENGTH: 11 m (36 ft)

WEIGHT: 250 kg (550 lb)

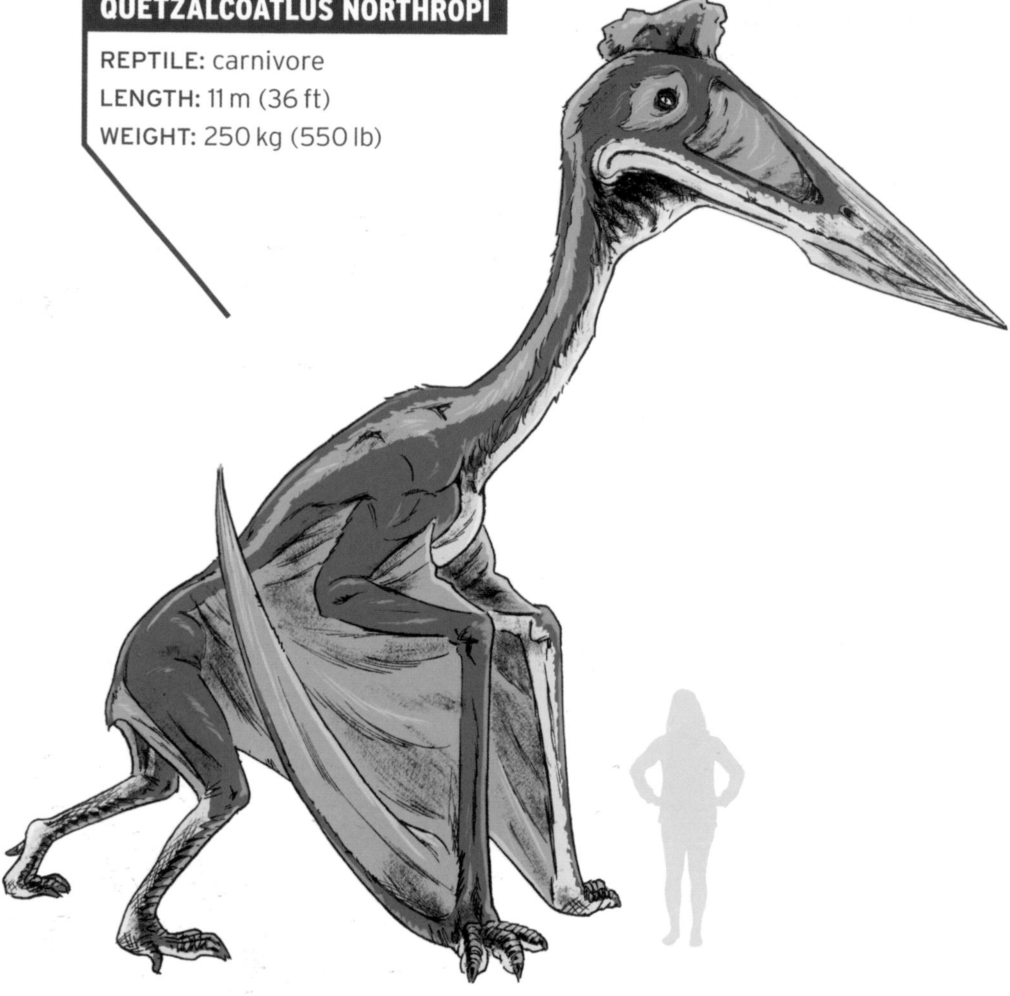

PTERANODON

REPTILE: carnivore

LENGTH: 5.6 m (18 ft)

WEIGHT: 25 kg (55 lb)

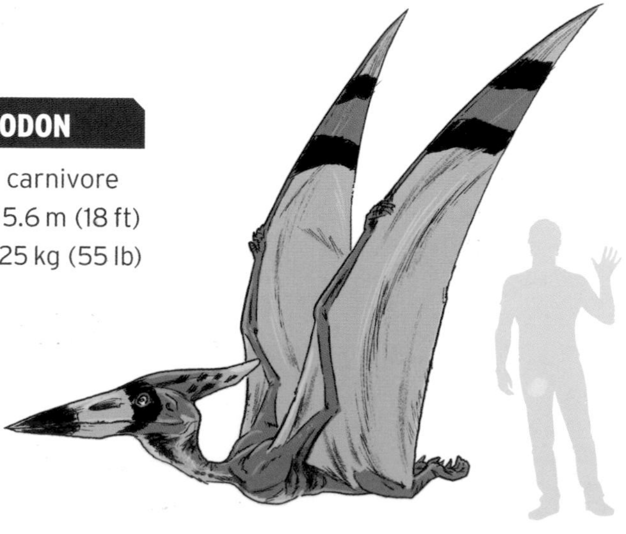

MOSASAURUS

REPTILE: carnivore
LENGTH: 15 m (49 ft)
WEIGHT: 15 tonnes

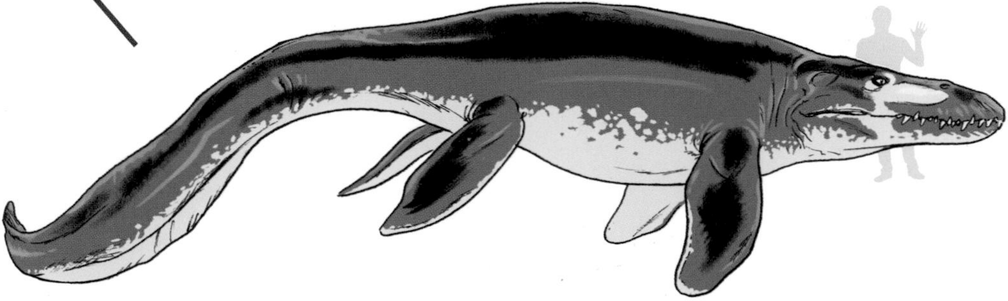

ELASMOSAURUS

REPTILE: carnivore
LENGTH: 14 m (45 ft)
WEIGHT: 3 tonnes

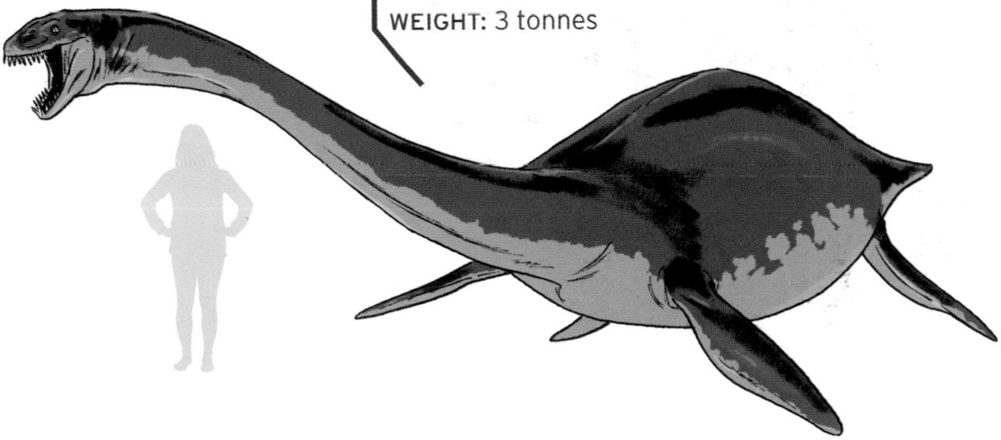

DEINOSUCHUS

REPTILE: carnivore
LENGTH: 10.6 m (35 ft)
WEIGHT: 8 tonnes

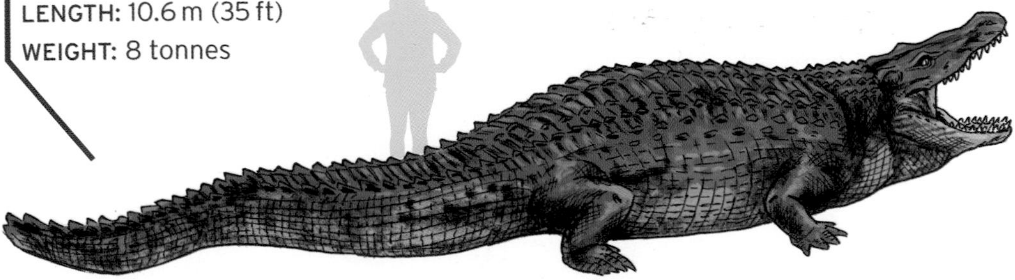

ARCHELON

REPTILE: carnivore
LENGTH: 4 m (13 ft)
WEIGHT: 2200 kg (4850 lb)

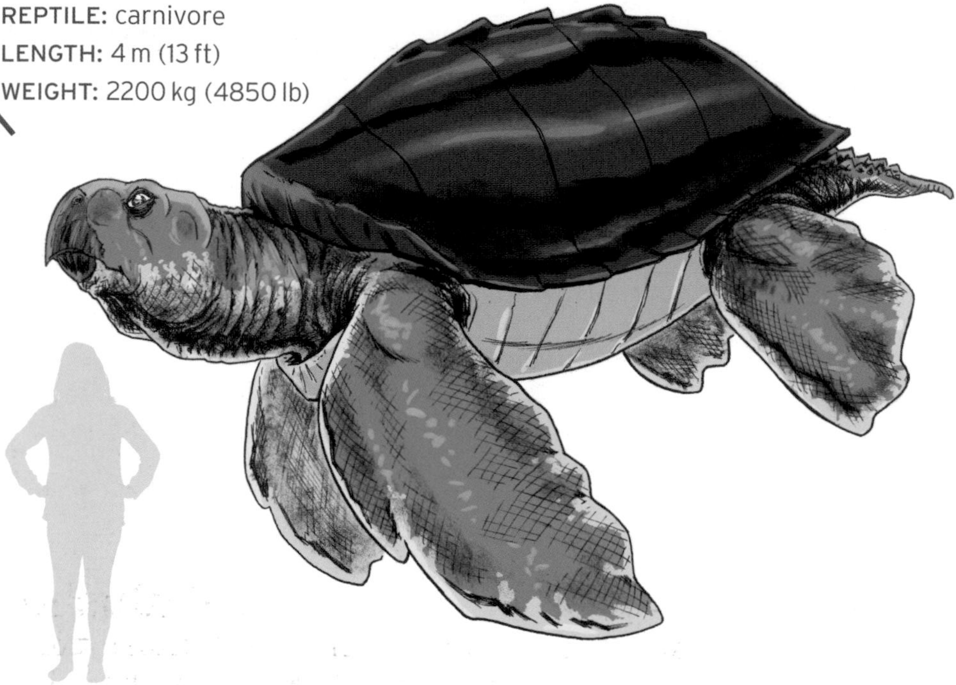

CRETOXYRHINA MANTELLI

SHARK: carnivore
LENGTH: 7.6 m (25 ft)
WEIGHT: 2.5 tonnes

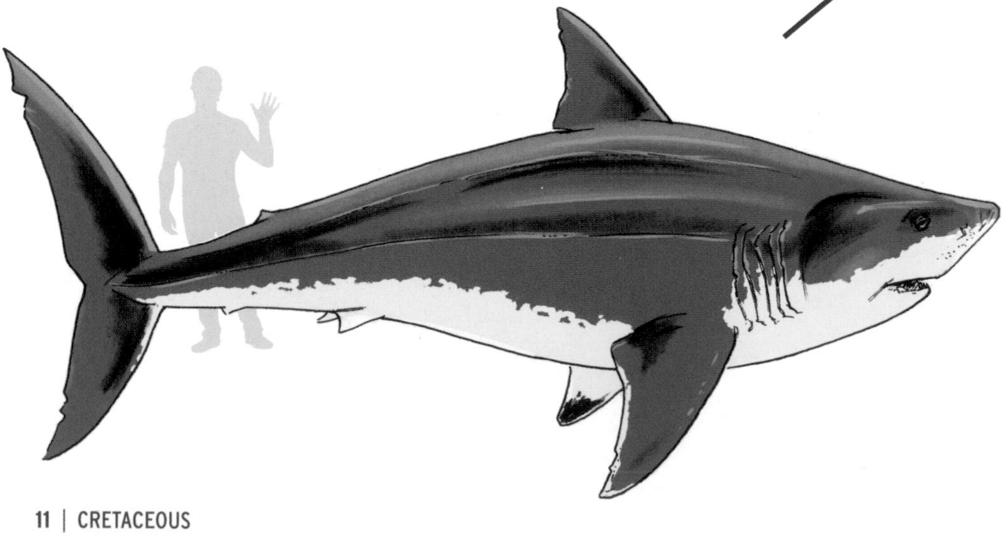

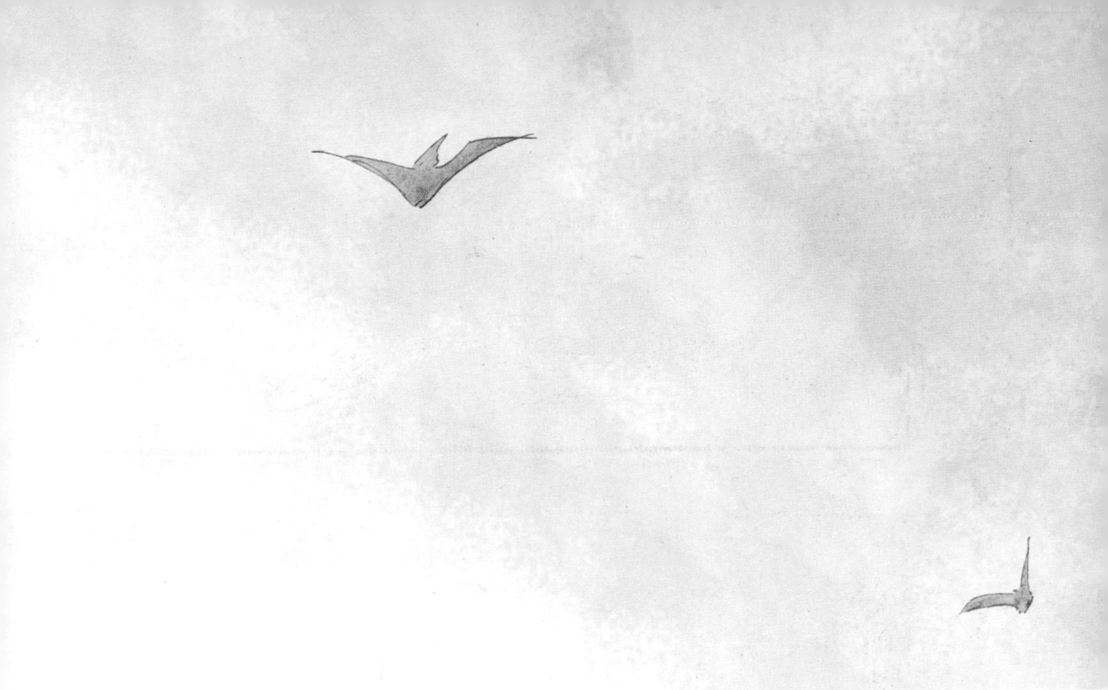

Tadd Galusha

is a Northwest based comic artist and illustrator. Creator of the web-comic *The Backwoods*, he has worked on numerous titles including *Godzilla* and *TMNT/Ghostbusters 2*. Tadd currently resides in a small town of Southwest Alaska with his wife and two dogs.

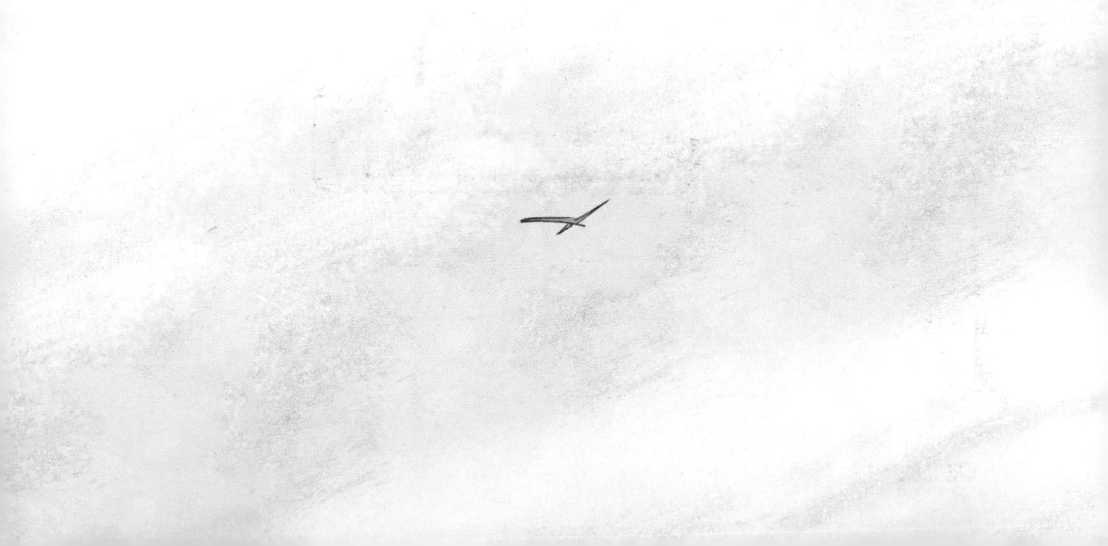

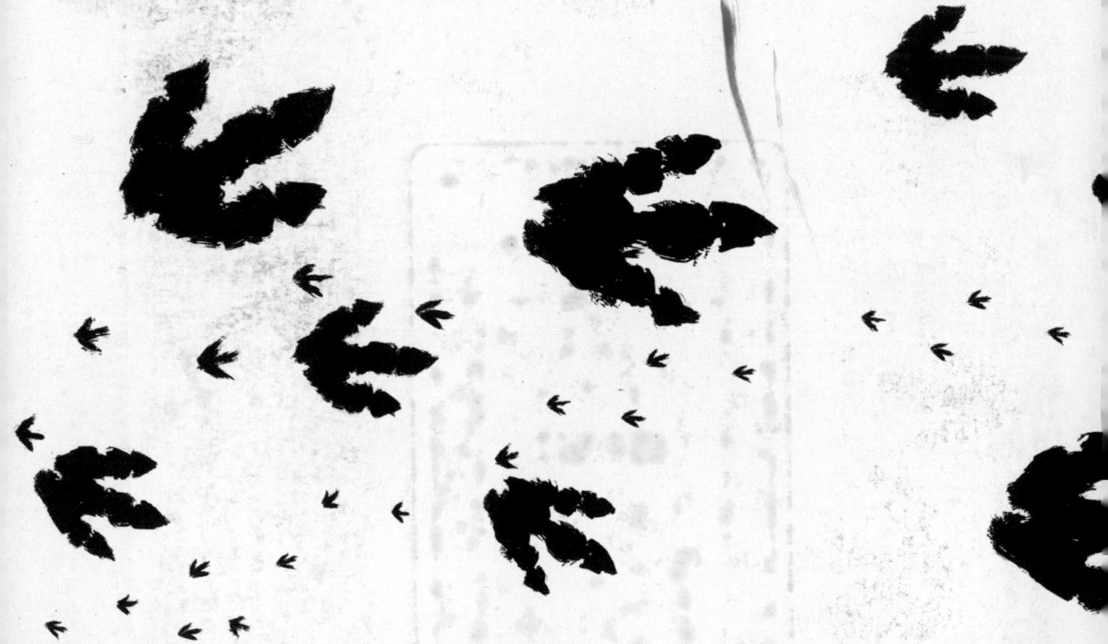